MALCHARIST

ADVANCE PRAISE FOR *MALCHARIST*

"If it weren't a cliché, I'd say *Malcharist* is impossible to put down. The prose is razor-sharp, and it has the narrative drive of a crime thriller. It is also extremely funny. If John Le Carré had the dark, lacerating wit of Hunter S. Thompson, he might have written a book like this."

—Carl Elliott, author, *White Coat, Black Hat:*
Adventures on the Dark Side of Medicine

"An engaging, fast-moving read that has the corruption in the clinical trials business down cold. It takes real talent to turn this subject into a page-turner, and that is what Paul John Scott has accomplished with *Malcharist*."

—Robert Whitaker, author,
Anatomy of an Epidemic, and *Mad in America*

This is a work of fiction. Names, characters, places and incidents are either the product of the author's imagination or are used fictitiously. Any resemblance to actual persons, living or dead, organizations, events or locales is entirely coincidental.

Quitting medications abruptly can cause serious adverse events and deprescribing should be monitored by a qualified physician.

Book design by Laura Drew. Cover illustration and design by Billiam James, adapted from photos "Woman," by Shutterstock and "Fearless Girl, New York City Wall Street," by Anthony Quintano.

Title: Malcharist
Author: Paul John Scott
ISBN: 978-1-989963-06-7
Publisher: Samizdat Health Writer's Co-operative Inc.
Categories: Fiction/Psychological
             Fiction/Thriller/Medical

First Printing, 2020
Revision: 2020-08-22

pauljohnscott.com
samizdathealth.org

For Leslie

MALCHARIST

a novel by

Paul John Scott

Samizdat House

Samizdat Health Writer's Co-operative Inc.

1

Mark Barry lurched forward in a panic, sitting up in his bed with enough force to unmoor the small queen from a headboard secured to the wall.

Another bad dream.

I guess you could call it that.

But he was having a hard time telling the difference lately—the difference between an ordinary nightmare and the darkness taking over his head.

A lifetime of good will had been erased in a week and four days. Misadventures in his grey matter had filled his waking hours with emotional numbing and existential dread, a torment-generating virus spiked with vibrations on the underside of his skin.

His descent had come on without warning, bearing hallucinatory visions remaking the farthest corners of his subconscious into a slaughterhouse.

The latest hallucination had placed him inside a small tower of corpses, clawing in desperation towards the light. His thrashing only caused bluey-ash cadavers all around him to shift into distorted new poses. A leg slipped onto his face, its hairy shin pressed onto his cheek.

In this dream Mark would grasp at a skull to pull himself towards freedom, only to feel his feet slipping deeper as the torsos below him shifted under his weight. The flapping sounds came fast. The smell lingered in his nostrils still now.

Insomnia always followed the night terrors, and Mark used his sleepless hours to burn off his new bad memory. He had never before paced a budget single-occupancy, but to relieve his warehouse of dark energy tonight he had compulsively lapped from 9:47 to 1:15, riding out three cable news hours and part of a house-flipping show before collapsing into the corner at 4,788.

So yes, he was definitely knee-deep in the hellscape now.

He was, if he had to put a finger on it, unsafe.

The question seemed entirely reasonable: Did any of this matter?

This room would be getting picked over by detectives in another twelve hours.

He called his wife.

"Marky?"

"Hey."

"So late. You OK?"

He was pulling the sheets off the bed. They were fascinating and valuable.

"Having trouble."

Mark didn't tell her the nature of his troubles. He couldn't produce words to describe them. He had begun to twist the top sheet into a rope, and didn't know why.

"Is something wrong?"

She would have been worried. Mark never called after ten while away on business.

"It's OK. Go back to sleep."

"Love you."

Someone in control of his arms hung up the phone. Mark pushed the top sheet into the wall safe where it would no longer tempt him. His brain had become a renter living upstairs from a meth lab.

He had hoped hearing the voice of his wife Susie would help him ignore the voices asking *what if a person sailed off the roof of this place, would five floors be enough?* He had attempted to watch these questions with detachment, but they were insistent he take them by the hand.

Driving down the interstate they had demanded *pull the wheel to the right.* They sought out high bridges. Industrial machinery. Weight-bearing cross-beams and sharp objects.

During a four-hour slog from Minneapolis to Madison it had become a heroic achievement for Mark not to search out the local hardware store, make a beeline to the box cutters, then carve himself out in the hand tools.

Mercy had prevailed, but the urges came roaring back after check-in.

Mark watched in helplessness as someone using his voice called down to the front desk in search of a hunting store, taking down the directions onto a scrap of a napkin before something furious inside of him flushed them down the toilet.

He had only been seen in this condition once.

Not two hours in on I-94, he had needed to park and sob at a rest stop outside of Eau Claire. He lost time for a few hours, then pulled himself together for the trooper who had approached his window.

"Afternoon."

Mark wiped his eyes.

"Officer."

"Someone called about you."

"Family crisis."

License, please. Proof of insurance.

No, he hadn't been drinking. No, he didn't need a ride.

Mark didn't tell the trooper he could not imagine life as salvageable for much longer. That he felt dead first, bullied second, agonized third, from the first thing in the morning until he could no longer stay awake. How his days had been spent delaying suicide in six-hour intervals, his nights fighting something worse. He couldn't tell his Susie, that would terrify her. He couldn't go to the emergency room. They would admit him. He needed to figure this out.

Running through his chronology of decline and despair while unpacking his things into the Americinn West Madison, he calculated his last moment of non-misery on the Sunday before last. So by that count, it had taken eleven days for his mental state to deteriorate from fair, to something's not right, to wanting to jump out of his skin, to bottomless pain.

Could it have been the drug?

A week and a half earlier, Mark had gone on a trial of bone-building drug he had seen advertised at the bottom of his homepage. The box had appeared after he typed a question about trail running into a search engine. A couple of calls later he was pulling out of an office park, having registered for a study of a drug which had already been on the market for a couple years.

It was hardly the place you'd imagine when picturing a clinical trial. The person in charge was wearing designer sweats and a golf visor facing backwards. The kid had enrolled him after a few general questions on his health.

"Why a new trial," Mark had asked.

"They already got it approved for people with injuries," the golf visor told him. "Now they are seeing if it prevents injuries in the first place."

Something fatal about that exchange now caused Mark to see his life speeding towards the past tense.

Why, why, why did he sign the forms? It seemed so reckless to him now. He had only wanted to complete a triathlon, OK, to really run it, this time, to not just start training and quit with sore knees. He could have managed.

Instead he had read the insert, agreed to take the pill once every twelve hours, to call back with questions if he had them. He called last week to ask if the terrors could be a side effect.

"So, it's Bricen? This drug doesn't give you nightmares, does it?"

"Why do you ask?"

Strange answer.

Mark had dialed the 800 number after spending four days on the drug and feeling his aversion to violence wash away on day three. He was too ashamed to tell Bricen about the nightmare itself, a short feature starring Mark, a woman in a Dunkin' Donuts outfit, and a shovel. Bricen attempted to reassure Mark there was nothing to be alarmed about.

"It's a drug that is going to deliver protective benefit for athletic performance and healthy lifestyles," he chimed, stumbling over his copy. "You should be OK. Give the medicine a chance to work." Bricen had said that like Mark was taking the medicine. Would that mean Mark was on the drug and not placebo? But why would Bricen have known that? Was there something about Mark's question that gave him away?

Mark had decided to quit taking the pill. That was eight days ago. He hoped that quitting cold turkey after three days on medication hadn't triggered anything he couldn't handle. He seemed to recall it was sometimes dicey to stop taking a drug on a dime. Maybe that was a fuck-up.

Only now it had been eight days off the pill and the head games were unyielding. Deprived of the chemical, his body was apparently pretty goddamned steamed.

He should have tapered.

So. Was he going to do this, or not?

The unthinkable began to take shape. All this pacing. He couldn't do it any longer. No one could. Name one person. The large movers of his arms and his legs were kicking just to kick. Even if he could outlast the agitation, the scraping under his skin was intolerable, totally unreal. His last nightmare had tried to tell him as much. He was already in the ground, he just hadn't accepted it yet. His body had become crushed underneath a stack of corpses. This had to end.

I have been poisoned.

He wrote down the realization on a note pad by his bed.

1) Who did it?

2) Is there an antidote?

3) Can I stop it from happening to someone else?

4) If I do this, will they know I never meant it?

A shaking on his insides began to gather in waves. He picked his wave and pulled up on the board. He got into his pants, found his way to the lobby, and paced in this malevolent state of non-thinking straight on through to the parking lot. He could hear freedom in the distance. His legs felt lighter with every step. It all made sense now, this hotel so close to the interstate.

It would be trucks. No families at this hour. The drivers would be going seventy-five. They would be guys who could deal with it, guys that had mown over animals, served their country, seen dumpsters full of death. They drove rigs that said *Mack* on the grill.

Should he turn around?

Here came his ride.

Mark's sight became acute. Time slowed to a crawl and he began to notice the smallest of details. His heart was awash with gratitude and as he saw the span of his 34 years in high definition. There, on the tallest exhaust pipe, a spear bending to the side of the cab. It was a small, beautiful, deceased dragonfly. He saw that his driver had a beard running down his neck, in a sweatshirt and battered glasses. He saw that his driver looked scared.

Should he go back?

You will be better off without me, Susie.

The horn started blowing. The lights grew brighter, then they became a Christmas tree he remembered his dad putting up the last year before he left.

That's funny. Mark was wrong about this.

The grill said *Peterbilt.*

2

You weren't supposed to look for work on a Monday. After fifteen years of trial and error, Griffin Wagner had sold enough words to acquire that Zen koan about freelancing for magazines. On Mondays, your editors' in-boxes will have filled up like a bathtub, and your pitch will sink like a stone. He had read that somewhere.

Just in case it was wrong, he ran the mantra by a Star Wars toy on his desk.

"Pitching on a Monday," he said in his best Yoda voice. "Try that, no one should."

He tossed a pen towards the bobble-headed Jedi.

"Do. Or do not," Yoda replied from the talking collectible. "There is no try."

"Interesting," Griffin remarked in the direction of his roommate, an adopted black lab he had named after the Six Million Dollar Man himself, Lee Majors. "Yoda thinks you ought to pitch on Mondays."

The steady stream of advice for underemployed writers had been meant to soften the blow, but no one could help us now. Griffin knew that. The assignments were gone. This was a crater, and there had been a bomb.

And it started out looking so rosy. Fresh out of college, Griffin wanted to work for the legacy brands, then-fat, now-emaciated glossies asking questions like:

"Are Americans Too Fat?"

"Is Ringo the Happiest Beatle?"

"What did Jesus Really Say?"

Time. Rolling Stone. Newsweek. At 22, this had seemed like an excellent idea. Now 36, the dream had made Griffin one of the last men on the Titanic.

Fleeing the bartending life in Minneapolis, for five years in New York he had worked as an intern, fact-checker and freelancer, picking up bylines for his clip book back when a struggling writer kept such a thing.

For a half-decade Griffin had maintained the conviction he could live in the center of all media on low pay and long hours. Then, after the websites had vaporized the print ads, and after his smart and funny article editors were replaced by kids optimizing content, Griffin packed a truck and headed back to the Midwest.

He had taken Lee Majors for a run in the new snow before grabbing a shower just after nine-thirty. He looked down at a glowing six on his phone. A half-dozen calls and one message. They must have rolled in since he set down his mobile around eleven. Looking them over as he toweled off his shaggy brown hair, Griffin only recognized a couple of the numbers.

Four showed area codes from Minneapolis (612), one from the western suburbs (952), and another from St. Paul (651). He could identify digits from his cousin Sarah, b-ball partner Ben and his younger brother Roger. The mystery hang-ups were another matter. The practice almost always signified late night impulse, callers too shy to state their purpose. The list of suspects was long.

Griffin had his father's broad shoulders with his mother's dark features, long eyelashes and large blue eyes. He knew he'd been dealt a good hand, but liked to think he had played it with care, opting more to be pursued than to pursue. But in keeping his options open while living in the bars, Griffin's social life had become complicated.

There was Katie, a waitress at the C.C. Club with a porcelain doll face and a highly inconsistent apartment situation. They had fooled around a few times, but fearing it was only the deep feeling he saw in those eyes, Griffin would crash with his clothes on and only once had taken Katie on a proper date. He had mistakenly promised to cook her risotto but hadn't yet delivered on the offer and she wouldn't let him forget it. He needed to get better about that.

There was Brianna, another friend from the business albeit with a toughness about her that played with his desire. She had a shimmering street fighter energy that had him wasting far too much money at the pool table during her shifts at Red's Roost. She'd once passed him her number and wasn't shy about calling, but like Katie, had enough men coming at her that she could drop off the radar for weeks at a time. All for the best. He really just wanted to hold her, and she would surely end up hurt or mad about it.

Now that odd and suburban 952 was harder to place. Laura? After five years at a mortgage company, she had ripped up her life to study oil on canvas and deliver flowers. Upon bumping into her at an ice cream shop by the park, Griffin felt something stir in him as she laughed about this small downfall. It did not help that she'd become a dark and beautiful set painter living in an apartment owned by her dad. An outsider just like him.

So when she had floated the idea of their driving to an old warming house to buy hot chocolate and rent ice skates, he said, *for sure, we need to catch up*. Even worse, she was now terrifically hot, and had recently broken it off with a longtime flame. A twirl on the ice in new snowfall with this one could put him knee-deep in conversation and candles and presents at Christmas. All when he was so very, very broke.

Griffin knew he was lucky in love or some approximation. But it had started to feel worrisome, here on the backside of his 30s and still scraping to make rent, that love was all it seemed he had. "Love is all you need," as the song goes. But a part of him, the part with an eye on a leader board now rapidly slipping into history, definitely needed more.

He hit the playback from his only admirer who'd felt the courage to drop a proper message. He listened to the sleepy chatter as he poured from an enormous bag of dog food into a bowl by his refrigerator.

"Hey, cousin, it's Sarah. You took off on us last night…We missed you! Did you pay the check? Someone paid our check and we couldn't figure out who."

Griffin had met up with some girls to see Spoon at a club uptown. He'd planned on a fun time, but the band took forever to come out, his booth mates all had crushes to sort out, and he had been sandwiched inside of their conversations for over two hours. After excusing himself to hit the bathroom, he paid for their beers and slipped away without the hugs.

"It wasn't bad," Sarah said. "They played like, side one of 'Ga Ga Ga Ga Ga.' The encore went on for three more songs with the lights turned up, and the place went crazy for 'Cherry Bomb.' Anyway, we closed it down and it didn't get ugly. Let's get out some time when we can talk? Love you."

Click.

"Well, we love you too, Sarah," Griffin said in a doggie-voice to the snout of Lee Majors. He was kneading the fur of his friend's neck with a slow, rigorous two-handed massage as the dog looked upward towards him with soulful, grateful eyes. "When are you going to leave that film student for someone with the funds to cover a pitcher of Rolling Rock?"

Griffin dropped to the floor to bang out his push-ups, mulling over who he could pitch and how much the gig might pay. Though they were offering a third of what he'd made in the day, the local magazines were still solvent, should his checking account dip into the red.

He hit 50, felt his arms begin to wobble, and got up to pull on a collector's-issue Fran Tarkenton. He had purchased the pricey so-called throwback Vikings jersey on a whim two years earlier, a splurge after cashing a big check during the good times.

It wasn't especially flattering, but on days that were dull, it reminded him he still had heroes. He told Lee Majors he would be right back, pulled on a pea coat, grabbed a shoulder bag off his coat rack and pushed the door open to his second-floor exterior staircase, whereupon he stepped out into the ten-degree bullshit.

The city was covered in new snow, and that always gave him a shot of hope. At the bottom of his stairs, Griffin walked a familiar fifteen paces through an alley and into the back of Muddy Waters, passing an entryway cluttered with news of band gigs, apartments for sublet, and lost pets.

Griffin started most of his days in this little coffee shop, the first stop on a freelancer day-circuit spent hopping from one temporary desk to another. He worked in a sequential chain of cafés, diners and libraries, spending just enough cash to non-loiter his stay. At the counter, he ordered the light roast and pointed at a scone.

"Wags."

He turned around. It was Pevin, a friend on his floor back in college. It had been years. Pevin now sported blocky horn-rims, an expensive arsenal of weather protection, and the blank look of disappointment that passed for happy in the region. He appeared to have filled out considerably.

"Or should I say Mr. Cream Cheese—I thought you moved out east?"

Griffin had once filled a hole in the wall of Pevin's dorm with bagel spread. They had needed to pass end-of-year inspection for a road-trip to some enticing music festival.

"Yeah," Griffin muttered quietly, "I must have had enough of the struggle. I moved back a couple years ago."

But it had been seven.

"You're still at the nonprofit?"

"Sort of," Pevin replied. "We are partnering with the MNHS."

Griffin scoured his brain for the meaning of the acronym. Nothing was coming.

Pevin began banging his mittens on the radiator. Pools of new snowmelt would soon be forming on the stacks of *Real Estate Shopper* and *Vegetarian Times.*

"Sorry, MN what?"

"Human Services."

Dave Pevin was now surveying the bakery case.

"It's a state agency, mental health referrals," Pevin said. *"Excuse me Ma'am, does the peanut butter in these contain trans fats?"* A clerk in cargo pants gave Pevin a look and a shrug. He charged forward with a daft dietary homily.

"It's a Franken-food used to extend shelf life in processed baked goods," he offered somberly to the blankest of stares. "It lowers your good cholesterol and elevates the risk of heart disease."

Griffin stifled a laugh, and kicked him in the boot.

Pevin handed her a five.

"Here. It looks like you probably use something heart-healthy," Pevin said with a wink.

He turned to Griffin. Griffin resigned himself to the fact that the young clerk was going to think he was friends with this guy who had just winked at a girl selling coffee.

"So what are you doing, still writing?"

Same old question.

"Sort of," Griffin replied. He paid for his coffee and the scone.

"I write for the men's magazines these days."

"You mean like, *Warrior Drum*…the zine?" Pevin asked.

Zines. Wow.

Now there was a blast from the past. Small, early-Nineties, DIY-scene. Sort of the canary in a coal mine for the coming curse of digital, if Griffin had to put his finger on it.

"No," Griffin replied. "I mean the magazines out of New York."

"Sweet. Loves me some *Esquire*," said Pevin. "Written anything for them?"

Griffin scrunched his face, then looked out the window with a short shake of his head.

"Really?" Pevin asked. "You'd think that'd be every scribe's dream."

"You'd be correct," Griffin said.

He stole a look at his watch.

"That place is impenetrable," Griffin added.

"What about *Harper's*?"

"I don't know," Griffin replied, "they are kind of obtuse."

Truthfully, Griffin would have killed to have something in *Harper's*, but they had never responded to any of his pitches.

"How about *The New Yorker*?"

Hey Pevin, ever try out for the number three job at the State Department?

"Yeah, that's another fortress."

"Lately I have been digging *The New York Review of Books*."

This endless parade of smarty magazines that did not publish Griffin, answer his emails, or make passing contact with anyone he had ever hoped to know.

"That's cool."

"So tell me where can I find your prose then, my man, *GQ*?"

"No, I wish. I write for *In the Zone* mostly."

Griffin's paying work came by way of a half-hearted relationship he had carved out with a well-paying bro-title called *In the Zone*. Thanks to its dozens of ad pages each month for cars, clothes and shaving cream, *In the Zone* could run as thick as a pine board in the fall and early summer. In exchange for this support from the male consumer-goods dollar, *In the Zone* stuck to workouts, man-toys, sex, and not much else.

In the Zone cover lines included "Shoulders, Arms, Abs and Ass, No BS!" And, "Six Tricks to Rock Her World—And Your Bed!" #*iTZ*, as it had recently taken to tagging all tweets after the explosion of the new micro-blogging platform, had a special interest in the sustained condemnation of visceroptosis, otherwise known as the sagging male stomach.

Every second *In the Zone* cover made a case for this towering mission, including Griffin's personal nadir, a story under a headline written by the *In the Zone* brain trust crowing "About that Gut: Are You Pregnant or Wut?"

As it happened, this *eye-popping look and feel* of his employer's shouty, shirtless method had garnered only praise within the industry, fielding accolades from *In the Zone's* peers at the annual magazine awards luncheon. Overcome with pride, corporate eventually had the best of it stenciled on a wall behind the reception desk.

Upon departing the elevator on 23, all visitors to *In the Zone's* Midtown Crib, as the magazine taken to calling its offices, were greeted with an eight-by-four-foot blow-up of the magazine featuring a shirtless actor whose action-hero franchise had recently reached its 4th installment. Below that:

In the Zone…a sexy read that punches you in the face and then pours you a Manhattan.
          —Magazine Market Monitor.

All of which is to say, Griffin could not have picked a niche less well-situated for the bro-bashing, New Voices-embracing, patriarchy-smashing reversal of fortune which had begun to remake the publishing landscape.

Dave cleaved a massive corner off his peanut butter bar and began eating it while standing. A piece of crispy rice became lodged in his beard.

"*In the Zone*, haven't seen that one."

Griffin had learned to expect the awkward pause that inevitably followed all mention of his brotastic employer when speaking with the well-read denizens of South Minneapolis.

He waited for the question that always came next.

"So, are you freelance," Pevin asked, "or do you work on contract?"

Check.

"Yeah, the whole industry is freelance," Griffin replied.

The piece of crispy rice in Pevin's beard had now drifted southward and was looking precarious.

"I blog sometimes," said Pevin. "Wordshark dot com. Transit policy, climate hacks, responsible food practices. You should check us out."

Griffin nodded and told Pevin he had to go. He felt a familiar panic setting in. He knew better than to ask Dave Pevin about his blog. He slipped out onto the sidewalk to make the call.

"Trevor, it's Wagner, you got a second?"

"Grifter! I got one for you but not much more."

"Just wondering what you thought of those pitches."

Trevor Drake, editor-in-chief of *In the Zone*, had been Griffin's boss and long-distance banter-mate for seven years. Their writer-editor bond was once a smooth pairing of Trevor's editorial expediency and Griffin's financial desperation, but over the last few years, things had changed.

Trevor had become subservient to Nigel Butler, an editorial director five years his junior and the slumming scion of a Melbourne fast-food fortune. Nigel, moreover, was the new breed of editorial flim-flam man. He had moved up in the magazine through the division for catalog copy.

In other words, Griffin's boss was Trevor, but Trevor's boss had ascended the masthead with no discernible interest in journalism, just a clean streak of nepotism and impossible-to-top stories from the VIP party scene in the South Pacific.

As a result, Trevor now said yes to Griffin's pitches only after consulting with Olivia Newton-John, as the two had taken to calling Nigel. And Nigel only said yes to story ideas that had already run in competitor magazines.

"Remind me again?"

"You know, a profile of the guy who invented the proton beam, an expensive cancer radiation treatment now being built at $150 million a piece."

"Oh, yeah...I don't know...Ha-ha...Not relevant for our guys," Trevor said. "If you are getting radiation, that's kind of heavy."

Death. It wasn't relevant for *In the Zone*, of course not.

"What about me asking why disposable razor blades run thirty-three dollars a pack?" Griffin knew this one wasn't going anywhere, either. He only continued to sell it because bailing on your pitch too quickly made you look weak.

"It's about forty cents worth of mass-produced plastic," he added. "How do they get to thirty-three dollars?"

"Womp-womp." Trevor said. "That thud you hear is the sound of Crikey falling over on his geriatric treadmill desk if we ever do anything to make the shaving ads go away."

So, Olivia Newton-John had now become Crikey.

Griffin labored to keep up with all the nick-naming. He decided to try a joke.

"You don't want to go out in a blaze of glory?"

Trevor paused, waiting for Griffin to speak.

It's possible he may have been digging for something in his desk.

"I mean, you know, ha-ha, make a statement?"

"Anything else?

"How about the death of Hemingway? You know, the lion in winter, life at the bottom of a bottle, that whole pizza." This one actually had potential. Griffin was dealing with a recognizable masculinity icon. A famous romancer of beautiful women. The author of hard-boiled prose. Plus hunting.

"Wasn't he like, 60 when he died?" Trevor countered. "That's kind of old for our demo. Hey Griffin, weren't you going to try out for that semi-pro arena football league?"

Trevor did this sometimes. Just changed the subject like an ADHD-afflicted editor eventually does. Griffin had no choice but to let the idea drop and follow along.

"Are you kidding? I weigh 170. Those guys would flatten me."

"Yeah. You don't have the sack for that."

Griffin pretended not to hear that. Training. He thought that might work.

"I did infiltrate a Parkour scene once. That would jack up the fitness well."

"Bunch of guys jumping from building to building like Spiderman," Trevor said. "Let's give that one the slow clap and move on. I'm going to need to wrap this up."

Griffin heard a buzzer go off in his brain. Garbage time. He observed the words leaving his mouth with the feeling someone else was saying them, a freelancer far more desperate for paying work of any kind.

"Six essential moves for a lobster bake on the beach?"

"Holy Shania Twain," Trevor barked, "that sounds like something we could use."

Of course, it does.

"Let me run it by Crocs and get back to you."

"Sure," Griffin exhaled. He made a mental note to remember that Nigel also went by Crocs. "Thanks."

He hung up and watched Pevin pull open the door to Muddy Waters, then saunter past him without looking up from a wilting *Vegetarian Times*. As Pevin dropped into a Volvo that looked expensive, the vehicle sagged.

Fuck me. Lobster bake.

3

The text announcing her change of plans came through five hours after UK-native and Manhattan-dwelling corporate scientist Shivani Patel, 37, turned off the recorder. Orders out of her product-development supervisor and dark pharmaceutical sales overlord Seamus Cole, 57, arrived at 6:10 a.m.

They said that Shivani, a high-flying expat and veteran ghostwriter for Deadline Medical—*scientific communications, on demand, with discretion*—a wholly-owned subsidiary of Krøhn-McGill pharmaceuticals (NYSE: KMP)—that she was to skip her previously-assigned work order for the early morning hours.

That one, slated for 9:00 a.m., was a rubbish workshop entitled "Emerging Treatments for Social Anxiety Disorder."

Shivani (Sheevi G. to her friends) was also to ixnay her late-morning assignment, the one requiring her to infiltrate a talk called "5-HT Transporters in the Treatment of Sleep Dysregulation: New Directions in Best Practices."

Her new job according to this text had become "Med-Ed," shorthand for Medical Education. Seamus had directed Shivani to brief a fresh batch of so-called Key Opinion Leaders, suggestible and cash-strapped young MDs presumably one Shivani-powered training from agreeing to hump Krøhn-McGill medicines for side pay.

Here was how she learned the news:

> shivani.
> team has recruited 26 KOLS.
> need u in the Duke at 9.
> gonna train bioferex for prophylactic.
> analytics has identified
> future Rx in psychiatry

Shivani didn't get it. This was a psychiatry meeting.

Bioferex was a drug for hairline cracks of the femur.

She hadn't imagined a room full of shrinks would care about a new pill for the repair of stress fractures.

She thought about the KOLS. They gave her a headache. She thought about the early-century namesake of the ballroom where she now would be asked to mingle, the only word Seamus had chosen to capitalize properly. The Duke of Windsor, a face-saving honorific for King Edward VIII upon abdication of the throne in 1936, had been a crushing disappointment that the crown had been lucky to off-load in the lead-up to the Second War. If ever there was a fitting gathering spot for the crowd she was about to face, this garish ballroom honoring the Duke was the place.

Thumbs flying, Shivani fired off her reply.

> So I am giving the bone drug
> talk even though the KOLS
> are from psychiatry?

Maybe they were trying to expand the new pill. Get it written for a more lucrative market. It's hard to make bank treating splinters of the femur. Shivani knew the end game, how her employers had hoped to move the bone pill on to everyone signing up for the gym.

Seamus must have decided she would explain to psychiatrists that exercise helps with depression. That would allow them to start jamming a bone drug into their medicine bag. Seamus' reply had confirmed as much.

> This is the plan.

Sitting upright in bed with a coffee and a scowl, Shivani looked with confusion at the party number balled up on her dresser. Her raven black hair was hanging in front of her light green eyes. She must have made her way in from the couch sometime after one. She offered her best impersonation of enthusiasm for the switch-up.

> what about my q's for
> 10 am slp dsrders tlk?

She had just enough time to lean over her nightstand to dig out two Advil when she heard his reply ping.

> what q's?

Shivani propped herself back up against her headboard, tossed back the medicine with a pull from a bottle of Fiji, shook her head slowly and re-typed her gig.

> i'm supposed to push
> new use for zoloxetine?

Shivani had thought that by using *zoloxetine*, the generic name for the Krøhn-McGill antidepressant and billion-dollar category-killer known as Serotonal, she was being discrete. Seamus wasn't having it.

> chill.
> member about txt

"Oh, piss off," she exhaled, tossing the phone into her French bedding, closing her eyes and rubbing the first two fingers of her nightclub-stamped hand to a hangover-inflamed temple.

"Fuckity-bye to you as well, Seamus."

Shivani had been assigned to do a little of everything at the big meeting on her calendar for the day. But prior to being reassigned just now, her initial job for the morning had been to stake out a seat at the back of two drug education lectures, cool her heels until the portion saved for questions, then fire off a query to facilitate a speaker's ability to venture off-label.

After biding the tedium of the talk itself—she had invariably ghostwritten most of it, so a crossword from the *London Times* always seemed more interesting—Shivani was expected to pose as a curious bystander and ask whether Serotonal was effective in treating shyness, insomnia, or some other malady.

She could ask her staged question with any brocade of ad-libbing she cared to apply, as long as it helped to conceal her identity as a drug plant. Her mission was to introduce new uses of the pill to the crowd, and any phrasing would do. As long as the question enabled a big-game clinician to venture into off-label promotion, all was cracking.

The ruse was meant to wring new revenue from the drug, funds vastly more lucrative than those supplied by its FDA-approved function, and despite her employers having never managed to prove the drug was in fact safe and effective for those purposes. It's not like they were the only ones who did this. On some days, Shivani looked around and realized that the only questions asked during the Q&A were via proxies for the makers of drugs.

In the matter of being suggested pills for indications that hadn't had to pass the scrutiny required of hair coloring, America's millions of trusting medication consumers were getting played on the regular.

So it was illegal.

Sort of.

It was against the law for a manufacturer to promote new uses for a drug without having received formal FDA approval for that function. Doctors could always prescribe drugs for unproven uses. But the drug makers themselves could never market an unproven indication, not now anyway. Nor could an ambitious and hungry sales rep so much as mumble a distant hope for an unproven use.

Shivani's bosses could certainly never mention unproven uses for new drugs in their ads. All of this added up to a problem: doctors only tried unapproved uses after being told by other doctors it was a swell idea. This is why industry needed to get the gossip going. Even if they could only do so by answering questions from staff working under cover, today with a most unpleasant hangover.

To a lot of people, the ban on off-label marketing must have seemed quaint. Indeed, it appeared likely the United States Supreme Court would soon be invoking the assertion that pharmaceutical manufacturers held a constitutional right to free speech in the spreading of falsehoods.

For the incurious black-robes under Chief Justice John Roberts, this would likely be just another Tuesday, if Shivani had to guess, all in spite of the fact that the danger of pitching medicines for unproven uses was the reason behind the creation of the FDA in the first place.

For Shivani, the cost of taking part in these shenanigans wasn't so much the guilt as the hassle. It meant she had to throw her Deadline Medical lanyard into her $7,500 Botegga Veneta Cabat metallic calfskin tote prior to asking whether Serotonal could be prescribed for the treatment of some new discomfort or another. Anxiety, agoraphobia, dysphoria, whatever else they had thought of. OK, so maybe she harbored few regrets. For now, anyway.

Last night, more so. Feeling philosophical after an evening at the Roseland Ballroom with the bard of betrayal Leonard Cohen, Shivani had spent an hour alone on her couch, attempting to dump-truck her demons into a digital tape recorder.

She had been off of her face at the time, with predictable results, including teary-ness, nostalgia, and escapist thoughts of a reinvented life after leaving pharma for good, perhaps selling champagne mangoes on an island with no marina.

It was a sloppy test-run for going public about what it was that medical ghostwriters did. How the side effect seemed to be showing up everywhere. A confession ending in tears.

Only now it was morning. Shivani's desire for reform had faded. Work was work.

She threw on her best KOL-speaking outfit—Seamus had trained her to coach young doctors "dressed in something you'd wear to a third date." (Which meant what exactly Seamus, fuckable? Gross.)

She tossed a KOL-training thumb drive in her bag. She headed down two flights of marble-and-iron staircase, breezing past the cuter of her building's two doormen, then out into the bright sunlight of a late February thaw in lower Manhattan.

"Ciao Marco! The Bennington, please."

She couldn't believe her life sometimes. This was one of them. Marco hailed a town car and relayed her destination to the driver while holding open a door, leaning in to say goodbye with a gentle touch of his brim. "Have excellent day, Meez Patel," he said, flirting politely. "I know you're going to have a good one, OK?"

"How sweet of you, Marco," Shivani replied, handing him a ten and a small wave. "Get thee to the Ovaltine."

She had mumbled the joke under her breath, but when her driver looked in his mirror with confusion, she realized she had spoken too loudly.

"It's nothing," she clarified, applying eyeliner from a compact. Ovaltine was the nickname she'd adopted for *Novoamine*, an unwieldy tagline for the 42nd meeting of the American Association for Psychiatry.

"Off to recharge the fading hopes of the neurotransmitter era," she whispered a little more quietly, resting her forehead against the window and gazing blankly as a fillers-injected beauty pushed an imported stroller down Madison. "Beats changing diapers."

Novoamine, was ever there more of a pant-load.

Her elder clinicians might have caught the moniker's mash-up of the prefix "novo" (to renew), with the suffix "amine," (for the monoamine

23

system of brain chemicals affecting emotion, arousal and memory). But the tortured wordplay was surely lost on the young MDs it had targeted. Most of those eager ducklings, bless their hearts, would have neither understood nor cared what "Novoamine" was meant to mash.

Shivani herself had raised this problem during a meeting the previous spring, one in which planning had determined *Synaptica 2010, Receptor 2010* and *Membrain 2010* all stunk. "I like this one," Seamus had said, pointing at the slide for *Novoamine 2010*, thereby putting an end to the discussion. The day-long AAP Executive Summit had been booked into a private alcove off the Pool Room at the Four Seasons. The choice to go with *Novoamine* had occurred over a noon-hour meal of grass-fed filet served with a root vegetable trio.

Shivani had barely gotten a chance to digest her breakfast, so the very smell of steak at such an early hour made her gag. But Seamus was one of those ravenous steel town linebackers, and she knew her place. She had pushed around the heavy fare with an appearance of enthusiasm, and only raised her concern late in the process.

"So, Novoamine," she asked. "That's not too arcane?"

"Would it matter?" Seamus replied.

Shivani's commanding officer was now sawing into his braised Brussels sprouts with a fussy overcompensation. The intensity of her boss's knife-over-fork would have bothered her less had it not resonated with her memory of the pitiless old butlers who had populated her early years in the public schools of East Anglia.

Like every calcified headmaster who had walked out of a Pink Floyd lyric to correct her exams and mark up her essays, Seamus would have surely fueled his entire, clawing ascension with a poverty of self-awareness and a bottomless hunger for status.

Shivani's guess was a tyrannical upbringing in the rustbelt.

"I see, yes, exactly."

Shivani had no idea what she had just affirmed. That it was this ungainly *Novoamine* was moot. At 14,000 members, the American Association for Psychiatry was hardly struggling for credibility, much less cutting-edge branding. As the world's largest professional association for doctors trained in the provision of medications for mental illness, the AAP were largely untouchable in the eyes of the public.

This was indeed something. How the trade consuming her handiwork had needed only three decades of tacking towards neurotransmitters to cement its authority over the care of human distress. The guild had prevailed over literature, psychology, mythology, creed, folk wisdom and doctrine all by utilizing—well, you could take your pick from any of the neuro-neologisms one pulled at random from Shivani's cooked-up papers on dopamine pathways.

A remarkably seductive narrative had succeeded beyond her employers' wildest dreams. Showcasing one's familiarity with neurons, receptors, cortical structures and grey matter had become the one conversation shared on both sides of the now bitterly-divided political culture, having long since taken the U.S., then Europe, and finally her beloved United Kingdom with barely a fight.

So *Novoamine* may have been weird, but for AAP, weird was working. This never ceased to amaze her. Shivani had helped to craft their arguments, and knew all too well of the short man behind the curtain—the way in which brain chemicals fell impossibly short of their image as all-powerful mood governors. Shivani also knew these seductions had saved the AAP from its adventurous past.

Sure, a generation of children were on speed, a quarter of middle-aged women on meds that smothered all sexual function, and millions of veterans, the elderly and low-income preschoolers on sedatives that shortened lives through metabolic syndrome, brain shrinkage and heart disease. And yes, so some boys, OK, thousands, were taking a drug for disruptivity that had them growing breasts.

But any organization that spoke this conversationally of calcium channel ions and reuptake inhibitors had clearly moved on from those nasty forays into Oedipal conflicts, insulin coma therapy, Rorschach blots, frontal lobotomies and the institutionalization of women activated by abuse and bad marriage.

Plus, so very few members of the AAP even knew who wrote their journals.

How else could Shivani Gandha Patel, the prodigiously-published ghostwriter behind so much of the AAP's most influential research, just walk across the lobby of the Bennington this bright sunny morning without ever once being recognized?

4

The Duke of Windsor was a whale of a room, a pretty little princess done up right in full Trump-style. The prized ballroom for the historic Bennington Hotel on Park, it offered a fifteen-foot chando, elegant frescoes, gold-inlay ceiling panels, and of course the show-stopper itself, a glorious, life-sized oil of Edward VIII and Mrs. Wallis Simpson.

Seamus had always treasured the Duke for that amenity alone, having been moved to tears by the uplifting true story of the royal who had chosen love over kingdom. He had learned of it on Royal Originals, a cable network he'd watch if the day had been long and Marcita had made her signature crab remoulade.

Winners aren't afraid to spend a little cash, which is why Seamus didn't flinch from securing the Duke at the steep mark-up for having booked the glam beauty on short notice. He knew first-class KOL recruiting came with a price, but that it paid for itself one thousand times over here at the AAP.

Attention to detail had been a Seamus Cole specialty during his three decades in the industry, an unsurpassed run of excellence propelling him into a tax bracket commensurate with his commitment to health, cutting-edge science and the astonishing prosperity of the modern pharmaceutical marketplace.

As VP for Clinical Research, Krøhn-McGill Psychiatric-North America, Seamus knew AAP was chockablock with only the hungriest prospective Key Opinion Leaders. Aspiring KOLS of tomorrow could be recruited by the dozens at the annual gathering of psychiatrists, if one only showed them a taste of what they could expect for their time and expertise.

That said, Seamus also knew a few of them would be ungrateful for the good fortune he was here to shower upon them.

"I thought you said this was going to be over by 9:30," mumbled the bearded and well-fed shrink in the third row. It was normal to encounter attitude on these outings, but a bit early. New KOLS usually held their bitching until at least an hour had passed. It now being 9:10, Patel was officially ten minutes behind schedule. So much for good will.

"How does everyone feel about the sweaters, not too warm for your home climates, I hope?" Seamus had placed $500 silk-embroidered V-necks on every chair. They weren't his bag. He didn't personally ascribe to the notion of "casual elegance." Seamus knew you dressed to win. He was partial to a traditional product, three pieces, bespoke with hand details. There was no denying the quality of today's gifts, however—the thickness of the braid, the ribbed touch and feel of the fabric.

The loot had been custom-manufactured by an elite leisure-wear company in northern Ohio known as Mercy Creek Knits, and it served a dual purpose. By placing a Krøhn-McGill logo in delicate silk thread over the left breast, Seamus had, in the eyes of the IRS, effectively handed the doctors their own speakers bureau uniforms, rather than gifts. Uncle Sam wouldn't need to know that none of these guys would be wearing their "uniforms" while giving academic talks now being distributed on Krøhn-McGill thumb drives.

Nor that none of this comported with the Hippocratic oath—the outdated notion that medicine should be free of distortion by monetary or material enticements. But it had been decades since industry had made short work of the wall between AAP and the private side. Seamus and his competitors now conducted virtually all of the specialty's research, from bench science to the trials of new drugs, from start to finish.

Peel away the veneer of academic disinterest and the assertion of private interest was on full display throughout the day's meetings, whether via the private-public "partnerships" hoovering up public subsidies for brain sciences, or the Krøhn-McGill underwriting of *Black Tie & Candle Light,* the *Novoamine 2010* closing night gala. (Musical entertainment: Cold Play. Ticket price: $350 per person. Attendees on scholarship: 100 percent.)

The presence of drug sponsorship was omnipresent, inescapable, emboldening and yet somehow always unspoken. There was simply no awkwardness about it at all, and in spite of the towering Dopamine Biologics™ logo stationed behind the podium in ballroom A, the luminescent Krøhn-McGill™ swirl projected onto the dance floor at *Black Tie & Candle Light,* and the 2,000 plated-nickel coffee mugs noting the generous support of Hastings Neurobio™. Everyone had agreed to frame the glorious new hour as one of "translational medicine." In exchange, industry was granted control of all educational content.

When the KOLS had eaten their fill of salmon eggs benedict, drained the guava juice decanter twice and kept the Italian girl with curls steaming away loudly behind the Bugatti engineered to resemble a high-performance motorcycle, it was time for Seamus to tell them why Shivani Gandha Patel, now a half hour behind schedule, was well worth the wait.

"Where is she?" Seamus answered. "More like, '*who* is she?' Let me put it this way, there are medical communications specialists, and then there are VIP tickets to the sold-out stadium show. You want the best, don't you?"

"We are here to pick up the new talk, right?"

29

The remark came from a physician in the second row. He had bunched up his $500 silk freebie and stuffed it into a backpack, like a teenager. These guys. It never used to be this way. The new KOLS had once wanted to learn a thing or two. Ever since the Internet, they were coming in with all the angles. This one's tag read:

    Butterwood, Jared, Jr., DO
    St. Thomas Children's Hospital
    Orchard Grove, TN

So the guy was not an MD. Seamus noted the accreditation and adjusted his Prada eyewear, then rubbed his hand in reflection over his mouth. He hadn't slept well. Last night there had been a $1,806.50 charge on the bar tab at the Carillion Room, an unauthorized outlay at 2:45 a.m. for some sort of cognac that had caught the eye of Dr. Elton.

Maybe this was a KOL who had missed the cut, a Dr. Elton of tomorrow ahead of schedule in feeling fed up and eager to get some. It made Seamus sad. Seamus would love to have filled the room with talent. But Krøhn-McGill had needed to dig deeper of late, and for more than a few years running. Were they using an outdated playbook?

This being 2010, recruiting young doctors to give speeches to old doctors about the benefits of your new drug was becoming a thing of the past. For the competition, paying KOLs to speak had become kabuki. The bribery had gone operational. His competitors had reimagined the contract, with "speaking engagements" for KOLS having devolved into unadorned whoring. Only last week Seamus had given in and arranged a dinner connecting one of his high-performing prescribers with a rep recruited from a grindhouse outside of Fort Lauderdale. He wouldn't do that again. He was better than that.

Seamus had standards. He was still kicking it for the right reasons— today that being to seed the lands with disciples for Bioferex. So to start out his morning like this, with attitude from the farm team. How long until hitting his number freed him at last?

He checked his cash-out timer on his phone, an app that counted down the years, months, weeks, days and hours until he could pack it in. There were still two years, eight months, three weeks, four days and ten hours until his yacht steered into port and the KOLS could go jump in the lake. He had excellent plans for a place outside of Sarasota. It had a specified size. Fifty six thousand square feet. It would match the home of Andrew Carnegie.

"Dr. Butterwood, is it?"

The doctor nodded.

Seamus began to stall with a reply he could have delivered in his sleep.

"Excellent question. First, welcome to the Key Opinion Leadership breakout at *Novoamine 2010*—Nuvanami, man that's a mouthful." Seamus drew scattered laughs for the gag, and it was indeed an act. He knew every tortured deliberation behind the *Novoamine* tagline— including its correct pronunciation. He had signed off on its approval.

But he liked to raise the confidence of new KOLs by playing the fool. Seamus knew shy residents first approaching side money were sometimes wary by default, less-so lately, but that they would always feel the love if served with enough flattery. Seamus elevated new KOLs by diminishing himself. It sometimes surprised even him how little that cost.

"To answer your question, yes. I'm not an expert in psychiatry but I know that every one of you are destined for the very *top* of your profession, and more importantly, that we can learn a lot from you. We know your peers can learn from you, as well, especially when we arm you with cutting-edge scientific presentations to deliver at forums hosted by Krøhn-McGill Psychiatric. I think you will find Krøhn-McGill KOL status is not just an invaluable contribution of your expertise to the advancement of medical practice, but a reliable and generous second revenue stream and a feather in your cap that will quickly elevate your profile within the community of professionals."

"I was wondering about the dinners."

It was Jared Jr. from Tennessee. Seamus took no offense at the young osteopath now stepping on his speech. He knew the generation well, that they had been socialized to believe their needs came first, including the need to speak over others.

"I don't know anyone in our state association," Jared continued. "I wouldn't know how to do any of that."

"We already thought of everything," Seamus replied. "If you become a member of the Krøhn-McGill KOL network you can expect 360-degree coverage at a host of elegant venues."

"Where are those?"

It was the recruit rocking some blazing white, waffle-bottomed running sneakers in the first row. Seamus made a note to remind himself they would all be needing sartorial training and a Krøhn-McGill menswear account.

"We have the ADHD golf getaways at Pebble Beach," Seamus said. "But maybe you like the slopes? We have a mood disorders three-day in Aspen, conveniently situated just twenty-seven feet from lift number one. No waiting in lines, no shuttle to the hill, a valet to grab your gear the minute you tire of the world's most exclusive blue runs."

Seamus was riffing now. He knew better than to let this pitch see daylight.

"For KOLS working state hospitals, our severe mental illness oaked chardonnay tasting in Napa is the hottest ticket of the season. And pediatric specialists will tell you they swear by our conduct and behavioral disorders Insights Chautauqua hosted by the Inn at Sunset Ranch in Mountain View, California."

Their eyes had grown huge.

"But you don't have to identify in a specialty in order to help us move the needle on patient care." Seamus liked to hit the phrase "patient care" early and often. It could be the smallest mention of greater good that relieved a prospective KOL of his guilt over selling out.

"The emerging treatments salons in Palm Beach, Santa Barbara and at any of our specialty training convocations in Barbados, St. Thomas or St. Martin are all generalist-tailored and eager for the contributions of physician-servants such as yourselves. Some of the most welcoming resorts in the world have opened their doors to those courageous professionals willing to leverage their authority in the service of eradicating mental illness."

This was the line that usually knocked them over, due in no small part to its winning appeal to an aspiring KOLS' healthy sense of self-regard. Seamus had theories as to why the altruism framing closed the sale. There would have been adult-development delays, the brutal battering his young clinicians' self-esteem would have taken at the hands of fathers and father-figures throughout residency, the humiliating years of flying coach while undergraduate classmates jumped into management consulting and private planes, and far too many romantic disappointments to count.

Seamus had been clicking through slides of beaches, mountains, tropical sunsets and urbane doormen for five-star lodging. His outlandish offering of no-strings paydays had their undivided attention. He moved in for the kill.

"We handle your Linked-In profile, we Tweet for you, we update your CV with every new publication, and we schedule, promote, staff and populate your talks. Then we immediately compensate you for them. Cash or check, however you prefer."

Seamus had paused at a slide of a pool party at the Bellagio.

"You show up, deliver the data you are now about to hear described for you, then collect your fee. It's that easy. We fly, house and feed both you and your spouse—or whoever else you choose to bring along for the fun."

Before Seamus had lingered too long on the suggestion the KOLS invite a mistress on the road, he spotted Shivani at the back of the room. She had arrived as requested, the Brit they had groomed with such care. Tall boots, silhouette-cut PVC pencil skirt and black satin jacket over a white silk blouse. He couldn't believe his veteran ghostwriter was both a prolific producer of corporate science and such a captivating presence in the flesh. The fact that they had plucked her from obscurity with a note card on a job board at Johns Hopkins never ceased to amaze him.

They would have launched an eighteen-month search to find her mix of brains, style and raw drug marketing talent.

"So here she is," he said, "our Bioferex specialist herself, Shivani Patel."

The soundman hit his cue. Sub-woofer audio of Phillip Glass began filling the room, and all thoughts of Shivani Patel having made the young doctors wait began to fall by the wayside. Seamus relaxed in his faith in her performance. He was confident she would know her talk inside and out, deftly hewing to its overarching objective of teaching these doctors to sell other doctors on the FDA-pleasing notion of a statistically significant association in bone cell turnover within the 1,600 people who took the new pill during the Phase II, a trial known as "Rostangilorb (Trade name Bioferex™) for Osteoblast Proliferation at the Femoral Neck (ROPFEN)." He knew he could count on her professionalism, how she was in the end a true numbers rat, and that as such, almost certainly unfamiliar with the less-easily deflected measures required in easing new Krøhn-McGill products past the FDA.

He knew that Shivani from the immigrant quarters of middle England wouldn't be showing off recently surfaced photos of the mercenary locales where trial subjects had gone to have their bones imaged—how Krøhn-McGill had run most of them through a radiology lab next to a tanning salon in aging Cicero, IL. He knew his alluring and versatile ghostwriter could be trusted not to highlight the way in which the so-called "parabolic association" in slide seventeen, a datapoint purportedly validating treatment gains from Bioferex over time, was little more than a Jackson Pollock splatter in the results made to resemble a positive trend thanks to art having truncated both Y and X axes.

In short, Seamus had kept Shivani out of the circle of trust. As one of his last remaining holdouts from the unimaginative, pre-1990s Krøhn-McGill, she had preceded the harmonization of R&D with marketing. Shivani had come on line god bless her back when marketing would show up at the end of a disheartening process of science. Invited in like garbage after the guys with pocket protectors had solved a quote-unquote "medical problem." Shivani was in this way a relic from the weak, pre-industrialized evidence base, one of the few remaining data people who cared little about a balance sheet.

Their pills never made it rain. And their studies only sometimes produced the necessary safety and efficacy deliverables. Seamus had upended these inadequacies, the outdated notion of marketing-blind investigative science. Seamus had moved sales onto the ground floor of drug development, such that financials now determined the selection of illnesses to be treated, the design of studies, the patient advocacy needed to demand new drugs and the saturation campaigns needed to create new customers. Patel was something else entirely—a scientist first, with all the risk that entailed. She was, in short, not one of them.

Were she not so good, Seamus would have unloaded her ages ago. All of which was why he had been careful to place her in a box. Payroll kept her in golden handcuffs. Security flagged all signs of unwelcome curiosity within her emails. It was a given she would never be informed where the company stored raw data. That as selflessly as she had served the firm, no mercy would be shown should she ever make overtures to the press, regulators, or seek out legal or personal counsel outside the Krøhn-McGill family.

And all these measures had held, however, ensuring that she was, in the end, a professional. They ensured that Patel had Seamus's trust—his trust that she would refrain from telling the whole story, or half the story, or anything approaching the subject of Krøhn-McGill Psychiatric of North America in the slightest spirit of transparency. Seamus knew Shivani, and Shivani knew her job: to push a thumb drive in her laptop, then teach Junior and the rest of these fine young clinicians how to turn the world on to Bioferex.

35

5

The caller ID read 212. Seeing the Manhattan area code in his Minneapolis one-bedroom triggered a small shot of relief for Griffin, who knew he couldn't pay the bills with proceeds from his only assignment now in play, a demoralizing desperation pitch slated for June under the headline of "Lobster Bake on the Beach and Six Skills to Master for the Summer of Your Life."

He picked up the phone.

"Wagner here."

"Greg, E.J. Cerrano, I'm with Pagel-Simon in New York. How are you today?"

PR. Trevor must have given someone his number again.

"Yes, it's Griffin, actually."

"So sorry, I knew that. I love your work, truly."

She had no idea of his work. His own mother had no idea of his work.

"Do you have a second?" the flack continued. "I wanted to offer you a killer idea for a story. It's about a Krøhn-McGill drug called Bioferex, have you heard about it?"

"Umm, yeah, sure," Griffin lied.

There were so many ads for drugs. He could hardly keep up.

"It's for guys and women in training, anybody getting ready for a marathon, maybe a half, 10K or tri. Tri's are huge, you know, practically a rite of passage. Guys are doing Bikram, so are the very hottest girls, which is nice, am I right?"

"I'll say." Griffin felt embarrassed, more than a little patronized. These people tried so hard.

"And you write about guys, you GET them, man, so you probably know a lot of them develop stress injuries, hip and knee pain if they jump in too hard. You know how guys are, right, Griffin?"

E.J. Cerrano was waiting for him to say something.

Griffin was pruning his email box.

"They have the will to take on a top-notch endurance program," she continued, "but they might not have the miles under the hood to withstand the beating. The body needs time to adapt, as you know. Skip the base-building and you can be side-swiped by stress fractures."

She was right. As far as he could tell. He had heard all this years ago. Also, she had clearly rehearsed her pitch for days.

"Oh yeah, for sure."

It wasn't hard. A lot of mass-deleting. All he ever got was marketing.

"The pain of a stress fracture in the hip, femur or foot can be searing, and it shuts you down. And you know what that means: bye-bye registration fee."

Bye-bye registration fee? It sounded scripted.

"Bioferex has been proven in clinical trials to be safe and effective in speeding the repair of stress fractures. The FDA has approved it as an adjuvant treatment for the injuries. And recently—this is the key part for your story—doctors have begun prescribing it off-label for *prevention* of stress fractures."

OK, that would be notable. Griffin stopped deleting.

"Wow."

"Wow is right. It's only a matter of time before orthopedic and clinical sports medicine guidelines are going to include this category of intervention as a recommended preventative for population-based advisories on exercise. So, this is much bigger than triathletes, Griffin. It's going to be the drug that everyone takes to get off the couch."

Well. There was a publicist with high hopes for her pill. Who knew if it was warranted. Adjuvant. Strange word. Griffin had Googled the term while she was talking. *Adjuvant therapy—treatment given in addition to the primary or main therapy.*

"E.J., is it?"

"Yeah."

"What an interesting name."

"Thanks. It's short for Eileen Jane."

"Come on Eileen, I love that song!"

She didn't reply. Griffin silently cursed his unfiltered mouth. It was, if he had to reconstruct the lyrics, a song about lusting for your friend's little sister.

"So, Eileen, could you possibly send me a packet on any of this?"

Griffin knew the request was annoying. Everyone had stopped sending paper a decade ago. Griffin liked to ask for it anyway. He could read it in a bar, or on a bus. Circle the strange parts. Leave it out on his desk as a coaster, or a reminder to return a call.

"Done," Eileen offered. "Gonna get that Fed-Exed to you this minute. It will give you everything you need to report your story and then some. And when you are ready, we can put you in touch with Julian Powers, the endocrine researcher whose work helped to develop Bioferex. We can also set you up with some pretty amazing athletes who are taking it. You must know Jade Radcliffe, right, tight end for the Saints?"

"Oh, very cool," Griffin said. "I love that guy."

Griffin didn't know that guy at all. He pretended to keep up on the athletes, but they just kept coming, year after year.

He told her his address, said goodbye, then opened up an email window to bang out a pitch. He had to give Eileen credit: anything that combined medicine with endurance training was deep in the wheelhouse of *In the Zone*. He typed fast, hungry for paying work, cracked in a subject, "Bioferex story idea," and regurgitated her pitch.

Hey Trev,

Nice talking with you the other day. One other idea: how about 1,000 words on Bioferex? It's a drug to treat stress fractures for guys new to endurance training.

It's been around for a while, but it's prolly gonna be pushed for healthy people as a way to train safely for endurance races.

I can interview the doctor behind it, and Jade Radcliffe, and find some regular guys who are using it.

Promise I won't get too wonky with the science!

LMK, G

Griffin prepared to hit send, reviewing the Bioferex pitch one last time when he took note of the date: December 8, 2010.

It had been thirty years to the day since John Lennon died.

Griffin put *Abbey Road* in his CD player. Everyone had gone over to MP3s but he was slow to make the change. "Come Together" began to percolate in his speakers.

Here come old flat top,
he come, grooving up slowly.

He smiled at the climbing bass line, the word games Lennon had spun out to explain each Beatle in the four-verse mystery, starting with Ringo, then George, serving up harsh complaint about himself, and finally sadness about Paul wanting to break up the band. He reminded himself to go see Curtiss A that night at the Entry. His annual John Lennon tribute was one of the many small charms about life in Minneapolis.

Griffin had a couple of hours to kill. He decided if he ran some hoops down at the Y he would feel less guilty about his state of under-employment by the time they sang "Imagine." Enough for a Monday.

6

Shivani set out the door before dawn. She needed clarity like a junkie. She had hoped to find solace for an hour and ten at Yoga to the People, a boutique Ashtanga studio in her Gramercy Park neighborhood. The class had become her sole chance for getting into the office without crying most days. Today's outing, the 5:30 a.m. Advanced Inversions II, had started out looking like it would do the same.

During each return to Warrior I she had focused on her breath and the voice of Jin-Jin, her delicate and intuitive instructor. Rocking herself into frog followed by a headstand, Shivani had attempted to look with trust and compassion at the swells of panic inside of her. She vowed to accept the images of death at her hands as transient, mental clutter to be neither banished nor infused with selfish emotion.

She cultivated this practice for the full seventy-two minutes. At the end of her class, lying silently in corpse pose, Shivani committed with humility and acceptance to the fullness of her circumstance, honoring her good intentions and paying heed to her breath with arms supine, and chi-vectors externally rotated in palms-to-the-ceiling configuration.

As Jin-Jin then called her to seated pose, Shivani affirmed to herself before saying *Namaste* that all was right in this moment she shared with her fellow travelers, that she would seize her every breath with trust and an open heart. She remained seated like this in quiet contemplation as a Chilean flute track played over cocktail-hour beats mixed for the Saint Tropez poolside.

She thought about how much she liked those places, and how sorely she would miss them when she gave up her life as a drug industry whatever-she-was. She stared into the near distance as the harried professionals around her began wiping their mats, checking their phones and gathering sandals.

She sat with the responsibility of having been called upon to a make change in her life.

She exited her early morning retreat sore, sad, and prepared to do just that, harboring only loving kindness towards herself and the problem she carried within her.

She would embrace her openness to what comes.

Then, stepping out onto an iron-trimmed sidewalk along busy Madison Ave., she raised her eyes to the sight of a double-MTA as it roared by her with a vinyl wrap advertising the new product.

It was called Bioferex. Like all the drugs with an X in their names, it was trouble, beginning with its origin. Though a pill for the bones, Shivani knew Bioferex had been built to replace the losses of an SSRI about to go generic, an apocalyptic evaporation of revenue destined to flatten the balance sheet. Not just any depression med, this was *zoloxetine*, brand name Serotonal, a drug it seemed the entire world adored.

Back in the mid-nineties, Shivani had been the wordsmith on hand when Krøhn-McGill first muscled Serotonal into a crowded new market for antidepressants. Serotonal was a janky pill, however, one that Shivani and the telegenic doctor who'd begun signing his name to her writings had managed to push to the front of the pack.

His name was Jeremy Elton, and he always found time for morning shows and magazines. Together, Shivani and Dr. Elton had jumped atop a popular marketing message to persuade all doubters that Serotonal reset a so-called *chemical imbalance in the brain.*

Although it hadn't taken much work.

It was an intoxicating narrative, their tale asserting that one in ten Americans, one in five young adults, and one in four middle-aged women were suffering from a shape-shifting disorder of biology with no physical fingerprint of any kind.

A plague of mood disorders had swept the land, in this telling of the troubles all around them, and all that was required to arrest this great sadness was a lifelong commitment to the transmutations of industrial polypharmacy.

It resolved so many problems, their tidy narrative of illness and rescue. It muted questions of whether the triumph of technology had a role in the poverty of the times. It offered consolation to parents bewildered by their truth-telling children. It dispensed with grief in a consumer marketplace that careened from pleasure to pleasure.

And so it soared. The Serotonal messaging flattered a deep, unidentified hunger to feel an emotional sophistication required of the times, one Shivani found to be somewhat hollow. It told all acolytes they too could be among those for whom the neurotransmitter conversation was familiar. Nonfiction books were funded. Patient groups rose up to demand access. Political heroes jockeyed to disparage any insurer who appeared skeptical.

Mostly, Shivani disliked Serotonal's tendency to trigger a worrisome side-effect, one that, in a more careful setting, should have been disqualifying. Central among its collateral damages, Serotonal gave birth to high levels of akathisia—possibly as steep as ten to sixteen percent of all users.

Akathisia was a formal classification, derived from the Greek for *inability to sit still,* denoting dopaminergic depletion rendering Parkinsonian agitation complicated by immersive psychic distress. An eviscerating phenomenon of drug-induced rage combined with emotional distancing from the self, akathisia could lead to intrusive thoughts of suicide and by extension, the self-immolation of violent harm to strangers en masse. Shivani spotted akathisia in the crime pages like a Red Sox lifer reading the box scores.

Though akathisia had been on the books for a century, the clinical brigade had been coached to view it like a rash—your basic extra-pyramidal or motor syndrome, a Tourette's or tardive dyskinesia. And yet it took a person hostage in the furnace of their very soul. Akathisia was a special kind of monster, a pharma-cruelty set upon obliterating the human being.

Shivani's employers had managed to obscure this nagging conundrum by asserting soaring levels of unrecognized mental illness, and in its wake, ensuing suicidality. In this most audacious game of pharma-chess, all users of Serotonal that had come forward with a tale of something akathisiac were greeted with robust gaslighting.

What the victim had experienced was simply proof of their condition, delusions to be patiently deflected within the larger SSRI project. In the name of fighting back stigma, the testimony of the Serotonal-poisoned itself became the object of stigma, hysteria to be vanquished as the protestations of Luddites, therapy-phobes, anti-vaxxers, tin-foil hatters, Scientologists and those who would obstruct Access to Care.

Only when the deaths and the extraordinarily unpleasant manner of exiting among unhappy Serotonal customers became impossible to ignore—and there really was no precedent for the pre-teen hangings—were regulators forced to acknowledge a product defect. Lawyered language was placed within four lines on the label of all pills. Hedging their move, the CYA had been limited to a non-emancipated population, underaged persons for whom the pills would be offered regardless. And then the warning was packaged in language that warned of the warning itself.

Bioferex should not have harbored this side effect, however, which is why it had puzzled Shivani to learn one afternoon while buried deep in the data, that Bioferex seemed to torment more than just the standard five percent. It wasn't even limited to the Serotonal ten-to-fifteen. Shivani couldn't be sure, but for her money, Bioferex was wracking thirty.

Was that possible? A third was a lot.

But those were her numbers. If so, it was a large bug in the operating code, so much that one could call it a feature. A third of the population, in this scenario, seemed unable to fully metabolize the compound, leading to toxic build-up over the course of a three-to-seven week loading dose.

That, or a withdrawal syndrome was making itself known through post-market reporting pathways. So with the hour having arrived to make the science sing for this Serotonal replacement, a bone-and-fitness drug her employers had clumsily named Bioferex, the company sought out Shivani once again for her skill in polishing paper.

True to form as a child of immigrants, Shivani had put her head down and gotten to work, taking possession of summary numbers the firm had generated at dozens of nondescript trial centers, columns that were presumably mathed-up by unknown others prior to being presented to her in synopsis form only. Armed with these corporate data, Shivani had ghostwritten two indication trials of the pill, FDA-approval paperwork enabling Bioferex to gain passage for sale as a first-line treatment for stress fractures.

That was all easy enough. But stress fractures were merely the camel's nose at Krøhn-McGill. They were, to better quote the sales team, a *crowbar*, a perfunctory malady required to wrench open the more ambitious, lucrative, population-ready market that was, well, everyone. Bioferex had to become not so much a drug as toothpaste, something found in every home.

Shivani had delivered this work, because she was Shivani. She had done so overlooking some things, with the firm having withheld other things. She took consolation in the reminder that there was always a chance the data she had sought but never received was somehow exculpatory—in favor of Bioferex being safe. That being said, chances were great that the data was denied for obvious reasons.

Why do people struggle to be brave? Was it her love of nice things? Krøhn-McGill paid Shivani more with each passing year, and she had gone along and gotten along. Her mood darkened as she stared in mild panic at the oversize decal. It was scaled for the launch of a Broadway mega-production, this banner for her pill moving brashly down the premier roadway of the world's bright shining city.

She thought about the volunteers with unexplained calamity in the healthy user arm of the Bioferex trials. Their suffering made no sense. Why had so many of them undergone such terrible mishaps?

Shivani knew these fears were too big for Jin-Jin and crow pose to fix. Unless she could find a way out, she was going to search in horror for her handiwork as each new report of the signal appeared in the news. These thoughts seemed impossible to sustain for a lifetime, or even a year, no matter how much they were paying her.

7

Griffin got lucky.

Trevor called back the very next day.

"Seven hundred and fifty words on Bioferex works for me, Melanie Griffith, but don't take your eyes off the prize."

"Prize?"

"Our lobster bake for two?"

Griffin paused.

"Don't act like you forgot," Trevor laughed. "That one has it all."

"Go on."

Griffin despaired being chained to the likes of Trevor.

"It has connotations."

"Connotations?"

"Yeah, conno-fucking-tations. Lobster bake on the beach is going to get us some sunsetty fantasy shots. Layout says they are calling in their two favorite models. We're talking about a college girl in a spotted two-piece. It's still being story-boarded, but I'm thinking a Sarah Lawrence junior holding a couple of three-pound lobsters like a boss. You can see how this is a story that has it all."

Trevor was riffing, and now Griffin just had to listen.

"It's going to be hot as hell. Mad honeys, the full Abercrombie. Her hair is down to her ass and our guy is ripped. Thinking we're going to dress him in some droopy board shorts, rocking that iliac crest."

The men's magazine business was homoerotic AF.

"Trevor when do I get to see your iliac crest?" Griffin couldn't resist.

"And as such," Trevor continued, "lobster bake on the beach is far more useful to our boys than a pill for man-babies just starting to lace up their sneakers. It's especially more useful than a thumb-sucker on some returning Iraq vet who didn't get his old job back at the grain elevator."

Griffin had pitched that one a month ago.

"We'd all like to write a *Harper's Jottings* or a *Top of the Talk* or whatever it's called."

"It's *Harper's* Readings," Griffin said with bland deflection. "*The New Yorker* has a page called the *Talk of the Town*."

"Yeah, well, we'd all like to make out with Kate Upton, too," Trevor said. "We're trying to run a profitable men's magazine here. Think you can get your head out of the clouds and crank out a lobster bake for me? Like, right after this story on the bone pill?"

Trevor didn't need wait for an answer. Griffin was always hurting for work.

"Hanging up now," he said. Then he did just that.

Though Griffin had told the flack there was no need to rush, a Bioferex press kit came the next morning via Priority Overnight. It was a fifty-three-dollar mailing they had likely shipped at a premium to dozens of service-writing freelancers. *Christ, these drug people were tight with their cash,* Griffin thought as he wedged the box under his arm. *How come they didn't send it by helicopter?*

For a readership as large as *In the Zone*, PR would make it rain to get you to write up their account. Add in a drug budget to the equation and

Griffin was pretty sure that Pagel-Simon would have sent him to South Beach to claim his press kit had he only asked.

Free samples, speedy deliveries and fawning calls from charming women in PR were the dubious perks to Griffin's line of work. Four years earlier, he had taken an assignment on reviewing high-end cologne, a story he had pitched as a great way to get free body wash. Today, his closet still resembled the fragrance counter at Macy's.

Griffin had also forgotten to return three tennis rackets, six leather basketballs, four diving watches and more five-in-one tools than any man without a garage could possibly defend owning. His bookshelves were lined with high-quality hardcovers. His bathroom was filled with every skin cleanser sold to man. All of it had been dropped on his doorstep like magazine-writer Christmas, day-in, day-out, including this very package he now held for Bioferex.

He was rich in stuff and poor in cash.

୬

It said: *ROPFEN: A six-week, double-blind, random-controlled trial of Rostangilorb (Trade name Bioferex ™) for Osteoblast Proliferation at the Femoral Neck.*

Griffin read the drug's chemical name out loud, trying out three possible ways of pronunciation.

"Rostan-GI-lorb."

"RO-stangilorb."

"Ro-STAN-gi-lorb."

The article had run in a journal called the *American Journal of Metabolic Medicine,* or *AJMM.* The very title made him groan. Griffin turned on the TV, surfing to the highlights of last night's Timberwolves game. Eventually, when he could stall no more, he drifted back to this thing on rostangiwhateverthefuck.

Clearing his throat, Griffin took a sip of coffee and called up his best impersonation of John Cleese to better deliver his dramatic reading of the study's small, opening summary paragraph to Lee Majors:

"In a randomized controlled trial of twenty-six men with femoral neck stress fractures," he called towards the dog, *"we compared the rate of osteoblast production and millimeter expansion for bone modeling in users of Bioferex (50 mg) with placebo controls (n= 18) through CT imaging and cell dye phosphorous. Duration was six weeks. Bioferex was well-tolerated."*

"..And who the fuck knows what that means, Lee Majors."

At the mention of his name, the dog glanced upward without lifting his chin from his paws.

"…The treatment group demonstrated a statistically-significant increase in bone cell production, bone cell proliferation, and fracture closure advantage over placebo," Griffin's John Cleese continued.

"Earlier studies have noted that 50 mg Bioferex produces a similar rate of osteoblast proliferation at the femoral neck in healthy users, thereby suggesting a possible PROPHYLACTIC advantage in users at risk of femoral neck fracture…and in reducing the risk of repetitive strain fractures of the hip, tibia and navicular, etcetera, etceta and so on."

All jokes aside, Griffin took a small dose of pleasure in having followed the meaning of this deadly dull thingy. As well as he could tell, the experiment in question had shown that Bioferex made bone cells grow faster after a hairline crack had emerged in the hip.

There would have been some limitations to this finding. Bioferex may have only brought on these changes in a crack that never caused pain. The study never established that Bioferex decreased the time needed to recover from fractures. It only found that new cells were being spit out a little bit faster on the imaging. Through the magic of transitive reasoning, it appeared, this had been good enough for the FDA.

Griffin thought he remembered Come on Eileen telling him Bioferex sped the repair of fractures. But from what he could tell, it was clear the manufacturer had never shown that to be the case.

"Check this out…The flack and the abstract did not match, Lee Majors."

49

The dog looked up at him from the floor once more, then began licking his paws.

"Imagine that, but don't have a heart attack, or get jacked, Mack, cause we need you to show some sack."

The dog stopped what he was doing, dropped his head to the floor, closed his eyes and signed off with a swift exhale.

Griffin thought it interesting that Come on Eileen had exaggerated what the drug did while reading from a script.

"If I didn't know better, Lee Majors, that means the people at Pagel-Simon were putting a fib into a marketing plan."

Which was of course illegal.

Though the act routinely went unnoted, Griffin knew it was against the rules to promote a drug for treatments that had not been proven effective in the eyes of the FDA. Eileen's bosses would have likely assumed there was no penalty in overselling a pill to a hack for *In the Zone*. And they would have been correct.

Griffin threw the folder into a pile of other press kits. The sooner he wrote this up, the sooner it rolled through revisions, the sooner he could bill for it. Which, according to his contract, was worth 750 words at $1.50 a word, or $1125. That was enough to justify three, maybe four phone calls.

Griffin heard back from Dr. Julian Powers in three minutes, which had to be some kind of record. On the call, the metabolic disorders specialist had been careful to state the most granular details of his professional title—how he was *Julian C. Powers, MD, Ph.D., holder of the Garrett George Endowed Professorship in Metabolic Research, Harley James Cornwall Wing, Wilson University Memorial Medical Center, University of Dallas.*

And there was just no way whatsoever Griffin was going to get any of that in his article.

"It's not a cure for cancer," Powers intoned. "But when it comes to sports medicine, this drug really is breaking new ground. We've never had a metabolic protocol for people who train hard and play hard. This could be just that drug."

Powers was a decent fit for *In the Zone,* projecting the right mix of authority and guy-ness.

"Before now, you couldn't predict who would get a stress fracture," he had continued. "With Bioferex not only can we speed up healing, we are thinking of using it as a prophylactic."

Like the flack, Powers had made a casual assertion that research had shown Bioferex sped up healing time, when his study hadn't proven anything of the sort.

༄

The next interview was less worth the effort.

Griffin's ten minutes with Jade Radcliffe, All-Pro tight end for the New Orleans Saints, was supposed to have been arranged through Pagel-Simon. But after four emails then three phone messages, Griffin discovered he would need to go through the NFL team office. That person put him in touch with Jade's agent, Willie Jones. Willie Jones had his own media person.

Why was a football player even repping a stress fracture drug? Wasn't this a pill for amateurs? According to the Bioferex press kit, Jade had taken up ultra-endurance running for the offseason. Following a nifty fifty in the high desert heat, however, he had developed searing pain in his shins. Go figure.

"I had preseason camp in two weeks and I couldn't get out of the chair," Jade told Griffin during their six minutes on the phone. "I was taking all this motherfuckin' Advil and it wasn't helping, which was why I said fine, I would go on the Bioferex. It let me get back in camp in time. They were saying I was going to need 6-8 weeks otherwise."

Dang, a quote.

True, Griffin would need to remove Jade's delightful use of the *motherfuckin*. Buried also was this strange admission: *I said fine, I would go on the Bioferex.*

Did someone push Bioferex on a pro football player? Who?

※

Griffin read over his article one last time.

So it wasn't going to win any prizes.

It had all the usual clichés. ("The jury's still out.")

He had allowed the detestable phrase "game-changer" in there — the most irresponsible boast in all of health writing.

But he liked the way he had described the femur by invoking Fred Flintstone.

He liked the way he had named the drug maker—thereby pleasing the publicist—yet still managed to appear independent by making fun of its name.

It made the article look neutral, which it wasn't.

Griffin had essentially told everyone to go get on the damn pill. Because this was his role. Fuck it, a larger reality loomed: He had been sitting on this dull short for three weeks, and his bank account was running low.

Send.

8

Suzanne Barry found the last chair in the community room of the Powderhorn Park Co-op, a plastic seat next to a rack filled with brochures advertising mental health problems.

That's how the glossy, oversized sales pamphlets touting regional treatment centers within the Behavioral Health Facility Finder looked to her, anyway. Like advertisements for mental health problems.

So perhaps she had gotten cynical.

In those first, late-fall days after Mark died, Susie grabbed her short moments of forgetting where she could. She felt normal during sleep, then horror upon waking. Relief came when she had to do something abjectly parental, like helping their daughter Crystal off to school. These small actions allowed her to briefly forget the call saying Mark had walked in front of an 80,000-lb. semi travelling the posted 70 on I-90.

Parenting pushed all this briefly to the side.

It was during one of these fleeting moments of normal when a nurse asked if she had heard about MISA. Susie's eyes drifted across the photo-pin on her nurse's brightly colored scrubs. It was a picture of a happy family with two young children atop a redwood swing set. Susie knew it was there to humanize her provider. But the sight of an intact unit always triggered a new wavelet of pain.

"It can really help to be around others who have experienced what you are going through," said the young nurse, who reached into a drawer and pulled out a notecard titled *When "Being Strong" Isn't the Answer.*

Susie had taken the card, nodded politely, and begun praising Crystal on what a brave girl she had been to take the booster without shedding a tear. Susie restrained her dismay over how the nurse had said "what you are going through," as if Susie was going through something with an expiration date. Susie knew the loss would be with her always.

"I can't imagine what it's like," the nurse added.

No, she could not, indeed.

Well look at this the nurse was still talking about it.

"This is a place to go and remember that you are never alone."

Susie knew she wasn't alone. She had Crystal, who was in second grade. Susie nodded again, because people were just trying to help and it was now Susie's job to make helpers feel comfortable. To do that, she left with the brochure.

The name stood for Mental Illness and Suicide Awareness.

It was a local chapter of a national group. A box at the bottom said meetings were open to all, held every Wednesday. She and Crystal had downsized after Mark did that thing with the truck. Susie would have thrown the brochure away, but something made her leave it on the desk in the new place, right off the kitchen, a family pile cluttered with bills and children's artwork, whereupon it seemed to hang around.

Susie was intuitive. She looked for coincidences to help her make decisions. Over the next few weeks, the brochure had begun to appear like a sign. One day she gave in and decided to give the meeting in a crowded community center in south Minneapolis a try. They couldn't make her say anything. She could just listen.

୬

Someone passed her a clipboard.

"The offering of your name, email, place of employment and address is strictly voluntary," it stated along the top. Why not. Susie filled it out, handed it to the next person. She pretended to study the advertisements. One said, "Horizons," another "Beginnings," a third one "Prairie Sunrise." She wasn't sure if she had done the right thing. The clock hit 7:30 and the room began to talk in unison: *Depression was silent in those who left us, but we will not be silent about depression.*

"Thanks, everyone."

The voice came from a tall woman with blocky glasses. The woman was serious and practiced. Her eyes were warm, but the corners of her mouth were closed. She may have been secretly furious about something. She was not sad. That confused Susie the most. Who does this if they're not sad?

"I'm Charlotte to you all, first names only here, regional chair and certified group facilitator. We have some new faces with us today."

Susie saw Charlotte nod in her direction.

"To our new friends, you are free to tell your story, or share the gift of your silent fellowship. Speak when you wish, or not at all, but everyone together now: *When one voice speaks to the all, the all will hear through the one.*"

Another chant.

"I'll start."

It was a younger woman in a down coat clutching a Coach bag from the mall.

"Mya, please go ahead."

"I am really angry today. Angry at him. Angry at myself for not knowing."

Mya stared at her hands.

"That's all."

"That's the truth," Charlotte offered.

Charlotte waited a beat.

"Your truth…But your anger is at the *disease*," she added, "not him, isn't it?"

"No."

Mya was resolute.

"It's at *him*."

Well this was interesting, a rebellion. Charlotte jumped back in.

"Would you be angry if he had died of Lupus?"

Mya shook her head.

"More to the nitty-gritty," Charlotte continued, "if your husband had died of Lupus and had never been given the chance to be treated, would you be angry at him? Or would you save your anger for those who would deny him a *medical* treatment for a *medical* disease?"

The room sucked in Charlotte's analogy with a collective round of nods. Charlotte leaned back on her arms. "We talk a lot about medicine in here," she continued. "It's not because we don't support therapy or are patsies for pharma. It's because we won't be silent while others allow the lie to stand that suicide stems from failure. We stand for medicine because that is how we reject the blaming of those we lost."

It was quite a speech. But Susie wondered if it made any sense.

I saw what you did there, she wanted to say. It was the first Susie had ever heard it put that way. The straw man, that you would ever blame someone for taking their own life.

Susie didn't know anyone who would drag out a slur like *failure* in the presence of someone who lost a friend to suicide. And she thought it was another not very kind thing to say, the way this pivot seemed to materialize on the heels of jamming poor Mya for her anger.

Let the woman feel her wrath. Susie had felt her own recognition at Mya's confession. She'd had her moments of anger. It would have supportive of Charlotte to say Mya's anger was normal. This was a support group, after all.

꿈

"Mark wasn't depressed."

It had taken forty minutes, but Susie blurted that out.

"I just wanted to say that first thing," she said. "I've heard what depression looks like. I don't want to sound unsupportive, because I'm not. But I haven't heard anything about depression that sounds like our life."

"What was he, then?"

Charlotte, of course.

"I don't know what he had," Susie replied to her hands now, "but he wasn't depressed. We had just planned a trip to the Caymans. He had just put money into the college fund and signed up for a triathlon. You should have seen him telling stories at the dinner we hosted two nights before he walked out onto that freeway."

At the mention of Mark's cause of death, Susie sensed the others looking up from their laps. It confused her to think that a room full of suicide survivors would find the manner of Mark's ending startling.

"He never wrote a note," Susie continued, a little faster. "Just some… *weird* questions on a note pad. It's almost like it wasn't planned at all. So I have been really angry."

She looked over at Mya.

"It seemed like he didn't see any other choice."

The room offered Susie a moment of silence.

"It *wasn't* his choice," Charlotte said, "not with depression. Forgive me, because I say this from a place of compassion."

Susie nodded.

"But his life sounds a bit manic? A little bit grandiose. Triathlon? In our experience, that's depression before it flips into bipolar. It's OK to be mad. The illness fooled you. You didn't do anything wrong."

Susie hated that line most of all. She knew she didn't do anything wrong.

"He hid it from you," Charlotte continued, "and by hiding it from you, he didn't do anything wrong, either. He hid it out of love. If I can say this without causing offense, chances are you are *still* hiding the fact of his depression from yourself. And no one in this room would blame you. Here in this room, we hold each other up. Out there, the judgment and stigma flow. Everyone please all say it out loud with me for Susie."

The room joined Charlotte in a quick chant: *It's no enigma there's stigma.*

"Thank you everyone, I know you have busy lives and plenty of normalcy to get back to."

And then that was that. Susie got up to go, and her bag toppled a rack of brochures for MISA. As she bent down to pick them up, Susie saw the golden KM for Krøhn-McGill on the back of each one.

A memory arose from an hour spent cleaning out Mark's side of the dresser.

He had been taking a KM pill when he was training. Susie never knew.

That triggered another thought.

Depressed my ass, she thought. He was training for a triathlon.

9

Three weeks after Griffin sent in the Bioferex thing, Trevor responded in his usual magnanimous style.

Hello fucker. Sorry to take so long. Nice enough go at it, but a tad DULL. I realize it's only a health short, but could you please get me some regular guys who've taken this thing?

The piece needs a regular guy.

Better yet, why not take some of this drug yourself? There has to be a race for a fatty like you.

Griffin dreaded the request that he locate a "regular guy" who had taken Bioferex. Editors loved "regular guys," but they were a writer's nightmare.

You could find a "regular guy" who had used a product but didn't want to be in a magazine. You could find a "regular guy" who had used a product but was set on speaking with only important-sounding words.

A surprising proportion of "regular guys" were prone to thinking their opinions were more interesting than they were. And yet this "regular guy" supplied his editors with such a feeling of satisfaction.

Most likely, this stemmed from the need to keep the show going. The appearance of a regular guy left readers with the impression the piece they were reading had been generated from the ground up, rather than its actual pathway into the media, via a press release down.

And take a drug? For an article?

Score one for the nerve. The idea would be laughable, were Griffin not suspicious that his slippery and unknowable patron was in fact being serious. Journalism, it seemed, had increasingly become a stunt profession. Now you had to take the pill.

ℒ

Griffin came around. (Because money.)

Plus, Bioferex, now that he thought about it, was probably closer to, what, a supplement?

It was probably like eating your vegetables.

And, truthfully, he wasn't totally wrong for it. After all, what if this was a way to lose a few pounds? Get winded less frequently on the basketball court? He wrote the note without thinking. *I'm wondering if it is possible to get some Bioferex for myself,* he typed. *I understand if you can't.*

Send.

And though he half-hoped that Come on Eileen would blow him off, the flack replied with blasé efficiency within minutes, CC'ing "Bricen Hostetler, patient administrative liaison at RXS, a Krøhn-McGill partner located just outside of Minneapolis."

Well what do you know, right here in town.

"He would be happy to provide you with a sample pack after we get you a prescription, which also shouldn't be much trouble," Eileen continued in a happy tippity-tap-tap. "RXS has a network of accredited prescribers on call for this very purpose."

A second email arrived within the half hour from an MD sporting a surname full of consonants. The note to Griffin from Dr. Vargn

Puletzkinecz contained five screening questions, a quiz Griffin promptly demolished. No, he had never taken hormone replacement pills; No, he was not being treated for cancer. No, he had not been diagnosed with heart disease. No, he was not under the care of a psychiatrist. Yes, he was over 18.

"It's a 21-day sample pack," Dr. Puletzkinecz wrote. "We call it Three Weeks to Peak Performance. These will keep coming until we hear otherwise. Congratulations on an excellent decision to try Bioferex for yourself. We are confident you will love the extra intensity you will soon be feeling during workouts."

The parcel came priority overnight, from a return address labeled *RXS, Maple Grove, MN*. It contained a sample pack of Bioferex. The Bioferex logo had by now become familiar to anyone with a TV, showing up in magazines and online, with Bio written in italics, the X winding gracefully in a curve meant to suggest a pastoral running trail, as opposed to a fraying femur. Griffin tore it open and unfolded the package insert, a densely-footnoted tissue entitled,

DRUG FACTS: ROSTABGILORB 50MG.

It contained all the usual small-print advisories related to dosage, mechanism, indications and side effects, a blur of legalese of use to none but the lawyers. Griffin would sooner read the privacy agreement on his credit card statement.

He set the CYA aside and proceeded to examine the contents.

The pills came in a blister pack designed to represent a 21-day cycle. That would have suggested some kind of a ramp-up. Griffin only briefly wondered why a drug safe enough for the world would need to control the on-boarding slowly. But he did not hold this worry for long.

Was it all the products he had sampled through the years? He'd become such a sensible, trusting consumer. All the free skin creams, the free designer toothbrushes, the free high-end body-hair trimmers and the free power gels packed in foil. The decision must have looked, in that fatal moment, like so much more of the same. Punching the capsule marked DAY ONE through a thin sheet of silver before tossing it back with a swallow of water, it was all too easy. The thought came to Griffin only once and that ended that. This was America. People take pills every day.

Griffin's mood lifted enough to decide he did in fact want to take on Trevor's final request: finding a so-called "regular guy" who was busy taking Bioferex. How hard could it be? After Googling a few terms, Griffin spotted his first lead, a post on a blog called *Weekend Warrior*. It was an entry called "Bioferex: One Man's View." The byline said *Edward Salinger*. It was a year old.

Edward Salinger is a software engineer, read a caption.

He lives in Fort Wayne, IN.

Boom.

A regular guy.

"I am psyched to have learned about Bioferex for stress fractures," a hopeful Ed Salinger had written. "I had a stress fracture the last time I trained for a 10K. Bioferex is once-a-day, *and* expensive ($330 a month). But if I can get back in the game, I figure it will be more than worth it. I will be posting as my training progresses. Wish me luck!"

Oh yeah.

Regular Guy as fuck.

A bit colorless, but that was all very fixable in Griffin's hands. If anything, plain-speaking Ed seemed even more like the real deal than someone churning out smooth copy that smelled of PR.

As he looked for an update, however, Griffin realized no more posts had been written. That in itself wasn't alarming. Abandonment was ever the fate of most blogs. Still, something about his regular guy's disappearance was odd. Ed Salinger, enthusiastic at the start of his Bioferex trial, had really never posted a word about it again?

On a whim, Griffin typed Ed's name into a White Pages, quickly turning up no address. He added Fort Wayne. This too, was a bust. He broadened the search to all of Indiana.

Bingo.

Fort Wayne Journal Gazette.

Ed Salinger, 38, of Wildwood Park, died suddenly on Monday,
April 9. Ed was a father, husband and friend.

A graduate of the Indiana Institute of Technology, Ed
received his BS in engineering, and an MS in
biomechanical sciences.

As obits so often do, this one featured a selfie.

Dead Ed was smiling.

Griffin found him to be a likable, relatable-looking dude in a
biking helmet.

Ed worked for 10 years at Zenon informatics, designing
software for health IT. Beloved to his wife Kendra, Ed was an
avid cyclist, runner, and friend of the outdoors.

Services will be held 10 am, Saturday, April 14 at D.O.
McComb & Sons, Covington Knolls, 8325 Covington Road.

In lieu of flowers, memorial contributions may be sent to
MISA, Indiana Chapter.

It was sad and kind of weird, finding and losing a source in all of
two minutes. Since Griffin's day was slow and since he had been looking
forward to contacting this Ed Salinger, he decided to type the acronym
into his search engine. That's when things got heavy.

MISA was a support group for survivors of suicide.

Did he just find out that Ed Salinger killed himself?

Exhaling, then reaching for his coffee, Griffin leaned back in his
chair, sent a silent prayer off for the soul of Ed Salinger, then set down
his cup and went back to the search results.

The morning was getting late. He needed a regular guy before lunch.
But pretty soon he grew antsy and went back to learning what he could
about Ed. Before long, a new story popped in to his results, a short,
older item, it looked to have run in the back of the newspaper.

April 11, 2010

Body found near rail crossing is identified as Wildwood
Park man.

Staff writer.

The body found hanging in a nearby rail crossing has been
identified as that of Edward James Salinger, 38, of Wildwood
Park. Salinger's body was found Monday by a pair of cyclists,
hanging from the historic Williston Trestle. It is not certain
how long he had been there.

An investigation is underway, but the county medical
examiner says he does not believe foul play is suspected.

§

Welp.

Seek and ye shall find.

After lunch, Griffin returned to working the blogs for a regular guy,
someone happily taking Bioferex, ideally non-dead.

He eventually found one, and then a second.

The first one, unfortunately, seemed kind of new to the entire idea
of training.

"My doctor told me I needed to lose 160 pounds."

That was how Lance Shultz, a sympathetic, forty-two-year-old
window salesman from Port Lucie, Florida, had made it clear to Griffin
that he wouldn't be making the cut for *iTZ* under its decidedly shallow
editorial philosophy. The art department would need to be shooting
pictures of Griffin's "regular guy." Lance had learned of the drug in a
weight loss club. Ergo, Lance was fat. Hey, he had tried.

"We exist to lift people up, Waggity-man."

Griffin remembered Trevor saying that the last time he tried to

64

include a source with a body fat percentage approaching those outside of fashion.

Luckily his next regular guy, a Rick Price, age 38, had potential.

A 30-something living in Phoenix, Bioferex-using Rick Price had boasted to Griffin how he'd logged "a solid decade of ten-to-twenty weekly in the 90 degree heat." Then and only then did Arizona Rick develop pain in his arches.

Key takeaway for Trevor: not a slob.

In another plus, not dead.

♋

Griffin sent his rewrite off the very next day. It had been a moderately hell-holish process. Three guys who had taken the drug and said they liked it. One who had decided to hang himself.

His rewrite had also satisfied Trevor's request that Griffin go on the pill himself, and even unspooled a "scene" describing just that.

Trevor liked what saw. He got back to Griffin within the hour, signaling in his own dimwitted way that Griffin would soon be getting paid.

> Much nicer. We will take it from here & I will tell accounting to put through your payment.
>
> Feeling grateful I never let your halitosis get in the way of our friendship.
>
> I eagerly await your advice on how to cook lobsters on the beach. Crikey wants to rent the best stretch of Montauk for a weekend-long shoot.
>
> TD

10

Retail therapy, then therapy-therapy, that was the plan.

Thankfully, the SoHo office of Dr. Jennifer Chase, PhD, was located around the corner from Gjale, perennial Shivani haunt and flagship storefront for the coveted Danish beauty line.

Gjale audaciously offered three and just three personal care beauty trophies: eye-, base- and lip- Rejuvenation Organics.

Otherwise known as makeup.

Though Gjale was hardly a store, as much as a vehicle for the beauty press. The boutique routinely hired celebrity DJ's for buzz-building new product launches, moneyed parties peopled by A-listers. Shivani had enough friends in cosmetics to know that the bold-faced actors merely stepped out of town cars for a desultory walk on red carpet—soiled with stains if one cared to look closely—before leaving through the back with a check and a handful of Vicodin.

Shivani had no membership at Gjale and was therefore just the drop-in clientele.

She had a life. Or at least she wanted one—hence the appointment with Dr. Chase, a clinical psychologist in private practice.

Her sanity, she had to accept, had gotten wobbly.

Shivani selected three items from the juniper line, paying $175.50 for the lipstick, $430.00 for the eyeliner, and $668.75 for the 2.8-ounce base.

Having gamely handed over her Onyx card for the $1,200 impulse buy, Shivani departed southward onto Spring Street, terrified at the binge she had just exhibited but determined to sort out her worries.

Upon being buzzed into the lobby, ascending a marble staircase, filling out too many forms and taking a chair across from her small, mall-branded confessor, Shivani sat clutching her pricey new eyeliner. She felt warmed by its presence as she repeated the first of Jennifer Chase's frightening questions.

"What would I say is the reason I came here?"

"Yes. What would you say is the reason you came here?"

It was a fair question, given the circumstances and all. Why indeed had Shivani decided to go through with this plan to meet with a therapist? Was she here to practice coming clean? Was she out of her mind?

She looked around for something to hold her gaze, a spot in the near distance to anchor the decade-plus of secrecy at risk of being thrown out the window.

"And those are your parents?"

"Yes." Then another long pause.

Shivani heard a cab honking on Spring Street. Dr. Chase was showing a high comfort level with silence. Shivani spotted all the standard mood disorder manuals: B-B-B.

Barlow for anxiety. Burns for depression. Beck for CBT.

No dodgy goods on first pass, that was comforting. No *Listening to Prozac*, *The Noonday Demon* or *The Bipolar Child*. None of the popular valentines bestowed onto her industry courtesy of American self-help publishing.

Given this reasonable person's library, Shivani knew her confessor's training had been anchored in the standard and dutiful care of privilege. There would have been board certifications in all the manualized treatments targeting depression, worry, compulsion and low self-appraisal. Previous clients of Dr. Jennifer Chase would likely have spent hours reframing their thought processes, learning how to tolerate and grow bored with the demons, practicing self-care.

Shivani had come to know all the dominant paradigms well. CBT for mood, DBT for personality, IPT for relational struggle. She had set up enough comparison trials pitting these post-psychodynamic warhorses against her employer's pills to have long ago noted how, as a creature of pharma, she had clearly locked into a multi-year deal with the wrong baseball club. Shivani's determined handiwork in spinning these drug-against-therapy match-ups left her with the weakest of boasts—that drugs combined with therapy were the best treatments for the lifting of depression.

It killed, but Shivani knew it was all just a fig leaf—how readily were some intrepid fraud-buster to dig into her data they would happen across the less-inspiring take-home: that her employers' pills were riding the coattails of manual-guided therapies, and that it was the talking, not the pills, that had been the vehicle for the lifting of symptoms.

Sure, the drugs had helped things along with sleep, and offered an antihistamine's worth of depersonalization, maybe a Sudafed's worth of activation all wrapped up in a robust placebo effect. The blind was always broken given the telltale signs of dry mouth and failure to launch in the bedroom. For Shivani, the data purporting to support meds was reason she was here, in fact, rather than home taking one of her pills. She knew the numbers.

"The reason I came here is that I don't like my job," she lied.

"You don't like your job."

Dr. Chase was now skimming Shivani's answers to a biographical questionnaire, lightly touching the tip of her pen to certain words in the answers. It appeared as if she was planning to return to their contents. "Tell me more about that. It says here that you work in PR?"

"Sort of, yes."

"'Sort of.' I don't follow."

"I bet you still want to know why I am here."

"That would help me to help you." Dr. Chase smiled warmly.

"Well, the reason I am here is that, lately, but almost every night, my job has me feeling anxious and losing sleep, and I can't tell if that's because something bad is going on around me, or if it's all in my noodle."

Shivani had never spoken with a therapist. She felt her heart picking up as she opened up to the stranger, worried that she had disclosed too much. Maybe it was a British quality, the fear of saying anything personal, the horrible possibility of being boring, the withering vulnerability that would follow.

"Tell me more, what's going on?"

"Well, it might bore you a bit. One imagines your basic lower-Manhattan shrink has heard from hundreds of the work-obsessed, worried-well. Just think of all the brokers who must have bounced onto the street after the crash in 2008, needing to pull their girls out of Spence and the enticing prospect of ending it all."

"Financial sector employees in my experience are not interested in developing insight on their problems," Dr. Chase replied. "They tend to resolve conflict with externalizing behaviors."

"What's that mean, exactly—'externalizing behaviors'?"

Shivani loved new ways of looking at things.

"Actions lacking self-awareness," her therapist replied. "Drinking, drugs, affairs, petty retaliation."

Jennifer Chase was leaning forward with her legs crossed, fingers and non-manicured nails laced at the knee.

"…And a lot of them could care less where their daughter went to school."

She tilted her head.

"Can you tell me more about this feeling—is it worry?"

"Worry is close," Shivani said. "But worry is too containable. What I feel, when I feel bad, lately, is that when I do my job, and especially when we accomplish some highly-prized objective…I feel, well, I don't feel like I should."

"Can you be more specific?"

"If I am forced to be more specific," Shivani began, losing patience. She stared out the window with rising panic for the privacy being stripped from her by the second. "I would say that my work has begun to make me feel like a garbage bag full of diarrhea. Since you wanted the specifics"

It was a test. Shivani could never go through all this with a bore.

"Luckily, I have a manual on just that condition," Dr. Chase replied, handing Shivani a tissue in mock earnestness. "It's called explosive diarrhea mood dysphoria syndrome."

Shivani stared down the street. And now she needed that tissue, bloody hell.

She focused anew on a brave squirrel climbing to the sixth floor balcony across the street.

She thought about her trip to the ridiculous cosmetics store that had gotten the best of her once again. Why did she insist upon getting such expensive shit for herself? Perhaps this could be the place to sort that one out.

It would have been anonymous in here. She had found Jennifer Chase, LP, PhD without the assistance of Gmail, workplace search engine, health-plan provider screen or any of the other means that could have created a digital trail within security. She decided to ask anyway.

"Are you bound to confidentiality in every circumstance?" As she asked, Shivani turned from spacing out on a squirrel, to staring Dr. Chase straight in the eye. They were lovely shade of blue. Pale with black rings.

"I am bound by law in a few areas." Jennifer Chase was now removing her gaze to the ceiling. "I have to abide by reportable statement requirements if I learn a client's acquaintance is in danger," she continued. "Were one a danger to oneself, I would have to take certain steps. If a child is being harmed or in danger thereof, I will of course have to file a notification. Everything else is confidential."

"Fair enough," Shivani replied. "I am here because I think I have a shopping problem."

So she clearly needed to stall a bit longer.

"Tell me more."

Shivani pulled the three Gjale items from her bag. "Just now, I picked these up on a whim." Jennifer Chase tilted her head with a smile. The eyeliner cartridge was plated in platinum. The mascara came in hand-painted porcelain.

"Wow. I've never seen any Gjale up close. This is quite a thrill."

"Well if you come over to my place, I can show you hat boxes full of it."

"I bet the Birkin did not come cheap either."

Dr. Chase had noted Shivani's bag. Ever since the success of *Bringing Home the Birkin,* there wasn't a consumer of chick lit who hadn't been made aware that the totes can cost tens of thousands a throw.

"Oh, yes, I forgot about this one."

"So there are more at home?"

"Probably…seven. No, nine. Here at my place in the city. A couple more on Fire Island." Dr. Chase raised her eyebrows.

"Are you in financial trouble?"

"Me? No. I wish." Shivani let out a small laugh.

"How much do you shop?"

"A fair amount. A lot. Whenever possible."

"Well, if you don't have financial problems, but you don't like how much you shop, what's the reason for worry?"

"I don't feel bad that I spend so much money. What I don't like is *why* I shop."

"Why do you shop?"

"To take my mind off my work."

"Well, we can talk about your work, of course. But as a start, I would say that if you are not in financial trouble, maybe you can look at your shopping less negatively. A lot of people do it for a little distraction. If the money isn't a problem it's ultimately harmless. Is it possible you're being too hard on yourself?"

"Maybe." Shivani waited a beat, then mustered all of her strength to finish the thought. "But maybe…"

"Maybe what?"

"Maybe they are buying me off?"

๛

"What do you mean, 'they are buying you off'?" Jennifer Chase had begun taking notes in discrete little scribbles. "Who's the 'they'?"

"Can we linger on the why a bit longer?"

Shivani was back to taking courage in the example of the squirrel.

"I believe it was Upton Sinclair who wrote, 'it is difficult to get a man to understand something when his salary depends upon his not understanding it,'" Shivani said to the window. "So maybe they are buying my silence. They being my employers. So many euphemisms for this little move. Golden handcuffs. Keep her in nice things. Feel free to offer the standard reassurances: The world is filled with compromises, my dear. That's why they call it work, buttercup. Etcetera and so on."

"Actually, I was going to ask why your phone is blowing up."

Shivani had set her mobile down with the ringer on silent and vibration turned off. She hadn't noticed what Dr. Chase had seen, how her screen had become a ten-mile-an-hour credit-roll of incoming punctuated with exclamation points.

Shivani could quickly discern the gist of it: demands from corporate that she immediately return to the office. In a twist, they were being launched by an oppressive Krøhn-McGill goon she loathed more than all others, save for Seamus, a pompous Brendan named Dimitri Firth.

Dimitri Girth, as he was better known over the water cooler ever since a drug rep he had bedded once informed the office he possessed a knob as wide as a firehose, had never invaded Shivani's phone before. The thought occurred to her: Why was Dimitri Girth trying to get her back to the office?

"Can they track your cell to a precise location?"

The worry had just popped into her head.

"Again, who's 'they'?"

Shivani suspected the question had made her sound paranoid. The studied, unsupportive blankness of Jennifer Chase's second "who's they?" had left her certain of that much. Shivani didn't really care.

"Powerful employers."

"If by powerful employers, you mean you mean to ask if American corporations are using geo-tracking, I don't know of any. The NSA, sure, perhaps they spy on us through our phones. But I doubt employers in PR are sufficiently motivated to follow an employee on their devices."

"Well, if jealous husbands can do it," Shivani murmured. She began to wonder if Jennifer Chase was up for this, if she was a capable sounding board for the real reason Shivani had come here. Her story about the boy in the elevator.

"Anyway, it's a special kind of PR."

What the hell. Shivani told Dr. Chase she was a medical ghostwriter.

She explained the job, as well as one could explain the world's most influential academic fraud system to a believer outside the circle. She listed some of the research she had worked on, relayed a PG-13 version of what she did at some of the big meetings, named some of the bigger clinicians she had written for, and touched briefly on her work with KOLs.

Dr. Chase hadn't heard of Deadline Medical. She had heard of Jeremy Elton, of course, but probably not of KOLs, though Shivani noticed she didn't let on. Dr. Chase appeared to know all too well about the many different drugs Shivani had shipped out.

Shivani sensed her therapist had nodded a little too eagerly, in fact, at her each mention of some of the more popular psychotropic brands, a common source of consumer identity among the professional class and all the unvetted assumptions that went with it, i.e.: mental illnesses are lifelong brain diseases, the relationship of mood to brain matter has been described by sophisticated trials of uncompromising integrity, access to this model of care is the *sine qua non* of compassionate treatment for all who are suffering. Kill me now.

Shivani put aside her worries—'turning off the tapes,' as Jin-Jin had counseled. Self-forgiveness had become her lifeline when confronted by more dispiriting evidence of her employers' influence on the cultural belief system. Instead of retreating into the safety of her caustic internal monologues, she decided to try out the truth. She told Dr. Chase how she had been paid to spread falsehoods.

"What kind of falsehoods?"

Here, if she had to pinpoint it, was where the dam burst.

"Deadly falsehoods. Violence buried so cleverly in data. The pain of a society being turned out by iatrogenic torment. Buried in tables we sprinkle throughout the journals, filling the medical library stacks with fairy dust."

At the mention of fairy dust, Shivani had rippled her fingers like Tinkerbell.

"Iatrogenic?"

"It means treatment-induced. An old word that has fallen out of favor."

"'Fairy dust' Do you mean lies?"

Dr. Chase was efficient at spotting a dodge, then mercilessly repeating it. Whatever.

"Well, the figures saying what took place in most trials are not technically lies," Shivani clarified. "But they are the product of asking the right questions." She cocked her head. "And that's a more insidious kind of deception, isn't it?"

"'Asking the right questions.'"

Sigh. This incessant game of repetition.

"Lies of omission," Shivani replied. "A clever hand at statistics can introduce all sorts of formulas to move the needle in the manufacturer's preferred direction."

"For instance?"

Shivani had grown tired again. Time to apply another test, this one a little meaner.

"Well, I know we quietly skip effectiveness-determining, like the

Bonferroni correction," Shivani offered blandly. "I know we regularly gain positive findings thanks to our hacking of the p-value.

"I know we push back the start and truncate it early and introduce measures not on hand for the start of the starting gun known as the protocol. That all of these quote-unquote 'mistakes' can reformulate the outcome to our advantage without breaking a sweat. I've noted with some surprise moreover, how these innumerable shortcuts, cheats and end-arounds routinely go unnoted by our harried and overmatched opponents."

"Who are your opponents?"

Jenifer Chase's face had become puzzled more than inquisitorial.

"Regulators at the FDA," Shivani replied. "Al, Steve, Meredith, we're all good friends by now." Shivani removed her latest Gjale from its case and began to draw light lines on the back of her hand. It must have been the stress. She was admiring her stuff again. "All the advertising-dependent editors and easily-cowed peer reviewers, the grateful keynote speakers and compromised executive committees for our annual conferences, let's not get started on the self-serious health press readily lapping up our results.

"I almost forgot the doctors! We are always working to diminish the scrutiny of decent everyday physicians in the presence of our product lines. You really think this disparate cluster of humanity knows its way around our tables? That it has the time? That even if one did put our work under scrutiny they could find anyone who would care? America dislikes nothing more than a know-it-all."

"Well, the p-value I understand." Dr. Chase was looking more alert now.

"Great, yay, psychology, so the p-value is the yardstick…"

"…showing that what you found could not be relegated to chance."

Dr. Chase was establishing the fact of having gotten the Ph.D.

Having aced her A-levels at Cambridge, Shivani would likely have had doctorates in biostatistics, neuropsychiatry and the history of pharmacology had she not split for Krøhn-McGill during her M.Sci at Johns Hopkins.

"Correct," added Shivani, "and we get our much-desired p-value if we can show the event would have occurred less than five in one hundred times by chance under a null hypothesis."

"Point oh-five."

So Dr. Chase understood ninth-grade math.

"Right," offered Shivani. "And if a study comes in at point oh-five-one, or point oh-five oh-one..."

"You find a way to change something small and bring the result below point oh-five?"

"Bingo. We do what it takes to nudge lousy drugs under the threshold of so-called statistical significance."

"It's a recognized yardstick for an effect."

"And it was developed by an early twentieth-century fertilizer researcher and eugenicist, totally arbitrarily."

Dr. Chase was leaning forward in a manner that appeared to be no longer in the service of their therapist-client transaction. Her posture seemed to suggest the two had drifted, and that the hour was wrapping up. Shivani sensed a summary statement forthcoming.

"I can't argue these troubles and don't want to," Dr. Chase injected, "but isn't it possible you are being a bit hard on everything?"

And here it was, right on schedule.

"Science is surely messy," Dr. Chase continued, "but look at the big picture. Medical discovery has given us all the tools of modern health care, not to mention so very much research on the brain. We've come such a long way. You've been part of something vitally important and necessary. It's your job, you might as well own it. Think about it like this—they used to give people lobotomies for depression."

Shivani had heard it all before. The great march of progress.

"Now we give them Serotonal. Oh, the wonders of modern medicine. Sorry, Dr. Chase, I can't be quite as cheery about the work in these journals. I've seen what goes on behind the curtain."

"Such as?"

"Where to begin? '*Phenobarbitol for Anxious Underachieving Children in Foster Care,'* ten authors, half a conscience. *'Haldol for Stage Fright,'* because nothing boosts your courage like an intervention producing involuntary movements of the tongue. *'Unconscious Symbiotic Therapy for Poly-Dysregulated Neurosis.'* No thanks, I shall wait for the movie.

"These journals. They look good and proper, but it's not like you think, Dr. Chase. No one is minding the shop. Misspellings in the abstract. Citations taken on trust. All of it designed for somnambulation, with so many dull drug names, duller researcher names, deadly dull symptom reports and most dull-tastic of all, dates of sudden discharge reports from licensing trials A, B and C, reason unknown. Keep the literature impenetrable enough to hide a million crimes, and make the brand name catchy, like Serotonal. The world marches on."

Jennifer Chase had looked up from her notepad at Shivani's first mention of Serotonal, a drug that was surely in the handbag of hundreds of her patients. By this, her client's second critical mention of the antidepressant, she paused, placed her pen down, folded her arms and lifted her eyes to the ceiling. It was surely a small pose of protest, timed for Shivani's hottest blast of testimony.

"Made-to-look-dull reports of agitation, distress, fatality or homicide following a standard three-week loading dose. A dull parade of cannabinoid-like and emotionally-blunted states at work within children, teenagers, young adults and the elderly. You look skeptical, Dr. Chase. Do you want more? Because I have plenty."

"No, it's just, I don't' know how productive it is to…"

"Lone shooters who sing playground songs as they are taken down in a hail of bullets. Quiet men placing a shotgun inside their mouth under the management of a pill meant to kill the blues. Mothers expressing only love and tenderness as they hold their small, kicking child under the water. The airplane taken into a mountainside by a responsibly medicated care recipient. Keep moving, nothing to see here people. Always the hangings, of course, just so, so many hangings. How I wish I was making these up. To the media, they all have a certain look to them."

"Which is?"

"Societal decline."

"Well, we do live in a nation stocked with weapons." Shivani could see her psychologist channeling her inner progressive. "We have children raised on cable, the internet, and all the confusing information overload. Bullying has been weaponized by social media and digital isolation. We have widespread underemployment and the break-up of families. Could you allow yourself to factor in even some of these variables? How would you know to blame your drug, anyway?"

"Because it's there in the numbers, my dear." Shivani replied, her voice becoming both thin and kind of sad. "It's there and it's a problem to be handled before lunch or we are made to begin moving suicide into placebos, no reason given, allowing these unsightly outcomes to slip back under the surface in our tables." She paused only a moment before her last word of confession. "I have done this myself."

She hoped she had flown through the last admission too quickly to give much away. Surely the phrase "moving suicides into placebo" had made little sense to Dr. Chase, who likely only understood of clinical trials what she read of them in the *Times*. In case she was wrong, she began to overload the comment with a final blast of complaint.

"I know my onions, on this Dr. Chase, because I am the person who has written the authoritative clinical study reports on a murderer's row of blockbusters, a real Top-of-the-Pops. And if I never got the real numbers, no one within the FDA has them either. And I have never once gotten the real numbers. Still feeling good about that prescription in your handbag?"

Dr. Chase shifted uneasily in her chair. The patient had unloaded an unfathomably detailed, possibly fabulist and seemingly delusional narrative the psychologist would have been in no position to affirm or deny.

"It sounds like you are suffering," she said with bland neutrality.

Well, duh.

"I'm sorry," Shivani rushed. "I've given a speech. No need for that.

The point is, I have come to believe I have become something far worse than the pusher of new pills. This gives me guilt, and guilt, I have learned, never sleeps."

Prior to coming into the office, Shivani had written out a check to *Jennifer Chase PhD.*, although her bag from Hermes now appeared set on hiding the thing in its artisan-stitched interior. As Shivani struggled to ply free her payment and get herself out of there, she began telling the story she came there to unburden herself of in the first place, a doorknob confessional to end all doorknob confessionals. It was the tale of the boy in the elevator.

"It's just that I'm feeling rattled because of a child named Truman," she said quietly to the carpet. "I met him after we recruited family men we had signed up for triathlons. We were targeting young fathers to test the new bone drug, especially if they had recently returned from combat. Treating veterans poses a well-recognized marketing advantage, but I have since begun to wonder if there were less than honorable reasons why my employer had targeted such a fragile demographic to try out its new pill. They would have to have known that the public would not look accusingly at the pill if a combat vet who had taken it then became suicidal."

"Are you suicidal?"

Dr. Chase seemed to only know how to approach Shivani's story as a precursor to mental distress.

"No, you're missing my point, I believe am making *other* people suicidal—I think." Shivani told her of how she had met the boy after Krøhn-McGill had slapped together a patient advocacy group to promote its new baby. She said the pill was called rostangilorb, a new drug for the prevention of injury. "The advocacy group was a ruse," she added, "it was just a letterhead and a phone number that actually called into the same Krøhn-McGill liars."

"They do that?"

"*We* do that, yes. A lot."

"I don't get it. Why invent an advocacy group?"

"Think about it: Everyone hates the drug makers. We know that. You have to get the sympathetic to make your case for you. That allows you to work behind the scenes. We have an advocacy nonprofit named MISA, for instance."

Dr. Chase nodded, a little too eagerly.

"It is a patient and family group," Dr. Chase said.

"And we built it to move people onto Serotonal. But this other one I'm talking about, it's called Athletes for Bone and Cartilage—ABC, get it? It sponsors amateur races in tandem with health systems and big employers. We pay for the event, then use the sign-up page to recruit trial participants. It also helps us deliver users of the drug to be interviewed by overworked reporters filing stories." Shivani had been careful not to name Bioferex by the brand name, using its lesser-known generic name *rostangilorb* instead. Why invite trouble?

"So one day I had been assigned to host a fourth-grader named Truman on a thank you trip to the big theme park. Krøhn-McGill was footing it, because we needed Truman's father to talk with the newspapers in a board room at a drug meeting downstairs. To keep Truman busy, we lined up a meet-and-greet with one of the big child actors. Which was when I learned that little Truman was a pint-sized saint who just didn't care about celebrities. He just said 'no thank you.'

"Are you sure, I asked him. I told him we could also take him to meet some professional baseball players. Nothing worked. I tried again. When he could take it no more, he said in all politeness, 'I don't mean to be ungrateful, Miss Patel, but my dad has been in the Army for my whole life. Now that he's home, I want to see him as soon as he is done talking with the reporter. I want to be with him more than going on rides.'

"So we finished up all the PR for the new drug without ever rewarding Truman the great, who had me wait with him in the lobby for the duration of the morning so that he wouldn't miss a moment of time with his father. A day later, all the veterans flew back home on our dime, and a week after that, Truman's father excused himself from the dinner table to get something out in the garage. The investigation is still ongoing, but according to what we have been told, Truman's best friend and hero then fully severed his own head under a table saw. Which is pretty hard to do."

Jennifer Chase looked up from her notepad, then stopped writing altogether.

"He had been on the drug for ten weeks," Shivani continued, "a ramp-up we saw while creating this side effect in the Serotonal trials, though it has been looking far more pronounced among users of the bone drug. And now it has fallen upon yours truly to finish up the paperwork for population-wide dissemination of our inviting little gel cap. So you can see why I would like to quit shopping so much."

Jennifer Chase sat motionless. The honking on Spring Street became the only sound in the room. Shivani would have loved for a few words of comfort, but her therapist seemed lost. Shivani scribbled something final onto her check, then handed over a tripling of the pay Dr. Chase had requested. "I believe this surpasses the agreed-upon fee," Shivani said. "If you can forgive me, I still have to make it to midtown for a two-thirty and the trains are running slow."

Looking at the super-sized payment, Dr. Chase quickly rose from her chair and offered to schedule another appointment. Shivani said she would need to check her calendar, paused to straighten her sleeves, then discretely set her bag of Gjale onto the therapist's unoccupied chair. Turning to the door, Shivani said she wanted Dr. Chase to have it. "I have too many things and it would be such a lovely color for those pale blue eyes." Dr. Chase was distracted by the final three letters Shivani had appended to the signature. It now read:

Shivani Gandha Patel, AOD.

"What's A.O.D?"

"Angel of Death, of course. It's my job, I might as well own it."

၄

A block up the street, Shivani boarded the B line certain her hour with Jennifer Chase had been a bust, perhaps a blunder. It had felt good to unburden herself, but Dr. Chase looked run over by it all, at the end especially. She'd given Shivani the face you show a friend in trouble.

Back at her desk, Shivani gazed at the sight of eight shouty emails from Dimitri Girth, each containing the subject line "people don't care about that!!!"

It seems that corporate was not in support of Shivani having avoided proper channels. To better understand the data she had been paid to polish, Shivani sometimes sought out intake staff for a given patient record. Entry-level team members were sometimes stupid enough to oblige you—unaware of company policy forbidding ghostwriters access to patient data. Shivani knew she couldn't get fired for plying case report forms out of low-level staff. But getting caught did create static.

Dimitri had gone to the trouble of attaching Shivani's request to his email, then annotating it with mean-girl emojis and disjointed, long strings of interrogatories.

> Shivani! Why the negative questions about a product we all believe in??????
>
> We commit ourselves to this study!
>
> We expect that K-M personnel do so as well!!!
>
> ALL internal communications must express confidence in our shared K-M mission!

Shivani scowled, placed her purse in a drawer, grabbed a stick and jammed it into the main frame. Then she dragged the email onto her thumb drive. She had been storing evidence whenever the company blocked her from better understanding another fishy goings-on. It felt like insurance, even if she had nowhere to bring it.

It might have been a bad move. She didn't understand enough about IT to know whether they could track it if you transfer email onto a thumb stick. Shivani put away the thoughts and tossed the stick in her bag. She had fifty letters and nowhere to send them.

11

Susie hadn't dreamed of giving MISA another chance. The meeting felt cultish, and cringey. Plus, to get there, she had needed her younger sister to watch Crystal. Plus, she didn't like Charlotte.

So it surprised her to get a sizable flower arrangement the day after that first meeting. The gift card on the inside was an extra nice touch, redeemable at a cute bistro in Uptown. Susie had never heard of a support group that sent thank-you gifts. She said so to Charlotte when thanking her while they met up for coffee.

"Who did you lose," Susie asked after ten minutes of small talk. "If I can ask."

"My cousin's husband," Charlotte said. She was waving at the waitress while reaching into an oversized bag. "It sounds like that would be a distant relative but it really sent a shock wave over the entire family. I come from a small town. We were all close. Gavin OD'd. I had been working for a liquor distributor, and quickly learned the options for support groups were nonexistent. That's when I learned MISA was interested in opening a regional office."

"So this is your job?"

Charlotte nodded.

"It started part-time, then they sent me to a half-dozen seminars out East and in California. I learned so much. The need is so great and the work never ends. There's advocacy, media interviews, fundraising. I am at the Capitol twice a week during the session. Sometimes I go to the D.C. office to learn about new bills in Washington. During summers I travel the state to talk with all the local chambers. We've already set up campus chapters at all the big colleges. We are making inroads into the high schools next fall. Middle schools are coming. They keep me busy."

"What did you do in your old job?"

"Coordinated deliveries. All the big brewers. Went straight into it after high school. There were sixteen drivers and three hundred stops a week. It was a fuckton of work. I was glad to be done with it."

Susie was surprised to learn the regional chapter of MISA could be helmed by a person with no college degree, only a distant connection to suicide, and who had previously scheduled beer trucks. But it appeared to be working out for her. Charlotte had pulled up in a luxury SUV the size of Montana.

Susie studied her new confidant closer. Charlotte wore jeweled jeans, a Packers sweatshirt and had an all-around hardness about her. She was coarse, too. The whole "fuckton" thing.

"What do you do, if I can ask?"

"I work at one of the insurance agencies," Susie offered.

"Bet you see a lot of single-car accidents. The lone mortality kind."

"No, mostly fender benders," Susie replied. "But now that you mention it, I don't really check how often people die alone in a car crash. That's an interesting point."

"No one talks about it," Charlotte said, muscling her subject into the first mention of auto insurance. "When the papers say 'single-car accident,' I know just what the Sam hell that means. Same for alcohol poisoning. Most big drinkers know their limit. I always did. Ditto for quote-unquote 'died unexpectedly at home.' All the ways we protect ourselves from shame."

There it was again, the evocation of shame. The backdrop for all MISA messaging, something Susie had never herself experienced in any of this worthless madness of life without Mark, not even once. Susie remembered how Charlotte had seemed preoccupied with shame at the meeting she'd attended. Was it the childhood on a farm Wisconsin? You would have needed to undo a lot of shame to rebuild your life around an event that killed your cousin's husband.

"So tell me about Mark."

Susie hesitated. It felt like betrayal.

"Umm…I had no idea it was coming."

"None of us did," said Charlotte. "That's what we all discover at MISA. We never say it was depression when we get the call in the middle of the night, and that's because they only ever showed us their happy face. I still feel the pain when I think about Devin suffering in silence. I know my cousin Beryl has never been the same."

Susie could have sworn Charlotte had called him Gavin the first time.

"Does she come to the meetings?"

"Who?"

"Your cousin."

"Beryl? Nope. Still in denial. They say to her 'what did you ever do to make your poor husband into a maniac?' So she keeps saying it was *an accident,*" said Charlotte, putting down her coffee to claw out a pair of exaggerated air quotes.

"Beryl's not ready. But you look like you are strong and honest with yourself. It's why I sent you that note and those flowers. We know it's an enormous victory just to walk through those doors, even once. We just want you to do it twice. And then maybe once more again next month."

They ordered lunch. It was on to the Packers.

Susie liked that Charlotte did all the talking, and that she didn't have to think about Mark for a while. Mostly, it was the feeling of not having to get over it.

෧

Susie couldn't specify when MISA began to seem like a place for her to find herself.

The blog started a couple of months later—shortly after she read something out loud to the meeting that she had written about Mark.

"You have a gift," Charlotte told her in the coat room after that reading. "We need your voice of experience. People should hear your story in your words."

Susie said she would think about it.

The next day, an invitation arrived to submit a post for the website at the MISA national office. A month after that, Susie's blog had migrated off the corporate page and into its very own domain. A photo crew had been dispatched from Chicago. An editor cleaned up her typos and inserted references to studies, media stories, MISA video and web links. Her site had been assigned a webmaster who managed to engineer 10,000 views from her very first day.

Susie's columns had a comment section. Each new column drew hundreds of replies. Her assignment was open-ended. A week after her first post, a subsidy began arriving: $1,500 per column. Susie would have done the work for free.

Then came the invitations to travel out of state. Appearances at other MISA chapters. Participation in academic panels. Fundraiser walk-a-thons and MISA trainings in nice hotels.

MISA had become a lifesaver for Susie, a source of support and personal meaning during the pain of being strapped financially while ripped apart emotionally.

After a year and change, it was all she could do not to marvel. What would Mark have thought if he could see her now? Would he have been knocked out of his spiral by the depth of her love for him? It would surely have given him strength, in his final hour of need, to fight off the depression that killed him.

12

It usually gave Griffin a charge to see one of his articles go to print, if for no other reason than the fact that he would finally be getting paid. But when the dazzling print run of *In the Zone* containing his piece on Bioferex hit the newsstands ("March 2011 Special Report: No More St. Fatty's Day for You!"), the already-soft health short had become a real steaming pile of it.

Standing over his mailbox while skimming its pages on a back porch staircase overlooking slush, Griffin began to develop a headache.

First among its disappointments, the rewrite had spiked his lede about taking the drug himself. True, Griffin had only been on Bioferex for a week by the time he turned in his revision—but now it looked like he had subjected his body to Bioferex for nothing. At least it hadn't hurt him any. After a month on the pill he was running six miles a day without pain. But the article was a mess.

An eleventh-hour decision had swapped in a new headline that strained the boundaries of good taste, even by the tortured norms of *In the Zone.* Griffin's original title for the article was restrained and responsible. It said this:

That's the Breaks
Bioferex and Your Bones

In his infinite wisdom, *In the Zone* editor-in-chief Nigel Butler (AKA Crocs) had determined the article needed something manlier, however, and delivered a monster:

Crush the Workout, Not Your Bones
Time To Get The GROUNDBREAKING
New Drug Bioferex
Into Your Man-Plan, Bee-yotch!

Flowing immediately below this travesty, Griffin's dumbed-down story now cast the modest medication as a towering innovation on par with the discovery of penicillin. Griffin had given a cursory nod to side effects like dry mouth and diminished appetite, but Crocs had somehow brought the stupid to even that, brushing them all off with a terse declaration that seemed intent on setting some kind of record for dumb-headedness ("Side effects? Sack up, please.").

Reading this grim mush under his name only compounded Griffin's strange, new sense of unease, an emerging feeling of something's-not-right, coupled with unexpected and uncharacteristic bouts of irritation that had him periodically being hard on Lee Majors for no reason. He had mercifully come to his article's inane closer, another addition by Crocs:

"With a pill this awesome," it boasted, "the question isn't if, but when Bioferex is right for you. Who doesn't need Bioferex? Only a dumbass."

Griffin reminded himself to breathe.

It wasn't the end of the world.

He had written loads of garbage before.

Plus, writers had to get paid.

Plus, no one he knew would ever see this.

All that being said, Griffin couldn't seem to make a dark, face-heating question go away. He had taken this pill. He had told millions of readers to take this pill. He was still taking this pill. What if it had, you know, problems?

13

"Mr. Drake."

Griffin was employing a British accent on Trevor's voicemail.

"It's the lab calling. We have the results in hand of your STD workup, which I'm afraid has come out of the hopper a bit bent."

He was trying to channel Ricky Gervais. You'd probably rate it a so-so.

"Just cutting to the bangers and mash here, all of us are in concert that your urinary canal is bursting with a germy sort of rubbish, the likes of which we have never encountered here in the Cheeseborough branch. So we shall be sending it up to London first thing."

That should have been enough.

"Hey Trevor, it's Griffin. I know it's unconventional, but I wanted to write a follow-up to the Bioferex piece."

Even as he asked, Griffin knew this was a non-starter. Fuck it, sometimes you get lucky. He had his reasons. A follow up might let him be a little less of a cheerleader for the thing. Talk about other ways to prevent shin splints, or femur cracks, or whatever it was. To redeem himself for promoting a sketchy drug.

Still. He knew the suggestion of a follow-up for *In the Zone* was magical thinking. It just was. As he signed off and hung up the phone, he could practically hear Trevor giving him an iTZ shake of the head no.

Sure enough, an email confirming Trevor's disinterest pinged a few minutes later.

WAGSY ARE THE PRIONS CHEWING YOUR GREY MATTER?
THIS ISN'T THE NEW YORKER. YOU ARE NOT JEFFREY TOOBIN.
THERE ARE NO TWO-PARTERS HERE.

He had been reminded who his employers were again. Why did he keep forgetting? You don't get to fix your mistakes in this life, not as a hack.

14

As the co-pilot announced their descent into Chicago, Shivani looked out over a grim run of malls, lorries, car parks and double carriageways covered in slush. She had long since learned to kill time after the landing gear deployed by playing a game she had invented: spotting the clinical trial centers testing drugs on the down-low.

There were more than you'd imagine.

Once you got below 500 feet, in fact, a spotter knowing what to look for could readily nail the telltale details of a pharmaceutical lab hiding in plain sight. You had your two-story, frost-encased oxygen systems. Your rooftop smoke-break patios. Your skylights for locked wards and your eighty-twenty mix of beaters to BMWs in the parking lot. Put a doctor in a commercial clinical testing lab for his paycheck and he usually required a garage full of performance autos to get into the office on most days. The test subjects, they drove cars held together with clothes hangers and plastic sheeting.

Shivani's present out-and-back was being conducted in the service of another academy slog. A year had passed since she'd suffered her last bout of panic over the problems with Serotonal and Bioferex, a meltdown on the night prior to *Novoamine 2010*. It turns out that time flies during months marked by paranoia laced with dread. She had never the time to face her fears in any kind of tangible manner.

She had seen a psychologist named Jennifer Chase for all of one session, only to return to her tormenters as they chided her for seeking access to restricted data, showing Shivani her place. She pleaded ignorance while aware that they saw her for a liar, whatevs. They would not be toying with her for much longer.

Shivani was intent on moving towards a state of resolve, as Jin-Jin had counseled, on holding firm to her acceptance that a rocky path was the human condition, and that adversity could not be avoided. But she still felt confused how to do that. She hadn't notified authorities of missing subjects in Bioferex trials.

Nor had she acted on news of the approaching date for a federal health directive, the one mandating full Bioferex coverage within all six of the national provider networks, the remuneration gateway to their tens of millions of patients.

She hadn't so much as approached a reporter hoping for a scoop to get him into the Sunday magazine. As a result, her janky pill's preposterous destiny—an employer health mandate and the pending campaign for universal enrollment—all remained in play.

And of course here she was all over again, collaborating in another grim city lacking a hotel worthy of her loyalty points. The team had given this year's shindig another grandee title—*Receptor Vision 2011*—assigning her the same circuit of academic hand-holding. For now that meant ameliorating her primary charge: the guru of life hacking himself, Jeremy Elton, now marching freshly off the plane.

He had an exorbitantly-compensated keynote to deliver. Shivani had written all of it. The short blot would barely scan a word of it until the moment he set foot on stage, of that she was certain.

In support of his standard two nights of trawling there would be need for a private car. There would also be need for Shivani to bear witness as the forty-something charged *Receptor Vision's* five catered lounges in search of new talent. She would be reminded once again how even the toadiest male with graying temples could prey on the flesh of young professionals at the AAP, with Jeremy having the advantage of wealth, fame and good genes.

Fortunately, her boss had become at least five percent less gluttonous at these affairs, more of a fixer than a feeder, albeit in some capacity Shivani couldn't quite understand. Just last month, for example, she had figured out all on her own that he had been brought in on some Bioferex data collection going down at a rehab facility in the meat packing district.

Shivani had been coordinating safety metrics when suddenly there he was, America's Psychiatrist on all the emails, a consultant in some murky capacity that remained unexplained. Elton's involvement in the project flummoxed her. It was a bone drug and he was a TV shrink but whatever.

"Patel!"

And now here he was, her very own need machine, charging towards her from across the O'Hare concourse. Shivani turned in time to observe the slight as Jeremy breezed right past a driver stranded with a sign reading *Dr. Jeremy Elton, America's Psychiatrist.*

"I have limos for the next three nights correct?"

Jeremy had shouted the question to Shivani over his shoulder upon passing her. The two had not been at a meeting together for several months, she had written all of his papers this year, yet a proper greeting was not in his vocabulary.

"Why yes, Dr. Elton. Looking forward to it."

Shivani hated speaking loudly in public. When in Rome.

"I'll take my talks at breakfast." Jeremy was on the move, three paces ahead of her.

"I have them here now," Shivani offered, reaching forward with a stick from her bag.

"Breakfast."

Jeremy stopped to survey a luxury vending machine which had tempted him. It offered an array of German-engineered headphones and other high end audiophile paraphernalia with prices starting around $300. He slid his credit card in the slot for a quick purchase.

"Can I slip these talks in your bag now?" Shivani offered.

"That's OK," he said, shaking his head with the gentleman's refusal. "I'll get to those later. The conditions in First were not ideal. I am now interested in some much-needed pre-covery."

Pre-covery? Jeremy was always trying out some asinine new lifestyle phraseology. A loud thunk emitted as a robot delivered his new set of headphones and iPad.

"Aren't these grandiloquent!"

Jeremy had turned to her with an enormous smile. "Our rat race has us lining up at machines to dispense for us the baubles of consumer temptation. How long until they offer us a new-and-improved soul?"

Gag.

A few minutes up the concourse, he stopped briefly in mid-stride once again, this time to sign copies of his book on a table in an airport kiosk, an impromptu practice that Shivani found presumptuous, personally, as the gesture had been uninvited and appeared to have elicited only confusion and distress from a clerk wearing traditional clothing of the East African continent. Ten marked-up books later Jeremy was out of the store, and fifty feet after that, staring into a concourse mirror, absent-mindedly swirling his finger tips on his cheeks.

He did this whenever he wanted his pores tended.

"If I don't find a spa with an antioxidant bath," he confirmed with a stage whisper, "I will be unable to function in the morning, speech or no."

The chauffeur, having caught up to Shivani and overhearing the request, asked Jeremy if he would like the name of a nearby YMCA. Ignoring him, Jeremy turned the pricey electronics box over a few times to inspect the small print, before handed it off to his confused driver, setting off again towards the limo stand. "Be kind with my luggage," he called on his way out the door.

Hoping to repair the faux pas of suggesting Jeremy Elton should patronize a public gym, Shivani busied herself searching on her phone for locations in Chicago where he might find a reputable spa. But he was already gone.

15

Griffin was off to Chicago, armed with the dubious goal of interviewing anyone who would talk about the silver anniversary of the world's best-selling antidepressant. The money had run low again. He had taken another assignment generated by an advertiser.

As far as Griffin understood it, the genesis of his current contract to write 850 words about the quarter-century of *zoloxetine* ("Serotonal At 25—How Are We All Feeling?") went like this: the week prior, someone from the drug maker (Krøhn-McGill)—or more precisely, its PR company (Pagel-Simon)—pitched the idea to Trevor.

Trevor punted it up to Nigel, who took note of the drug-maker's generous *In the Zone* ad budget and promptly instructed Trevor to assign a story on the pill by the next month's issue.

Griffin figured the assignment was an opportunity for travel, in this case, an all-expenses junket to the annual AAP clusterfuck in Chicago, a nerd-blowout entitled *ReceptorVision 2011*. Clicking through the conference schedule online, he counted at least a dozen lectures with Serotonal in the title. From what he could tell, this meeting would feature all the early champions of the drug, contemporary researchers testing new uses for the pill, and he even stumbled across the bit of good news that a historian of medicine would be talking Serotonal, a Kiwi named Alexander Breton.

He drove to Chicago, checked in to the company hotel in the Loop, took his dinner in the bar, and on the opening morning took a head-clearing run along the shoreline. By about 9:00 he had somehow dragged his way into the cavernous atrium at McCormick place.

It seemed as though the entire meeting had been built to hump the big Serotonal 2-5. After signing up at the registration table, a pair of marketing interns produced for him a black leather shoulder bag branded with the subject of the hour. The base of the high-end tote had been stitched with three bands of yellow, and above that, the words *Serotonal AD, Coming Home With Health.* There was no way he could ever hide that, he thought to himself sadly. Because otherwise it was such a smoking bag.

And on the inside of this swag he'd been loaded up with even more small-bore bribery, including an AAP umbrella, a leather hunting cap with the name of some vagal nerve device firm, a high-end water bottle festooned with a polished-nickel insignia for Krøhn-McGill and a $25 gift card for the convention center Starbucks. Scanning his program, Griffin discovered he had accidentally timed his arrival to catch the opening keynote, a talk by a celebrity doctor, the famed psychiatrist Jeremy Elton.

16

Griffin peered with resignation into a convention hall packed with psychiatrists eating pastry. *Work was ever work.* He instructed this to himself as he weighed the decision of whether to stand as an interloper from the press along the side, or to demand his fealty proper and slide like a boss onto one of the high-end couches that had been rented out at a premium for the occasion.

As a working member of the media, Griffin knew he was not supposed to avail himself of the comforts at these affairs. You were not expected to write fully honestly as press—you should not lie, and you should never tell the the complete truth. But your actions were watched closely should you enjoy anything with honesty. His run had been long, however, and the luxury furniture looked really inviting. In addition to the tricked-out rental seating, high end party planners had arranged interlocking lounge sections at the rear of the room, glowy and tech-celebratory chill quadrants anchored by the aforementioned couches as well as tastefully-appointed area-lighting, searing chrome coffee tables, and bar-stools at stone-topped counters outfitted with charging stations.

It was killing him. In the corner, a cappuccino kiosk appeared to be moving the French Press.

Recognizing with sadness that low hipster couches would only make his back scream—and to be fair becoming at least eight percent nauseated by the entire moneyed spectacle itself—Griffin retreated to a back doorway. His eyes were fine.

At the front of the room, a glowing screen announced the imminent arrival of "Jeremy Elton, MD, PhD, Director of Clinical Research, University of Dallas, Institute of Brain Studies."

It was all unnecessary, however.

Everyone already knew him as America's Psychiatrist.

Griffin recognized the thirty-foot headshot as well as anyone else, having surfed past Elton's two Public TV programs ("Natural History of the Mind, Parts I and II"), and seen his face on a trio of nonfiction bestsellers on display tables at the front of bookstores.

To pass the time, he reviewed Elton's bio in his program while leaning against a sign for the drug he was here to hump, the mega-selling antidepressant and cultural force of gravity that was Serotonal.

And it was indeed a tall pile of CV. Elton's bio said he oversaw $36 million in NIMH grants, had co-authored ten textbooks, published three popular bestsellers and, was the author behind, wait what? *Six hundred* medical journal articles?

Jeremy Elton was also a paid consultant for six Fortune 500 pharmaceutical companies, holder of visiting professorships at universities in Europe, India, South America and China, the recipient of royalties from sixteen pharmaceutical patents and thirteen medical devices.

So yes, the Jeremy Elton resume was jacked.

But it required only a layman's gaze at that bio photo to see why the man was money. With a wavy mane of salt and pepper, piercing blue eyes and a gleaming set of chiclets, America's Psychiatrist was endowed with swagger, especially against the backdrop of the sad parade of undertakers who otherwise populated the high halls of medicine.

Had anyone from *In the Zone* ever laid eyes on him, Elton could have easily snagged a feature. Maybe he had? Griffin hadn't read his magazine in years.

"Good morning!" A stunner in heels had made her way to the podium as Jeremy Elton took a chair next to an end table on her side. Sometimes the camera lies, but this time the guy was all that, more striking in person than in marketing. You could even say it was intimidating.

Out of pure sublimated jealousy, Griffin did the masculinity math in his head: *How do you write six hundred papers, treat hundreds of patients, oversee dozens of trials, juggle millions of dollars in grants, run a top-ten research department, put out three bestsellers, do dozens of TV segments each year and still find time to hit the gym?*

"We are thrilled to have Dr. Jeremy Elton, a clinician who needs no introduction and whose gifts of compassionate pharmaceutical ministry have brought us closer with each passing year to much-needed treatments for the debilitating conditions standing between our brave patients and full, productive lives."

The crowd let out a roar, in celebration of their profession as much as the arrival of their speaker.

"As the lead clinician for the groundbreaking trials of Serotonal," the introducer continued, "Dr. Elton is here to discuss a trial asking not whether, but *how soon…*" Then she did the most curious thing. She paused and theatrically gazed upward before continuing. "Serotonal should be approved to treat *Ped-AAD*: Pediatric and Adolescent Anxiety Disorder!"

Robust clapping rang forth.

"Dr. Elton also intends to find out not just whether, but *how soon.*"

Sustained applause rang out once again, this time louder.

"Serotonal should be approved to address *G-D-D*: Geriatric *Depressive* Disorder!"

The clapping had transformed into cheering.

At her side, Jeremy Elton sat with a leg crossed at the knee, offering small waves to the half-dozen groupies who had moved to the foot of the stage for a selfie with the celeb himself.

Griffin watched with mild amusement.

He had no idea they got so charged up at these things.

"Dr. Elton also will ask not just whether, but…"

The announcer stopped in mid-sentence to cup a hand next to her ear.

In reward of the gesture, her crowd obliged her with a hearty response. *"How soon!"*

"Serotonal will be approved for *MDD*: Maternal Depressive Disorder."

The audience having hit peak Elton, his host turned to face the man of the hour, placing a manicured hand over her heart as if to say that he deserved one last small gesture that the room was fully his. In return, Jeremy Elton held his hands quietly palm to palm at a point just below his chin, then offered a small bow of his head.

"Give *yourselves* a round of applause!" the announcer interjected. "You did *awesome!*"

His room having hit 100 decibels, Jeremy bounded upward with a boyish grin and a wave of his head to say "Stop, *please.*"

"Everyone give your warmest AAP welcome," his MC now concluded, "to Dr. Jeremy Raymond Elton!" And they went there. A full standing O.

In the course of covering dozens of these meetings in his time, Griffin had never seen a doctor get the Elvis treatment like this one. He watched with admiration as Elton bounded to the podium, pulled the microphone from its stand and slid over to an adulatory perch at the front of the stage. Why couldn't every grim lecture kick off like this one?

Griffin would have taken copious notes of what this impossibly-beloved, crazily-credentialed, "secular leader of the compassionate-pharmaceutical future," said next, except that at that very moment his phone began ringing, and the caller ID said it was Trevor.

Trevor only called to offer work.

Griffin stepped outside the hall to take the call.

17

"Dawg," Trevor barked, "how's our Serotonal bullshit coming?"

"So it's Dawg now?" Griffin asked. "How White."

"Not going to get our ads pulled are you?"

"Nope. Dawg."

"I ask, because while we would still *like* you to turn in a Serotonal anniversary piece, I think it can wait a month. More importantly, in the mean time we have a feature falling apart for July. I think your Hemingway idea would make an excellent substitution."

Griffin struggled to remember the aforementioned pitch.

It was upon reflection a piece he'd actually *wanted* to write, as well as he could recall, although Trevor had sailed right past it at the time. Wily fox must have logged it somewhere in his towel-snapping brain? Sometimes these guys surprised you.

"Think about it like this," Trevor said. "July, 1961 to July, 2011. It's been fifty years since the great one left us. Can you say time peg? Get it to me in a week?"

A week, holy shit. That wasn't much time.

If an editor demanded you rush an assignment, "Yes" was usually the correct answer. It paid you faster, and gave them less time to change their minds. But Griffin had to say no. This one required reporting. Plus, he had already said yes to something else.

"Can't," he replied. "I have to extract twelve hundred words from my rear end on car seats for toddlers. Something I picked up from an editor for *Parenting Monthly* named Jill Bisonnette," he added. "I can get jamming on the Hemingway story a week after that."

"Come on, Wagner. Bro's before hoes."

"Wait, what?"

"If anyone asks, I never said that. Just do us a solid this one time, please? Crikey thinks the Hemingway idea only works as a tie-in."

"So what are you saying?"

"I'm saying that if you don't do the Hemingway story for us now, we probably can't use it ever."

Griffin thought it over. It wasn't hard. He really needed to get into the feature well at *In the Zone*. He was so sick of writing service.

"Fine."

He agreed to tell *Parenthood* he needed a few more weeks, then signed off with Trevor. Looking down, he realized a pack of latecomers were craning their necks to watch America's Psychiatrist on a flat screen set up in a back-of-the-room alcove for overflow viewing.

"Nice bag!"

It was a brunette in a wool skirt with one leg crossed over the other.

She made a funny motion as she said it, as if to show off her Serotonal swag like it was haute couture. If Griffin didn't know better, this attractive stranger was flirting. Somehow his clever reply just came to him like that.

"Already had enough of Sir Elton, have you?"

"I kept waiting for him to play 'Don't Let the Sun Go Down on Me,'" she said. "I am *not* sitting through 'Nikita.'"

Griffin laughed. She was fast.

"So are you a psychiatrist?"

It was dumb, this question he had asked of her, but dumb was safe.

"Psychologist, unfortunately." She looked down at his tag. "Uh-oh, a journalist. Who sent you!" Her delivery came complete with a nebulous Eastern European accent—like the femme fatale in a Bond film.

"A magazine sold in gas stations," Griffin offered. "And that's all I'm saying."

"Mysterious," she smiled. "I like that."

"So why sit out here," he asked. "Why not get your hands dirty and catch a glimpse of the rocket man for yourself?"

"Eh," she said. "I'd rather listen to people who write their own studies if you want to know the truth of it." She began scanning her program with a bored look of superiority.

As she did this, she lifted a strand of hair from her face. Griffin smiled, tilting his head in confusion. "Did you see that nonsense about six hundred papers?" she explained with a slow shake of her head. "What is he, forty?"

Griffin returned with another confused expression. Personally, he had rather liked Jeremy Elton, and that surprised him more than anyone. Yes, maybe the guy was a little full of himself. But he seemed to have ample reason.

He decided to play along.

"What do you mean?"

"What I mean, is, he uses *ghost*-writers."

OK, this was officially not boring.

"You want to get some coffee?" Griffin asked.

It surprised him how confident that came out.

"With your free Starbucks card or mine?" she replied

Why wasn't it always this easy?

They found a place to sit in the convention center cafe.

Her nametag said *Sedona Piper, PhD, LP, University of Wisconsin, Madison.*

"Sedona, so that's a name you don't hear too often."

"My parents were Outward Bounders."

"LP...what's that, licensed psychologist, right?"

"Long-play record."

Griffin would gladly suffer the deflection if it kept her talking. He had been slumming. It had been ages since he'd spent any length of time with a member of the opposite sex who had finished graduate school. Since, like, the late Nineties, now that he thought about it.

"So help me out. What makes a person choose psychology?"

"My totally biased opinion?"

"Seems like it suits you."

"The self-esteem necessary to earn two hundred thousand dollars less after training in therapy for twice as long."

Sedona was busy tapping her Starbucks card in a line-chopping motion. Griffin wondered if she had a bad habit.

"Technically, there are other differences," Sedona said. "Psychologists are trained in manualized talk therapies, while psychiatrists are trained by older psychiatrists as they try out all the dope meds...That was a pun by the way."

The mature part of his brain was taking notes on her answers. They sounded informed and layered, and she was indeed a character—just the way she'd thrown a two-fingered double tap when she said the phrase "dope meds."

The lizard part of his brain was picturing her at a nightclub, with ear-splitting techno making the glassware rattle and a fog machine turning the dance floor into a cloud.

"None of us have the corner on virtue," she continued. "Psychology has some amoral characters who helped the CIA carry out torture, and our literature has an embarrassing replication crisis. That being said, the other team has thousands of high-functioning practitioners who think nothing of drugging up a two-year-old."

She had quit chopping lines and turned her attention to tea, lifting the bag and setting it back down. "Hey Griffin. I don't know about you, but I am dying to see that swag-o-rama over on the exhibit floor."

Sedona was now pointing towards a cavernous showroom set up across the hall.

Sure, he thought, why not?

They departed the Starbucks and walked a ballroom to their left. A glowing information kiosk listed three hundred vendors, including booths for all the major drug makers in the center of the room with hundreds of smaller displays radiating out towards the perimeter.

"Slum through here and you get a feel for why psychology feels like a wallflower at the ball," Sedona murmured as they entered the carpeted hall. "The evidence shows our treatments work and their treatments work when taken alongside ours. Did I mention we write our own studies? Do I sound bitter?"

"A little bit."

"I'm so not bitter. I got to keep my soul."

"And psychiatrists?"

"Can I be frank?"

"Seems like it fits you."

"They have painted themselves into a corner."

Sedona had now stooped to trace her finger down a map showing where each exhibitor was located. Her finger paused at the image for Krøhn-McGill. It was a quadrant the size of a convenience store. She turned and began moving in the opposite direction. Griffin followed along.

"The drug industry hasn't introduced a new class of psychotropic pills since the Carter years," she said. "It's all the same compounds tricked out with various little tweaks to provide cover, with ever more promises about the glorious future that awaits. Now they are pushing all their chips on a portion of the craps table marked brain research. I'd rather give a guy some ACT and help him learn to live with his pain."

"What's ACT?" Griffin was looking at an enormous plasma screen with a film on loop featuring an animated journey into the center of the brain.

"Acceptance and Commitment Therapy," Sedona replied. "It's

Buddhism for mood disorders. Step one: chuck the Ativan and tolerate the discomfort until it becomes boring. Step two: learn to say 'Thank you may I have another please?' to your misfortune. Defang all those fears that the benzos tell you to avoid at all cost. ACT teaches you to say 'I welcome you today discomfort, for teaching me something new about the experience of life.'"

Sedona had paused at a crowd of unknown origin. Griffin moved in to find them swarming a gleaming rack of new jackets set up like a high-end garment shop. A clerk was handing out silk windbreakers with an AAP monogram and with the logo for Serotonal stitched on the back. "Free to all," he bellowed. "No need to be practicing yet. Just give us an email address and we are good. How about you?" the attendant asked him with a smile.

"I'm good, thanks," Griffin called, as the two kept walking.

"You sound like you want to drown every psychiatrist in the bathtub."

He had turned to offer the detail close into Sedona's ear.

Was he working her? You could get away with mouth-to-ear in a bar, but pulling the move at a meeting was new for Griffin. He was definitely reaching. She had glowing sheets of blue-black locks and long, luminous bangs. He was a little confused.

"Sometimes I feel kind of sorry for psychiatrists," she replied, a half-inch from his ear. "They were the embarrassing step-cousin in medicine for so long. They'd taken on all these barbaric treatments—insulin coma therapy—sure let's put grandma in a near-death condition to see if the depression lifts. ECT? Nothing to see here people, just mild electrocution. Ice pick lobotomy...Psychodynamic therapy... Mesmerism, sorry wrong era. Only when the meds came along did they finally get a place at the table. They gave up everything for drugs, except now their moment is passing and most of their patients are unable to get off pills that make it impossible to get laid. That's making them do terrible things."

"Such as?"

"Well, Dr. Elton is in there expanding Serotonal into the preschools and senior living centers. That's just tacky. They've drawn mistrust on themselves. It's made them shrill and defensive, as if it were all about *them*, rather than, you know, *kids, grand parents,* sad people. No, everyone in the way of their method are haters, bad players set on perpetuating the stigma of mental illness. They are staying on that horse as long as they can ride it."

Griffin and Sedona had arrived at a booth offering baskets filled with aged port and hard artisan cheese. Griffin welcomed the distraction. She was charming, but her lecture was getting tedious.

"You like camembert?"

The question had come from a show-model working the display for a company selling an anxiety drug. Griffin looked up to an oversized photo of an actor dressed as a harried suburban mom, an approximation of a fine-boned product of the Connecticut private schools, albeit staring glumly into a laptop while her children ran through an expensive home.

Sometimes it's more than just stress, the copy read.

Ask your doctor about Altruex™.

"Les Fromage?" Sedona clarified. "At this hour?"

The show model was all deflection.

"It's not FDA-approved for stress, but it does pair nicely with this Tawny."

She had smiled to the last word. "Say," the model added, "aren't you…" and she pointed at Sedona with a light wave of her index finger. This odd momentary gesture of recognition would have piqued Griffin's curiosity, except that before he could ask more, Sedona was off and on her way.

After pausing to grab some cheese and then giving the blonde a quick *thanks*, Griffin began running to catch up with Sedona, by now another booth over at a stand-up for a high-end chain of mental illness treatment centers. They were giving out free aromatherapy candles.

"I look at it this way," Sedona said, pausing to take in the scent of the expensive wax. "Serotonal sold seventy-five million prescriptions last year. There's not a lot of stigma in a drug with more users than all of France. So these guys are a new breed. Six hundred papers? That's rich. Jeremy Elton would have to have written a manuscript every nine days to reach a pile of authorship that tall. By the way, these are gorgeous," she added, holding the candle up to Griffin's nose. "What is that, rosemary?"

Griffin made a mental note to remember the 75 million prescriptions figure for his story.

He watched Sedona pocket three candles and turn to leave the hall. The door had taken them back to the ballroom, and the pair emerged by an opening near the side of the stage, taking a spot behind a glowing and concert-sized sound board where they could look out over the crowd. To their side, Jeremy Elton was still on stage, generating calm and seductive connection with his audience about a slide entitled *Success Rates for Serotonal in Treating Major Depression in the Elderly.*

The background graphics were an undulating wave of shimmering pixels, an expensive digital effect resembling the swirling of northern lights as seen from the arctic circle at midnight.

"If you can get past the intoxicating visuals," Sedona whispered, "take a look around the room. Let's see...there. That's her."

"Who?" Griffin was still back on the whisper. It was kind, and warm.

"The real author of his paper. I'm guessing, anyway, based on that look on her face."

Griffin couldn't make out anything special about the woman in question, other than she did appear to hail from the private sector, judging by her expensive threads. She seemed a little less enraptured, now that he thought about it, almost bored with Jeremy Elton's ostensibly captivating talk. She was stylish, barely looking towards the stage. She might have been 35.

"What kind of look is that?"

"Like she has heard it all before," Sedona replied. "Like she wrote it herself, a long time ago, and now he's here, getting the rock star treatment for battering it…Like she's required to sit there, should any remotely-knowledgable questions arise."

Sedona skimmed the pages of her program, arrived at the spot for the speech now in progress, and jammed her finger on the text.

"I bet this is her, right here."

She swiveled the catalog so Griffin could read it, leaned in and read the line in a smooth purr befitting a voiceover pro selling Jaguars.

"'We graciously acknowledge the editorial assistance of S.G. Patel at Deadline Medical Communications.'"

"Meaning?"

"She's the ghostwriter! Elton is sharp enough to answer his own questions, but I have seen a lot of guys like him just bring the ghostie up on stage."

Griffin had seen that as well, the way assistants were sometimes invited in to help out an academic answering questions. The whole ghostwriter thing left him cold, though. He was a writer. He knew it was a skill like any other. It didn't seem that bad.

"Not everyone can write you know," he said. "It's not a federal crime."

"You're serious?"

A roar came up from the crowd. The Elton talk had now ended, triggering an exodus from the hall. As Sedona had predicted, now that the room was reshaping into the departed and the clusters of participants, her presumptive ghostwriter was indeed there at Elton's side, doing, conspicuously, nothing.

"Hey, this was fun."

Griffin turned to find Sedona midway into a movement to signal she was moving in for an embrace. OK. So now they were hug-friends? As he leaned forward to reciprocate, his bag swung around and banged her in the side.

"Tagged by the swag," he said. "Super sorry. Really glad to meet you."

He had briefly thought to get her number, but decided that could have been goon-like. Besides, he figured he could always find her down the line.

And as it happened, it would take him a couple of weeks to make that search, only to learn she wasn't so easy to track down after all. That he wouldn't be finding her on the website for the University of Wisconsin, or the directory for the AAP meeting, or the entire fucking internet. Sometimes you just heard a name wrong.

With bodies moving everywhere, Sedona was then off in one direction as Jeremy Elton approached from the other. When the pair passed him on their way to somewhere else, Griffin finally caught a glimpse at the name on her tag.

Well, I'll be damned, he thought, Sedona Piper was right. The tag read *S.G. Patel, MS Deadline Medical Communications, Inc.*

18

Though he was the winner of three prizes for nonfiction science writing and the author of two counter-histories of his field, Alexander Breton, MD, PhD, professor of psychiatry and distinguished lecturer at the University of Christchurch, had only been slated to deliver his remarks from what was clearly the designated *ReceptorVision2011* speaking participant wasteland, a McCormick Place quarter-ballroom unceremoniously identified as 12-J-105B.

Griffin had learned just an hour earlier he now needed to write about the interesting death of Hemingway immediately, and only later about the uninteresting anniversary of Serotonal.

Since he was stuck here at the AAP, and since the program notes for this talk contained references to both Serotonal and suicide, Griffin opportunistically saw it as a two-fer. As they had scheduled the poor man in Siberia, Griffin was seven minutes late.

The scrape of a steel latch as Griffin entered the underpopulated quarter-ballroom scorched the quiet of Alexander Breton's talk like a dumpster being dragged along concrete.

"I see we have a latecomer," Breton chimed warmly to his thirty gathered attendees scattered throughout a hall meant to house a hundred.

Griffin winced.

"Perhaps you can find a chair!"

Though Griffin had seen Breton on book jacket photos capturing him in deep shadow at the gates of university libraries, in person he presented as uncharacteristically athletic-looking, sporting the build of an aging tennis pro, with dark hair showing strands of grey that ended at his jawline. Behind him, a screen had been cued to a slide that was all business, however, the meaning of which eluded Griffin immensely.

Moving the Bodies:
A Secondary Analysis of Adverse Events in Serotonal Trials.

"Before I begin," Breton offered, "I am obliged to inform you that I have received compensation as an expert witness in lawsuits against some of the drug makers whose products are about to be mentioned."

Griffin was familiar with this clumsy confession. A pre-lecture routine whereby speakers were expected to own up to all financial ties with the drugs they were discussing, it required otherwise unknowable academics to delve into any and all sideline revenue that should have rightly bought artisan-cut stone patios, commercial-grade kitchens, high-end rowing sculls for their Ivy League daughters and other assorted trophies.

Jeremy Elton's disclosure had listed 47 different drug companies, a slide he had flashed onto the screen for a tenth of a second. For his part, Alexander Breton had been required to name just one law firm and two drug companies, a measly haul if there was one.

"Lest you presume from my toil within litigation that I am a so-called drug scold," he offered unnecessarily, "as you can see, I have also been compensated by drug manufacturers as well. All of which is to say, when it comes to taking payment from parties who have an interest in the data you are about to hear, I have played both sides of the fence."

"Other than that, I have no conflicts to disclose, except for those with my spouse, which are deep and unyielding."

Laughter trickled forward from the middle rows. Although it

would be the last gesture of kindness offered to the weary champion of academic history for the remainder of the hour.

"The data I am about to share with you today," Breton began, "is derived from our recent review of serious adverse events within the clinical trials of a highly popular drug. We reviewed unpublished data filed within the FDA related to Serotonal's capacity to cause a most-unwelcome side effect."

And it was lightening quick, what it was that occurred next—and almost certainly tasteless if not unforgiveable.

With imperceptible speed Breton mimicked the act of pulling a noose while tilting his head to one side and concurrently projecting his tongue.

It seemed defiant, to say the least, as if years of some unknown unfairness had left the tall parson in no mood to compete for the moral high ground.

Just as quickly, the slide behind him changed to a shot of a male model sitting forlornly with his artfully-coifed head in his hands.

"Sorry, guys," Breton called to a trio of suits in the back row. "I realize I should have asked for permission to use one of your adverts."

They must have been industry, Griffin thought.

"Be our guest," one of the suits replied.

And then a reply came so fast that it seemed like there was more to the relationship than that seen here.

"Not sure if I'd be so cheeky if I were you," Breton said with a smile, "but *THANKS!*"

First Sedona, now this, Griffin thought.

These people were wild.

"It's no secret," Alexander Breton continued, "that for children and young adults, antidepressants raise the risk of suicidal events." (Because of his New Zealander accent, here he had pronounced the word as "*a-VEENCE.*")

"Although it is not on the label," Breton continued, "antidepressants appear capable of this same quixotic manifestation in adults—at least if we are to trust the judgment of corporate counsel who've authorized wrongful death payouts over the last two and a half decades."

"And by the way, happy silver anniversary Serotonal!" he called to the suits. "Shall I send you a fruit basket?"

"We're good, thanks."

"Very well. But for all its longevity, it's well-accepted that your drug routinely produces thoughts of self-harm"—(a word Breton pronounced *sef-HAHM*)—"as well as attempted (ah-TEEM-ted) and completed (com-PLAY-ted) acts of harm and suicide."

"Well that's the entire kitchen sink, isn't it?"

The remark had come meandering Breton's way from somewhere in middle of the room.

"This list of so-called 'suicidal events'" the commenter continued, "is surely far too heterogenous for consideration as a singular side effect?"

It was awkward, this business of butting in so early. Breton had been talking for all of three minutes and yet was already being cut off by members of his room.

Briefly tilting his head to one side and then the other, Breton engaged in a performance of consideration.

"In our practice we see patients trying to harm themselves *daily*," his critic continued. "It's not always a desire to die. Some of these acts of self harm are just kids being bored!"

Alexander Breton's critic leaned back in his chair with a look of satisfaction. Breton gazed over his reading glasses at the vest-bursting 50-something. The moment dragged on a bit longer. Griffin heard a chair squeak as someone shifted their weight, and then Alexander Breton finally spoke up.

"Well, my new friend," Breton offered with a small laugh. "Objection *noted*. Though if the suicidal event is happening within your patient" (a word he had pronounced "PEH-shent"), "..and that patient is a healthy college woman newly placed on Serotonal for a mild case of social phobia before being driven to search out the lethality of pain pills"—a phrase he pronounced "pen-pellz"—"the events don't seem so easily given the wave of the hands. But thank you for your comment."

Breton looked down to his laptop in detectible weariness.

"So…do these suicidal events among depressed users of Serotonal stem from everyday use of the drug, or are the drugs as so many believe merely taking the blame for underlying misery in already-suicidal patients? I believe that's the gist of our critics' objections?"

It was like throwing chum into a tank of sharks.

"Suicidal events in a trial of antidepressants," a different audience member called out, "almost *certainly* stem from the underlying illness of depression."

Griffin looked for the source of this new attack but couldn't find him.

This time Breton just ignored the remark.

"All participants in the Serotonal trial *did* of course have major depression," Breton continued. "It was a condition of being enrolled. What we discovered, however, was that the excess of suicidal events in these trials was *demonstrably* linked to the drug and not underlying depression. Moreover, we became quite certain the drug maker knew about the side effect going in."

And though he had finally developed some momentum, now Breton paused to stare with momentary joy at the laser pointer he had been given.

"Well, look at this one," he offered with quiet surprise. He turned to regard the sight of the suits again in the back. *"'Laser in on Serotonal?'"*

"A little on the *nose*, wouldn't you say?"

After that, he tossed the pointer into a bin.

"Right. I shall now point with my hand, like a pauper. So. One might ask: How did we determine that the drug-maker for Serotonal knew that its antidepressant was dangerous? Did we catch them by planting listening devices in the Krøhn-McGill boardrooms? Did we climb through the air vents at company headquarters? The answer is no, we did not spy on their deliberations, and we did not need to, because data tells all secrets. And the data in this trial tell us quite clearly that researchers studying Serotonal sorted suicidal events in such an odd, guilty-looking fashion it simply made no sense other than as an effort to conceal drug-induced gestures of self-harm."

Breton paused here for emphasis.

"Anyone care to jump in?

"Very well, we've all played to a tough room before, so I won't ask for your sympathy. Let us now carve up some numbers."

Then he put up a new slide, one showing the abstract for an academic article.

"This is the published version of the study in question, a paper titled *Serotonal*™ *in the Treatment of Major Depressive Disorder,* though inside the company, this paper went by the thoroughly more bland-sounding designation of 'Study 463.'"

"Study 463 was helmed by a team of Krøhn-McGill-funded foot-soldiers, chief among them, our colleague here at the AAP and a well-known cheerleader for the compound, the ubiquitous America's Psychiatrist himself, Dr. Jeremy Elton."

It caught Griffin by surprise to hear Elton's name brought up in a critical light. He had just seen him work a room like Bon Jovi. These people all seemed to be fighting with each other.

"Study 463 was blind," Breton continued. "It included 2,761 subjects with depression, 1,387 of whom took the placebo and 1,374 of whom were given the active drug."

Griffin pulled a pad from his bag and began hastily taking notes.

"It was one of a dozen, identically-constructed studies performed by Krøhn-McGill on the effectiveness and safety of Serotonal. It was also one of just two studies that managed to find the drug both safe and effective. Not surprisingly, it was quickly submitted to the regulators as proof of the compound's readiness for market."

Griffin knew most of this already, how the studies we so often see heralding the success of a new pill are merely those that a drug maker chose to make public. It was unusual to hear the dodge being aired so conversationally in a lecture. Most researchers steered clear of the suppression of data and all of the mistrust it created.

"And in the two decades since its publication, Study 463 has been cited thousands of times," Breton said. "But hey, those are the rules, so, no quibble here. What we wanted to know was this: what did 463 really find?"

Breton now changed his slide to a three-column table, a slide titled *Suicidal Events.*

Study 463: Suicidal Events

Placebo (n=1387)	Serotonal (n=1374)	Total
Suicidal Events: 5	Suicidal Events: 6	11

Suicidal Events: Suicidal nightmares, thoughts, statements, acts, self-harm, suicide attempts and completed suicides.

"As you can see, when the final publication saw daylight, in study 463, five suicidal events anchored the placebo group, versus six within the group taking Serotonal. Which comes out to a tie, statistically. A tie of course suggests that while Serotonal doesn't exactly *reduce* suicidal events, it doesn't increase them either, effectively making this finding a win for Krøhn-McGill."

"You may now break out the champagne."

Breton paused for effect.

"No one?" he continued. "Very well."

"But what happens when you look at the *timing* of these events?"

And then Breton put up his second slide, an image entitled *Suicidal Events By Week.*

"Here we have broken down these same 11 events according to when they took place during the study. Pay attention now to the harms noted in placebo column, if you will. Specifically, the bad experiences have now shrunken considerably, from 5 to 3."

Study 463: Suicidal Events by Week

	Placebo	Serotonal
Week 1		
Week 2		3
Week 3	2	2
Week 4		
Week 5	1	
Week 6		1
Total	3 suicidal events	6 suicidal events

"So this finding—three suicidal events on placebo versus six on the antidepressant—it would have been a problem for Krøhn-McGill. The drug is supposed to look better than the sugar pill. How did Dr. Elton and his colleagues get away with telling the FDA that a doubling of risk came out to a tie?"

Breton touched the laptop in a showy outstretching of his pointer finger. He seemed to have few fucks left to give. His third table included a new row, one at the top, a row labeled *Two Week Pre-Randomization*.

If Griffin read this one correctly, the row represented a period of time prior to the start of the trial.

Study 463: Suicidal Events During "Pre-Randomization"

	Placebo	Serotonal
Two Week Pre-Randomization	2	
Week 1		
Week 2		3
Week 3	2	
Week 4		2
Week 5	1	
Week 6		1

"As you can see, now that we have included suicidal events which took place in the two weeks *before* the start of the trial, our missing two placebo-related adverse events have returned."

"The problem is, adverse events that occur within this period are grossly inappropriate for inclusion when it comes to judging the performance of a drug under study. Does anyone care to explain why that is?"

A short silence ensued, and finally a volunteer raised her arm.

"It's because experiences before the start of the trial are representative of neither a drug effect, nor a true placebo effect," she said.

She wore a plain skirt and carried her things in a shopworn backpack. She could have been a grad student. Breton seemed to have no other allies in the room.

"Exactly," he said. "Thank you, Elaine. We don't include adverse events from the weeks prior to the start of a drug trial, for the simple reason that patients who take part in our trials are almost invariably going through drug withdrawal when they sign up to study something new, and frequently agitated as a result. So anything that happens in this unwelcome window of deprescribing is related to neither the drug being studied, nor representative of the placebo. ...And bad things are almost *always* happening during this window."

Breton stopped, picked up a glass of water and took a thoughtful drink. His talk was venturing into unfamiliar territory, and the room was becoming quieter. The speaker was erecting a complicated case, and he seemed to have learned of the need to build in breaks for letting his audience catch up.

"Now for some reason," Breton noted with feigned befuddlement, "Krøhn-McGill *really wanted* to label the suicidal events occurring during pre-randomization as placebo-related. We know this is true, because the company *specifically asked* the FDA to allow them to jam them in the placebo column, a petition the FDA granted without comment."

"Those patients weren't on any drugs." It was another interruption from the audience. Some kind of agitator in the middle, again, trying to throw the guy off his stride. This one was all alpha, leaning forward with his finger pointing directly at the lectern. "It seems to me," he added, "that makes them fair game."

"Interesting choice of words," Breton replied after a short pause, putting his elbow on the podium and his chin in his palm.

"What words?" His combatant was looking keyed.

"Well, you just remarked that this study was, what did you call it,—oh yes, a *game*."

"You know what I meant," replied his adversary, flipping his hand in frustration.

"But is this a game?"

And now Alexander Breton sounded sincere.

"Is what we do a game, or is it science? Although it is true, as a literal fact, that these clinical trial subjects were not taking drugs leading into the trial, that hardly makes them a placebo group. They were normal comparison subjects only if one were to dispute the well-recognized rise of suicidality that occurs during drug withdrawal."

"Studies are filled with little decisions like these all day long, Dr. Breton," a different audience member said with amusement. "There's really no point in reading intent to them."

Breton put down his glasses.

"The movement of withdrawal events onto placebo is no neutral act," he said calmly. "It changes the context in which we are attempting to understand the safety of Serotonal. It creates a new normal, one wherein ordinary life for subjects on placebo has come to seem just a little more suicidal—just enough, in any event, to mask the rise in torment created for a portion of those taking Serotonal."

Griffin paused to let the argument sink in.

He had never before given thought to the relative nature of harm. In essence, Breton was saying, if you were a drug maker, you didn't have to show your drug was safe. You only had to show it was as safe as a sugar pill. And if you couldn't make your drug look as safe as a sugar pill, you only needed to make life while on a sugar pill look a little more dangerous.

"The manufacturers of Serotonal," Breton concluded, "hid the suicidality of their drug in plain sight. They slipped it behind the placebo suicides."

That last line caused a listener to lurch forward involuntarily.

"You can't prove they did this on purpose."

"Do we have to?" Breton replied. "It seems like Krøhn-McGill requested a steep departure from protocol, one granted only for this drug. These trials hid a lethality of antidepressants. Whether they designated the wrong events as placebo-related by accident or design may be meaningful in a legal sense. But all we are interested in as researchers is the scientific truth. No one from inside of these trials has ever come forward to tell us what they were up to when they miscoded run-in suicide events. I doubt they ever will. They all sign NDAs, for one."

Griffin noticed a pair from the suits in back had begun aggressively texting.

Breton called up another slide.

"I am truly almost done here, but I did want everyone to see what happened at the end of the landmark Serotonal for the treatment of depression trial. Again, this is only made possible because we requested so-called proprietary documents filed within the FDA. They are not visible to any doctor who chooses to prescribe these pills, much less the consumer. The investigators who have placed their name on this study would not have even seen these. Once you see them, you might agree that by shelving them, Krøhn-McGill did the right thing for the success of their stock price."

Griffin needed only an instant to see how much trouble the fourth table had created.

In a new row along the bottom, one entitled *Two Weeks Post-Trial*, three more suicidal events had been added in the column for events while on Serotonal. It suggested the suicidality associated with Serotonal was worse than a doubling of risk.

Study 463: Post-Trial Suicidal Events

	Placebo	Serotonal
Run-in	2	
Week 1		
Week 2		3
Week 3	2	
Week 4		2
Week 5	1	
Week 6		1
Two Weeks Post Trial		3

"As you can see," Breton said, "three more suicidal events were recorded after the trial ended, and all of them among those assigned to the Serotonal group. The period immediately following a trial is another window of harm, one in which the active drug is no longer being taken, but can still be causing agitation, dysphoria and impulsivity by way of withdrawal."

"Though none of these events were added to the public tally of problems caused by Serotonal, they clearly belong to the hazard of choosing to take the drug, especially because a subset of patients within the U.S. who go on to take Serotonal will likely go off the drug every day. Krøhn-McGill neglected to include these events into their assessment of harm, but we will."

"Add these withdrawal events to the drug-using group, take away the pre-trial suicidal events from the placebo-using group, and our final safety score comes out to nine suicidal events in the drug group, compared to just three in the placebo group. This means Serotonal was not simply equal in riskiness to placebo, or even doubly dangerous as doing nothing. No, what this table is telling us is that depressed patients taking Serotonal were actually *three times* as likely to experience suicidal events than were depressed patients on placebo."

"Now. Just one more."

Could it get any worse? Griffin shook his head at this catastrophe unfolding for the attendees to *ReceptorVision2011* hoping to celebrate the gift that was Serotonal.

Somehow it then did get a bit more worse, as Breton pulled the curtain back on data supporting the safety of the best-selling drug in the country.

"So, were these all just bad thoughts, or did people actually die?" Breton asked. "I know that's a meaningful question to a lot of people. It is common to assume, as our first commenter here suggested, that we may be making much out of nothing."

And there it was, the holy shit slide.

Study 463: Which ones Actually Died?
Non-Fatal Suicidal Events (NFSE) vs. Completed Suicides (CS)

	Placebo	Serotonal
Run-in		
Week 1		
Week 2		3 (CS)
Week 3	2 (NFSE)	
Week 4		2 (CS)
Week 5	1 (NFSE)	
Week 6		1 (CS)
Washout		3 (CS)
Totals	Non-Fatal Suicidal Events: 3 Completed Suicides: 0	Non-Fatal Suicidal Events: 0 Completed Suicides: 9

"So as you can see," Breton continued, "The final score is nine to zero. When you get specific about the adverse events themselves, and do away with this convenient euphemism that is quote-unquote 'suicidal events', Serotonal appears to have a lock on completed suicide."

"While three depressed patients taking placebo had experienced non-lethal suicidal events—empty threats, half-hearted overdoses of non-toxic drugs, calls to suicide hotlines or acts of self-harm—nine depressed patients taking Serotonal took their own lives. I'm struggling to find a non-alarmist way to put this, but I can't. Serotonal, the most popular SSRI in the world, is grotesquely lethal."

As his table faded, an image of America's Psychiatrist came into focus—the same photograph Elton himself had projected just an hour earlier.

It was a rugged, outdoorsy shot, a heroic image of Jeremy Elton stepping onto a rock while straddling a tributary in the wild, hands at his side.

Only now the photo had been altered to include hundred-dollar bills fluttering from the pockets of his high-end rafting outfit, with the elephant-headed god Ganesh placed beneath the researcher's tricked-out rafting shoes.

A bit on the nose indeed.

"So you can look at it like this," Breton concluded. "If I am selling you a drug that causes death, and I want it to appear protective, I have two choices. I can make people on the drug look better. Or, I can make people on placebo look…"

"Worse."

Griffin said the word to himself, taking in the full weight of the deception.

"Yes," Breton said while looking at him. "Exactly."

19

It was crickets for the Alexander Breton Q&A.

The audience began adjusting their belongings as a handler made a meek plea for engagement.

"If anyone has any questions at all," she offered, "please don't be shy."

More silence.

"No one?...Now is the time...Dr. Breton has travelled *such* a long way to be here with us."

After another interminable twenty seconds, she put up the white flag.

"Very well then," she said, "thanks everyone."

Griffin moved towards the front of the room as the small crowd move quietly towards the door. Breton was staring at a cable connecting his laptop to a sound board. Griffin reached down to unplug the correct one, saying he enjoyed the talk immensely.

"Here for the wake?"

Griffin laughed and introduced himself, sheepishly naming his magazine and reason for being there.

"I was originally supposed to write about Serotonal's quarter-century of success."

"It has made them a lot of money in twenty-five years."

"But this is quite a new wrinkle, your finding that it is nine times deadlier than a placebo?"

"Well, I wouldn't worry about anyone beating you to the story."

"Can't really go there right now anyway," he replied, "because now they have put me onto the death of Hemingway."

"It was horrible? Yes, that's been the consensus."

For a minute it was so quiet you could hear the sound of the fan in Breton's laptop. Another awkward pause.

"Reserpine," Breton finally added, this time looking up towards the ceiling. "Now there's a drug one doesn't hear about often."

"I'm sorry?"

"Ernest Hemingway took reserpine, pretty sure I read that somewhere. It was an early drug for hypertension. But it had the same problems as Serotonal."

So now Hemingway had died of drug-induced suicide as well. OK.

It was disappointing for Griffin, the possibility that Breton was given to seeing his side effect behind every act of self-harm. He seemed a little paranoid.

"In the Zone," Breton added, "I can't say I have heard of that one. How would you describe it?"

"It's for men in their twenties and thirties."

Griffin started to wonder if he could ditch this guy and still snag an interview with Jeremy Elton if he tracked down his publicist. The magazine would love him.

"Well, if a lad magazine wants to ask me about the diagnostic error at the creation of the monoamine hypothesis, that's a first."

And what on Earth did that ever mean?

"But to answer your question, reserpine was a mid- 20th-century hypertension drug, one now largely decommissioned except for third-world health systems."

Griffin realized the suits were now hovering behind them, very likely glowering. He dropped back a step to let them all have at it. An argument right now could go to good use in an article some day.

"Dr. Breton, Seamus Cole, Krøhn-McGill Pharmaceuticals, welcome to Chicago."

Griffin suppressed a small smile at the charm offensive. They had just had their drug compared to something from the Cabinet of Dr. Caligari.

"Thank you," Breton said, gamely shaking the meaty palm of a stocky man with a strong jaw and a combed back helmet of silver grey hair. "The drive in from the airport looked lovely."

"Sure is. Listen, I just wanted to let you know we follow your research closely," replied the suit. Griffin took note of the man's gold-plated cufflinks and a hefty Rolex. "In fact," the man added, "we have read everything you have ever written."

Breton seemed taken aback.

"Well, that seems unlikely," he replied. "But thank you, I think. I hope you found the lecture intriguing."

"That's one way of putting it."

The men wished him well and wandered off, leaving just the two of them.

"Do drug execs always treat you like an old flame at the class reunion?"

"Not sure I get the reference, but sure, it's unflaggingly pleasant. That said, I could see how one might expect otherwise. How the reporter who has watched a crime procedural or two might imagine our relationship in adversarial terms. In the real world, life on opposing side of the drug makers can be a bit dull."

Griffin had pointed to the hall and asked if he could walk with him.

"So they don't make threats, try to get you to stop what you're doing?"

They were walking now.

"Nope."

"Send you the head of a horse?"

"Nope, sadly."

Griffin and Breton had entered a hallway. Breton paused to lean backwards on a glowing oversized vending machine selling nothing but bottled water. He appeared to have nowhere to go.

"Oh the Godfather, funny. Yeah, nah. To the contrary. In the real world, intimidation and personal destruction are carried out with all the courtesies of the sort you just witnessed. You may have heard the expression: 'keep your friends close, and your enemies closer.' Well, that is our little arrangement."

Breton was scanning the hallway as he spoke, distracted. He now looked exhausted.

"They come to all my talks," he said with a sigh and shake of his head. "They always come up to say good show, mate. They make sure there are painfully few in attendance and that those who do arrive will enjoy the complaints of planted critics. So, no, the true penalties for my research take place through conversations, not violence, conversations I am never allowed to hear."

"How would you know?"

"How would I know a drug maker has chopped me off at the knees?"

"Yeah. What happens?"

"Well, it's obvious, mate. Despite years of productive publishing on other topics, I am suddenly no longer able to get an email returned from the *Journal of American Psychiatry*. Or my application for funding goes unprocessed. Or my talk at the APA is scheduled over the lunch hour, in this Falstaffian outpost right here."

Breton had turned to look at the number.

"*12-J-105B*. Charming."

"My research assistant can discover her application to graduate school has become lost, yeah that's happened. My secretary can receive unsolicited job offers from angel investors seeking her out at a tripling of her salary. It's quite creative and effective. Prior to raising this topic, I once gave talks in ballrooms of the sort commandeered by Dr. Elton."

Breton leaned towards his research assistant who had briefly emerged from another cluster of attendees, before the two exchanged a few words and she headed off towards the center concourse.

"Back when I first began to root around into this material I was quite naïve," Breton said. "I had spotted my patients experiencing frightening episodes of agitated depersonalization after going on the drug, upwards of thirty percent. I said, 'wow, let's see what happened.' So I took them off. Tapered, right, because a hard stop can make things much, much worse."

Griffin suddenly remembered he had quit Bioferex all at once.

He hoped that wasn't a mistake.

"I watched the adverse effects wane, which would suggest it was indeed a drug effect, then put my patients back on the drug, and watched the side effects come roaring back, which pretty much seals the question. It's called challenge, de-challenge, re-challenge, and it's sort of the gold standard for spotting side effects. Or it was, anyway, before the manufacturers realized they could ride the celebration of randomized control trial design to hide side effects, put an end to clinical observations and invalidate all other evidence. Nowadays doctors only look at the cautionary statements, which have been written by industry. So for most doctors, if it is not on the warning label, they will say your side effect is impossible. Anyway, once I started writing about this in the journals, the wheels began to come off."

"They came after you?"

"Oh, quite the contrary," he laughed.

He pointed towards the main concourse and Griffin nodded.

"At first, they tried to bring me into the tent. I believe this is what Americans call the 'good cop' routine."

"Is that why you said you had been paid by the makers of the drugs?"

Griffin was taking notes as they walked, not sure what he would ever do with them.

"Yep. Bastards bought me off for cheap. I was designated a key opinion leader, sort of a vanity title that had me speaking at lavish gatherings in gorgeous locales."

"Did you feel like a sell-out?"

"Are you kidding? I travelled in the front of the plane. Took a private driver. Enjoyed long dinners on the dime of others and faced down more empty afternoons in marvelous resorts than I can count. My wife misses them very much. Let me tell you, you haven't lived until you've seen the sunset from an ocean-side balcony at the Mauna Lani Bay on the Kona coast of the Big Island."

Griffin was scribbling as fast as he could.

"But, what you're saying is, you took the money."

"With pleasure," Breton said. "'Consulting fees' is I believe the term. I do not discriminate against those with means. And it was all going great until I continued writing papers that my patrons did not find to their liking. They then began to roll out the bad cop routine, to tell my peers that I was on the take from the lawyers. Which was rich, truly, because I had been on their tab for far longer."

"Were you?"

"Did I receive compensation for my time spent testifying on the nature of side effects?"

"Yes."

"Why of course. I believe science is vital in a nation of laws."

"The attacks on your character, that must make you resentful."

"Nah, It's juvenile. I always get invited somewhere. They make sure it's a lonely, hard-to-reach affair."

"And the suits in back?"

"The detail men do not need to threaten me when they can fire off a text and remove ten percent of all funding from any journal considering my work. They keep me out of the best publications. That's the entire ball game, if you haven't heard."

Griffin and Breton had reached the lobby. Breton was moving towards the elevator. Griffin hadn't asked him anything about Hemingway.

"One more thing about reserpine?"

"If you buy me a pint in the lounge upstairs," Breton said, "I will tell you more than you care to know."

༃

133

The elevator opened to reveal Jeremy Elton and an assistant, the woman Sedona had pointed out as Jeremy's likely ghostwriter.

"Alexander," Elton said tersely. "Pleasure to see you again."

"Jeremy. The pleasure's all mine."

Breton began to pick at a piece of lint on the shoulder of his jacket.

A smile crawled across Griffin's face. Breton had just spent an hour dissecting Elton's biggest trial, knee-capping it all with a mock-up lampooning Jeremy Elton's apparently towering self-regard. And now here they were fast friends trading pleasantries.

"I missed your talk," Elton said. "I understand you took a deep dive into some old number laying around the FDA?"

Breton nodded. He was staring at the numbers designating the floors.

"You could say that."

"I hope my name came up."

"Oh yes." Breton smiled.

"Credit goes to those who take it."

"You were credited, mate."

Breton smiled harder. The elevator door opened. Griffin and Breton got out, then walked towards a bar off the lounge. Griffin had to ask.

"OK, that was awkward."

"Oh no, we go back."

"And he knows you have named him as a participant in the thing with the placebo patients?"

"This 'thing,' probably not," Breton said. "The news may take an hour to reach him. Then again, he may have known about my talk prior to my having given it. You never know what you're getting with that one."

And now they were reading Breton's emails. He seemed paranoid all over again. They went for a table. Griffin forgot to ask how far the two went back.

୬

Once their interview turned to the death of Ernest Hemingway, even the controversy-seeking Alexander Breton began to choose his words with care. Griffin told him all that he had learned about Ernest Hemingway's medical history and the timing of his mental decline in relation to getting ECT. Breton said Griffin might want to track down the letters from his Mayo Clinic psychiatrist, a doctor named Howard Rome. "A bit of detective work," he said, "but well worth your time."

"What will they say?"

"What?"

"The letters."

"Nothing, really. Just that his care team thought Hemingway was depressed and agitated on account of reserpine and Ritalin, an early monoamine cocktail they were starting to understand to be trouble."

"It would have been compounded by alcoholism," he added. "Not to mention a lifetime worth of head injuries, the CTE, dementia and all the impulsivity and agitation this can accelerate. But there's dementia, and then there's the side effect of reserpine, which presents as paranoia, restlessness, passivity, grief and the entire seductive tunnel-vision of a final escape. To me that sounds a bit like the side effect we see with Serotonal."

"What side effect is that."

"It's called akathisia, technically. You'll have to look it up."

Griffin started writing the strange word down, next to "reserpine" another strange word he'd never heard before. "Underline this one," Breton said, "A-K-A"

"A-K-A"

"T-H-I-S"

"T-H-I-S"

"I-A."

Griffin was humoring him. Aka-whatever sounded arcane, irrelevant. The electroshock, now that interested him.

"What about the ECT?"

"What about it?"

Breton seemed indifferent. He was perusing a bar menu.

"Well, sure, twenty treatments for six seconds at four hundred and fifty volts with a ball in your mouth," Breton finally offered. "It does seem to get one into a grand mal seizure—'It was a brilliant cure but we lost the patient'—I think it was Hemingway who described it like that. But it was reasonable of them to try."

Griffin raised his eyebrows.

ECT was a treatment that society had come to view with horror.

"Electroshock was sometimes effective for snapping a person out of akathisia, mate."

There was that word again.

"Maybe if we called it the Hemingway effect, the awareness of akathisia would have survived the passage of time."

"So you think it's true, then?"

"That reserpine killed Hemingway?"

"Yes, I mean," Griffin mumbled, "not to single out any one drug or anything."

"Why not single out a drug?" Breton replied. "They make sure to single them out when they advertise them to us."

"Do you think it's true Hemingway killed himself because of a side effect called aka…"

"Akathisia."

"…Aka-thisia, and not depression?"

Griffin wanted Breton on the record for this. His Hemingway story just got interesting. But it would need an authority on the record to say the words: *Medicine did this.* That would be big. It just may have been, now that he began to think about it, the reason he was here.

"No. I won't say that," Breton said with a shake of his head. "I don't know enough about Ernest to say whether it was true, and neither do you. But I think reserpine rises to the top of the list of probable causes. It was a nasty bit of pharmacy, especially for people without depression."

"But you just said we should call aka-, aka-thisia, that we should call it 'the Hemingway effect.'"

Griffin wasn't going to let him wiggle out of this.

"Not really. What I meant when I said that was that—the real Hemingway effect—that would have been something much worse. That would have been the way they all thought reserpine caused depression, instead of madness. It was an early, pivotal diagnostic error with unforeseen consequences to this very day. When they assumed reserpine had caused depression, by extension, that created the fallacy that depression was characterized by a deficit of serotonin. And all of that, now *that* was catastrophic."

Griffin knew he was never going get any of this granular history of neuroscience into a magazine with scented inserts. He bit his lip and looked to the floor as Breton continued

"If they had properly noted what really happened, how reserpine had caused akathisia, not depression—a condition whereby *both* serotonin and dopamine had plummeted, shutting down access to the frontal lobes and ushering in a profound and profoundly fatal combination of disaffection, numbness, dysphoria, impulsivity and the urge to take action—we might have averted the suicidal antidepressant era now engulfing us. Now there's your Hemingway effect, mate, and it's astonishing, if you think about it. In taking on the wrong lesson from the reserpine story, they provided the ideological moorings for decades of drugs that brought on the same problem."

The pause was lengthy.

"Listen," Breton finally offered in a parting note of sympathy, "I wouldn't expect a story about Hemingway dying from akathisia to go over well. I suggest you write the piece your editors probably wanted, the one about the ECT. Trying to change the story of Hemingway's ending is itself career suicide. The only special interest more effective at shutting down opposition than the drug bosses are probably the literary bosses."

Griffin laughed.

"I think I can handle a bunch of Hemingway fans," he said. "Besides, if a story of mine is published and I get paid, that experience is going well enough as I see it."

Griffin watched as Breton let out a small shiver of disbelief, then looked down at his watch. Griffin felt briefly exposed for his sharing of an unflattering characteristic—a tendency to being unserious about everything. Meanwhile, the person across from him had traveled halfway around the world to deliver bad news about a popular drug to a chorus of hostility.

Griffin sensed something within himself loosening its protective grip on the defense of pretending to not care. It had been so long since he acknowledged how much he really did care. He had faced insurmountable prospects in publishing, and for long enough that he had resigned himself to whoring. They in turn had trained him to comfort himself with the idea that nothing fucking mattered. This caring part, if he could do more of it, felt like the return of a memory.

"I think we need to wrap up," said Breton.

"Sum up your thoughts on Hemingway for me?" Grifin got ready to write everything down. Breton didn't disappoint.

"Reserpine would have likely triggered the 180-degree transformation in Ernest Hemingway's personality, taking him from fearless to fearful. The weight of this anxiety would have darkened his outlook. Mayo as I recall were wise enough in that day—they were not afraid to talk about side effects then—to take him off it. Once through with ECT, he would have been prescribed an early antidepressant. Given his previous sensitivity to the effects of reserpine, under the antidepressant the side effect would have reemerged. Add in his CTE, alcoholic dementia, life regrets and isolation and that would have been the final nail in his coffin, so to speak. Major despondency and suicide at the first chance."

"So the first antidepressants could accelerate suicidality as well?"

"Oh, yes," Breton said as he rose from his chair. "This reaction has always been with us. Though they haven't always called it suicidality. It's been called all sorts of things: 'psychosis,' 'abnormal thoughts,' 'abnormal dreams,' and 'agitation.' The makers of one popular product once famously called it 'emotional lability.' But it all means the same thing."

"Which is?"

"Better to find a GP who can get you onto a beta blocker, maybe some nicotine or an antihistamine. The alternative is torment that only outwardly appears to have been the product of free will. Your mourners will say 'such a pity, we never knew he was depressed.' But the internists will keep giving out the drug that did it, possibly even to your widow and orphaned children. The public can only guess why so much madness continues to proliferate. Toxicology reports can only mention quote-unquote 'therapeutic levels of prescription medication.' One can never name the pill in our time."

Breton was now walking away.

Did this guy know how to get off the stage or what.

Griffin looked at his notebook. It was all too much. That lecture to the room full of trolls. This wild, fucked-up conversation just now. A surprisingly plausible rewriting of the most famous suicide in American letters. It took a few minutes longer for Griffin to realize he had never asked Alexander Breton about Bioferex.

20

Griffin made his way over to Elton's second talk of the day. It, too, was held in the largest room in the building. A stage call somehow even more showy than his first, this time America's Psychiatrist had come to sell the room on a Krøhn-McGill pill for Alzheimer's. Griffin took a seat near the back. Sedona Piper was nowhere to be found.

"We are here to disrupt the flywheel of thought dis-aggregation." Griffin had heard Elton saying, "node, lobe, and network."

It was hard to say what any of that meant, but the man was still pretty badass, in Griffin's mind, anyway. Griffin knew that Alexander Breton saw him more darkly, having suggested that Jeremy Elton had put his name on an early Serotonal trial that had concealed a deadly side effect. He'd even made Griffin re-evaluate his passive acceptance of working in high-paying drivel. But Griffin was still keeping an open mind about everyone. It's possible this whole place was filled with weirdos. As America's Psychiatrist began to deliver his talk, Griffin turned the comforting thought over as he got lost in a slide appearing behind Jeremy Elton, a video animating the activity of billions of brain cells lighting up in rapid sequence.

"Science has begun to identify the mid-brain mechanism underlying all neuropeptide signaling," Elton continued. "We speak today of the intersection of mind and body, the gateway to a transformational psychiatry, mental health, and the advent of all human potential."

It went on like this, peppered out with charts and bar graphs, and it killed, somehow even more-so than the previous Elton speech. It was confusing, yes, but Elton had a way of bounding from one arcane scientific term to another, then inserting all the little touches that papered over the tension, from the self-effacing joke to the personal story from his clinical practice to the broad and inspiring appeal at the end to rethink the nature of suffering. It felt like a sermon and a motivational lecture all in one.

When the talk reached its close, Griffin hoped he might slide in to ask Jeremy Elton a few questions on fly.

࿅

"I can get you ten minutes," Elton's publicity handler had told Griffin after intercepting him on approach. "You can have your time at 3:40 pm, room C-17. Please arrive early. We ask that you will tape Dr. Elton's comments."

At the appointed hour, Griffin and the infamous Dr. Elton had barely shaken hands when his source had begun managing the terms of their conversation.

"As you may know, my title on first mention is 'Jeremy Elton, MD, board certified clinical psychiatrist.'"

This happened sometimes: A source gets bossy on you.

To help build trust at the start of these interviews, Griffin always scribbled down these kind of demands, nodding yes even when he meant no. That said, he would not be using any of Elton's lengthy title.

"On the second mention, it is customary to refer to me as 'Holder of the Nathan Daly Endowed Professorship of Psychiatry and Chairman,

Department of Psychiatry, University of Dallas, the Institute of Brain Studies.' Now. When shall the article be published?"

Welp.

"I can't say for sure when the article comes out," Griffin offered gamely. "But I will be sure to let you know."

Truthfully, that too was false.

Given only ten minutes to work with, Griffin knew what he was here for.

He wanted to ask Jeremy Elton about Serotonal and suicide, or rather akathisia.

He had Googled the word on the way over and found it was indeed a thing.

"I will make note that you have agreed to send me a copy."

Yeah, no. Elton was still talking in terms of his own imagination.

"We can do that, of course," Griffin said.

At least Elton didn't demand to see the article in advance.

"...In advance of publication."

Griffin pretended not hear him. It was time to start in.

"Thanks so much for talking with me, Dr. Elton." Griffin leaned forward as he spoke. "I am reporting a story on Serotonal. I know you were investigator for the first study."

"As principal investigator of SITMADD," Elton offered, "the landmark 1998 clinical trial of Serotonal, a double-blind, randomized controlled trial of Serotonal in the Treatment of Major Depressive Disorder, research we published in a special issue of the *International Proceedings of the National Academy of Psychiatry*, we were able to demonstrate that Serotonal was safe and effective in the treatment of major depressive disorder to a statistically significant margin."

Griffin scribbled away.

It was all unusable, but he figured he could wrestle control of this thing after giving Elton a few more sentences to blow hot air.

"...We reported that Serotonal lowered depression scores on the standardized Hamilton-D scale of depression by an average of fifty percent in the first six weeks. Now the question for your magazine becomes…"

All the bigs did this. Buried you in blather, regurgitating the prepared message.

"Does Serotonal have a problem with suicidality?" Griffin asked.

Elton stiffened. He paused, turned to look at his assistant, and turned back to Griffin

"There have been no suicidal actions," he replied slowly, "only suicidal *thinking* in the trials of Serotonal."

Griffin raised an eyebrow at the suggestion you would ever diminish the fact of a person wanting to end their life.

"Yes, but Serotonal comes with an actual suicide warning," Griffin replied.

Elton paused, turned to look once again at his aide, then returned to looking at Griffin. He was the picture of calm, thoughtful medical compassion.

"Responsible reporters like you," he said with a kind tap on Griffin's knee, "know about standard warning language, how you would write that to address the inevitable, tragic self-harm that arises in the study of psychiatric patients. And you know what? The press has been admirably, heroically restrained up until now, thank goodness, in not giving a forum for the sad pleadings of the anti-psychiatry mob."

Griffin looked down at the small glowing dot indicating his recorder was working and he was indeed getting all this down. He was pretty sure Alexander Breton had just presented data showing nine people had died of suicide in the Serotonal trials, a seemingly scandalous tally of gravestones given that the placebo group had lost no subjects whatsoever.

"The black box warning was an overreaction, Mr. Wagner. If patients frightened by its message go un-medicated, we will see *more* deaths by suicide. Most of all, what really has me worried the most, is that the warning places a stigma on the drug precisely when we need to *reduce* the social cost of depression, not spread false alarms about rare events."

Griffin figured he had three minutes, four tops. The next question just came to him.

"Not to be difficult, Dr. Elton, but couldn't a person just as easily argue that it is stigmatizing to tell patients they have a brain disease requiring lifelong use of medication?"

Griffin hadn't prepared to ask that one. It just had always bothered him.

"I mean, in the past," Griffin continued, "depressed patients were told they were going through a tough time in their life. But they also were told that nothing was permanent and that they were resilient. That isn't a more empowering message? At the very least, it's hardly stigmatizing, right?"

"Oh, no, seriously, you do have to understand this next part," Elton said. "Since their introduction, antidepressants have brought on a *drop* in suicide rates, here and across the world." He smiled with a warm measure of consolation. Sure enough, there it was.

"Now I'm sorry to say that I probably only have time for one more."

"Yes," said Griffin, who suddenly remembered a piece of data he'd gleaned from one of Breton's books. "But suicide rates have been dropping for thirty years, right, and antidepressants came along in the middle of that trend. Which brings me to your trial of Serotonal."

And suddenly this was it, the question Griffin came here to ask. He decided to say it and not say another word no matter how long the silence.

"So, I don't know how to put this, Dr. Elton, so I will just say it: why did you move run-in suicides into the placebo group in the Serotonal trials?"

Griffin had been careful to put the assertion as a given, just to rattle his subject, then to study Elton closely. Preposterous charges, after all, are generally greeted with laughter. True to his guess, Elton seemed to brace himself, adjusting his entire mid-section upward in an instant. His face was careful to remain neutral, but he looked toward his assistant. He looked down at his watch. He was doing all that he could to make Griffin jump in. When he could bear the silence no longer, he pulled his head back in a pantomime of confusion.

"Excuse me?"

It was the first time Elton had hesitated the entire conversation. The pause sent a chill up Griffin's spine.

"It has come to my attention just an hour ago," Griffin said, flipping through his notes of Breton's talk, "that in the earliest trials of Serotonal, which were your studies, investigators moved run-in suicidal actions into the placebo group, ignored treatment patient suicides in the early weeks after the trial ended, and grouped both lethal and non-lethal adverse events under the same vague terminology, effectively camouflaging the lethality of Serotonal. This data says that nine patients taking Serotonal took their lives, while three patients on placebo experienced suicidal gestures. I wonder if you have a comment?"

Elton had stopped moving altogether.

"My *comment*, Mr. Wagner," he finally offered, slowly and with a gentle shake of his head, "is that our drug was well-tolerated and effective." He then got up to leave, and nodded to his assistant, who promptly told Griffin they were finished.

"As a side note," Elton said, turning towards Griffin, "you are surely citing the work of Dr. Breton. I think I recall seeing the two of you earlier today in the elevator. I need to confide in you that responsible journalists always note he is a controversial figure in our field. It's quite sad. One could even call him an outcast. It fills me with sorrow, really. He was once a great leader and visionary in the academy but indeed he has fallen far. In any event, what matters for you as we part today is that his views simply do not carry the respect of his peers. I would hate to see such a bright and promising journalist risk his reputation by reporting with credulousness on such an outlier."

OK, this got to him. Griffin had to admit it.

Elton was sure of this, and no longer transparently guilty looking. You were always questioning whether a source was solid. Most of the time there was no way of really knowing.

"So you deny it then, just for the record and all," Griffin said, now feeling like kind of a bluffer.

"Deny what?"

"That suicides were moved into the placebo column in your Serotonal trials?" Griffin asked more quietly. "Because, I mean, not to belabor it and all but...I didn't hear you say that?"

Elton was walking out the door, his jacket fitting him like James Bond. He turned his head only halfway for his response.

"A true signal cannot be hidden by manipulating a few events in a heterogeneous group of patients."

Wild, Griffin thought. Another non-denial.

21

Shivani awoke to 622, the suite she requested at the Worcester House in Washington, D.C., for the Deadline Medical discount of $850 per night. She used to put in for 736, but one day it was booked and providence yielded 622's chocolate-leather headboard, Iranian silk rug and plum-colored bench. Game over.

Shivani was needed in the District every fifth Thursday to update the FDA on the status of whichever trial her employers were roto-rooting through the regulatory pipeline. Seamus and the other nobs took rooms up at the Mayflower, where they presumably paraded in its mid-century lobby, a facsimile of Napoleonic splendor, hoping to talk to Russian models. K Street was like high school and Shivani wanted to keep as far away from it as she could. That rendered this boutique hotel in the gay neighborhood north of the White House her best hope of protection while on business in Gomorrah.

Mercifully, her bureaucratic inquisitors at these affairs were your basic public servants, sharp and well-meaning, but invariably overmatched and underpaid, resigned to keeping the meeting moving and hear only enough from *SG Patel, Clinical Trials Liaison, Krøhn-McGill Global,* to check off all their boxes and flee their federal real estate in time to beat the traffic. If all the questions were getting answers, in her experience, no matter their value, things were copacetic with the feds.

This time, Shivani was here to update the reviewers about the trials meant to green-light Bioferex for a fitness-promotion indication. Valuations were hard to nail down, but following federal approval of this indication, Krøhn-McGill was situated to become better monetized than the collective GNP for all of northern Europe.

Shivani's testimony fulfilled a statutory requirement for the oversight of manufacturers engaged in clinical trials. The FDA needed the cover of having asked industry for its explanation, for instance, should a study appeared to have cut corners. Shivani delivered her cover stories with flying colors, offering up just enough mumbo-jumbo with bored-looking panache to win the day.

Just last month, for instance, after the chair of some committee had asked why a new antihistamine was undergoing testing on an abbreviated timetable, Shivani spontaneously improvised how "we took that step after concluding that three weeks is the optimal incubation framework for assessing peak eosinophil rate-limiting enzymatics."

It was a small masterpiece of unassailable confidence. It sounded deeply scientific. Parts of it were even valid, which gave her weary conscience a small measure of peace. And it all played so much better than it would have by telling them that the trial in question had been shortened from ten weeks to four thanks to a five-alarm fire they had discovered very late in the process.

After twenty-eight days on the antihistamine, it turned out, seasonal allergies came roaring back with the strength of ten dinosaurs, filling subjects with congestion like cement hardened for the core of a nuclear reactor.

A month on *Inhalatin EC,* it appears, had super-primed their sinuses for pollen, with her Krøhn-McGill headmasters having invested far too much bling to pull the rug on the pill for a side effect as nebulous as the sniffles. Shivani had rewritten the protocol to shorten the trial to a four-week window in which the drug actually seemed to work.

Like all of her fibs, the dodge felt defensible enough to let Shivani sleep. The regulators, bless them, moved right along as well. Small crimes like this came easy enough to her by now, but something inside of her was fighting the prospect of being a tool in matters greater than seasonal allergies.

The state of her health was changing. Worried that she was flirting with perjury, research fraud or felonious indifference to adverse events in the rostangilorb case report forms, Shivani's body had begun fighting back.

Her hands shook at odd times. She rarely slept more than three hours at a stretch. Food tasted like cardboard and she sometimes heard bees, whales or helicopters where they did not exist.

This was how her beloved 622 had come to play such a restorative hedge against her slow-motion landslide. She had developed a series of calming rituals. Upon arrival, Shivani would drape a piece of embroidered silk fabric over 622's 63-inch plasma flat screen, an HD disseminator of all the usual sociopaths holding court on cable, not to mention the commercials selling poison. Thirty-second spots for Bioferex were running three times an hour these days, and it was no longer sufficient for Shivani to simply hit mute. The mere sight of their location shots had become a trigger all on their own.

She knew what kind of money was being spent for helicopter footage on Pacific coast roadways, the aerial splendor of secluded island beaches and craggy mountain ledges—the jaw-dropping imagery required to make her adopted nation comfortable with her employer's repurposed compounds. It was all money they would be needing to earn back, money dependent on her now-overdue paperwork.

Here in 622 with the television covered Shivani could pause upon rising and read a page of Tich Nat Hahn and take an egg with gratitude before putting on her FDA clothes—off-the-rack so as to not rub it in with her classmates who had gone on to serve the nation in regulatory affairs—and find the strength to go do the devil's work.

༄

Shivani saw him around 6:00 after a long day on the FDA campus had wrapped, go figure. Shivani had made her way back to the Worcester and repaired to the lobby to get a glass of something with bubbles before hiding in for another night. This crowd had no ties to industry, so it was odd, to say the least, to bask in the sight of the boss of all federal mental illness research himself, National Institutes of Mental Health Director Roger J. Trestle, MD.

Shivani had been sitting in the Worcester's glam hanging Lucite chair when Trestle entered in possession of his high-end road bike. A person she had only ever seen on the front page of the *New York Times,* Dr. Trestle was now dressed like an actor auditioning for a commercial advertising medication serving the prostate.

Shivani had tasted enough bureaucratic stiff-arming in her time to know this was indeed a moment—her only chance. These guys were unreachable for persons hailing from industry, encircled by battalions of bureaucrats who intercept any pleadings that may give the appearance of insider-ism. Shivani knew she would never again snag an opportunity to tell Roger Trestle himself about the signal she had witnessed—high levels of suicides and unexplained violence in the user arm of Bioferex data—a spike her bosses had effectively buried in the tables with protocol-shifting and miscoding.

So here she was, a glass of champagne having dulled her loyalty, steeling herself to charge a chief of all oversight with the power to delay wider use of the drug. Shivani began to rise from her chair, then froze at the second bizarre sighting in her path that very same hour—the appearance of none other than Jeremy Elton himself.

He too was now clad in this garish road biking nonsense.

So were the two of them boning?

Taking in this sight of the middle-aged turds parading through her sanctuary in lycra made Shivani's head swirl. She had lifted bucket upon barrel for Jeremy Elton, providing emergency surgery for his lay-press books, writing his pandering speeches for MISA meetings, and briefing him with bullet points before his appearances on every news show that came calling. Now *he* had the ear of her target audience.

Positioning herself back in the hotel's sleek Warholian chair, Shivani knew she was invisible. Were you not scheduled on their mobiles, men like Jeremy Elton and Roger Trestle would not see you within inches of their faces. After a few minutes longer, after she watched Elton peel off from Trestle to take a call, Shivani re-seized her moment. The last honest man in the regulatory pipeline was once again alone, relaxed, and hopefully open to hearing her story.

Of all people, surely he would listen.

"Dr. Trestle!"

It was her sweetest voice possible, and Roger Trestle barely looked up from his phone.

"One minute is all I have," he replied, nodding to acknowledge her as if being accosted by young women in Washington hotel lobbies were a commonplace event for men with his pull. "I just got back from a thirty-mile sprint and need to refuel," Trestle stated, pausing to snort an upsetting obstruction of post-exercise congestion. "Do we know each other?"

"I don't believe so," Shivani fumbled, extending a manicured hand that he returned with his biking-glove encased paw. "My name is Shivani Patel. I work in trial design on the industry side. Confidentially, I have been hoping to get your thoughts on whether we might ever see regulatory support for a few safety questions we never seem to nail down."

Roger Trestle stared at her. It was the clumsiest opener ever. If she could start over, Shivani would have told the federal chief of all mental illness research funding something much more direct: that he should not trust her handiwork, that her employers cared only about sales, and that her trials were likely causing waves of people to kill themselves. Yeah, that would have worked.

"Well, everyone has suggestions," Trestle said. "At the NIMH we are excited about the Brain Initiative."

Shivani hated the so-called Brain Initiative. It was the latest big idea. Instead of blaming brain chemicals for mental illness, psychiatry had shifted to the search for brain structures and the supposed genetic machinery of mental illness. Shivani knew it was all merely an exit plan for the dried-up fortunes in monoamines.

"Of course," Shivani lied. (You had to sound like a team player.) "There's an ongoing issue, however, one in which serious adverse events flow into differing post-market surveillance silos, with data getting fragged in such a way that it disappears on paper, if not in the field."

Trestle looked to the ceiling.

He may have been admiring the modernist oversized toaster suspended in the atrium. He offered a perfunctory side-to-side bobbing of his head—a patronizing pantomime of weighing her position before pushing it swiftly into the garbage disposal.

"What's your point?"

"Thanks for asking, Dr. Trestle. Sorry not to be more clear. My concern is that interrelated adverse event reports never achieve a critical mass under this framework, especially if the side effect is rare. This makes it hard for regulators to act. I think the NIMH could play a much-needed role here."

Trestle began struggling with his biking gloves.

"Industry has well-developed protocols for noting adverse events," he offered.

"Yes," Shivani continued, "but as it now stands, my employers do not ask questions addressing problems they do not benefit from resolving. You understand."

All this coy wordplay.

I think Bioferex might be causing an epidemic of extra-strength akathisia.

She could have said it like that.

I think Bioferex takes a problem we barely acknowledge with SSRI's, and renders it much, much worse.

That would have been a direct statement. Why couldn't she just spit it out? Probably because she was a scientist, a professional identity given to understatement, and there was so much that she still didn't know. She didn't know if suicide was happening outside of the trials. She didn't know if her employers had manipulated their numbers out of incompetence, or on purpose.

"These signals teach us a lot," Trestle said. "Side effects can have extraordinary commercial potential. An adverse event can trigger a host of new uses for a compound. The urine retention wrought by SSRI's can open the door for new treatments targeting incontinence. Agitation wrought by psychotropic medications can open the door for treating depression and lethargy. Libido-diminishing side effects can be used to treat sexual pathology.

"We don't need to hound our partners out of the free market," he continued. "I don't want to drop names, but I know the researchers behind these projects. I'm here right now with Jeremy Elton. He does a *phenomenal* job of following what goes on in a trial."

Shivani died inside.

Roger Trestle, the currently sweat-encased boss of the NIMH, clearly had no idea of what bastards she and her pack of fuckwits could be, foremost among them, Jeremy Elton, now busily carrying forth with a mobile call on the drive, stepping in the blooms.

Was Trestle thinking of all the money on the private side that awaited him upon retirement? It would be maybe five years max until a guy of his age and stage cashed out and went over to the dark side. Then again, it was possible Trestle knew Shivani's people quite well, but just didn't care about the same things. There was glory in announcing new cures. It put you on the front page of the Times. Announcing the news of newly discovered side effects, however, was like farting at the dinner party.

Trestle picked up a placard for happy hour dining in the lobby bar.

"Fig and roasted nuts," he said, "this could get me some replenishing protein."

Shivani looked up at Elton, still gesticulating on the lawn out front.

"Now if you'll excuse me," Trestle said.

"Of course, thanks."

"I have got to try out some of these canapes before the Krøhn-McGill dinner tonight. They do know how to lay out a spread, but the food doesn't arrive until well after the academic talks, and I am famished."

22

Armed with the words of Alexander Breton and those of several confused and skeptical Hemingway scholars, Griffin filed his story on the author's death in one week's time, in fine shape for publication.

Trevor did his part as well, getting Griffin's copy expedited through editing, art, and layout in time for "*the July issue, baby, the motherfucking 50th anniversary.*"

That would be the 50th anniversary of Ernest Hemingway's suicide.

These guys, the way they talked.

Everything was another fast lane for braying and boasting.

The story had its holes. Griffin had never been able to nail down Alexander Breton's parting question: whether Hemingway had been given a vintage antidepressant in the months prior to his death. A rush-order of photocopies from the Hemingway collection at the Kennedy Library in Boston had indeed confirmed that the author had been taking the reserpine-based hypertension medication known as Serpasil for five years prior checking into Mayo.

It also confirmed that the eminent Mayo psychiatrist Dr. Howard Rome had indeed blamed reserpine combined with Ritalin for Hemingway's downward turn. But it said little about his care after that.

Rome would have pulled Ernest off the Serpasil in January of 1961, presumably without tapering. If doing that had made America's greatest living author suicidal, would he remain suicidal in July?

Griffin had his doubts. While akathisia can last months, so much remained unknown.

But no article settled all questions. At best, the good ones raised them. It was surely enough for Griffin to have reported that Mayo Clinic had been certain by the start of 1961, that reserpine was making Ernest Hemingway suicidal, and that they took him off the drug and gave him ECT. Griffin used conjecture to assert that Hemingway likely received imipramine or another early antidepressant along with the ECT, pills that can also cause akathisia.

Griffin had no clue why he would have been the first person to make these claims, as a lengthy series of searches showed to be the case. He had decided to let go of his doubts, to trust the unknowable Alexander Breton, and just go with his gut. It felt like a story the world could believe in.

Which is precisely, for once, what happened. Following the week Griffin's article hit the newsstands, "The Side Effect that Killed Ernest Hemingway" began to gain the kind of traction that had eluded Griffin over 15 years of journalistic grind and toil.

The day his story dropped, Griffin received calls from an entertainment executive who optioned content for TV, and a documentary filmmaker wrote to ask if the two of them might be able to get together and talk. *In the Zone's* publicist quickly booked Griffin on three segments with regional news anchors. And in a development Griffin would never have been delusional enough to imagine, *Full Aperture with Harrison Reed* called.

You cleared the schedule for an interview with the global cable news network TPN, Harrison Reed's late-night interview show especially. It had an audience with interesting jobs and long attention spans. The program served a much higher class of clientele than his readers of *In the Zone*. Griffin had, it appeared, arrived.

Better work, and better-paying work. Could this be his ticket? Griffin had always wanted better work, but had pretended he didn't care. He'd wanted it ever since leaving New York. He had been stuck in his one-bedroom over the coffee shop pretending otherwise, avoiding his friends, working for Trevor.

On the day of his interview, Griffin tried hard to take it as nonchalantly as possible, leisurely picking out a blazer, a cleaners-pressed shirt and then driving over to St. Paul to be wired up for his interview.

At the studio, a doorman showed him to the elevator, where he rode up to the third-floor taping room. A lone greeter took him into the strangest of places, a ten-by-ten module for people being connected to the coast.

Behind him, the skyline of downtown St. Paul glowed from an oversized vinyl backdrop. Off-camera, his sightline ended at five feet, where it collided with brutality to a cinderblock wall covered in coffee-stained carpet. It felt claustrophobic and designed to quash all confidence.

"Who are you?"

The twentysomething sent in to wire up Griffin was lovely in a broken way, with big eyes, dark lines of mascara and a tattered leather jacket to comfort the chill of her shift in an old building. She seemed to have no idea of why Griffin was here, and less interest in finding out.

After leading Griffin to the far side of the glass, the studio hand pointed to a stool in front of the backdrop. Griffin would sit here and talk into the screen alone, she said, adding that she would sit inside the sound booth. "You need to look directly at the small monitor and ignore the camera on the tripod," she said as she clipped a small microphone onto his lapel. She handed him an earpiece and sauntered back to a control room behind a dull glass partition. There, he watched as she picked up a battered copy of *Harry Potter and the Sorcerer's Stone*.

Griffin swiveled once on his stool out of nervousness.

"That's going to make a squeak." She had called it through a studio console microphone without looking up from her book. "Try not to do that."

His studio hand's indifference to Griffin's big break helped to neutralize the jitters. But soon enough, the persistent appearance of snow on his monitor restarted them. Seconds before going live and still no connection to New York, Griffin briefly felt the air leaving his death chamber. A voice of self-doubt popped with alarm into his head: *What are you doing?*

A clock on the wall said he had four seconds to air time when his monitor finally kicked in. As it did, Griffin took in the familiar sight of none other than Jeremy Elton, currently being wired up by an assistant to *Full Aperture* in New York.

They must have picked him for the next segment?

Griffin was too stunned to consider the alternative, that Jeremy Elton had been invited onto his interview. It was hard to say what that would have meant.

"We're back." And there he was, Harrison Reed in person. Griffin felt a small thrill. He had been interviewed before about articles, but never by anyone famous. He wondered if his parents would be watching. Maybe his editors, too. Then again, it was a Sunday. They were probably watching the NBA.

"Tonight, we take up a perplexing question," Harrison began. "Did a prescription drug lead Ernest Hemingway to kill himself?" Harrison began to read his TelePrompter copy with somber affectation.

"Just over fifty years ago this month, the Pulitzer Prize-winning author of *The Sun Also Rises* and hard-drinking icon of American letters returned to his home in Ketchum, Idaho, where, as magazine journalist Griffin Wagner writes, 'he waited until the first opportunity to remove his Scott rifle from a nearby cabinet, placed the barrel in his mouth, and pulled the trigger, very likely with his toe.'

"But while the facts of Hemingway's suicide are well known," Harrison continued, "the controversial assertion you will hear next is new. In a recent issue of the men's magazine *In the Zone*, Wagner argues that Hemingway may have been driven to suicide not by depression, as has long been assumed. Instead, Wagner has argued, the author had suffered a side-effect from reserpine, a common medication of the era and one he had been given during the mid-1950s to combat hypertension. Here tonight to discuss this provocative article, please welcome to Full Aperture, Griffin Wagner."

Griffin heard himself mouthing a dry-tongued reply.

"Thank you, Harrison, it's great to be here."

"I'm going to ask the hard question first," said his host. "By the end of his life, Ernest Hemingway was an alcoholic, frightened, anxious, shell of his former self. He was the product of a father who took his own life. Friends and biographers who knew him have described him as broken and depressed. Why should we blame this terrible event on a pill?"

At least Harrison had come prepared.

"Thanks for having me on."

Griffin was determined to tread carefully.

Trevor had even texted him beforehand:

> re-MEMBER, my man
> NO one likes
> a know-it-all!

"If it's OK with you, Harrison, I would just like to reply to that question with a different question: What would you say is the amount it increases a person's risk of suicide if a member of his immediate family has taken his or her own life? Twenty percent? Thirty percent? Fifty percent?"

If it irked Harrison Reed to field a question from his guest, he didn't show it.

"I would imagine at least thirty percent," he said, "possibly higher."

"So, having a first-degree relative who has taken his or her own life increases your risk of suicide by fifteen percent," Griffin said.

"Now that may sound like a lot, but it is a fifteen percent rise in the overall risk of suicide, which is already quite low, roughly 10 in 100,000. In other words, for Ernest Hemingway, having a father who had killed himself would have inched up his risk from just 10 to 11.5 in 100,000."

Griffin hadn't known any of these facts before diving into research.

He felt a little like a fraud, speaking so authoritatively on something he'd only just learned. Then again, he knew everyone new to a topic felt this way at first, at least if they were being honest with themselves.

"So if I get what you're saying," Harrison replied, languidly setting aside the point with a wave of his long fingers, "the impact of genetics in suicide is overstated."

His chin was now in his hand, and he was peeking down at some notes.

A copy of *In the Zone* sat on his desk, probably for the first time in all of TPN history.

"Fair enough, point taken," he continued, "family history may be less important than we think. But Hemingway undoubtedly sought out danger throughout his life. He took a host of anxiety medications signaling problems with mood. There was his legendary alcoholism. He'd had multiple head injuries. Shouldn't his risk have been higher than average, fully independent of the side effect you posit?"

Griffin thought about how little he had been served by the rest of what he had been advised about live TV by Trevor, who had also written an email saying:

1) DON'T BE A JACKOFF!
2) ALWAYS DO PUSHUPS BEFORE DOING TV
3) WEAR AN OPEN COLLA
4) KICK SOME ASS!!

"Those are good points," Griffin conceded. "But Hemingway's physicians at Mayo singled out reserpine combined with the stimulant Ritalin as the reason for his agitation, paranoia and despondency. They told him this in letters now stored at the John F. Kennedy Library in Boston, all quoted verbatim in my article."

"In the fifty years that have passed, nothing about the evidence concerning this drug, or our ideas about depression, has changed. Reserpine and even Serotonal can have this effect on some patients, though reserpine has thankfully fallen out of use."

"Harrison, if I can just jump in…"

Well, that didn't take long.

It was Jeremy Elton, his patience having apparently worn thin.

"Given the controversial nature of this topic and the critical need to provide balance with such a very sensitive subject," Harrison said, "we have invited the author and psychiatrist Dr. Jeremy Elton to offer his perspective on the side effect you mention. Dr. Elton welcome back to the show."

"Thanks, Harrison," Elton said. "It's so good to see you again my dear friend."

Elton patted the news anchor on one of his outstretched hands.

Harrison let out a warm smile.

Griffin felt powerless.

"Do you know what troubles me most about an article like this?" Elton said. His hands had merged in a pose of prayer, his voice having dropped to some kind of TV-savvy stage whisper.

"The very implication that *any* pill can cause suicidal thinking."

Elton wasn't speaking as much as calling up a soft homily, a preemptive strike that Griffin would be admiring for days to come.

"We have to balance this well-meaning but ultimately reckless focus on side effects with the genuine harm that can arise by leading readers to question our tools."

"But the FDA has issued warnings on antidepressants," Harrison jumped in.

The news anchor had fully abandoned the subject of Hemingway, and though Griffin did not yet know it, for the rest of the segment.

"They did, after all, place a warning on the entire class of antidepressants."

"And it's not just antidepressants, Harrison." Griffin was officially jumping back in, hopefully not too eagerly. "Some form of suicide warning applies to drugs for thirty-eight different conditions," he said. "These include treatments for asthma, obesity, epilepsy and smoking cessation."

"Well that seems careless," Elton said, still exuding warmth but ten percent less. "Come visit my clinic sometime and tell me these drugs do not save lives. I work with patients, Mr. Wagner. I see the benefits of these pills *first hand*. The effectiveness of these treatments is not parlor talk for some us. We are on the front lines of care."

Griffin thought about Sedona Piper and Alexander Breton, the outsized scorn they had expressed for Jeremy Elton who nonetheless seemed unflappable and formidable. Griffin weighed the abstract possibility that his opponent may indeed have been a front man for others. He let out a small laugh and shook his head. He knew in his heart that TV was a poor medium for what he was about to say next. But he couldn't stand being lectured.

"Well, as long as we are on the subject of your work, Dr. Elton, I hope it's not parlor talk to ask why a study you authored on Serotonal has a placebo column containing suicidal events that do not appear to belong there."

Somehow that came out easier than he thought.

"…I know your critics assert that these steps were highly irregular."

Elton seemed to stiffen. It was one thing to have swatted down this assertion at an interview with Griffin alone. He did not appear to like it being stated on national TV.

"He's talking about serious adverse events, Harrison," Elton replied to their host, "a common obsession with the anti-psychiatry mob, and if I can add just one comment, a scare tactic that only reinforces the stigma experienced by those who would step forward to bravely seek help for mental illness. Given twenty minutes and a white board I could explain how the argument Mr. Wagner raises is so very misleading. But this is obviously an inappropriate venue for parsing the sophisticated details behind multi-million dollar clinical trials, studies that provide our very best hope for bringing lifesaving medications to market. People in need turn to us for clarity, and we owe them that at the very least."

It was quite a speech. Jeremy Elton was like no one else on the spot.

This was, after all, his medium. Griffin suspected with resignation that he may have just gotten his ass handed to him. They hadn't mentioned Hemingway in several minutes, and Harrison Reed appeared to be desperate for a way to bail on the entire segment.

Sensing his time was running out, Griffin decided that if Harrison Reed and Jeremy Elton weren't going to let him talk about the reserpine that may have killed Hemingway, he might as well ask them why.

"That's fine, Dr. Elton," Griffin said. "But if I can ask, how did you end up on this show?"

"Excuse me?"

Griffin straightened, absent-mindedly scratching his chest, bumping his clip-on microphone and sending a crackle through the audio from St. Paul to New York. The tech turned to wag her finger at him, the universal symbol for *that's a no-no*. She had black-painted finger nails.

"I mean, I know how I ended up on this show," Griffin added, extending his hand from the microphone, palm-up. "I'm here because I wrote an article, and you found it interesting Harrison. I don't think we have talked about it very much, but perhaps that's the price of raising a subject which has apparently been off-limits for the better part of five decades.

"What I want to know is, why did your producer contact Dr. Elton to offer this so-called 'balance' to my article? Why add a rebuttal at all? My article is just a theory, you know, one about an old drug at that. You could have picked a Hemingway scholar to counter my points, or a historian of pharmacology, or an expert in suicide. Why Dr. Elton?"

"I don't see where this is going," said Harrison Reed.

"I ask because a sizzling plate of spin went out last week by Pagel-Simon, a public relations firm for the makers of Serotonal."

Elton began blinking with both eyes.

"It confuses me why anyone would jump to the defense of reserpine,"

Griffin continued. "And yet their press release did just that, stating that *In The Zone* had published a quote-unquote 'controversial' article—their words, not mine, though I noticed that you used them, Harrison—and that Dr. Elton would be available for interviews to rebut these points.

"So I look at this robust attempt by a drug manufacturer at counter-messaging a story about the death of Ernest Hemingway, and I ask myself why would a modern-day drug giant go into damage control over an article in a men's magazine about a fifty-year-old drug? And all I can think is, they must be nervous about any mention of this side effect, no matter its date of origin, no matter the drug of origin."

Shoot.

Griffin had given a speech.

He was pretty sure that violated Trevor's first rule of TV: (DON'T BE A JACKOFF!).

Harrison's face seemed to combine both pique and resigned enjoyment at the sudden arrival of live television jet fuel in the form of person-to-person conflict. This clip was the kind of thing that ended up on YouTube.

"Very well," Harrison deadpanned. "You are the scheduled guest, if you would like to wrap up, Mr. Wagner, you may have the last word."

Elton pulled his head back, as if to say, *him? Really?*

"Ok, well, thanks for having me," Griffin offered. "I'll just propose that maybe Krøhn-McGill wants to stifle any reporting on akathisia because it is a side effect that accompanies Serotonal, their best-selling drug. Dr. Elton, as you may know, has collected over $1.5 million in consulting fees from Krøhn-McGill. That hardly makes him an unbiased resource on the safety of Krøhn-McGill antidepressants."

Jeremy Elton made a light shake of his head.

"And for the record," Griffin continued, "I got three thousand bucks for this piece. I might get thirty thousand for the year if I can stay in the good graces of my editors."

"Well," Harrison said with a laugh, "we aren't going to get into the booking process for this progr…"

"I *am* well-compensated for my expertise," Elton injected. Apparently he'd heard enough once more.

"Moreover, I don't create the free market, but neither will I apologize for it. My disclosure is made available to editors whenever I publish."

"But your editors don't publish that number very often, do they?" Griffin replied.

Harrison Reed must have wondered how the wrapping up of his show had suddenly come unraveled.

"…The very idea that my judgment can be purchased for a few coins," Elton said, "is simply laughable."

"Coins?" Griffin looked confused. "Is that what they call a cool mil-five these days? Keep moving, doctor."

Harrison leaned forward and began tapping his papers.

He then placed his copy of *In the Zone* upright in view of the camera for the agreed-upon three seconds, before dropping it on the floor beneath him, a little too vigorously.

"This has been an interesting ten minutes," Harrison concluded. "Thanks to you both for your time. I hope we can continue the conversation another day."

Griffin heard the sounds of the Harrison Reed theme music, then the soft hum of his live connection leaving his ears, then watched a red lightbulb go out in his studio, the signal that his feed had been turned off. He began to unclip his on-air mic when Jeremy Elton looked into the camera.

"Hey," he said to Griffin. "You'll regret this."

Griffin laughed with disbelief. They had been sparring on collegial terms. This seemed comically bent on intimidation.

"Krøhn-McGill is going to think closely about ad spending for *In the Zone*," Elton continued. "The more you attack us, the more we fight back. This is about people's lives."

Elton looked over to his side and started talking to someone off camera.

"OK," Griffin said. "This is getting weird, Dr. Elton. Thanks for your time."

"He can't hear you now, just so you know," the tech told him. "Your mic is cut."

Griffin got up and looked out the studio window at the glowing First National Bank Sign across the street. He felt about as far from the world of cable news programming as possible. He felt invigorated, moreover. He was pretty certain he had just demolished Jeremy Elton on an influential interview show. Did he mean to do that? Was that the right thing to do? He had after all, more or less always liked the guy, at least initially. Still, taking down a giant like America's Psychiatrist… in the world of health journalism, that was kind of like harpooning a whale.

On his way out the door, the tech gave Griffin a wave. She seemed to see him differently this time.

"Nice job," she said.

"Really?" He leaned against the door to talk with her a little longer. "What did you like about it?"

"Well, for starters, *super* cringe-y."

"Thanks," Griffin said, "I guess."

Then she scrunched up her face. "But ick."

"What's ick?" Griffin asked.

"Just that guy. Something about him."

23

Shivani did her best writing after six. Her brain moved like the trade winds when her office began to quiet. Motionless to begin with, the Deadline Medical suite had been soundproofed to monastic standards during an extravagant renovation three years prior, a year-long upgrade and the most transparently obvious pretext for a surveillance install ever imposed onto a workplace.

Over the course of a month, Deadline Medical had relocated all two hundred of its New York personnel into temporary space "up the block," a make-do that turned out to be floors sixteen and seventeen of the Plaza Hotel. The clear-out allowed design gurus to mount an assault on the firm's midtown headquarters, commandeering it for round-the-clock construction that would transform her workplace into something best described as a ski lodge built for the Sultan of Brunei.

In its aftermath, Shivani now produced her words beneath ten million dollars worth of barn beam cross-hatch. Her re-opening day tour explained that each of the sixty-four hand-sewn timbers had been carefully archived following appraisal and curatorial reclaiming from abandoned sixteenth-century Provençal country estates. At the time, Shivani had been slated to crank on the approval application for a prostate drug, so the tour was a welcome diversion from her normal midday low.

"The lot survived a competitive round of bidding at Sotheby's," she remembers Seamus boasting. "You'll notice an eclectic trio of curated lighting statements, just our little way of putting it over the top." Each passage deeper into the firm's newly overbuilt headquarters took her Deadline Medical colleagues through hand-blown glass by Chihuly, gem-cut crystal from Swarovski, and at the apex of the firm's power center, walls lined with backlit early-century originals by Luis Comfort Tiffany.

With the entire complex tricked out in four kinds of polished hardwoods, the only reasonable explanation for the mish-mash of money wasting design chaos lay in the possibility that her employers' "discrete boutique in partnership for your challenges of scientific argument" had needed to clear as much cash from the books as possible.

These were the sort of red flags she tended to let drop.

She was, after all, busy enough enduring the install men, a half-dozen goons who, when they did speak, shared a Slavic dialect of unknown origin. Her workspace had clearly become loaded for recording every kind of data, with sensors logging audio, video, movement, body temperature and presumably high blood pressure. It was a given that Shivani's bosses had tapped into the cameras on her computer. Which was exactly what she stared into all day.

Unless she was in the field, Shivani saw so little beyond the monitors required to meet her daily quotas. On any given day, she could be facing down a lead article for the *Journal of the American Medical Society*, a featured comment for the *American Journal of Geriatric Nutrition*, and on the 37-inch LCD, a seven-hundred-page CSR to be filed in support of FDA approval for Bioferex as prophylactic for stress fractures.

Her bosses held high hopes for this last one—a meticulously-controlled dataset certifying the bone drug was safe and effective in the prevention of jogging-induced bone fractures among the overweight and untrained. It was an understatement to say it would trigger an avalanche of revenue like no other product in the firm's history—at least $22.5

billion stateside and $75 billion globally once the EU came on line.

Curiously, no Bioferex analytics were ever made available in the firm's two stateside databases. For reasons that eluded Shivani, the firm appeared to store data offline and somewhere out of pocket, possibly overseas, though, as to where, she could never figure out. This was a frequent source of frustration, as finishing the Bioferex CSR had become the Holy Grail within the firm. It was the last hurdle needed to classify the pill as duly indicated for anyone joining any gym.

Finishing this phone book would allow unprecedented riches to rain forth. The day she turned it in, Shivani well knew, the work would unleash the extraordinary profit-taking created by putting every American in marginal physical condition on a drug that cost $330 for 30 days, and a wonder-drug insurers would surely trample over one another to reimburse, given their longstanding endorsement of healthy lifestyles and regular exercise. It went without saying that Seamus was following her progress closely.

Did he know she was stalling?

Why *were* all those spying portals installed? Did they know what she knew, that once approval had been granted, there would be no putting the genie back in the bottle. Shivani would have pondered these questions longer, but now here he was, Seamus himself, calling her into his office.

"Who is this little shit?"

Seamus was seated behind a preposterous Louis XV Provincial farm table, a desk reclaimed from what were surely the vilest artifact mercenaries stripping the French countryside of all legacy infrastructure.

"What little shit?"

Shivani was self-protective enough to affect chumminess with Seamus.

There was no other way to work with these tossers. Your affect was the tell.

"Him."

Seamus pointed to a big screen that had lowered from the ceiling. It was a news hour featuring Jeremy doing TV on a Sunday night, the oversized hi-def magnifying each hair on his rakish mane. Elton was wearing the standard pose he had acquired in media training, a resting of his chin on the top knuckle of his pointer finger. And there on the other side of the screen, a fresh young face was talking with palpable defiance. He had dark features and broad shoulders. He looked maybe 30. He was to Shivani a dish.

"Saint Paul, MN. Griffin Wagner, *In the Zone*" read the chyron.

Shivani had never been to St. Paul.

Notably, this little shit, to use Seamus's words, did not appear as deferential in the presence of America's Psychiatrist as was the norm. One could even say he seemed somewhat cocky. The corner of his lips had a slight curl to them.

"You heard of him?" Seamus asked.

"No, why?"

"We sent Chip out on this story about Hemingway and side effects."

"Why that one?"

Shivani thought the subject lay well outside of Jeremy's zone of expertise.

"No reason. Just to keep him busy."

Seamus was lying. They never sent Jeremy out for no reason.

"But he's been stepping in it this entire program," Seamus said. "I mean, who would figure he'd be having a hard time with someone from, what is it, *Maxim*?"

"I believe it is a publication called *In the Zone*," Shivani replied, smiling at the dopey employer of the cutie chewing up the telly. She secretly felt elated. This moment, it was still young. But she began to harbor the hope of an answer to her looming problem.

"So," Seamus said, "how's that Bioferex CSR coming?"

ॐ

170

Back at her desk, Shivani opened her purse and set it on the floor, leaving the bag ajar at the top. She already had filled a stick with embarrassing emails. She wouldn't dare try downloading trials, as that would trigger piercing alarms within the system in seconds. But she needed to get 90 percent out of here. She had to prepare to be gone in an instant.

As she reached up for the frame she kept over her desk, a photograph of her late dad, she made a slight show of looking at it for a beat before letting her arm drop gently and casually, whereupon she placed it in her bag. Cameras only kicked on in response to sudden or deliberate movements.

There was still the scarf. There was the second set of keys (now copied by others?). She packed away her old ID on a lanyard and a swipe card that had preceded the biometric updating. They would have forgotten she still had that one. Who knows, maybe it still worked somewhere within the system.

With a reporter finally in mind and no more time to stall, Shivani was unofficially gone. They could find some other sinner to finish the CSR, and it would take that person months if not a year. At the bottom of her drawer Shivani found a wrinkled and yellowed updating of her employment agreement, something they had sent for a signature a few years back and stupidly forgotten to retrieve.

Legally Binding Non-Disclosure and Confidentiality Agreement.

The buyout of 2006 had triggered a scramble for NDA's, especially after the new owners discovered their highest-security writer was under no orders to keep her mouth shut. But that was five years ago.

She had never signed it.

24

An hour after Griffin wrapped up with *Full Aperture with Harrison Reed,* the ping sounding email via his website made Lee Majors' soft ears perk. It was from Shivani3890@yahoo.com with the subject line, "TPN just now."

Hi Mate!

Caught you giving Jeremy a pasting on the telly. Well done.

You should know that Serotonal has gotten Jeremy minted.

He's the proud owner of two Bentleys and I get the feeling he has been collecting beach homes. You don't make that kind of cheddar from selling books on Channel 13.

You surely know how they invented a drug called rostangilorb. Does it have a similar malfunction? I'd want to know if I were you. Better yet, is it worse in people who are not depressed?

Sheevi G.

ᔮ

Griffin read it in confusion. He'd pulled his share of flake-mail over the years, but this one had all the signs of being legit. The author had called Bioferex by its generic name (rostangilorb). That question at the end seemed a little too pointed. His curiosity was killing him.

Who are you?

Griffin.

The response arrived in another half hour.

I can tell you I work for a firm which provides professional services for Chip, though I think you know of him as Jeremy Elton. And that we service a variety of drug makers, but mostly Krøhn-McGill. And that as part of that work, I have had suspicions about the studies that got Serotonal placed on the market.

You are correct that suicides which were not proper placebo events had migrated into the placebo column. It's been a while, but as I recall these decisions were imposed upon us from on high. No one ever told us why these were requested, but I would be lying if I didn't admit we could see the false appearance of normalcy it had created.

I am not in a position to go public. I can meet up if you come to New York, but I can't say if it will be productive.

Sincerely, Shivani

Griffin had to read the note once more to be sure it was real. His source, whose name seemed to be either Sheevi or Shivani, had not only worked on the Serotonal studies that Breton had sounded the alarm about, but wanted to talk to a reporter about doing so.

Well, well. That would add a little punch to his piece on Serotonal at 25.

25

It didn't take an hour for Griffin to realize his fifteen minutes of fame on *Full Aperture with Harrison Reed* had grabbed the eyeballs of his bosses at In the Zone. Two minutes after the show had wrapped, Trevor fired this pointed analysis Griffin's way via text:

> G-DUMP!
> Who the fuck
> goes rogue
> on TPN?

As he would soon understand, the argument Griffin had picked with Jeremy Elton inadvertently delivered a long-awaited beat-down to a media hound ripe for cancellation. That Griffin had accidentally awakened a groundswell of Jeremy Elton fatigue became eminently clear the next morning, when his Twitter following multiplied from 346 to 13.7k overnight. Over in his in-box: 375 new emails.

A morning that would ordinarily have been given over to skimming career advice on *Media Bistro* was instead spent clicking open fawning requests from producers for morning TV. With nothing on his schedule, Griffin could have gotten on a plane that afternoon, but decided to ignore all of them. Surely something better could come of this.

He was still wondering what that would look like when, a day or two later, the better offers arrived. By early the next week, he had heard from editors at the *New York Times Magazine*, the *Atlantic Monthly*, *Rolling Stone*, *Harper's* and *Esquire*, the final note almost bringing tears to his eyes. Each of these new contacts had laid out a plan of action for how their publication could make the best use of him. All of them dangled smart, interesting bids.

The moment was bittersweet; all were magazines he had pitched relentlessly over the years. His sudden desirability exposed the decidedly unimaginative business plan behind magazine publishing—how every-out-of-work freelancer was invariably chasing some editor too busy chasing someone with buzz. Moreover, these towering publications not only hunted down the writers they wanted and ignored all the rest, they hand-fed their catches fully-fleshed story plans accompanied by generous budgets for travel.

After years of getting no work, now there was suddenly too much of it. Griffin knew the swarm would soon fly somewhere else. His big moment had only gone down after he'd veered off script on a radioactive subject—hidden suicides in the early trials of Serotonal—and impulsively roasted a famous poser as a hired gun for Krøhn-McGill. It had been, as far as he was concerned, an abject failure.

Griffin had never made TPN properly alarmed about akathisia, much less the possibility that the side effect was still with us today. Jeremy had too efficiently wrestled Griffin onto the trap door that invariably dropped open should a curious person ever question the risk-to-benefit ratio of America's beloved mood meds.

And that mattered to Griffin, he had to admit it, because somewhere along the way, this had all grown personal to him. He started to ask Lee Majors what to do next, when he received a text from someone he did not know.

Griffin,
Got your number from Trevor.
It's time to talk about your future, as in,
the big picture.
Do u like steak?
-Mitch St. Germaine,
Word Management Worldwide.

Griffin had to Google the name of the firm, "Word Management Worldwide." It appeared to be some kind of privately-held, highly-capitalized entity with offices around the globe.

As for what it did, the digital storefront said only this:

Exclusivity and Talent Representation.
Monetizing strategies for digital, print, film, unscripted content, social media, personal branding, viral invention, public speaking and paid appearances.

So, yes, whatever the fuck all of that meant. He did like steak.

26

It was an inauspicious cluster-fuck of shambolically bad timing.

Jeremy Elton's departure for the keynote at a Himalayan three-day happened to have been scheduled for the morning after his catastrophic drop-in on *Full Aperture with Harrison Reed*.

The night had been unpleasant. Jeremy had suffered fitful sleep at the Lancaster, and thanks to a misunderstanding between his travel assistant and the front desk, the tight choreography of personal care which should have fulfilled Jeremy Elton's preferences for wake-up had gone awry.

An unseasoned assistant named James had swiped in to Dr. Elton's suite ten minutes later than requested, leaving the care team for America's Psychiatrist with barely enough time to draw a bath, open the drapes, turn on "Reflections of Passion" from Jeremy's travel collection of Ecuadoran flute CD's, then fan three newspapers on the credenza prior to overseeing the presentation of pain au chocolat and seasonal berries with crème fraiche.

In the face of young James's interminable delay, Dr. Elton sat patiently in his humiliation, stoic and cross-legged on a tufted bench at the foot of his Luxe bed in a plush Lancaster robe, committed to remaining a force for kindness and humility.

Jeremy gazed contentedly in the near distance with equanimity and poise. There was so much to do in this day that lay ahead. He still needed to catch the town car to the airport, board a first-class seat to New Delhi, with that to be followed by a rooftop riding compartment on the Kalka-Shimla, the four-hour rail passage to the Mondari's towering lodge within a forested mountaintop in the state of Himachal Pradesh.

These events all passed, because all things must pass.

Dr. Elton meant no harm to any living creature, which was why it had been his express parting wish for the Lancaster that young James—the father of a Jets fan (Bodie, 7)—would not learn of his demotion until Dr. Elton was high above the Atlantic en route to the fragrant continent.

Thank Shiva that all of these distractions were as hidden from view as the eviscerating eruptions happening at that same hour without Jeremy Elton's knowledge on social media, an unprecedented fallout from his disastrous appearance on *Full Aperture with Harrison Reed*.

"Jumping Jeremy, Jacked" the *Daily News* had crowed, invoking the manner in which Dr. Elton had seemed to leap from his seat when the interview had ended but the show's theme music was still playing.

"America's Psychiatrist, Your Credibility Called, Says it Only Wants to be Friends," the *Gawker* offered in another simmering bucket of snark.

It would be 36 hours until these insults had made their way onto the device owned by Jeremy Elton. By then America's Psychiatrist had travelled halfway around the world, #JumpingJeremy was no longer trending, and all texts from Krøhn-McGill media relations rolled helplessly into a file he rarely bothered to check.

For his part, Jeremy Elton only remembered the interview going well.

Corporate had asked him to appear alongside a magazine writer. Jeremy had performed as he was told and was now off to assist in the launch of KM+Healing & Leisure, a private equity-funded health-tourism subsidiary created within Krøhn-McGill as a hedge against the coming collapse of American healthcare, a death spiral which forecasting dated at a point when Bioferex reached peak consumption and annual company revenues soared past one trillion dollars.

With all available capital for healthcare having been exhausted in the states, the Indira Gandhi Hospital would be necessary as one of the firm's thousands of emerging Krøhn-McGill ATM machines, outposts serving all one percenters who, like Dr. Elton, periodically required leave of the bustle and distractions of Manhattan, Singapore, Orlando, Palm Beach, Las Vegas or London.

The need to enjoy restorative spaces for attention to health was only growing stronger, of that there was no quarrel. Spaces like the Lord Kitchener Suite, his room here for the afternoon, would remain protected by the economic and social disorder his employers' untrammeled profit-taking had unleashed, sickness of the sort already emanating outward from the American Bible Belt.

"So, as you can see, touch, and intuit without disruption of our essential life energy, in this rigorous analysis, MacrocilinXR has outperformed all other bacterocidals and bacterostatics under review."

This was the moment in the new antibiotic talk where Jeremy often held his hands in the supplicant pose. Becoming only briefly like Christ, he let his gaze drop downward in acceptance, not simply invoking but *inhabiting* abject humility. It was important for the audience know that these words were placed in Jeremy's care by forces bigger than all of us.

"As such, there seems little question that MacrocilinXR should be considered not only as a first-line defense for aggressive infection control," he continued, "but a preeminent tool for the devastating mood-management comorbidities which can accompany gastrointestinal presentations in the population of Himachal Pradesh."

Time and place are only an illusion. In spite of young James's insults and the various Harrison Reed inconsiderations, Jeremy had fought his way here victorious—through the churning of the Manhattan roadway, hours locked in an airway cabin with only simple fare for replenishment, the traversing of two oceans, followed by a hired car to the teeming north Indian station and then upward by rail before settling in at the Kitchener and finding his way downstairs.

Jeremy Elton had done all of that and made his way to this podium, having at last arrived at his final slide, the pinnacle of a talk the ungrateful Shivani Patel from Deadline Medical had messengered to James, the former executive butler at the Lancaster and surely a wiser man thanks to the growth experience of setback courtesy of Jeremy Elton. All of this had transpired so that Jeremy could give this enlightening homily to a welcoming room of South Indian and Malaysian medical professionals. The world was an unmitigated marvel.

The meeting had been planned to promote Serotonal, a compound close to exhausting its patent protections within the U.S. and therefore poised to enter pharmaceutical maturity, an end-stage product phase in service of secondary global markets with nonconforming regulatory characteristics. Upon his arrival, however, Dr. Elton learned from a coarsely-truncated Seamus Cole text that he should instead initiate India for off-label use of the wholly unremarkable Krøhn-McGill knock-off MacrocilinXR—a narrow-spectrum antibiotic—for, did he read that correct? Mood disorders?

Jeremy had never heard of something so preposterous.

Who promotes an antibiotic for mood disorders?

And he might even have protested, had not the Luxe bed at the Lancaster followed by twenty-four hours of travel imposed such horrific penalties on his spinal L3, L5 and sacrum. Jeremy decided that Patel's slides would need to explain themselves, in the end, and indeed they had. She'd even included a friendly Post-It, an odd quip notifying America's Psychiatrist in confidence that "only a fool stays in a suite named for Kitchener," as she put it. "Sir Winston himself lamented the slaughter unleashed upon the Dervish by his incompetent Field Marshall."

Elton had no idea what any of it meant, but he did like Patel's handwriting.

180

Perhaps he would encourage her to be his lover the next time they were in theater together.

"Excuse me, Dr. Elton, surely you have heard of NDM-1 of course?"

Elton had reached the end of his talk when an impertinent young physician from one of the nearby hospitals had raised his hand to ask the intemperate question, complete with an acronym of no matter to the keynote.

Someone had to say it: Though they were his spiritual brethren, the people of the subcontinent were hopelessly behind in matters of medicine. Perhaps this reference to NDM-1 was some sort of primitive numerology? Folk medicine derived from Ayurvedic oral history? Jeremy elected to hear the man out, a token show of interest before graciously moving along.

"Of course," Elton replied, "your point?"

"Well, it's just that you have proposed something quite astonishing," the doctor continued. "If I am not mistaken, you have proposed without being facetious that physicians in this impoverished region begin prescribing *antibiotics*, for *mood disorders*. As you know, Dr. Elton, NDM-1..."

"I'm sorry I'm not familiar with the term."

"New Delhi Metallo-Beta-lactamase ?"

"Yes, of course, go on."

"As you know NDM-1 is an antibiotic-resistant virus in our midst, soon to become the world's worst, one now ravaging our countryside. Only two antibiotics remain that can even hope to tame it. Though even they should be used sparingly, lest the virus adapts and they also become ineffective, those very antibiotics are being profligately prescribed in the dozens of pharmacies owned by Krøhn-McGill, now ringing the hospital where your firm intends to base its new health-tourism initiative.

"Why on earth would we prescribe these last arrows in our quiver for mood disorders," he continued, "something they are patently unable to treat, when their overuse is already poised to recreating untreatable forms of illness last seen in the Middle Ages?"

Christ.

Elton had been told he could give the talk and explore the grounds.

"How," the doctor continued, "are antibiotics even considered effective in the treatment of mood disorders?"

And here it was, another Third-World practitioner with opinions.

Elton had tennis in an hour, followed by billiards and the spa. During the latter, a bead of oil was to be dribbled upon his third eye. He made something up.

"The use of MacrocilinXR will prevent gastro-intestinal infection, a potent trigger for mood management challenges. You would know that if you practiced in the West, so of course I understand the unfamiliarity implied by your question."

The doctor blinked with both eyes, holding back his rage.

"Dr. Elton, if anything, the gastro-intestinal infections you cite are on the rise from the overuse of the Krøhn-McGill acid-suppression pills. The idea that infections cause mood disorders is, to be generous, mistaken. We have neither used nor needed these costly interventions, and yet they have been marketed to us relentlessly by Krøhn-McGill, though perhaps bribery is the better word. In so doing your patrons have invited the sort of pharmaceutical bioterrorism that could prove catastrophic within the sanitation challenges we face."

Elton sighed. He looked out the window at a forest of towering cypress. They used to know how to treat a gentleman in the colonies. He had been to Bermuda more times than he could count. Now there was a place where staff still cared for human needs. He contemplated his schedule. Tomorrow there would be a four-hour flight to the south to oversee the launch of Pentix, Krøhn-McGill's sprawling new Contract Research Organization in Chennai, Tamil Nadu. Corporate would soon be outsourcing all clinical trials into Pentix. It gave Jeremy a shiver to wonder what that development meant for his lucrative placebo consulting work.

He took in the soaring view. He thought about the tragic loss of Jack, his younger brother who died from a fall when they were both just boys. His parents had always loved Jack more, that was never less than obvious. When Jeremy's jealousy became too much, Jack fell from a ledge during a long family hike. Jeremy remembered Jack's face after he had pushed him off that path in the trails overlooking Santa Barbara, just before his parents came around the bend. He remembered it just like it was yesterday. He vowed to call Krøhn-McGill and ask why they seemed so intent on placing him in situations where his authority was continually challenged. It was as if they wished to see him fall as well.

"Doctor, your question is eminently worthy," Elton said, feigning concern while wondering who else but he could tolerate such disrespect from the likes of these muppets. He'd already refuted the insubordinate know-nothing and dismantled his amusing questions. That would have to be that. There would be no more interrogations today about the wisdom of prescribing antibiotics in rural India for mood disorders.

27

Mitch St. Germaine, corporate counsel and recruiter for creative at Word Management Worldwide, slipped into a steak house the pair had agreed upon over email.

As a fair-skinned product of the New England prep schools, Mitch was an hour into making first land contact with a state shaped in right angles, having trouble getting his bearings. The streets were so wide. The people as well. But meals were hard for Mitch in any locale. All St. Germaines found it excruciating to eat, and Mitch had his standards The sight of so many 200-pound humans here in the cornfields had him worried for the chance he would ever find something edible, let alone his preferred arctic char with lemon foam.

And yet Griffin Wagner had chosen this ridiculous chop house.

Perhaps he'd imagined it would test the load limits of the system now courting him?

If so, they were going to get along just fine.

This room couldn't come close to the check averages Mitch routinely absorbed before sundown, let alone those rarified outings requiring Mitch to bury a receipt in his expense report. This was a chain steakhouse. They might has well have been making the deal at a food truck.

With an hour budgeted for changing, Mitch had arrived over-dressed, as was his preference. Today he had chosen a $450 weave by Paul Stuart—it would catch the eye of a local from the men's magazines. That said, Mitch was partial to a well-worn Oxford. He paired the Italian shirt with a fitted jacket from the back of his travel closet, a waistcoat you could fold into the carry-on without worry. It might have been Ferragamo, he couldn't remember.

Upon meeting in the lobby Griffin Wagner appeared to be a likably rumpled Midwesterner, and after the maître d' escorted them into the dining room, the two settled into a quiet table in the far corner. For the first twenty-five seconds, Mitch remained immobile, running through the many personal disagreements he had discovered with the configuration of his place settings, anxieties he kept to himself.

Silence at the start of meals was fine by Mitch. He had grown up under the unknowable family patriarch that was Ellis St. Germaine, a remote father and celebrated author who tormented Mitch with ruthless cruelty. He'd by then become lost in his fame. In the late Seventies and early Eighties, a byline by Ellis St. Germaine had become must-read commentary in the *Village Voice, The Nation, Dissent, In These Times,* and *New York Review of Books*.

Busy with the construction of his searing eviscerations of Gerald Ford, Jimmy Carter, Ronald Reagan, and then George Herbert Walker Bush, Ellis was deeply unavailable for the young child with a cough that he had sired with his student-turned-lover Vanessa. When Mitchell had become ten he had taken to derisively quoting poorly-constructed paragraphs in Ellis's magazine, leading Ellis to threaten to kill him.

Like all products of resentful patriarchs whose best work is three decades in the past, Mitchell fled the nest in Burlington with extreme prejudice at the earliest possible convenience, which, looking back, was middle school. That was 1986. He would cast his first vote as an adult for the second Bush, and upon graduation from Georgetown would hit the capitalist candy store running. Mitch set out to overturn every value held dear to Ellis, hoping only for the good fortune to do so before the patriarch succumbed to the rare cancers that seemed to claim all St. Germaines. His goal was of ensuring that his father stayed alive long enough to witness all of it.

By the time when, in early 2008 and right on schedule, Ellis passed away from a carcinoma of the soft tissues after excruciating bouts of pain, Mitch had become a kingmaker within his father's field of publishing. Yet where Ellis had sought to compose argument in the service of social justice and impressing his college-aged lovers, Mitchell had shown a monastic rejection of such vulgar temptations, committed only to serving any unwashed systems of capital intensification he damn well pleased. This had led Mitchell St. Germaine to the top of Word Management Worldwide, a bullshit operation if there ever was one.

Griffin ordered the New York, 16 ounces, medium rare. It was $76. Mitch went for a petit filet, six ounces, rare ($92) then asked the apron to come by with still water ($26), braised Brussels sprouts ($22), and to hold the bread (complimentary). "I like this place," Mitch said. "I can appreciate its assertion of nostalgia while accepting that the room's a pack full of suits."

Griffin looked around. It *was* all salesmen.

The speakers were playing Sinatra and the wine glasses descended as big as fishbowls, goblets of Amarone quickly refilled when you weren't looking by men in starched butcher's apparel. A glass door separated the dining room from the cigar lounge, a creepy grotto lined with dark bookcases and leather armchairs.

"Besides," Mitch added, "I know you have written about how to cook the perfect steak."

Griffin made a note to scrape some of the garbage off Griffin Wagner.com.

"I'm sorry to hear you know that," Griffin said.

"No way. I've read a lot of your clips for *In the Zone*. It's been a pleasure—all the clever pieces on how to survive falling through the ice, getting in a bar fight, talking your way out of a tax audit. I liked your profiles, too. Though I don't know if I would have called Vince Vaughan the next De Niro."

"Yeah, I would gladly take that one back."

Griffin had never taken dinner with anyone who knew their way around his website.

"But I thought the one you did of John Malkovich was fresh. So was the piece on sex in the NFL. Speaking of the old gridiron, it's sad to hear the news about Jade Radcliffe. And right after you interviewed him."

"I must have missed that."

A fan of the NBA, Jade was perhaps the only NFL player whose name Griffin recognized, though that too had begun fading.

"Murder-suicide? Yes that was it. Ran over his fiancée with a Bentley. Beautiful girl, from the picture in the paper anyway. Sorry, I thought you heard. It's all over cable right now. More money, more problems, right?"

Griffin felt the blood draining from his face.

Now a pounder from the NFL was dead. Was this more of the Hemingway effect? Really? *Another?*

Waves of guilt began washing over him. He had promoted the drug in a magazine sold to the most suggestible readers known to man. Was it going to keep killing people in ways that could never be traced?

Relax.

He took a deep breath, then let it drain out of him slowly. It was a coincidence. He had taken Bioferex himself. He had even quit cold turkey just two weeks ago. And here he was, *fine*.

But Jeez, the guy drove over his girlfriend in a Bentley?

"How did he kill himself?"

"Who?"

"Jade. Jade Radcliffe. I mean, after he drove over his girlfriend."

"He shot himself in the middle of an intersection, screaming at a police officer to do it for him."

Griffin thought about how Mitch from Worldwide Whatever seemed to want to help him do big things, and could probably even make some of them happen.

He drank some more of the expensive wine.

He decided he would use this Mitch to write an article that would make Bioferex die.

"Of course everybody starts out paying dues."

Mitch, who Griffin hadn't heard talking as much as providing background noise to his harrowing thirty seconds of panic, was officially blowing the smoke his way.

"The good ones make paying their dues look interesting. You did that, that is what I would say." Mitch had picked up a hand-rolled breadstick and was now tapping it against the side of his glass. Griffin let the pause grow long. Finally he spoke up.

"So. Did you take me out for steak to tell me you liked my article on how to win a bar fight?"

Griffin smiled.

"Because we could go find some trouble. I mean, I could show you what I learned. It mostly came down to evasion, going for the balls, that sort of thing."

Mitch smiled.

"I thought it would be smart to get to know you, is all," Mitch said. "That came out funny. I mean, I know you are looking into this whole clinical trial business. Moving things around to hide side effects."

Mitch had waved his hands in a diminishing way at the last sentence, looking back into the cigar lounge. And was that ever odd. Mitch St. Germaine seemed to get the idea of side effects a little too well.

"Wow, so you caught that," Griffin said. "I didn't get too blamey about the subject on TPN. I never said it was intentional.'"

Griffin briefly considered telling Mitch about his email from a ghostwriter, the woman named Shivani, the woman who wanted to take him on a guided tour of pharma chicanery. Something inside of him told him to save that conversation for an editor.

"…Though I did bring up the subject once with Jeremy Elton," Griffin added. "Are you two friends?" Griffin had said it as a joke. The blank look on Mitch's face suggested Griffin had inadvertently connected actual dots.

"Well, everyone knows everyone, you know," said Mitch. "Jeremy's got, like, three bestsellers. His agent works down the hall from me. You ruffled some feathers, sure, nut-punching him like that. But you also moved the needle, advanced the narrative, however the saying goes. It's why I'm here. We need more conflict in publishing. Publishing is dying, you know."

Griffin stirred his drink. He moved the silverware around his plate in slow motion, like longboats. It felt important to watch what he said next.

"I'll cut to my pitch," Mitch said. "There can't be much money in those articles on your website. I notice you aren't on contract with any of the big magazines."

At the mention of contract pay, Griffin felt exposed and defensive. His inability to land salary from a national magazine, despite slavishly trying, had been one of the great disappointments of his professional life.

"You have the chops to work at a higher pay grade," Mitch said. "That's obvious. You don't have to live like this, you know, check-to-check."

Griffin made a face.

"I saw your car when you pulled up." Having cut his steak in two and pushed half to one side, Mitch had begun pre-sawing the cubes designated for ingestion into two lines of small battalions, an elaborate ritual of some kind. "What's that got, 300,000 miles on it? We develop creators for peak performance. We control production and inject stimulus into the market. We place writers in scoring position and service

189

an eye-popping roster of technology CEOs in need of speeches. We're talking high rollers who don't think twice about dropping $15,000 for five pages of platitudes on futurism. How'd you like to drive something with working windows?"

OK. This was getting effective. Griffin knew what was happening, that he was being seduced. Because that's the thing about seductions, they're rarely secret.

"Some of them take you on their travels to fetching locales. Vineyards. Surf Meccas. Almost always, these outings entail plenty of downtime. You can do this kind of side work and still write for magazines. I'm just throwing things against the wall here."

By the end of dinner, Mitch St. Germaine had offered to sign Griffin under contract as a writer with Word Management Worldwide, an offer Griffin accepted on the spot. It was far too easy.

Griffin knew he should have been skeptical. But try as he could, he saw no downside at all. It was just a giant showering of cash, no strings attached. And of course, the wine had played a role in his deliberations.

In exchange for exclusivity in representing his work, Griffin would receive monthly commissions from WMW totaling no less than $10,000. He could reject the corporate work as he pleased. Word Management Worldwide didn't take a commission.

They would give him a health plan. They would prepare his taxes. It's possible they sent over a cleaning lady. Griffin couldn't make sense of the firm's Santa Claus financial model. When pressed, Mitch would only allude to a convoluted funding mechanism.

"We are retained by clients in service to a host of fiduciary objectives," he offered while picking with a desultory grimace at a pear poached in Calvados with a dollop of nutmeg-scented clotted cream. "We provide them with a stable of multi-platform initiatives." Griffin had no idea what any of that meant either. "All the folks in midtown keep haranguing me to bring them more writers from the Midwest," Mitch explained, casually alluding to something deeply enticing, close relationships with the editors of the magazines who had never answered Griffin's pitches.

So, yes. This was going down. Griffin yielded to the concept of taking help.

Things had gone badly for a long time. This felt like a possible pause in things going badly, an end to being all alone in his work, to living so very broke.

After some celebratory single malt and a cigar in the lounge, Griffin and Mitch shook hands, shared a fist bump that they exploded in cool detachment, and Griffin left the ridiculous dinner with the first steady income in his writing life. It was a tripling of what he was now making, all of it for side work, with the added hope of making connection to the magazines he'd always dreamed of one day breaking into.

If he hadn't just learned two people had come to a violent end, quite possibly from a drug he had taken and promoted, it might have all seemed perfect.

28

Griffin woke up on his kitchen floor, butcher knife in hand, more than a little confused. Lee Majors, who normally slept on a dog bed next to the couch, was now curled into the closet near the back door, hiding in wait to get outside. The clock said 3:47 a.m. What the fuck. It appears Griffin had made his way out of bed, across the apartment, and begun rifling through his kitchen drawers. "Come on Lee," he said. He was going back to bed.

Lee Majors didn't move.

The next morning he made plans to fly to New York, booking a flight for the following week, with the goal of interviewing the medical ghostwriter who had written to him from Shivani3890@yahoo.com. It had been three days since his meeting over steak and Amarone with Mitch St. Germaine, just enough time for Mitch to have taken a lunch with David Nichols, Editor-in-Chief for *Esquire*. The pair left that lunch locking in a feature from Griffin titled "The Rise and Fall of Jeremy Elton," a narrative to include extensive commentary from Elton's ghostwriter, a woman Griffin had assured them who would be willing to talk on the record if she could remain anonymous.

A crumb of apprehension spiked within Griffin's suddenly unpredictable cerebellum as he hit the button to pay for his nonrefundable ticket. He hoped he had tied this first assignment to something solid, that his source was who she said she was, but knew he couldn't say that for sure.

So far, the human being behind Shivani3890@yahoo.com appeared to be the real deal. But it bothered Griffin even he didn't know her full name. After sleeping on it a few days, the sleep getting more and more unpredictable, the mystery became too much. He wrote and told her so.

> It looks like Esquire will let me keep you anonymous. But for me to feel confident in you being who you say you are, I need to know your full name.

Shivani replied about two hours later.

> So, I don't want to talk on the record, because these people are starkers and seem quite skilled at retaliation. I'd rather not learn about that first hand. But just between you and me, my name is Shivani Gandha Patel.
>
> Everyone calls me Sheevi G.

Esquire had passed Griffin off to an editor named Ryan D'Ambrosia. The change was a breath of fresh air. Where Trevor had controlled the construction of Griffin's articles with an iron fist, Ryan had prepared just a thought or two of pre-reporting guidance.

> Hello Griffin,
>
> Nice to meet you. It's great news that your source is going to spend a day with you in Manhattan. My first impression of this

one, however, is that, given her status as Anonymous British Brainy Lady, it is going to be kind of dry?

It's just the nature of the subject matter – academia and whatnot. Also, Jeremy Elton is ZZZZZ.... If she turns out to be interesting, you can just as easily make the story all about her.

Try to hang out with her and go do things. Go running or something. Get her talking with sweat trickling down her face, standing over her stove in what I am sure will be a nicely-appointed kitchen, all of it paid for thanks to her skill at writing drug studies in a way that looks sciencey while making sure to sell more medications.

But it's probably going to be less grabby if you can't get her on the record. Think you can change her mind? I don't see this working with a mystery source. Just being honest. I will circle back as more thoughts come to me, but feel free to check in and let me know how everything is going.

Ryan

PS Minnesota? Sounds tranquil!

Interesting. *Esquire* could care less about Griffin profiling Jeremy Elton. *Esquire* wanted Shivani to go public. Plus, "scenes." Griffin still had no idea how he was going slip in the suggestion that people had died from Bioferex. How he would get away with using *Esquire* to kill the drug. Were this the movies, some sort of John Grisham novel they all run out to buy in hardcover, he would need to get his hands on some incriminating paperwork. But he had no idea what that would look like.

Griffin mounted a digital search of "Shivani Gandha Patel" in all of its variant forms. Though the name took him through pages of bright and ambitious-looking young women stationed in corporate posts across the globe, the search to confirm his ghostwriter didn't check out as easily as he had hoped. There was no one with her name and employer on LinkedIn, Facebook, or Twitter, much less on the webpage of any Manhattan-based medical communications firms. He did eventually find his verification of her work history, but only after he had migrated onto Google Scholar, whereupon her name appeared here and there in the credits of differing medical papers.

"The authors would like to thank S.G. Patel of Deadline Medical for editorial assistance," they stated. So, yes, phew, she had really ghost-authored papers.

՞

On the night before he flew to New York, Griffin fired off a text to the only person he could think to ask his one other question:

> Dr. Breton,
> Griffin Wagner here.
> I'm about to interview a Serotonal
> ghostwriter.
> What should I ask her?

His phone chimed in ten minutes.

> Well that's interesting.
> Ask her to get you
> the raw data, mate.
> Some of the scribbles they
> never show anyone.

Scribbles? It sounded gravely imprecise. Griffin was going to get an afternoon with Sheevi G, maybe two. They would not be digging through piles of drug industry paperwork. He needed specifics.

> Sorry...
> How would I
> know what to

look for?

This time Breton needed ten minutes.

Patient has
withdrawn,
N.R.G.

It had to be the middle of the night in New Zealand. Griffin thought he could get away with one more question, max.

What's NRG?

He was right.

No Reason Given.
Have to go, it's very late.
Good luck.

29

Griffin and Shivani agreed to meet the next Tuesday at Michaels, the midtown spot where Mitch St. Germaine had secured the very same *Esquire* assignment Griffin had flown here to report.

He was supposed to be getting a travel card from WMW, but in the meantime, all of these costs were his alone, so Griffin was watching his wallet. That created its own set of problems. Prior to settling on a locale for their meeting, Shivani had thrown out the names of half a dozen places with check averages that left Griffin shaking.

"Should we try Le Benardin?" she asked.

They were on the phone, their first ever call. It was the night before his departure, Griffin was packing, and Shivani was finishing up after a long day at work. Even Griffin had heard of Le Benardin, a legendary money pit.

In its day Le Benardin would have been the Sistine Chapel of gastronomic pleasures across Manhattan. And yet Shivani had suggested the locale like it was to swing through a Wendy's drive-up. Besides the prohibitive cost, Griffin knew better than to meet his source in a dining room that would be motionless except for the sound of silver on china. He'd just been through all that with Mitch.

"What about someplace livelier?"

Shivani followed up with four other equally insane alternatives.

"There's Le Cirque, Jean-Georges, Aquavit. Gramercy Tavern hasn't gone downhill as much as everyone thinks."

Again with the four-star places. Was she testing him?

Griffin countered with the only dining room he had ever heard of in Manhattan.

"Should we go to Michael's?"

"Think we can get in?"

"The magazine has a table."

Griffin had no idea if *Esquire* "had a table," at Michael's, let alone if he could claim it.

He had been rattled by her suggestions and succumbed to an overpowering urge to appear connected. He was, after all, trying to get a highly-paid corporate insider to rat out her employer. You didn't land that kind of cooperation after picking up a tab at Chili's.

Waiting at the *Esquire* table for his ghostwriter to arrive, Griffin began to experience a creeping sense of doom. Those old Minnesotan doubts. This wasn't going to be like impressing Katie at the C.C. Club. He looked down at his dress shoes. They looked like dead turtles. He gazed out at the crowd. The room was jammed with designer threads. He didn't even know what it was that a medical ghostwriter did. He had overpromised.

Last night was another weird one. What was it with these fucked-up dreams of late? He'd felt blood splattering in his eyes this time, then woke up rubbing them. Lee Majors had been hiding. It looked as though he had kicked off his sheets in a rage.

The flight out to New York had been characterized by intense feelings of claustrophobia and a parade of mildly unbearable thoughts emanating from some bomb shelter in his hippocampus. Weird zaps rocked his head for reasons unknown. Standing in line for security felt like the Gulag. He had rocked from side to side swell enough to cause TSA to pull him out for hand screening, an experience made just fantastic by the fact that he'd become overwhelmed with an urge to pace and pace and pace.

He looked up and he saw her. He thought it was her, anyway. A woman with South Asian features was approaching their table with the host, an older man in a short jacket and tight pants. Griffin rose to greet her, but then the pair swooshed on past. Turning his head in confusion, Griffin pivoted back to find a a far more captivating presence who had approached just behind the both of them, all on her own. A demure beauty of maybe 30, long, dark eyelashes, with piercing green eyes. She was giving him a little wave.

"Down here," she said with a laugh. "I would never wear flats."

His first thought was that it was indeed her, S.G. Patel, the ghostwriter pointed out to him by Sedona Piper at the AAP, although now her hair was flipped upward in a pile skewered by bamboo needles with a lone pair of strands framing her face. Better yet, the business threads she'd worn at the big meeting in Chicago were now swapped out for heeled boots and a green silk top over black tights. Was it her day off?

"Sore-ey," she chimed, a little breathless. "Just got out of a meeting and made my way over stat. Grifton, is it?"

Close enough.

He was charmed. Griffin started a handshake but Shivani rolled her eyes, waved him off, then added "let's not look like strangers in this place," fish-hooking her upper lip as she slid into her chair. "We've infiltrated quite the piranha tank."

"Print person piranha tank, there's a nice alliteration. I suppose we should figure out how you want to be identified."

Wow. Griffin couldn't believe he actually said, like, *that*.

It was a wildly operational question, straight out of the gate and all.

As if to confirm his fears, he watched in regret as Shivani processed his demand by imperceptibly shrinking in her seat.

"What if we talk about something more pleasant," she finally offered with a weak smile.

Shivani had picked up a menu and begun scanning it with detachment, mumbling something Griffin could not quite hear, though it could have been "goat cheese, thou fate is ever thine."

A waiter swooped in, Shivani ordered a Pellegrino, and Griffin asked for a Diet Coke. As the waiter peeled off, the pair sat for another long silence, an excruciating lull causing Griffin to become aware of conversations all around them.

He had been off his step like this with everyone lately, a heightened neuroticism and socially-penalizing insensitivity to nonverbal cues. Here in this context, it was officially hurting him. Shivani seemed to be waiting for him to take the lead, and normally he would oblige, he did these things well back in the tap houses of his home tundra, but here he was drawing blanks.

"So tell me a little about yourself?"

It was for now the best that Griffin could do. It was as if his brain had become permafrost.

Shivani gazed at the menu some more.

"Five-seven, allergic to walnuts," she finally offered, wide eyes now more interested in the street.

"Seems like a nice neighborhood," he said, hoping the redirect might work in his favor. He could see the towers on Sixth Avenue from his chair facing east. "Are your offices around here?"

"Yes," Shivani said flatly. "Deadline Medical is two blocks towards the park."

She waved a thumb to the north.

They let another five seconds pass, then she continued.

"We have offices on sixteen through eighteen. The Krøhn-McGill headquarters is just up the street. The primary plant is out in New Jersey, but they sort of own us on sixteen on up as well. Is your magazine located around here somewhere?"

Relief. She had tossed him a question.

"I believe *Esquire* is somewhere on fifty-seventh," Griffin replied, uncertain which magazine she had meant. "My invitation to the holiday party keeps getting lost in the mail. My other magazine, *In the Zone*, has an office somewhere around here, too. But strangely enough, I have never been there either."

With the confession, Shivani raised her eyebrows in mild surprise. Another blunder. She may have wondered how low on the food chain she had agreed to give up her life story and possibly her career. Griffin should have pretended to be better-connected than he was, but bluffing left him exhausted. It was one of his liabilities. Shivani returned to looking at her menu.

"How about I skip the small talk," he tried. "I bet you don't have all day."

"Wonderful," she replied. "Not my cup of tea as well."

"Why are you doing this?"

"Thinking about ceviche?"

"Talking to *Esquire*."

"I wish I knew the answer to that myself."

Shivani set down her menu and gazed to her left, chin in hand, looking out at the room. She stole a look at her phone, then put it back in her purse. She looked at her nails. Their lunch had begun to feel like a Tinder match from hell.

"That's alright," Griffin said. "Maybe this is a better question: How did you get into ghostwriting—is that what I call it?"

Shivani picked up her purse and began digging around for something.

"I saw a card on a bulletin board," she replied drably, still digging. She began unzipping and re-zipping the interior compartments of her bag before finally locating what she was looking for. It was an eyeliner, and it had a funny word on it: Gjale. She then pulled it open and began drawing lines on the back of her hand. The color glowed on her olive toned skin. Griffin wondered if he had travelled to New York to profile an introvert having second thoughts.

"I mean, what attracted you to ghostwriting?"

The waiter returned with two drinks. Shivani smiled. The pair stared at the waiter in silence.

"I can give you a few more minutes," the waiter said.

"Splendid," Shivani said. He left.

"What attracted me to ghostwriting was that I wanted two thousand quid to finish grad school. Once I started getting the work, I thought I had found my people. Back then, the industry was filled with guys like my dad."

"Your dad?" Griffin felt relief. Personal history was a writer's best friend. A couple at the table next to them got up and left. Shivani reached over to grab their untouched ramekin of butter.

"My father read sciences in Emmanuel at Cambridge," Shivani continued, placing her purse back on the floor, then plucking a knife from her place-setting and, yes this was weird, gently knifing a small morsel of the other table's butter onto her lower lip before touching it with her tongue and bringing it lightly into her mouth. Griffin smiled in surprise. "Fear not," she said, with a momentary widening of her eyes, "the data slandering animal fat is garbage."

"No argument here," he said. "But you were telling me about your dad."

"At Cambridge, he would free-climb the five hundred-year-old colleges on the down-low. No gear, no rope, no fancy footwear. Sneakers and wool pants, just shimmying up the spires at midnight. St. John's, Trinity, all the gentry cathedrals of literature and science, ten stories up the tallest tower ordered by Henry VIII. 'The ground is precisely one hundred feet below you,' was how his pal described scaling King's with nothing but a friction hold and a 35-degree footrest. 'If you slip, you will still have three seconds to live.' His book was called 'The Night Climbers of Cambridge' and it's still in print. Anyway, I liked the way those guys saw things."

"Do you mind if I take notes?"

Griffin had no idea what was up with the story about her dad climbing Hogwarts, but he needed to get some of this down. Shivani shook her head slowly back and forth, then knife-tipped another gram of Irish butter onto her lovely lower lip.

"Not here," she said.

Well then what the fuck were they doing here?

Griffin decided he would try to compile notes in his head.

"That's cool," he said. "Keep going."

"Well, dad would pose little empirical questions and ask for our hypotheses. You should have seen the science fairs when I was growing up. The other kids were testing foods the gerbil liked best."

"That would have been me."

"Well I was putting spores under the microscope. Is it osmoresistant? A toxin? When I met people in pharma in the early Nineties I fit right in. Back then scientists were still around who knew that all observations were valid. That if something in the data wasn't right, one could say just say, 'hey mates, this is off.' It was all about the numbers."

"What's he doing now?"

"Who?"

"Your dad."

Shivani's face sagged and her eyes returned to the window.

"He passed away."

And here Griffin thought he was rolling.

"I'm sorry."

That didn't sound trite at all.

"Can I ask how?"

And that didn't sound journalistically exploitative, no sir.

Shivani stiffened, then looked back at Griffin with dull scrutiny.

"OK. How did Daddy die? Let's see. I was ten. We were driving home from dinner. Everyone was laughing. Daddy was doing Monty Python. 'Just a flesh wound!' We got home. Daddy pulled the car over to let us out at the garden path. We stepped out of the family car, he fanned the auto perpendicular for approaching the driveway backing in, and then an Austin-Healy came roaring around the corner."

Griffin tried to think of something. Nothing was coming.

"Mummy remarried after a year," Shivani added, her voice rising in labored cheer. "A dull bloke with an unmemorable face who pulled a good paycheck when he wasn't spending it at the pub. My science projects were confusing to him. I kept my head down and left for the States as soon as I was able."

She didn't say anything for about ten seconds. Griffin had begun nervously folding and unfolding a calling card he'd taken from the host stand.

"So, there's that little scene you wanted," she offered. "Be sure to get it down all in your noodle."

The waiter returned.

"Why not get something," Griffin suggested. Changing the subject was sometimes the essence of kindness. "It looks really good."

"It does," Shivani replied. "You go ahead." She then turned to the waiter. "I will just have some more butter please."

Griffin stifled a smile. He liked her.

"A bowl of soup?" the waiter offered.

Shivani looked at the waiter.

"What's your name?"

"Roan."

"Hi, Roan. I'm Shivani. Do you have the bisque?"

"Of course. Should I bring two?" He looked at Griffin.

Griffin started to nod slowly.

"I don't want any bisque," Shivani said, causing Griffin to slowly shake his head no to his order as well. "I was just curious," Shivani continued. "I'll have a glass of the Russian River."

Aaand now they were drinking.

"Peroni for me," Griffin said, moving his Diet Coke to the side of the table.

Roan disappeared. Shivani put her chin in her hand and began talking to the window.

"I adored ghostwriting when it was run by researchers. But the brain trust went to rot during the Clinton years. Every last scientist in production was replaced by a prize idiot. Believe me, I dated a few of them. Handsome. A bunch of guy's-guys. They really liked your magazine, too. That's how I knew to look for one of your kind."

"My kind?"

Chin in hand, Shivani allowed her captivating green eyes to finally slip towards his, offering the burn that followed thereafter slowly and with great care.

"Writers, with the means, to reach certain men."

"Which men?"

"Men not complicated by the burdens of self-awareness."

Fine. Griffin pulled out a pad and placed it on his lap, then on the table. If he was her designated super-highway to idiots, he'd earned the right to take some notes. He produced a pen and raised an eyebrow.

"I'm thick," he said. "The memory needs notes."

Shivani nodded and leaned forward on her elbows, pushing the bread basket in front of his writing arm to block the view of the pad from the rest of the room.

"We started having drug-development meetings," she said, running her manicured nails through the strands on the side of her face, "crude strategy huddles run by guys out of refrigerators, auto-detailing, liquor distributing, the military. They weren't too worried about the science. They were keen on sales, or commissions more precisely, only now they were our bosses. The R&D budgets began being diverted to golf weekends and champagne lounges. Moral decay, how original, right? They started telling us what we could and couldn't say. It took about six years for the industry to become fully commercialized. No more answering to PhDs for you."

"What's it like now?"

Griffin was still taking down her previous answer.

"You know, they made the studies a win-loss type of thing. It was all about the boo-yah. No curiosity. *Grab that cash with both hands and make a stash…* I think that's how the lyric goes, Griffin with an F for Pink Floyd and one more. But the poor little tools, their time is passed and they don't even know it. Some real prize robots are preparing to eat their lunch. Guys who are far more Machiavellian."

"So, what, the drug companies in Europe?"

"Oh one wishes. Germany invented the pharmaceutical industry. No, I am talking the Baltics. China. My ancestral homeland. Ever heard of Chennai? It's Detroit of the south Asian continent. The frat boys who destroyed medicine are going to get postered by the oncoming waves of low-pay nerds from Tamil Nadu."

"I barely understand science myself," said Griffin.

He did understand what it meant to be postered, a term for a basketball player being dunked on so hard the image ends up on a poster.

"Yeah, well, science is about trying to disprove a finding, not doing whatever it takes to come up with a financially desirable conclusion. The only way you know if a drug works, remember, is to try your hardest to prove that it doesn't, then face-plant. Failure is your friend in the lab. If a finding survives your best effort to prove it wrong, that's a thing of beauty. I believe Daddy called it 'a page torn from the master plan for the universe.'"

"Doesn't sound like something you could prepare for in refrigerator sales."

"The guys now running my life think a good scientist will have shown 'product disloyalty' if she identifies a flaw in the trial."

"Did that happen to you with the trials of Serotonal?"

"What part of the trials?"

Shivani had shifted in her chair as she returned his question with one of her own.

"What do you mean?"

"I'm going to need that you get more specific, sorry."

"OK…" Griffin felt the table becoming a showdown again.

"These irregularities are highly technical," Shivani continued. "Not to be unkind, but you work for an unserious magazine. Explaining the math here in a way the larger public might have a chance at absorbing is a challenging task, but it's critical if this overture of ours is to succeed. It's not clear to me that you are up for it."

"OK," Griffin said. "Try me."

Shivani smiled, then pursed her lips while she thought over her options.

"Serotonal trial irregularities, let's see. You had improper latency upon initiation. Improper disqualification from surveillance. Noncompliant status in outcome coding, efficacy measures during diagnosis, the specious use of relative versus absolute risk in SAE reporting, and let's see, use of the HAM-D for diagnosis of Intermittent Depressive Disorder against countervailing norms, that was *quite* improper as well."

Shivani began scanning a menu as she continued, but speeding up.

"The use of the highly suicidal Intermittent Depressive Disorder as proxy diagnosis for harm following treatment of subjects with Major Depressive Disorder, that's of course a grotesquely obese thumb placed on the scale. The use of irrelevant subgroup analyses in the abstract, can you say ugh. A failure to reproduce subgroup analyses in the abstract, the use of subgroups with no intergroup corrective calculations, data dredging, selective publication, abandonment of negative trials, the *total* disregard for the subjectivity of global ratings scales, my *god*... There's still the erosion of blinding thanks to benign side effects, I could go on. Should I go on? Or should I stop here? Are you good with these concepts?"

Griffin wondered how things had suddenly turned contentious.

"Me, no, not too good."

He pointed a finger to his temple, as if to say that he was not the brightest bulb on the shelf. Shivani had clearly studied circles around him on her path to the apex of medical ghostwriting. He knew there was no point in bluffing.

"Well, that worries me," Shivani said, putting down her menu. "You will need to wrap your head around subjects more wily than the honing of a jump shot if I am going to entrust you with my thoughts on the movement of suicides into placebo columns. Because if you get this wrong, you see, we're both fucked. I have a lot to lose. I'm betting you do as well?"

Griffin had seen sources go cold on him before.

This was the first time one had ever done an about-face.

"You contacted me, remember?"

"I do remember," Shivani replied. "I'd had a bit of wine and was feeling tragic about life."

"I'd say maybe don't disregard that feeling," Griffin said with a small smile. "We're not so different, you and me. You work for idiots, I write for them. My guys are *all* wiping mustard on their pants."

Shivani nodded. A small smile fought to say hello.

"We could skip the technical problems you just listed and talk about the paperwork on individual people," Griffin said, "I think they call that raw data, right? You must have stories about raw data? People are people. Everyone understands stories about people."

"Well," she said.

"What?"

"It's just, this question: 'Can I see the raw data?' The names, dates, statements and actions detailing the experiences of test subjects. It's charming."

"What of it?"

"The naïveté. Really. Just what do you imagine happens, Griffin Wagner, if you are Shivani Patel, you ask to see raw data, and they have decided you have begun to show product disloyalty?"

"I suppose they call you in for a conversation."

"More like I am to approached as though I have been caught holding bags of cash and a plane ticket somewhere warm. The raw data, my god, the very question is a riot. Those are trade secrets."

"Is that what they called the suicides moved to placebo while testing Serotonal? 'Trade secrets?'"

Shivani paused at Griffin's second mention of Serotonal.

"That would be their legal status at the present time, yes."

"Alexander Breton said I should ask you to show me raw data on placebo suicides."

"Well-well, the intrepid Professor Breton. I can't say that I know him other than his reputation precedes him, but, sure," Shivani said. "I haven't seen raw data since the Nineties."

She brushed her brown strands behind an ear.

"I will be sent a spreadsheet if I'm lucky," she continued, "a big ledger of 'trust-me' numbers to be taken on faith. Problem is, by then all the secrets have been baked into the cake."

"Well, where is it?"

"What?"

"The raw data."

"You think I know?"

"Does the author know?"

"Who do you mean?"

"Does the person who writes the articles about the trial know where they keep the raw data?"

"The person that writes the articles about the trial would be me," Shivani said. "What is it you think I do?"

"I thought a doctor or researcher writes an article, and you come in to, you know, punch up the prose a little?"

Shivani put her face in her hands. She shook her head as she said it:

"You're fucking kidding me."

"Not really."

She looked up in exasperation.

"If you mean the doctor whose name goes at the top of the papers that I write, I can't say I have ever even met a quote-unquote author during the period dedicated for my writing of his paper." Shivani ran a finger over her lower lip as she thought about the process. "They don't shop for that bloke until our paper is all buttoned up and the journal is awaiting signatures. No sir-ee, the lucky winner gets my article with a cover letter and a stamped envelope addressed to the journal expecting the thing. Once the author signs it, a check is mailed to the author's house as well as that of the journal editor."

"How much?"

"How should I know, probably twenty grand? Fifty for first author? The price is never enough, considering it's a human soul, but who am I to talk, right? Once the thing is published, yeah, maybe then the so-called author and I will meet if they need to launch the thing at a meeting."

Griffin was writing it all down, albeit illegibly.

"Because?"

"Because they don't know what their own paper says?"

Griffin looked up and started tapping his pen. This was getting beyond preposterous.

"You're serious?"

"What?"

Griffin began tapping his pen faster.

"I mean, that's not even ghostwriting," he said. "There's nothing collaborative about it."

"They have us write papers. They go out and find doctors to claim authorship. They pay them for their signatures. I can't imagine anyone is surprised by that."

"I wish more people knew about this."

Griffin leaned back in his chair.

"I wish we had a world-class aquarium in New York."

Shivani began digging around in her bag again.

"And they don't have anything to do with the study?"

"The famous authors of clinical trials, no, no to all that."

"No to all what?"

Shivani looked up, getting bored.

"No. The so-called authors of clinical trials are not finding the patients. Not talking to patients about their problems. Not handing out questionnaires, filling out forms, prescribing drugs, giving placebos, tabulating results or writing conclusions.

"No, the famous doctors whose names grace my papers are not

sending their study off to a journal and waiting with fingers crossed in hopes of inching forward the state of care. No, no, and no. Pharma hires a contractor to do all that. A private contractor knows what its job is."

"Which is?"

"It will give you what you want out of a trial, then send me the data to be written up, whereupon a famous doctor will put his name on it and a reputable journal will publish it. Eventually, all the lesser journals will publish spin-off versions of the same dodgy pant-load. Clog up the pipeline with enough baby studies and you birth the appearance of an organic march of scientific advancement, rather than the one-author marketing plan it always and ever was."

Shivani had been looking in her wallet.

"Here, this one is something else." She handed Griffin a card that read *FJT Therapeutics: Data, Performance, Results.* Griffin looked at the card. He was stumped.

"Don't worry, I don't know what it means either." Shivani smiled and took a sip of her wine, then turned a bracelet on her wrist, looking around the room nervously. "It's an outfit that ran one of the trials I have been ordered to write up later today."

"And to think I imagined drug trials were run by scientists."

Shivani laughed. She leaned in.

"Look at it this way: You're Krøhn-McGill. You have 47,000 employees. Are you going to trust some dodgy academic with bad breath when it comes to the fate of a molecule that can send your stock soaring? You want his signature and a couple of his patients to piggyback on the respect garnered to his ivory tower employer. Beyond that there are far more mercenary systems for the testing and collecting of clinical data, most of them conveniently off-shore"

Griffin paused. He barely knew what to ask next.

He was writing as fast as he could, but it was getting beyond complicated.

He hadn't even gotten to his Bioferex questions.

"For me, the final straw was the marketing of a drug for dementia,"

Shivani said. "These papers of mine were going to run all over the world as letters to the editor, review articles, trials or sub-analyses of trials. Chop and parcel them long enough and you can easily poop fifty articles out of the same weak study when it's all little old me, writing feverishly under other people's names like the Wizard of Oz."

Griffin had seen how search engines can turn up dozens of entries on a new drug. He never imagined they could have all sprung from a single, insanely-productive writer-for-hire impersonating a field of research.

"But I realized I needed to ask someone at the contractor if they knew the outcome beyond six weeks for a blood problem the competitors were going to ask about. I thought I would euthanize it in the Discussion section. I tracked down the tragedy where the study had been conducted. I asked. I'll never forget the answer. Bloke in charge said, 'who the fuck knows, Ms. Patel'"—and now she was leaning in with an emphatic head-bob that charmed Griffin immensely—"'I'd ask those chaps how their cholesterol is looking, but they are all back under the overpass.'"

Then she leaned back and ate some more butter.

"Mind you," Shivani added, "it had been a fortnight since the study ended, and the CRO."

"CRO?"

"Contract Research Organization, clinical trial chop shops—the CRO had no idea where all the patients had gone. We studied the drug for six weeks and put that pill on the market. Does it blow up in your body on week seven? Who knows, we lost track of those people once they claimed a check. It's a business. One of the biggest CROs is run by a guy who used to own a chain of mattress shops."

Griffin was three ideas behind her.

"I thought this was going to be about how the doctors whose names are on the top of clinical trials have not actually written them."

"Yes, guilty as charged. But not only do the docs not write the papers or conduct the trials, they couldn't get on the phone with the people who conducted the trials if they wanted. The CRO runs the study, yours truly writes it, a big-name doctor trades his name for pay, and the drug company treats us all like children."

"I didn't know doctors were so lazy."

"They're not." Shivani paused to look up from her butter, a small dot of it perched precariously on her upper lip. The seriousness in her eyes stopped Griffin in his tracks.

"I hope you didn't think this was your little chance to write an exposé on the fallen state of modern physicians," she said. "If some MD has an attack of conscience and tries to write his own paper, my bosses will need all of five minutes to find someone more malleable."

"Who ends up taking the work?"

"The principle investigator is increasingly someone easy at a middling university who's happy to have his name in a journal. You know, like Julian Powers."

Griffin looked up. Powers was the expert he'd quoted for his article on Bioferex.

"I checked you out." Shivani smiled. "That's a fit looking picture on your website."

"Thanks."

Strange. He had not expected to find her a flirt.

"The selfies with fish lips weren't getting me much work."

The waiter walked up and Shivani gave him a little shake of her finger as if to say *can we have just another minute*. So he left.

"You know what?" she asked, "this was bonkers."

"What?"

"Me, talking to you, here. I haven't quit my job. The office is blocks away. You are not exactly anonymous, making your name on TPN as a tormenter of my boss. Others could walk in on us at any time."

They *were* seated at ground zero, and for publishing as well as Pharma. Griffin dropped a fifty on the tablecloth—more money than he would dream of spending on two rounds in Minneapolis—and the two of them got up to slip out. He hadn't even gotten his tape recorder running. He had to get this thing going.

ꙮ

On the sidewalk, Griffin and Shivani turned to their right and began walking east towards Fifth Avenue. The streets were pristine in the banking part of midtown. Griffin was looking at her hair, her stony face, all of it just stress and unshaken confidence. They would have loved to shoot a photo of her. It was a shame that hiding her name would likely tank his *Esquire* contract. Griffin needed her to come around on that.

They crossed Fifth, turned south and Shivani froze.

"Holy buckets," she said quietly. Griffin followed her gaze to the source of alarm. Ten feet to her left, a hired car had pulled up in front of the Lancaster. Shivani turned her back to the limo and in an instant her face had moved towards Griffin. She pretended to look for something in her bag. Griffin saw a driver walking around to open the passenger side door.

"It's Rene," Shivani said quietly into her coat.

"Who's he?"

"Our driver for Deadline Medical. We always chauffer Jeremy and he always stays here whilst in the city." Shivani backed into an alcove while pulling Griffin against her, out of the sight of the witnesses.

It all happened so fast. As he returned Shivani's kiss, Griffin's brain took in all the shimmering sensory data. An expensive scent. Locks of her hair in his face. Some sort of straightening product. Strands catching in their mouths.

Vaguely, and from the corner of his eye, he caught sight of a tousled mane of salt and pepper. He could have been wrong, but it sure looked like the familiar head of none other than America's Psychiatrist.

Jeremy Elton may have been looking their way, but for now, Griffin couldn't be sure of anything. Shivani Patel was touching the tip of her tongue to his teeth.

30

When the limo pulled away, Shivani extracted herself from Griffin's face, prepared her defense, and laughed quietly. "That was acting, by the way."

"I don't know," Griffin said. "Seemed legit to me."

It had been ages since Shivani had come across a shy man.

She hadn't planned on this, but two glasses of white wine on a stomach lined with butter had gotten the best of her. To her surprise, this Griffin in her life seemed flustered, and that seemed to her like intel in favor of character, or at least chivalry. It seemed like enough to trust him with a slightly longer conversation and a deeper version of the facts as she knew them.

Shivani had become jaded. She had been in New York for too long. Maybe she did like him a bit. After years in the orbit of predatory English boys and their preening ways, Shivani had come to enjoy the value of an uncomplicated male. This Griffin fellow wouldn't be reading too much into the fact of her locking on his face. He had an air of experience and a lack of need about him. He wouldn't be sending her a dozen roses at the office, making more of it than it was. Then again, if this one was truly naive enough to report on her story, could he be smart enough to get it right?

Shivani had tried to test him back in the restaurant, only to come up empty-handed. She wanted another drink, this time somewhere dark. She knew he would be pressing her to flip on his recorder. She knew it had been manifestly unfair to tell him those secrets while demanding he refer to her without identifiers. As Shivani thought over what to do next, the two walked a short block to Fifty-Fourth, where she remembered a pub that would be just right. Noisy, unpopulated with spies.

"Let's go here," she said pulling open the small door to the Hotel Elysee, "to the Monkey Bar."

"Sounds like a fun place," Griffin said.

Shivani thought he had said it like he had no idea what she was talking about.

"It can be," she said. "It's got a history."

They were seated in a front booth, looking at the murals of monkeys when Shivani glanced at her phone to see a text from the insufferable Seamus.

where are you?

As if he owned her.

She put the phone in her bag. Just above them, a chimp in a three-piece was mixing Manhattans with a glass shaker.

"I was hoping to get you on to Serotonal and Bioferex?"

As predicted, Griffin was doubling down on the meaty subjects. Shivani had hoped she might get to talk out the clock, regaling him with the shady side of ghostwriting while leaving the incriminating chapter and verse on the sidelines. Only now he wasn't having it.

Shivani sipped her drink. The vodka settled her. Griffin had pulled out the bloody recorder although thanks again, vodka, now it didn't bother her as much.

Still. Fuck the recorder.

She shook her head no.

"OK," Griffin said, putting it back a little less easily. He was starting to look nervous, or perhaps frustrated.

"I will have to keep good notes in my head," he added. "Here's the question of the hour..."

"You're kidding."

Shivani had said the comment to her boss, now busy harassing her via text.

> Are you on a date
> at the Lancaster?

One thing was for sure, Shivani didn't have long, no matter if she trusted this fetching bloke from a shopping catalog or not. She took another sip of her drink and set it down. Time for some courage.

"Do they have the same side effects?"

She leaned in close.

"Bioferex," she whispered, "is Serotonal's little baby drug."

Griffin gave her a funny look.

"Krøhn-McGill knew the Serotonal money was going away," Shivani added, making a small gesture with her fingers denoting scratch.

"The mighty zoloxetine patent was closing. They had nothing in the pipeline. They were about to lose billions. Marketing was sending these unpleasant emails. It was *all hands on deck!* They called it the Serotonal Time Bomb, the cratering of 2012, and said that it would bankrupt the firm within twenty-four months. They demanded we find a way to re-purpose it."

"That was the big plan, find another use for an antidepressant?"

"Not just any use," she said. "They wanted something horizontal."

"Horizontal?"

Shivani waved her hand slowly across the table, leaning back in her booth. She pulled the olive spear from her drink and bit slowly into the salty garnish, both seductively and skeptically. A thought came to her: What would he be like in bed? It had been sort of a long time.

The lights behind the bar began to form double images. Things were going to get ugly if she didn't find some food. Then again, look where acting rationally had gotten her. Shivani felt the way she had felt the night she cried into her recorder. A waitress had begun speaking. Shivani handed their menus back to her.

"Cute dress. No food for us. Just keep them coming."

She leaned forward and tried not to slur.

"They wanted a drug that could be taken by everyone and grandma. Black, white, young, old, sick, healthy. Medicine doesn't make money anymore by treating the sick my dear Griffin if you haven't noticed. This whole idea was about plugging a four billion-dollar hole."

"So they decided to medicate, what," he said, "the need to run three miles without knee pain?"

"They started thinking about ways to do that, yes. You know—'hey gents, wouldn't it be money if we had made a pill that everyone had to take before signing up at the gym?' A pill for every last chap in the Tough Mudder, that bloke waving shipping ropes up and down inside of a CrossFit, the gal hoping to lose four stone on the treadmill and the lad toeing the company wellness mandate. Someone in the lab figured out Serotonal had an isomer that improved the markers for bone density, and that gave us Bioferex."

"They're iso- what?"

"Isomers...Reverse images of the same drug."

"Does that mean they do the same thing?"

"Sometimes. Sometimes they don't. Or they do, but they act funny."

"So…you won't believe this, but I actually I took Bioferex for a while."

Shivani paused, then leaned in close again. She loved this weird little room, its heady mix of Chanel, cigar smoke and alcohol.

"We all make our choices to get by, love."

She hadn't really heard him. His mouth was more interesting.

"But to answer your question, Mr. Wagner, I have no clue if the isomer of Serotonal increases suicide."

"Good answer for a chemist," he said. "But what's the ghostwriter think?"

Shivani realized he wasn't getting nearly as hammered. She heard a ping. Another text on her phone. It was Seamus, who else.

> I trust you are familiar with
> our confidentiality agreement

"Ha!" Shivani showed Griffin the text.

"Quite the head-fakey, wouldn't you say? Excuse me for a second. I know it's rude to text in close company but this is too rich to let pass."

Shivani began feverishly typing with two thumbs.

She paused to smile. Proofing what she wrote, her euphoria slowly wilted.

This was a decisive moment. What she was about to do, it deserved a second thought. She could come to regret it. She showed her reply to Griffin.

> Why yes, my dear Seamus.
> But I am worried I never signed
> my nondisclosure agreement.
> Could you be a dear and find it for me?

She had not yet hit send. Doing this was big.

"This is the fantasy reply, you know," Shivani said, staring fondly at her kiss-off. Boasting of your failure to sign an NDA was war. Tantamount to lunging across the conference table, then burying a knife in your boss's Adam's apple.

"This is one of those texts you write in order to feel good," she sad, "then delete before sending. That said, it would be *such* a fuck-off."

"I don't get it."

"They botched it," Shivani said with a sigh. "They never got me to promise not to spill."

"Do it."

She stared at Griffin. He was now locking into her. She felt as though he seemed like a real person, a person worthy of her secrets.

"Seriously?"

"Seriously."

Griffin leaned back and laced his fingers behind his head. Shivani considered the thought of her liberation from the planetary weight of Krøhn-McGill in her life. He couldn't have possibly known the penalty of committing betrayal with Krøhn-McGill, what it would unleash from the Death Star that had shadowed her every step for the past fifteen years.

Her entire working life had been defined by Deadline Medical, later Krøhn-McGill. Now came the possibility she could reclaim it for herself. She had heard it all before. But now she felt ready to receive it.

"Think about it," Griffin said. "You can't stand these people. You don't like your job. You told me this gig was a drag before we had ten minutes in the same room. Why do you think you wrote me in the first place?"

If only he knew. But Griffin was right. She needed to put distance between herself and the beast that was her life in their image. Shivani stared at Griffin. She leaned forward and kissed him, surprising him, warming her.

"If you send me roses I will never speak with you again," she said. Then she held up her phone and hit Send. The instant it left, a force inside of Shivani that still liked nice things put her hand over her mouth as she turned to look helplessly out the window.

"My god, what have I done?"

"Are you OK?" Griffin asked.

She looked at him.

"I've never been better," she said turning back. "You can use my full name. Shivani Gandha Patel. Let's have another."

"Did you hide a spike in suicides in the users of Serotonal?"

Griffin felt terrible putting the crime in her lap with such finality, but they had already kissed twice and fled two bars.

It was four in the afternoon. He knew his time was running out. His instincts told him she would be the disappearing kind. Just that strange little fight she had picked with her boss, for example. How was that not a red flag of some kind?

Combine it with all of the drinking, and none of this bode well for how Shivani Patel would be feeling about their project in the morning.

"Turn off the stick," she said.

"I never turned it on," he replied. "You banned it, remember?"

"Well that's peachy, because when you start talking about hiding side effects ..."

"Those tricks that you wrote me about . . ."

"Those tricks that I wrote you about ..."

"...and which I have never admitted to fasili...fac*ilita*ting by intention."

"Yes."

"*Off* the record."

"Yes."

"Because this is where the going-to-jail part starts."

"Go on."

Shivani then changed the subject.

John Lennon. They must have talked about him for blocks.

Since slipping out of the Monkey Bar, they had walked four short streets north, then one more west to the park. When they had arrived at the west end of the green, near Strawberry Fields, Shivani blurted it out.

"In the safety trials, they told us they were getting a signal."

"A what?" Griffin asked.

"It means numbers that stick out from the norm. It's much better than saying a pill is killing someone who's only taking it because they need an easy five hundred in a hurry. In this case, the drug was spinning off too many reports of a call to the trial administrator from the next of kin. It was going to look bad, to show up as a doubling of the risk."

"So," Griffin tried gently, "is this when you would have helped to move suicides into the placebo column?"

Funny way of putting that—"would have"—Shivani got up from the bench and started walking in the other direction. They *had* gotten a bit trolleyed.

"I want to watch the artists now," she called over her shoulder.

☙

They sat on a bench in front of a man drawing a sketch of a mother and her daughter.

"Let's say I saw it happen," Shivani offered.

"Ok, let's say you saw it happen. What's the it, by the way?"

Griffin had tried to ask the question with blasé affect. After starting cold in Michaels and warming up in the Monkey Bar, Shivani had grown cold on him here in the park.

"Let's just say the Bioferex spreadsheet was all out of whack."

Bioferex? He had asked her about Serotonal.

"Actually," Griffin said, "I think I remember reading that paper."

"Yeah, well, the data showed guys taking the bone drug had three times the suicidality as the people taking sugar pills. That they were doing Z-L-E-S."

"Zlezz?"

"Zombie Life-Ending Shite."

Shivani reached in her bag and pulled out a cigarette. She lit it, pulled a big drag and blew a slow train of smoke as she explained. "That was the term around the office. Z-L-E-S. I never saw any paperwork with my own eyes, but I heard enough to believe it."

"Such as?"

She pulled her cigarette to her lips and squinted as the smoke curled around her eyes.

"I don't know. How about a guy diving in the city wood chipper? Is that magazine-y enough for your boss? Maybe a soccer dad cutting into his femoral with a Bic?"

She tossed the smoke to the ground, then hit a tear quickly at the corner of her eye with the back of her palm.

"All anecdotes! The girl drinking petrol straight from the pump. An elective forearm amputation, self-administered without anesthesia. Our coders had done their loyal best. Called this one 'agitated' instead of suicidal. Called those episodes nightmares. Impulsivity, that was a fine bit of hand-waving. For me, impulsivity is a new bag at Bendel, not sucking back a gallon of bleach."

"What did you do?"

"Not we. They. Discharged them. Backed them out of the trial. Called them "de-consented, NRG.""

NRG. That was the acronym Breton warned him about.

"How many of people on the drug were moved into the placebo group?"

"Probably two. I never see stories, only numbers. They're not boneheads. We don't get any details. I didn't even *get* it. I asked one of the guys if they were taking agitated people during run-in and calling them placebo. I had never seen that kind of move since the Serotonal trials."

"So you now you're saying the Bioferex trials had moved suicidal events to placebo as well? You wrote to me because you said this was a problem with Serotonal…"

"It's a problem for both drugs," Shivani said. "But outside of the trials, they haven't seen suicides with Bioferex.

"You're sure about that?"

"No. But Jeremy was on the emails and that's *not* his area. I need someone to pry this open in the news. It's why I wrote you."

31

Jeremy Elton was officially getting his hands dirty. This despicable task atop the nation's greatest waterway. It was almost ten, he was thoroughly famished, and yet the final placebo suicide required for FDA approval of Bioferex for prevention of bone fracture—Patient 447 in federal trial registry number NCT00699837228—it had simply become impossible to produce through any other means.

This one, the suicide of Placebo Patient 447, known as Danny Bryan, 26, no known address, would need to be recorded in the CSR due at the FDA's White Oak complex by week's end. Doing so would remove the final obstacle delaying certification of Bioferex for prevention.

That report, a dense regulatory doorstop entitled *Rostangilorb (trade name Bioferex™) in the Prevention of Stress Fractures: A Six-week, Multicenter Trial,* after interminable delay in the hands of Shivani Patel before her foolish decision to leave the firm, would get Jeremy's employers off his back. The death of 447 would also unleash tens of millions in new revenue and insulate Jeremy from unwelcome questions vis-á-vis the Serotonal debacle.

It would do all this by pulling the signal below the all-powerful cutoff that was statistical significance, a threshold signifying events which happen rarely enough to be classified as chance, and somehow the receptacle into which all of Jeremy Raymond Elton's once-lofty therapeutic dreams had collapsed.

So no, he didn't need this, not one bit.

Jeremy would much rather have been back in the Chilean mountains, an all-expenses retreat he had left early in travelling to Saint Paul this morning in order to step forward and finish what others had started.

Instead of the Patagonian highlands, in her exquisite cruelty, fate had delivered him to the Lafayette Bridge, a wind-whipped, six-lane Mississippi river-crossing with a cracked roadbed, accumulating drifts of snow, and an over-trussed under-rigging he'd never hoped to see again. Life comes at you fast.

Jeremy and his charge Danny Bryan had begun to trade small talk. The pair looked at the old buildings along the shoreline. Jeremy needed the patient to stop daydreaming. The requisite correction to this behavior was ordinarily well within his grasp. Getting him up here had been painless. Just seventy-five dollars was all that it had taken to convince this tousled and unemployed occupant of *New Changes* to partake in this ruse, which was what again? That's right, an impromptu role-play for *fully informed compassion in the face of a suicidal imperative*, a burden shared by all residents of Danny's facility.

Jeremy periodically invaded an assortment of resources like *New Changes*, but this center had been unusually well-stocked with the ideal client: no immediate family, prone to recklessness and frequent self-harm, journal recordings of their nightmares and intrusive thoughts of ending it all. The problem was, this time, he needed more than just a suicidal gesture. He now needed a placebo-ingesting subject to cross the threshold.

Alexander Breton had correctly identified a jarring absence of suicides in the placebo arm for his previous trials of Serotonal. The FDA would eventually start looking for placebo suicides in the trials of Bioferex. The fate of Bioferex mattered to Jeremy, because Bioferex was, of course, an isomer of Serotonal, which itself was but a minor tweak of a compound isolated from the dried, root structure of the woody plant *rauwolfia serpentine*.

Rauwolfia, a folk medicine and sometimes wily sedative known as *the serpent* within ayurvedic medicine after the snake-like coils of its root structure, was a viper in more ways than one. A Janus-faced entry into the pharmaceutical story, it appeared early as the doomed hypertension molecule sold as reserpine. Few knew that a chemical cousin of the serpent had given the world its favorite antidepressant. Jeremy preferred to keep it that way. That project was becoming inherently more challenging, moreover, because the serpent was poised to become Bioferex, a pill for everyone.

"Come on, Danny," Jeremy said with quiet forcefulness, "this is no laughing matter."

Jeremy felt hopeful, as though things might finally be taking shape. Then again, this boy was so unlike the wrecks he ordinarily recruited from *New Changes* for his self-harming placebo arm. This one seemed thoughtful, confident, and not at all sad.

This work! All to save a *gym* drug. Jeremy knew this problem of runners becoming blunted while wracked with torment would not be so easily brushed aside, dismissed with the usual waving of hands. The side effect would lead to questions about Serotonal, and after that, its origins in the serpent.

People knew about the serpent. Rauwolfia had become a shorthand in his psychiatry texts for the ability of a compound to scar the human psyche. Now that legacy would become Jeremy's problem. Eventually, all of Jeremy's problems would become America's loss.

He was, after all, their psychiatrist.

Which was, in the end, why he had gotten on the plane to Minnesota.

Krøhn-McGill had discovered their scaling paradox so very late in the process.

To produce the appearance of a benefit, they would need to test Bioferex on thousands of patients. Conversely, a large trial virtually assured the appearance of a signal.

It was the classic good-bad conundrum. To show medical benefit, you needed a large trial. To hide a side effect, you needed a small trial. You can't have them both. Given the size of the trial they needed to launch—2,293 subjects in 42 trial centers—a side-effect within just five percent of users would produce almost 100 acts of self-harm or violence.

Try creatively miscoding those reports in the data.

"The akathisia will show up once we get over five hundred subjects, gentlemen."

Mitch and Seamus had given Jeremy a full hour to make his case. He had wasted little time putting the facts on the table.

"You're asking too much of this pill," he had told them. "It's only Serotonal. It's not going to prevent stress fractures. Antidepressants are *sedatives*, functionally, with a little activation and emotional blunting thrown in for good measure. Serotonal's not even an especially strong antidepressant. Sure, it's made us all a lot of money. We've had a fine run in the meadows with this thing and we've even helped a few patients. But it's a *sloppy* pill. It throws a *bowling ball* into the monoamine system. You may tell yourself it's the Eucharist, but I can assure you, Serotonal does not target disease proper, and its strongest effects are *side* effects.

"You want to market Serotonal for something new? Call it an anti-aphrodisiac, then give it to sex offenders. Eucharist, hah! This pill is more like a *mal*charist. If your subjects are like 20 to 70 percent of users, they will lose all genital sensitivity within weeks, some of them for good. At least a quarter of them are going to get the nightmares."

Jeremy had said all of this to Seamus and Mitch during their meetings in the penthouse at the Lancaster. He had repeated it to them during their stolen conversations at the AAP. The pair remained immovable, and continued their orders that he build a trial big enough to cause Bioferex to appear effective in preventing stress fractures.

Should Jeremy fail, it was implied if never stated directly, regulators would get to run loose on his early work for Serotonal, a drug about to go generic and therefore one they no longer needed to defend in the marketplace. Jeremy had hoped that his speeches would have turned the tide. If anything, his protestations had led Seamus and Mitch to begin viewing him with suspicion.

Their betrayal galled him. Did they not appreciate *all that he had done for them?* They couldn't possibly understand how these medications worked. Mitch and Seamus barely understood how to test them. Krøhn-McGill had left it up to *him*, Jeremy Elton, to shepherd their tweak of reserpine through the early Serotonal trials—the worst of all CROs. Now it had all come down to this: getting Danny Bryan, his final placebo suicide, onto the books. It was all *his* job, here on this *highway* bridge, in god-awful *St. Paul.*

The hell with it. Jeremy had come up with this plan on his own.

Someone had to live in the real world. America's Psychiatrist had been needed once again, this time to bridge the gap between the promise of their beloved drug's financials and its disappointing safety profile, ensuring for them in so doing his status as a researcher in good standing and a force of healing above all suspicion, a healer in pursuit of the betterment of humanity.

So, yes, his purpose was clear.

He needed to get this noncompliant daydreamer, like, now, to jump off the Lafayette Bridge.

∽

"What are you thinking, Danny, now in this troubling moment."

Jeremy had taken care to use Danny's name early and often. He had made sure to touch the side of his arm as well, at least twice. Human contact is a powerful force.

"Can you verbalize your thoughts?" Jeremy continued. "Feel free to step closer to the edge, if that helps. Because we need to really *understand* your thinking, Danny, were this final choice to be thrust upon you. Then you can help others.

"Does it feel ennobling, somehow? Remember, if we can just tap into your state of mind at this very moment of crisis, we can use that information to help others prevent the terrible mistake of considering suicide in their lives. So, are you thinking, 'just get it over with?'"

Danny was bobbing his head from side to side, like ear buds set on the B-52s. Jeremy peered into the darkness below, thinking only of the Buddha, centering himself as he had learned to do during times of high stress. He had noted with frustration that Danny's head was no longer bobbing, but was now rotating on the frontal plane. It had become a silent protest, in other words, a disastrous no meaning *no*. Danny was now smiling.

"You're high."

"Danny."

"Think of what you're saying, Dr. Fuckendorfer."

"Danny."

"Standing up here, I'll tell you what I feel, I feel like shitting my pants, if you really want to know. That's one long drop."

Danny looked up at him with a shake of his head.

"Dude it's windy," Danny laughed. "I'm not going anywhere near that fucking ledge."

Elton felt the first traces of panic. Danny was the last Number Needed to Harm. He was a final placebo death on the books to get the filings within acceptability ratios. But he was nowhere near being talked into it.

"Danny, let's reframe for a moment," Jeremy said calmly. "Look at the illuminated bank over there."

Elton pointed at the old First National Bank, a glorious tower of stone with a soaring, "1st" from the 1920s. As Danny turned his head in the light, he kept his feet pointing towards the road. *At least I won't have to see his face this time,* Jeremy thought, as then he pushed the boy backwards in the center of his chest.

Because his feet were facing the road, Danny managed to elongate his tumble for an instant, teetering, swinging his free leg forward, then cart-wheeling over the rail. One leg briefly pointed straight down, with the other back at Elton. Then he soared like a bird into the night.

It wasn't as bad as he thought. Certainly not like the last time he had done this, back when Jeremy had to push his older brother to his death as a child. Jeremy comforted himself in the thought that came next: *No one would ever understand the toil that Jeremy Elton had undertaken to reduce the stigma of mental illness.*

He departed the bridge, free of his task, eager to record the death and set the books right for Bioferex. His heart was racing; the blood began to rush to his face. He began practicing a set of calming rituals he had acquired at a workshop in Santa Barbara. Then he looked up to see a shambles come bounding down the riverbank.

Jeremy wrestled his breath under control just long enough to tell the man about the tragedy, making sure to use all the wistful wordplay that had dazzled supplicant Jeremy Elton interviewers all these many years, explaining his brave role in attempting to right the universe to no avail. Much to his relief, the shambles didn't appear to recognize him as America's Psychiatrist.

In another win, the kid smelled like weed.

Up at the street, Jeremy spotted an illuminated delivery sign atop the young man's beater. A poorly drawn logo: *Waiter on Wheels*. The relic reminded Jeremy of still another pressing problem. *He'd* never gotten any dinner.

Reaching inside the Kia, there awaited his prize. Jeremy smiled at providence in the form of a biodegradable pod of take-out, all of it placed here for his nourishment. He got into his Lexus and drove away.

32

Griffin returned from a long run with Lee Majors when his phone began to wail like a dying person in terrific pain. He was feeling jittery and thought a breather might erase the murderous browser history of his soul, but no. He had begun pacing his apartment when he picked up the call and dropped to an arm of his couch, his left knee bouncing.

"'Shello."

"Gavin Wagner?"

"It's Griffin. Griffin Wagner. The only name I got."

"Oh, sorry, I knew that. That came out wrong."

"No worries."

"Whit Pearl, Hearst Media."

Hearst was corporate for *Esquire*. The December issue would have shipped by now. It gave Griffin a small feeling of confidence to imagine the clock-tower gears of Hearst publicity grinding in coordination, all to hump his word dump on medical ghostwriting. The caller's blasé mangling of Griffin's name did manage to return him to his properly small place in the movement of the planets.

"So we have been getting a little bounce here in the office from your feature, the one on the ghostwriter, what was she, something medical you said?"

Bounce, funny.

That's all Griffin could do these days. Bounce. Pace. Anything to relieve the compulsion.

"Oh, good."

"Sure. Bounce is good. So, you are free to do media this week?"

"You mean talk to people?"

The idea was alarming.

"We have requests for TV, yes, and we—I'm in publicity, sorry I didn't say that right away. Sorry, also, I haven't read the piece yet, probably obvious, but I'm looking forward to it."

Griffin knew this apology well. Everyone says they haven't read your article but are looking forward to reading it. They never read it.

Was any of this worth it? His life had been such a long series of failures.

"But we have pushed the story to all the top venues and there's interest in network radio. What else...I think *NPR* got back to us, a couple of newspapers, some regional morning shows. We didn't try to put you on the morning shows, not thinking that's a good fit. They don't tend to go after the sponsors, you know. Looks like here's a few AM stations. Says here Harrison Reed wants you on again."

"All sounds great," Griffin said.

Harrison Reed, that happened.

"Sorry, Gavin, could you hang on a second?"

Griffin heard Whit Pearl cup a hand over the phone, then the sound of muffled commands. *Whit Pearl,* exactly what kind of psychopathic name was that?

Griffin's *Esquire* fixer had apparently hailed from three generations of Manhattan publishing, the snake. Probably had grandparents on Central Park West.

Whoops, Whit Pearl was back on the phone. He couldn't read a person's mind, right?

Right???

Griffin should have been happy. Yet here he was less than nothing.

"Yeah, that would be cool." Griffin said.

"How about you go talk to Harrison sooner than later?" Whit offered. "If he likes you, he can pull you on to the Morning Show. We will get you in-studio this time—no link-up."

The fuck. Now he had to fly again? Griffin realized he could throw his face inside the oven—it's not like there was a law against it or anything.

They traded details and Griffin hung up. His leg was bouncing, and he had kicked at the crate that served as his coffee table. If he didn't get off this couch and start moving soon he was going to smash it into pieces.

თ

Getting his story into the Hearst publicity office triggered Griffin's recollection of his other encounter with a back room for the storied publisher, the strange way in which the estimable *Esquire* fact-checking team had focused on what seemed to Griffin like the least-important facts. Griffin's article on Shivani had suggested a powerful pharmaceutical manufacturer manipulated a trial, misleading the FDA to approve a pair of drugs that were deadly. Those assertions seemed inherently worth vetting.

Instead, the chief of research at *Esquire*, a woman named Claire Tracy, had kept Griffin on the phone for several lengthy calls probing anodyne matters like, "whether we can really describe an osteoblast as a single-cell organism?" Claire wasn't sure. "What's the proof," Claire had demanded in this same phone call after much shuffling of papers, "for your assertion that 10K's are the most popular of all the so-called 'weekend warrior races'?"

Griffin was stymied.

"And does the midtown tavern where you interviewed Ms. Patel really sell Maker's Mark single batch? Because the bar manager told me it might have been the blend."

"I would be so much more comfortable," Griffin had replied at the time, "if we spent our time making contact with my sources. Did you ever get a hold of Shivani Patel? I'd love for her to have looked at some of the math."

Claire paused. Griffin had awaited her answer with a slight case of the nerves. He had never spoken with Shivani after their walk in Central Park, and they had only communicated by intermittent text. As he suspected, Shivani had more or less disappeared on him. He had never before closed a story without a primary source on hand, even just for email.

"Oh, her?" Claire replied. "Yes, we talked about whether to contact her. My editor-in-chief believes that since Ms. Patel has emailed us that she is traveling and unable to be contacted by phone, that your hand-written notes are good enough. Though we all felt it would have been helpful had you tape-recorded her."

"What about her bosses," Griffin said. "Did they ever call you back?"

"I am still waiting," Claire had replied. "I've left two messages and sent three emails. But as long as we tried to contact them, we are covered legally."

Strange. Griffin had never known a company to snub a call from fact-checking. On the bright side, Claire Tracy had agreed to keep the line about the 10K. She had finally confirmed the detail after searching the website of the *American College of Sports Medicine*.

"I locked it!" she wrote to Griffin 1:45 a.m. on the night that his story went to print. "I'm going home," she wrote. "Yay!"

Fact checkers were always nicest to you right before they put the piece to press.

"I hope you have a wonderful night!"

Reading his piece that night for the very last time, Griffin had taken a parting inventory of his story. He had included his failed attempts to speak with Deadline Medical, Jeremy Elton, and Krøhn-McGill. Claire had inserted the word "allegedly" in front of each suggestion of wrongdoing. The entire piece had been vetted from top to bottom. So maybe he could relax? After all, he normally did just that when a story went to press. Except with this one, he couldn't stop thinking the article possessed an enormous weak spot.

It all rested on Shivani's word.

༠

The issue of *Esquire* featuring Griffin's byline finally surfaced in the grocery store. He grabbed a copy for Ron and Catherine, a copy for his coffee table, and a third to toss into a trunk.

"Did you mean to take three?"

The checkout guy was fucking with him.

"Never mind I don't want them," Griffin said.

He left the magazines on the counter and headed for the door.

"Hey! I just was making sure you meant to buy them?"

"Fuck straight off."

Jeezus, where did these people come from?

༠

The next morning Griffin took a call in his cramped Minneapolis kitchen at 6:47 am. The dreams were weird again last night. He had woken up crying. Now he was foggy about everything.

"So we are here with Gilman Wagner, boy that's a great name, and he's calling us from New York where he has written a heck of an interesting piece asking important questions in this month's *Esquire*: How is it that drugs today work? *Do* they work? Are you getting your money's worth? Or is there a *better* way to treat our illnesses?"

Guy Raymond on KNSZ AM out of Wichita—Voice of the Heartland—was talking in a stagey basso. An assistant had put Griffin's call through to the studio line. Guy had clearly not so much as skimmed Griffin's article and come on like they were old friends.

There were sixteen interviews calling in before noon. Griffin had been lingering over the terrible mistakes in his past.

"That's a great question, Guy," Griffin started. He was walking a part of the apartment where the floorboards wouldn't yell. "I'm so glad you asked…"

Full Aperture with Harrison Reed had booked him for the next evening. Griffin flew out at lunch Sunday and touched down at LaGuardia by three, whereupon he caught a cab to the studios in Times Square. The flight had toyed with him. He had been confined to a window seat and had prayed for a crash. As the cab let him out on Forty-eighth the woman sent down to grab him appeared to see the garbage in his soul.

He had no idea how to answer her questions.

"Whatever everyone else does is fine," he said.

"Well, most people here for TV arrive with their own makeup tech."

He looked at his hands.

"We can find someone upstairs."

"Be sure to not bob your legs while you're on the air," Trina said. Griffin must have been bouncing his knee while Trina powdered his face. He had needed relief from the axe scraping out the inside of his kneecap.

They got out of the room with the mirrors surrounded by lightbulbs. She pointed at a green room, then headed in a separate direction.

On the famous Harrison Reed set, Griffin gamely grabbed the celebrity's outstretched paw and shook it though his fingers trembled. He tried to ignore a powerful sensation of wanting to leave. It appeared as though Harrison, busily flipping through the pages of the *Esquire*, was on the other side of a river. Griffin remembered how you made conversation, heard the soundtrack to the show, then watched the lights go dark as his knees began once again to bounce.

"We're here again with Griffin Wagner," his unknowable host intoned, "the author of a new article in this month's *Esquire* entitled 'The Lady Who Makes Your Drug Appear Safe Wants to Go Forth and Sin No More.'"

"And I must say, that's quite a long title, Griffin Wagner, welcome back to the show." Harrison smiled. It was a warm smile. Griffin did not want to kick the table leg any harder than this little bit. It gave him just a taste of relief.

"Thanks, it's great to be here."

"So, medical ghostwriting," Harrison said. "Tell me about this?"

The words came out. Griffin saw them on a wall, read them, and tried not to interfere.

"Well, Harrison, the pathway to market for everything you find at the pharmacy begins in medical journals, as scientists publish their findings on the experiments that broaden our understanding of human health."

Harrison was looking down at his notes.

"So I learned a great deal about how much these papers are the work of hired guns," Griffin continued, "science written by marketing professionals posing as clinical researchers. It's troubling. This process of creating evidence for the FDA seems have become a pantomime of science."

"A pantomime of science," said Harrison, "explain that, please."

Harrison was letting Griffin say it. That felt nice. This was different than last time. Last time they'd done this show, Griffin was already on the defensive. A camera man moved closer. Griffin felt a sharp zap in his head and it shook him.

"What I mean by pantomime of science," Griffin stated through the pain, "is that we want to make sure these articles are written by scientists, not salesmen. And it turns out that they are almost entirely written by salesmen."

"You mean ghostwriters."

The pain was holding. Cauterizing his brain.

"Exactly, Harrison. There is a robust industry of so-called medical communications specialists who are contracted by drug and device firms. They write academic papers and scientific presentations. It looks like the work of clinical researchers, but it's all done by contractors for hire, with the end goal of making it appear as though the researchers themselves had conducted all the studies."

"And they have not?"

"No, to the contrary, the contribution of most academics in these cases is limited to having rented the use of their name."

"And this is common?"

"Very. The majority of medical literature on new drugs is conducted in contract research organizations, or C.R.O.s for short. Their results are then ghostwritten into papers for publication."

"And this is all legal?"

"It's not against the law or even the ethical codes that govern practice in the various specialties. Think of it as a loophole big enough to drive through with a bus wrapped in vinyl humping Bioferex."

Griffin had seen a bus advertising Bioferex on his cab in from the airport. Harrison didn't look amused.

"Your source?"

Griffin felt the vastness of New York falling on top of him. He took in the thought of his comic vulnerability here in the backfat of Midtown, all of its makers who could wish him harm.

"The existence of a medical communications industry is uncontested," Griffin replied, "though they tend to keep a low profile. But hey, my story had the participation of a medical ghostwriter, a charming and brilliant person with a fat pile of academic papers on popular drugs. Her name is Shivani Patel. Gaining her participation was invaluable. Ghostwriters never talk about what it is that they do. Most of them are tied into long-term confidentiality deals."

"What's her story?"

Griffin thought about how best to answer that.

What did he really know about her anyway?

"She's British. She has had her hand in hundreds of papers. I supposed she decided she had enough."

"But she didn't come on the show with you today," Harrison said.

That's true. She had indeed been hard to track down over the last couple of weeks.

"No," Griffin said. "That's...I mean, she is a source, and has her own life."

"Your article supplied no photographs of her."

"Right..."

Where was this going?

"I understand her conversation with you is the only contact she has had with the media?"

"Correct, I think she was..."

"Because we are hearing something different about this sourcing from a researcher whose work has been implicated by your piece. Following publication of the article we were contacted by someone you had engaged with on our show a few months ago."

Harrison turned to look at an in-studio monitor.

For fuck's sake.

"Remote from Vail, Colorado, where he is attending a high-level gathering of clinical trialists, we are pleased to welcome back Dr. Jeremy Elton. Dr. Elton, welcome to the program!"

Griffin was dumbfounded. He steadied himself in his chair, grabbing his knees to stop their moving. It felt like ants.

They had seated Jeremy in front of a backdrop depicting a craggy Alpine tableau not unlike that welcoming Julie Andrews in *The Sound of Music*. With his rugged suede overcoat and ruddy glow, America's Psychiatrist looked as though he had just stepped off of a freshly-groomed blue run with Robert Redford.

"This article runs headlong against a host of statutes concerning intellectual property and publishing, Harrison," Jeremy said. "I'm sorry, I just have to be honest."

What?

Griffin moved to speak up in his own defense, but heeded the long fingers of Harrison Reed signaling he was still talking.

"You weren't contacted for comment?"

"We tried to contact you repeatedly, Dr. Elton." Griffin said.

"And how exactly does the article run into publishing case law?"

"Where to begin," Elton offered. "The disclosure of trade secrets. The breach of confidentiality agreements. The clinical study reports quoted are explicitly nonpublic by statute and the references to case report forms is *highly* worrying…And for the record, I don't know anyone named Shivani Patel."

Griffin felt as if he had flown through a windshield and delivered his body onto the pavement, rolling, rolling, flesh and bones in a pile, an event he'd been forced to watch intrusively over the last few nights. The last of these charges was beyond belief.

Now they were denying the existence of Shivani Patel?

"That's…*strange*," Griffin said, leaning forward on Harrison's table. "I saw her working your side at the Chicago meeting of the American Academy of Psychiatry."

"Perhaps you presumed you saw her," said Elton with a small laugh, not missing a breath. "Had you tried to confirm her existence with her supposed employer you would quickly have found they have never employed anyone with that name. Really it's remarkable to me Harrison this article ever made it into print. My lawyers will find ample grounds for legal action."

The next few minutes felt like hours.

Cross talk.

Elton was a wall of sound, conceding nothing, countering Griffin's every reply.

He had learned you could say anything, that TV was an exhaust fan.

Griffin's tongue had gone dry. Staring into his TPN coffee mug, he saw that it had never even been filled with water. Had he been sent out here to die?

"Let's hit the pause here, gentlemen," Harrison said. "And pick apart some facts."

He reclined in thought, then allowed Jeremy to careen back into more of the same.

Griffin had made up Shivani Patel.

Just, made her up, like a plagiarist-fabulist, con-man.

It was now on TV, so that made it true.

Griffin felt his face become hot, his palms grow moist.

You had to know this would happen.

The thought came to him out of nowhere.

You write for bro magazines. You should have stuck to cologne. You should die.

In the distance, Griffin could hear Jeremy blasting away. In the monitor, Griffin's face appeared as wide as the screen, even though moments earlier they had shot him from three-quarters.

"OK, I don't know what's going on," Griffin interjected, holding up a hand to signal a pause, only to notice it was shaking. "But this is *insane*. I spent *hours* with Shivani Patel. We had drinks. We walked throughout Central Park. I can get you the receipts and introduce you to the waiters."

Drinks, that sounded great.

Harrison jumped in.

"You had drinks with this person?"

"Yes."

"And you have tapes of your conversation?"

Fuck.

Griffin shook his head no.

"But you must know where she lives?"

"Like I said, we met in Midtown. You can Google her."

"We will," Elton said.

"Did you see her in her office?" Harrison asked

"The two of us saw *you*, Dr. Elton—you were coming out of the Lancaster."

Jeremy laughed, running his hand through his hair.

"Well, if you saw me on the street, you should have come forward and said *hello*. If she really knew me, she should have greeted me. Why didn't she greet me?"

Why didn't she?

"Because she was with me, presumably."

Griffin almost winced.

"Was there a *problem*?" Elton was now whispering, marshalling a pastoral voice of kindness. "You didn't think I had some kind of grievance with you, I hope? Son, I talk to reporters twenty times a week. I doubt I would have remembered you."

Son. He was good at this.

"Very well," Griffin said. "I will call up Miss Patel after this show is over and we can verify her existence." His voice was now quivering. "Then you can apologize for the suggestion I created my primary source."

"Correction," Elton said with palpable sadness. "Your *only* source."

Harrison tapped his papers.

"This is clearly a contentious topic, gentlemen," he said kindly, "one that will develop over time." Harrison Reed then cut to the break, and an assistant swooped in from the shadows to remove Griffin's wire. Though he was just five feet away, Harrison Reed didn't so much as offer Griffin a nod goodbye.

Griffin began walking towards a coat rack. The TV studio melted into a cubicle hive, and he escaped through a set of doors. He looked downward to recognize a text that had come through from Trevor:

> Wagner.
> what the fuck was that?

Dialing Shivani's number before he had hit the elevator, Griffin's call rolled into a recording, whereupon he became nauseous.

"The number you have reached," a voice offered drably, "is not in service. Please check your number and dial again."

33

Jeremy Elton was uninspired by the offerings at his lunchtime rest stop, a luxury dining lodge 11,000 feet up the Vail range of Colorado. For optimal comfort during his clomp through the mountain-pass chow line, he had unbuckled the latches of his $1,295 Lucite-and-carbon ski boots. His feet were now comfortable if his mind was ill at ease.

Seared tuna with wasabi and mango, where had he seen that before?

Lobster bisque with sherry, so nothing for the locavore?

The non-GMO-conscientious?

"Can I help you?"

Jeremy was still wearing his ski helmet and bearing the weight of this lunch. The clerk had dark eyes, thick, lustrous hair and olive skin. Her name tag read

Angelista
Buenos Aries

She could have sold skin cream at Barneys.

It was Jeremy's turn to make a selection, and while a haggard lane of famished Republicans had snaked behind him, a thought from the heart had stirred within.

Ignoring *Angelista* and the 10-person tray-line hoping just to pay, with a single pointer finger Jeremy typed a 140-character homily to his 667.2K Twitter followers in the US, Europe, Australia, Singapore and the United Kingdom.

> @DrEltonMD: Enchanting back bowls can't compete with the sounds of woodpeckers in the Aspen. #AAPA2011 #alltitudeattitude #alwaysbepresent

"Sir?"

Jeremy Elton looked over his Tweet once again for misspellings. He changed "enchanting" to "beguiling," then back to "enchanting." He accepted the Tweet button.

The moment should have spiked his outlook, but as he knew, wherever you go, there you are. And he was here. Abandoning his position, Jeremy clomped across the slate to *Santa Fe Crossing*, a grilling station moving southwestern fare. He sampled the soup, derided it as briny, then signaled to

Rex
Brisbane, Queensland

to ladle up a serving of High Desert Buffalo Chili.

A description noted the soup would require $14.95 a cup, $25.75 a bowl from his Krøhn-McGill Emerald Card. Inspired, Jeremy instructed Rex to load up his bowl with shredded Manchego and ancho-lime sour cream, which he had duly pronounced "crema."

"Pleasure, sir," Rex chimed, building the serving with care before wiping all stray droplets and finishing the presentation with a sprig of cilantro. Taking it all in, Jeremy winced. Something wasn't right. Holding the carefully-constructed meal with palpable grief, America's Psychiatrist had no choice but to abandon the food there on the counter.

The chili looked fine. It just wasn't a chili day.

He could not have known that until he held it in his hands.

"Always be present," Jeremy reminded himself, feeling only

compassion for Rex and more importantly, Jeremy Elton. Yesterday he had been called upon to once again derail a broadcast interview on *Full Aperture with Harrison Reed*, a thoroughly unpleasant task involving the despicable journalist who had lured Patel out into the open.

He had three talks to give, the snow on the back bowls was icy, and he was barely being paid. Compounding his burdens, Jeremy would be working with slides prepared by Patel, meaning any questions addressing data were now on him.

Clomping back to the sushi station, Jeremy settled on the Sustainable Harvest Rainbow Rolls, adding a bowl of Tom ka Gai and an overpriced bottle of San Pellegrino to his rapidly destabilizing tray. Waiting to pay, he grabbed a pair of cookies from a basket stationed at the checkout.

"Seventy-seven dollars and ninety-seven cents with tax."

This one had a name tag that read

Catherine
Adelaide, SA

Jeremy handed over his card as his phone began vibrating.

The ID said MSG.

Jeremy took the call, smiling warmly at Catherine's offer of a slip for him to sign, but making no move to receive it. The line could wait. They would get to tell their friends *you'll never believe who we saw while waiting to buy lunch.*

"Yes."

"Jeremy. It's Mitch. The skiing is good, I hope."

"It's a fine meeting," Jeremy replied. "But the snow is rutted on the front side and the village is overrun with families."

Mitch met the comment with silence. All these coastal fops were partial to icy and uncivil Vermont.

"What can I do for you?" Jeremy said as he signed for the overpriced tray and began his clomp into a dining room with a cathedral ceiling and an enormous boulder fireplace.

"What was that last night?"

Mitch was peeved. As Jeremy had guessed he would be.

"That was a TV interview, of course," Jeremy replied.

He was wandering the hall as he talked, this Cirque du Soleil of sushi and Thai in both hands. He had slipped the cell into a strap positioned across his chest. The accessory transmitted their battle into a $400 headset he'd fitted inside a $900 helmet. He'd learned to provide psychiatric sessions during blue runs but wasn't ready to address Oedipal conflicts while navigating moguls. The black runs tended to require his full attention.

"Jeremy. You made a decision without authorization to deny the existence of your personal ghostwriter, someone we have employed for decades and who has been credited in hundreds of papers. You do realize she has been at your side at dozens of academic meetings?"

Fucking Mitch. Such a weak man.

Jeremy shook his head at the loss. His time in the service of these people.

He knew what this was about. Payback for his doubts about Bioferex.

"Patel played a small role," Jeremy replied. "She's now in the past. The reporter is a nothing and a nobody. This story is over."

The room was noisy. Jeremy was yelling into the translucent air of Colorado.

He had returned to the checkout line.

"Sheila!"

Catherine from Adelaide looked up at him.

"This cookie has three M&M's."

Jeremy had taken note of the low candy count and become enraged. He tossed the snack in her cash drawer, breaking pieces over the slots for fives and tens. "I'm trying the peanut butter now," he said, then picked up a replacement and clomped away.

"Let's hope she's a nobody and a nothing," replied Mitch, who, if he had heard the fracas was not letting on. "I fail to see why you boxed us in on live TV. We now have to roll back her digital footprint, an unfathomably expensive errand, given her thousands of credits scattered across the internet. Security will have to locate her physical person, then financially or otherwise persuade her to become invisible."

"I hardly think it was helping to leave your ghostwriter's credibility intact upon the conclusion of that interview," Elton said. "But, sure, what do I know? I'm only the author of your most important papers."

Mitch remained silent. He would have needed to stifle reflux at the notion that Jeremy considered himself an author in the proper sense.

"That's right, what do you know?" said Mitch. "The *Esquire* story would have been a small curiosity in the unending landslide of magazine pap. Now we have a bona-fide media drama. Your allegation that a reporter made up his source has a considerable half-life in the news cycle. This was an unforced error. You're better than that."

"Clearly I was on the show to discredit him," Jeremy said, staring at a condiment station. "What's it matter if I did so by erasing her? I chose a permanent solution. You're welcome. Nobody recovers from that one."

"Let's hope you're right," Mitch said. "This crossed a line. I won't mince words. You're officially on notice."

"I'm on notice," Jeremy laughed. "That's rich."

He made sure to hang up first. It was but a tap on a button in his chest strap. Although he missed the button the first time, causing audible sounds as he hung up of Mitch saying "Jeremy, the thing is, it comes down to this…"

The room entirely full, Jeremy colonized a tile in front of the condiments station, placing his tray in front of the pumps for ketchup and mustard. Removing his ski helmet and shaking out his hair, he picked up his chopsticks and began devouring the rainbow rolls, oblivious to the arrival of families seeking access to the napkins and mayonnaise he had taken out of service.

A family guy stared.

"The fuck you looking at?" Jeremy barked.

Leaning backwards, he tilted his head to signal his relinquishing of the napkins for a father of two small tots.

"Sorry," Jeremy offered. "There's nowhere to take your lunch in this place."

34

"Did a novice reporter impugn the nation's leading scientific journals by inventing a so-called 'medical ghostwriter'? That's the troubling question raised this week during a curious interview on *Full Aperture with Harrison Reed.*"

Griffin heard the buttery intonation of a public radio lead-in while making a fried egg sandwich in his apartment. It was late in the morning and he had been up for three and half days, most of it spent walking circles in his apartment, tamping down thoughts of getting split open by the rail lines along Hiawatha.

He had ruled out a hanging. Though it sounded like relief, a noose would require rope, and he had not left his place since crashing on his return from New York.

He had used the time to think over a plan, one in which he could take all the money he'd earned from his break by way of Mitch St. Germaine, then drive to the coastline and walk straight into the ocean. It felt intuitively, mythically seductive—as though this ending would free him of all pain, releasing it below the deepest shelf of the Pacific where it might never hurt anyone again.

Unfortunately, while Mitch had promised him the world, Griffin's *Esquire* check hadn't arrived, and now he wondered if it was never coming. With forty-eight hours of trying to make his arms stop flaying, Griffin had just enough in the bank to get him to Utah, considering all the alcohol he'd need in order to stay breathing until Wednesday.

Now he was home and really going mad. Making breakfast, Griffin had mistakenly tried three wrong nobs before killing the burner to hear a man destroying life as he knew it. As he listened, Griffin watched his hands become the shaker at his paint store.

"Good morning, this is Robert Rice."

"Lee Majors," Griffin asked, "are they really talking about me?"

But Lee Majors had now taken to hiding when Griffin was home.

"Earlier this week, a reporter named Griffin Wagner encountered the explosive charge of inventing his source in the latest issue of *Esquire*. The story, one challenging the credibility of nearly every clinical trial, was based on an interview Wagner said he had conducted with a supposed medical ghostwriter named Shivani Patel. The counter-charge, that Wagner had fabricated all of it, was levelled by noted psychiatrist and bestselling author Dr. Jeremy Elton, who, we should disclose, is a regular contributor to the popular National Public Radio series 'Lives of the Mind.' In the program's pivotal exchange, Dr. Elton asserted that Patel simply did not exist."

Griffin heard the report trigger Elton's whopper to end all whoppers.

"For the record," listeners heard Elton say all over again. *"I don't know anyone named Shivani Patel."*

And then it was back to Robert Rice.

"This morning, we talk to the editor of that magazine."

Like the Elton ambush, Griffin had no idea that this take-out on his flame-out had been coming. *Don't they call you for comment anymore?*

And what was this business about him being a novice reporter?

Griffin looked around the living room, spotting his phone in the cushions of the couch. As he listened to the Rice interviewing *Esquire's*

David Nichols, Griffin pulled up his call history only to discover three messages had rolled in to his voicemail from a number in 202. That would have been NPR. Had he muted? Griffin didn't remember ever doing that.

"To be honest, we haven't had a lot of time to get to the bottom of this," Nichols told Morning Edition host Robert Rice. "But our fact-checking team vets every article inside and out. We have full confidence in both the piece and Griffin Wagner."

"Tell us more about him, if you wouldn't mind," said the host. "He doesn't write for you very often, isn't that correct?"

"No this was our first article together."

"For the record," Rice interjected, "We reached out to Griffin Wagner for comment but were unsuccessful…"

"The fuck you did!"

Slumped into his couch, Griffin shouted his retort in full-throated objection, then heard Lee Majors dart behind a door in the hall.

Who turned off his phone?

The story went on a bit longer, then mercifully came to an end.

Just the facts about a lie. Nothing about his story on academic fraud. Nothing about the manipulation of clinical trials. Nothing about Serotonal, Bioferex or the side effect.

"This would appear to be a fine moment," as Rice had sagely concluded, "for society to ask how much of what is reported is safely known to be true."

"Indeed it would!" Griffin called out to the ceiling once more.

He turned off the radio and looked at his phone. A handful of messages had appeared on his voicemail. He listened once more to the clip from Whit Pearl.

"In light of this episode," his *Esquire* contact had stated only hours after the program, "we have decided to part ways until all the dust settles."

A separate recording was logged by a seventeen-digit caller.

Griffin told himself he would take just this last message, then go buy ten feet of rope.

251

"Mr. Wagner, it's Alexander Breton."

It jolted him to hear the academic's New Zealand accent just as Griffin's life imploded.

"I caught a clip of you just now in my morning news feed," Breton continued.

So, even New Zealand.

"Keep the faith," Breton said. "This move—destroying a journalist on live TV, it seems new for them. You must have damaged them in some way that has got Jeremy Elton freelancing. More importantly, have you taken something? A drug, I mean. Because at the bottom of my screen I saw that your hand appeared to be shaking. In a signature pattern."

Griffin's hand had been jerking like this for so long he could no longer even see it anymore. Right now, for instance, his phone was moving, but as all the other markers of his decline had accelerated he'd just accepted it.

"You didn't go on to one of these and quit cold turkey did you? You know quitting requires a lengthy taper, right? Because if you are indeed rattled, you need to find yourself some kind of cold medicine straight away. Over the counter will do it. If you can't get some of that go find a cigarette. This thing is going to go to work on your head if it hasn't already. Has it? How *is* your head? Even a benzo. But don't take those for too long or you will have a new problem on your hands. Get going."

Griffin found a drugstore and bought two bottles of cold pills. He took a double dose by the back door and felt his darkness lifting within a half hour. He felt a growing horror over what he had escaped. The signs had been all around and yet he'd taken up its logic as that of his own free will. Once he got home, Griffin couldn't believe what had become of his apartment. On a spot over his television, two knives had been driven into the wall. Is that how had he made Lee Majors so frightened? Who had shattered his remote?

Wired up on cold medicine, Griffin fell to his bed and slept without nightmares for the first time in weeks, and for twenty-one hours. Still knocked out on antihistamine, he managed to pick up his phone as a reporter called just after 9 am. Griffin listened to him explain his purpose, while drinking a glass of water with two more antihistamines, staring blankly in the distance.

The *Times* had put two reporters on his story, one asking the questions, the other listening in. Griffin had been given a half hour to explain his position when they finally showed their hand.

"So, do you have a recording you could share of your interview with her?"

It was an embarrassingly proper request.

"...Something other than notes from your memory?"

Griffin cursed how stupid he had been, failing to record Shivani whoever she was. He ran through the reasons in his head: he had wanted not to scare her off. He was not used to cagey sources. There was all the drinking (what was that about, and in the afternoon, no less).

She had kissed him, gotten him loaded, and done away with the norms.

Had she done all that on purpose? The dead air as he pondered those matters had grown long.

"Griffin?"

"I don't have a recording of the interview,' Griffin finally said. "I realize that looks bad. But she does indeed exist. There has to be proof of her work online."

"I have looked with great care, actually," said the second reporter, very likely the grunt in the operation. "I have searched for the name Shivani Patel on Google Scholar, PubMed, even our terminal here, a private news database known as Lexis-Nexis. There's nothing stored with her name in the digital realm."

Griffin noted how young the grunt sounded.

How had he gotten into the field, and at the *Times*, no less, without ever writing bro-service?

"Well, she's got to be somewhere in the stacks," Griffin said to the lucky bastard. "They can't pull her out of every musty journal on the shelves."

"Richard?" The grunt was handing that one off to his boss.

"Sure," his boss replied. "It's possible her name is printed on paper in some journal. That would be great for your defense. But the only way to find those articles is through search engines, and they do not know of her."

Griffin wanted to smash something. A leftover craving.

"Libraries don't have card catalogs?"

"They got rid of those years ago."

Griffin thought this was again the grunt speaking, but the connection had gone bad.

"Did you look her up at Hopkins?" Griffin replied. "She would have gotten a master's degree in the nineteen-nineties."

"I don't see how that helps establish," said the more seasoned of the two *Times* gunners, "that you interviewed a medical ghostwriter."

"I honestly don't know what to say," Griffin said, feeling aware of a powerful sleepiness coming over him again. "You found me pretty easily, but you can't find her. They must have done something to scrub her from the internet."

"Well, that would be a first for me," said the first reporter.

"Mr. Wagner the web is a decentralized network," added the kid. "You cannot turn someone off."

"Perhaps you have some of her papers in your possession?" said Griffin's designated good cop. "Something you can make available to us?"

All these Monday-morning realizations.

Shivani had shown Griffin her paperwork in read-only PDF while leaning in close as the two drank it up in midtown. "I wish I could give you this," she had said with a laugh. "But sending files triggers alerts."

Griffin's interrogator had heard enough. The story had officially become one now asking if Griffin Wagner was even a real reporter.

"Wade," he said to the grunt, "I think we're good here if you want to jump off the line?" The grunt said goodbye and then departed.

"One more thing… Can I ask about your previous reporting experience?"

Here we go.

"Fire away." Griffin said. He stared sadly at Lee Majors, wondering if his companion would ever feel safe around him again.

"Your previous work, for *In the Zone*, it seems kind of, how should I put it. *Irreverent?*"

"How do you mean?"

Griffin wanted to hear this part put into words.

"Well, I see you have written 'Decimate Your Belly,' by Griffin Wagner. And here is another story called, excuse me for asking, but these *are* your bylines, 'Is She Faking It, Or Are You Quaking It?' So I wanted to ask, was this your first experience in serious reporting?"

"No," Griffin clarified. "That first one was part of a health package. I wrote about chin-ups for that issue. The second one was about sexual intimacy, if you had bothered to read it. I don't write the headlines. Are we about finished here?"

The reporter spent a final few minutes detailing a trove of bawdy *In the Zone* titles published under Griffin's name, the sort of work one presumably does not stoop to accepting upon leaving whatever the fuck Ivy League courtyard in which his accuser had trained.

It had been a feast of bad piecework, this roster of Griffin's Greatest Hits, all of it culminating in a grim assignment he had taken during a stretch of exceptionally tight finances wherein the magazine had assigned him to rank 48 euphemisms for the word "boner."

"That story wasn't all bad," Griffin said. "I got to learn a lot of new slang."

After an hour and change, his humiliation was apparently final, and the reporter ended the call. "I can't say for sure when or if this story will run," he offered. "We interview 20 or so sources a week and are lucky to get a story assigned every fortnight."

Fortnight.

Griffin turned off his phone and pulled down his shades. It was, as far as he could tell, noon. This would have to do it for the day.

∽

He took two Valium and slept another 24 hours. He spent the next day trying in vain to track down proof of Shivani. Weeks earlier, a search for "S.G. Patel" would have pulled up dozens if not hundreds of scholarly articles crediting her assistance. Griffin had seen them himself. Now her name no longer triggered publications of any kind.

What were these guys, the Illuminati?

Who did he really meet?

∽

Friday, Griffin faced a third round of blowback. Compared to the throat punch he had endured on public radio, it should have been easy to open up the paper and see his name derided in the local daily. And yet something about the shot launched his way on the Minneapolis opinion page stung a bit worse. Over his morning coffee, he stared in dumbfounded wonder at a prim homily invoking the name Griffin Wagner as the face of unethical journalism. Topping it all off, the piece was signed by his old college pal Pevin.

"When Reporters Lie," the headline belched. To illustrate this minor and yet strangely painful hit-job, the paper had accompanied the Davester's tome with a grainy freeze-frame from Griffin's interview on Harrison Reed, a tight screen-cap of Griffin's face in an unflattering grimace and to his left, the peaceful, handsome and contemplative gaze of Jeremy Elton.

256

"Journalism scandal engulfs Minneapolis shock scribe," read the subtitle.

Shock scribe? Was that even a thing?

"The state of Minnesota embraces the use of lifesaving medications like Serotonal," Dave's commentary began. "That's why so many of us who work in public health are deeply troubled that Minnesota-based magazine writer Griffin Wagner has chosen to undermine confidence in valuable treatments for mental illness."

It went on like this, punishing all the familiar straw men, trading in high-handed tropes and rhetorical furrowed brows en route to its penultimate pounding of the gavel.

"We cannot all take up this work," Dave had concluded in a most Dave-like of endings. "But we can all try harder to support those who do. Journalists included."

⇚

Griffin tried to keep busy.

He spent long afternoons compiling notes on what Shivani had told him about her back story. He searched for evidence of her life as a child in England, at the primary school she had attended near Leeds, the company that employed her father and her years at Cambridge.

He'd found websites for all of these places, but never a Shivani Patel.

Had she even been who she says she was?

Mitch had called to say Griffin's WMW contract was being held up in legal. Upon sending out a dozen pitches, Griffin realized his editors were not simply too busy to reply, they were saying no.

Esquire had of course moved on, but in more ways than one. Within weeks, Griffin's article on ghostwriting was no longer online, nor were any of his stories for *In the Zone*. That may have stunned him the most. That such a down-market title had now found him beneath their good name.

And then that was all. There would be no more disruptions to the great and mighty freeze-out that had descended upon Griffin's professional life, a career that was most certainly now a thing of the past. What's the phrase again, life comes at you fast?

His sentencing to total isolation would provide Griffin with a fast instruction in the reality of what it meant to be under suspicion, the terrible quietness of trouble. He had always assumed falling into scandal would feel somehow noisy, dangerous and chaotic. But the cloud now hanging over his name had created something quite the opposite—the withdrawal of what little contact the outside world had ever offered him.

35

Griffin had never felt a moment when it announced itself. His descent into despair had crept up unnoticed, with none of the overt madness he had endured under the torture of Bioferex withdrawal. That, after all, was a drug condition, a cruelty from the darkness of bad places. Whereas this, what he felt now, it was an ordinary if painful human response to loss.

It created a fear of thinking too long. A need to stay busy. An elusiveness of sleep. Instead of laconic depression, Griffin's remorse was a decidedly spry kind of desperation two-step. He found himself wanting to drink more, run more, chase women more, do anything to push up the dopamine.

That was as fertile as it ever was. The women in his life didn't care how he'd gone from flailing in a failing industry to becoming its poster child for irresponsibility. No one serving pitchers at the CC Club knew he'd spent his way through the entire *Esquire* check. That the corporate pay promised to him had been rescinded in a two-sentence email.

When his parents learned of his troubles they had not so much as blinked. His dad merely said they would need a couple of days to get some money together in order to tide him over for a while. Griffin knew what this meant, they were cashing in the retirement. "Don't worry," his father added. "We are pretty sure we can always get a second mortgage on the house if you end up needing more."

જી

Tired of the hate mail from strangers, Griffin began to explore the possibility of pulling down his website. Although once he began to tinker with his online storefront, he became puzzled that he had ever taken it seriously. *Look at all this crap*, he whispered in silence to no one. Service writing. Product launches. Contrivances.

His website, now that Griffin thought of it, was little more than a digital shrine to a good life squandered. Far from teaching him how to be masculine, the life skills he mastered as writer of guy's-guy skills now seemed like little more than the honing of jokes, massaging of nut graphs, and tweaking of stale copy.

His life had been spent, if he had to face facts, in the service of cultural pollution. Even his "take," against, against, against. What was that all about? And what *was* his obsession with the drug industry? Wasn't that just a way for him to reject the corporate people who had never given him a job?

The freelance life had only underscored the fact that he just wasn't company material. He had deluded himself into thinking he had been merely slumming when maybe the low-IQ content under his name was correctly assigned all along. He had never belonged in the smart magazines. He knew that now. The world had reminded him of his place. He deserved this.

જી

Though mild compared to akathisia, depression was a prison all its own. Starting with the matter of sleep. Griffin began to sleep in a way meant to make up for years of lost sleep. He began to catch up on sleep he'd missed during the Eighties. He could usually pull himself out of bed before noon, but then a week came along where the weather cleared, and for some reason, the sunshine just made him really fucking tired.

The hate mail had mostly stopped. It had been three months since he had been ritually sacrificed on *NPR*, *Full Aperture with Harrison Reed*, *the Star Tribune* and by a pair of writers who had deemed his story not worth pursuing for *The New York Times*. One of the clickbait sites had given Jeremy Elton a lengthy post to slander Griffin all over again—HuffPo? He couldn't remember. He did remember the reader count on that had rivalled the population of greater Minneapolis. After Krøhn-McGill had boosted the link, Jeremy's takeout on Griffin had been shared 465,000 times and that precipitated the unsigned emails telling him YOU SHOULD THINK TWICE ABOUT THE HARMS YOU HAVE DONE ITS HERTFUL TO SAY GARBAGE THINGS ABOUT ANTIDEPRESSANTS.

Griffin would try to eat something, but food began to hurt his stomach. His mind had become flat, perpetually hungover, noisy. He watched TV for hours on end, switching channels, losing time. His cell phone, the bill on his coffee table told him, was set to be shut off in one week. It was on a night after another day like this, a half hour after all the second-floor lights up his alley had been shut off, with the acid of worry rising in his stomach, that his phone rang at an odd hour. A girl? The ID said Blocked.

What the hell.

"Hello."

"Griffin?"

"Yes, who is this?"

"It's Jeremy Elton."

36

"I saved your number from our conversation in Chicago."

This guy.

Griffin was too stunned to say anything.

"Soo," Jeremy said, "I'm calling, because, well, I want you to know something. I want you to hear it from me that I hold nothing against you for being deceived by the antipsychiatry mob. I want to tell you that I know you only did what you thought was right."

Griffin let a small laugh fall to the floor. Lee Majors was chewing on a ball. Griffin picked it up and began bouncing it off a nearby wall. Lee began to dive and miss, dive and miss.

"What's more," Griffin absent-mindedly heard America's Psychiatrist saying into his phone, "from my understanding, nor does Krøhn-McGill hold you responsible. Just between you and me, while they briefly considered their legal options in the wake of your release of proprietary safety data, I am told that in the spirit of forgiveness, they now feel inclined to let these opportunities pass—considering your precipitous loss of stature and the like."

So, that was rich.

"A spirit of forgiveness," Griffin repeated

"Exactly."

Griffin waited some more. Jeremy appeared to have finished talking.

"If I hadn't been accused on national television of making up a source, Dr. Elton," Griffin finally said, "my release from worry over being charged with, what again?"

"The release of proprietary data."

"Proprietary data. Is that your term for side effects now? If I hadn't been accused of making up a source, releasing your data would be a badge of honor. Thanks to you, no one believes me. You, my friend, are a highly-skilled liar."

"I lied?" Elton replied. "How did I lie? I'm sorry the interview didn't go well for you, but I only told the truth. I simply do not know a Shivani Patel, or whatever you said her name was."

"You don't hire ghostwriters?"

"Of course I work with ghostwriters. The whole industry uses them. Your source got most of what she said correct, whoever she was. She just wasn't a ghostwriter herself. There's no way one ghostwriter could do all the work she took credit for producing."

Griffin paused. Shivani's claims to productivity were wildly off the charts. Elton's position was worryingly plausible. Still…He couldn't bear the possibility he had been wrong to trust her.

"Dr. Elton, it's late. How can I help you?"

"I want to help *you*, if that's possible."

Griffin laughed. He threw the ball harder, causing Lee Majors to gallop across the darkened floor.

"That's, wow…Why?"

"Because you are in trouble," Elton said. "And because we have met. And because I didn't get where I am by taking the actions of others personally. I have a temper. I am human. I can succumb to ego and pride. But I don't abandon relationships because someone writes something I dislike. We are both part of the same human journey. If our paths should cross, that is part of the plan."

You have to be kidding.

"Jeremy."

"Yes."

"Can I call you Jeremy?"

"Of course."

"We don't have a relationship."

"Fine! Believe as you wish. But you are being misled."

"How am I being misled? I saw you walking alongside Shivani Patel at the AAP meeting in Chicago."

"People follow me around at meetings all the time. That does not mean I know them, or even that they are who are who they say they are."

"She had a name tag."

"Name tags are just paper. Not all is as it appears. Listen, if you hadn't gone to see Alexander Breton that afternoon, you would have never been pulled into this unfortunate circumstance to begin with. It's not your fault. I just wish I could have warned you about him. He can be powerfully seductive at first glance."

Now Elton sounded plausible again. Griffin didn't know what to make of anything.

"Why," he sighed. "What have you got on Alexander Breton?"

"Did he tell you he was fired for concocting papers to fit expert witness testimony."

"Nice try."

Breton seemed like the last person alive to have baked his data in order to pocket fees.

"Listen to me. I treat patients. In the course of that work, I need to study drugs. Alexander Breton does this all from reverse. He approaches firms specializing in wrongful death, seeks out opinions they require, then reverse-engineers a host of papers about the harms of a given drug. That's why nobody publishes him in the good journals."

"Jeremy, do you have a place in Kona purchased by Krøhn-McGill?"

Griffin had no idea if it was true. Breton had told him this.

"I do!"

"Busted."

"Breton has one in the Maldives. Did he tell you that? And it's bigger!"

The guy had an answer for everything, some of them too precise for comfort. But how *would* Jeremy Elton know what Alexander Breton's second home looked like? Were these people all just friends? Was Griffin's rise and fall collateral damage in a pissing war among allies? He realized Jeremy was still talking.

"...Sure, we go back. Breton is brilliant. But he has had genuine struggles with paranoia, episodes that have sidelined him for years on end. These problems have affected his reputation. It's beyond repair by now. He is not the spotless academic you perceive him to be."

"It's getting late." Griffin was punting now.

"You are seeking affirmation," Jeremy intoned. His voice sounded kind and reassuring. "You are a creative soul, and a force for good in the conversation. What I hope to leave with you tonight is a sense that your obstacles, Griffin—this entire Krøhn-McGill baggage in your story—it is all only an apparition."

"No," Griffin replied. "It's actually a 57-second appearance on a cable show that's now been viewed over 3.4 million times."

"Listen," Jeremy said. "Cards on the table, now. I'm not interested in our lives intersecting in the courtroom. Krøhn-McGill wouldn't want that outcome either. Do what you will with that information."

Griffin made a mental note to figure out why Jeremy Elton would be afraid of going to court.

"Well, thanks, I guess. Do what you can with this information, Dr. Elton: Fuck off. Verily. Please hold for a brief survey about our service."

Griffin made sure to hang up first.

Jesus. Now he had to worry about both Shivani *and* Breton?

37

Shivani missed her fish, but not as much as she thought she would, given the many nights she'd spent drinking Barolo in the glow of their aquatic paradise while imagining what would become of her life after ghostwriting.

Now that the day of Shivani's independence was here, it was all anticlimax. She had sold her five by eighteen aquarium in a package deal that unloaded her place on Gramercy Park and put most of her things in storage.

The brokerage had agreed to require her buyer to either take out a service plan with Aquatic Discoveries of Westchester, NY, or arrange for the safe transfer of its contents to a Princeton, NJ, sanctuary for rare coral fish. She figured if she didn't they would all quickly die, given the kid who was moving in. A Chinese shipping magnate acquired Shivani's beloved apartment for his nephew to utilize while in town at NYU.

Shivani was supposed to clear $2.6 million after paying off the mortgage. She'd thought the cash would get her through uncertain times now facing her, seeing as how she had left Deadline Medical on bad terms and could no longer find work.

Her betrayal in *Esquire* and their staggering counterattack on live

TV had the intended effect of convincing Shivani she was clearly in grave danger should she do anything but flee, slip off the grid and start over.

And it would have gone smoothly, except for the claw-back now underway. As her closing agent explained via long-distance connection while Shivani sat in her mother's small garden, "it appears a legal firm that ordinarily works for Krøhn-McGill had inserted a poison pill into your original mortgage application, Miss Patel."

Charming. Back when she first bought the place, Shivani had thought the legal review offered by her new employers was a mere perk of some sort. Now came news they had retained power of attorney over her apartment the whole time. Upon word that her place would soon be changing hands, Seamus had quietly exercised their option, placed all proceeds into her pension plan, then immediately cancelled the account.

"Who was that, dear?"

Shivani's mother had been washing windows in a small greenhouse.

"Oh, no one. Just a realtor."

"What did he want?"

"Nothing. They basically stole my house and savings."

Shivani put the phone onto an iron table and picked up a kitten she had taken on for company. She stated the next detail to the kitten in kitten talk.

"They made sure, Mr. Biscuits, that if I ever left the old place without saying goodbye, it would be just you, me, and mummy without a shilling in our pocket."

Her mother stared with confusion.

"They can do that?"

"They can do anything, Mr. Biscuits," Shivani said to the cat.

"America is such a strange place," her mother said.

It was all too rich, almost as rich as Shivani's realization that she had gone out for lunch with a cute reporter, gotten slaughtered on Ketel One, spilled the company secrets, then took an axe to her future with a one sentence text.

That was three months ago. In the first hours after Jeremy had denied her existence, Shivani had closed down her cell, stopped all her credit cards, moved her cash into her mother's name at the council bank of Leeds and booked a one-way flight to England.

It had been twenty years and a lot had changed.

Her friends had finished school, become Yummy Mummies and moved to the suburbs. She had pushed drugs and they had built lives while taking them. England had changed, as well. It suddenly looked a lot more like America. The same chains, the same fascination with digital toys, careerism and pills.

When the *Esquire* story dropped, Shivani read it twice, the first time for shock, the second time for acceptance. Griffin, bless him, had dragged her sorry mates. Though she'd had early concerns he was in over his head, he'd gotten most of it right. But her hoped-for feeling of redemption was still on order.

Rather than cleanse her of all guilt, blowing the whistle on Krøhn-McGill had given her a taste of what was possible, and what remained undone. She had been forced into hiding. Griffin had been thrown under the bus. Bioferex was still out there.

And here came the money troubles, for the first time in her adult life. After settling into a flat near her mom, then taking a job as a volunteer at the pet shelter, a series of unexplained credit failures began mounting, and for the smallest of purchases, causing Shivani's mother to ask when she would be getting back to the pharmaceutical business.

"They have drug makers in the UK you know," she told her. "Maybe you're ready to get back in."

"That would be lovely, dear," Shivani said. "We have missed each other, the handbag shop and I, but I'm trying to follow Dad's lesson."

Her mother looked confused. The second marriage had fallen apart years ago. Shivani and her mum had yet to repair the damage. "Well," she said, "your father was no opponent of a nice living."

"He would be if he knew what it was that the drug companies did these days."

"Oh, I don't know about that."

Shivani resigned to acceptance of her mother's inability to understand who Shivani was, or why she had torched her life. She also made a plan to head back to the States the next day.

38

"Dr. Powers, please."

Griffin had blurted it out in a rush.

"Who's calling?"

"E.J. Cerrano," Griffin lied. "I'm with Pagel-Simon."

He had no choice. He had already left three messages as Griffin Wagner. He had to get through to Julian Powers. If Jeremy Elton had been called in to help gain the expanded approval for Bioferex, Julian Powers seemed like as good person as any to tell him how.

In a rare moment of success, Powers was finally on the line.

"Eileen, are we still on for Minneapolis?"

"Oops, sorry, Dr. Powers—this is Griffin Wagner. Maybe your assistant got our calls mixed up. I interviewed you for an article on Bioferex?"

Griffin heard an audible sigh.

"Oh yes, Mr. Wagner, I have been getting messages from you. It's a busy time right now."

"That's OK, I will be quick."

"Sorry, I did a lot of interviews. Who are you with again?"

Weird. Powers really had no idea who he was. He hadn't been avoiding him.

"I am a freelancer," Griffin said, which was eminently true, now that no magazine would take his calls. "I am trying to get to the bottom of something about Bioferex."

"Well, it's a medication for speeding the repair of bone fracture brought on by running."

"Right. Did you ever assess for suicide?"

"Suicide? It's not a psychiatric drug."

"No, I mean, yes that's correct. But lots of drugs for medical conditions do that."

"Listen," Powers said, "is this something you can put in an email?"

"Of course," Griffin replied.

Powers would surely be ignoring all new emails from Griffin.

That's OK, Griffin told himself. He just learned something important: Julian Powers was coming to Minneapolis.

Why?

Powers's name popped up on a webpage for a drug industry awards gala called *The Health Advertising Honors.* The organizers apparently called their own little Oscars the *Jerrys* for short, in honor of the late Jerome Wilton Greenbriar, "the father of pharmaceutical advertising." Because the *Jerrys* rotated a med-tech circuit, this year it would be descending upon the bio-med hotbed of Minneapolis.

"Sorry, the *Jerrys* are private," said a harried flack when Griffin called for credentials.

"No worries, have a nice day."

All that meant was that now Griffin had to rent a tux.

The *Jerrys* had rented out the Wyman Building, an old monster in the warehouse district on the north end of downtown. On the night of the affair, Griffin put on a three-piece and strolled in with the salesmen.

Inside, planners had trucked in a half dozen couches, chrome-and-glass cocktail tables, and a dozen glowing blue columns. In one end of the bar, a ski jump ice sculpture had been erected for rocketing 80-proof anisette into the mouths of drug marketers hoping to cut loose. They had all labored for another year of their drug-promoting youth. By 8:30 the bar was three-deep with drug pitchmen wearing black tie.

Griffin kept his eye peeled for the tinted aviators and shaggy grey mane of Julian Powers. But the awards show became morbidly fascinating all on its own. The first trophy of the night went to "How's it Going in There?" a series of spots for Flovac, a drug for constipation. Each ad featured an embarrassing moment of being stuck in the john—on an airplane, at the office, with friends over to visit—followed by the side-splitting kicker: someone at the door, asking, "How's it going in there?"

Best Brand Awareness went to an agency that revised a famous bandage company's iconic logo. The new design, "boldly reimagined by an upstart team that has been taking the industry by storm," had remade a 1930s image of a farm boy with a fishing pole into a stick boy and stick dog, so by all means, call the fucking papers. Griffin lost interest and flirted with the help. Eventually, at 10:32, the moment arrived to catch the *Jerry* Griffin had hoped to witness up close: *Best Non-Branded Campaign.*

The award was designed to recognize doctors who did media in the service of "illness awareness," sort of advertising without the ad. For drugs targeting new illnesses they invariably needed a doctor to go on TV and tell everyone about the symptoms. Griffin knew this should have triggered a stage call for Julian Powers. When the prize went to Bioferex, "the drug that ignited our passion for preventing stress fractures," Powers strode briskly to the stage to accept his *Jerry*.

"It was my great pleasure to help Pagel-Simon build awareness of Stress Fracture Risk Syndrome," Powers drawled compliantly, before gazing with gentle amusement at the trophy, a ten-inch pill bottle made of Swarovski crystal.

The applause died down, a band counted in the first four beats of the Huey Lewis and News mid-Eighties hit "I Need a New Drug," and before anyone noticed, Powers had slipped through the crowd and headed towards his seat.

It was not lost on Griffin, how this cheesy celebration for reporter manipulation had recognized the same illness awareness campaign that had snared his services that Monday morning, alone and mildly panic-stricken from a lack of paying work.

As he wrestled with his regrets for having been suckered, Griffin watched as the man who had just won the biggest prize of the evening casually deposited his large crystal hardware on a blue column, paused to shake his head with resignation, then made a beeline for the door.

§

Griffin found his victorious escapee taking a secretive smoke on a third-floor terrace.

"Hi," he offered, approaching him in the dark. A stream of cars snaked along First Avenue two stories below them. "I interviewed you once for a story on Bioferex."

Powers looked at him funny.

"I didn't know they let media up here."

"No, not working right now. Just came out to meet you."

Powers made a face at this weird bit of news.

"Don't worry," Griffin added, "I'm not a murderer or anything."

"Sorry. Didn't know I was this important."

"I have been kind of radioactive since my last piece came out." Griffin realized this was an awkward opening admission, but as a perk of having been blacklisted, he had started to care a lot less what anyone thought.

Powers tilted his head, then looked to the side.

"I don't read the papers," he finally said.

Griffin filled him in—how he'd learned Bioferex was really Serotonal, that Serotonal was dangerous, possibly Bioferex as well. How a ghostwriter for both of the trials thought someone could have buried a signal of harm in the data.

"They do that how?"

"By inflating suicidal events in the placebo arm," Griffin said. "Makes normal life look more dangerous, and that makes the problem on the drug look more like normal life. I can't get anyone to hear me out, however, because my ghostwriter only showed me these docs on her phone, then ghosted me."

"How appropriate."

Powers gave a little laugh at Griffin getting ghosted by a ghostwriter. Griffin had little energy for banter.

"I have been blacklisted in my field," Griffin said. "You're the only person I know who was there for the testing of Bioferex. So you can see why a night spent watching ad-men getting shitfaced would be worth it for me to ask you this question: Did you ever see anyone moving suicidal events into the placebo column for the Bioferex trial?"

Powers paused, holding his cigarette and standing very still. He looked at his shoes. He reached out and ashed his cigarette over the balcony, put it out on the railing and tilted his head to look at Griffin. The naïveté of the question he then offered felt astonishing to Griffin.

"Wait," Powers said. "Bioferex is an antidepressant?"

"Wow," Griffin replied in restrained wonder, "I sort of assumed you knew that. It's, you know, a race mate. I'm thinking that's what you guys call it. Isomer. A mirror image."

Powers had become perfectly still. It might have pained him, to be so far out of the loop on the drug he had spent a year humping in the papers.

"OK, sure, I remember that part," Powers said. "I had this once in chemistry. It's a chimera."

Powers put another cigarette in his mouth, then placed his hands together in prayer, squinting as the smoke curled up into his eyes.

"Just like my momma taught me growing up in coal country. Two hands. They overlap, but they don't match when you flip them palms up."

A layman's touch on the wonders of science.

It suggested a certain openness to Julian Powers.

Powers leaned in close. The smell of smoke on his breath was strong.

"Krøhn-McGill brought Jeremy Elton in at the eleventh hour," he said in a low voice. "They flew him up to Chicago every morning, then flew him home to Dallas every night. My job was to review the biomarkers of function. He had a suite at the International. I could never figure out what that guy did."

"You didn't ask the sponsors of your paper why they brought in a psychiatrist on a trial of a bone drug?"

"They don't pay me to ask questions," Powers replied. "They said he was experienced in managing controls."

"Controls?"

"Placebo-takers."

"Isn't that part of the trial supposed to be blind?"

"The term is double-blind," Powers said. "But it's a business. You know how these things work."

"Actually, I don't."

"Well, you get used to holding your questions."

Julian Powers began walking back inside.

Griffin had one more question. He called it out as Powers pulled open the double doors.

"Do you know Mitch St. Germaine?"

"Everyone knows Mitch," Powers drawled, pulling one last inhale from his cigarette, then tossing it the ground and putting it out with his foot. "Mitch works for Krøhn-McGill."

"I thought Mitch worked for WMW," Griffin asked.

"Yeah, that's part of Krøhn-McGill."

∽

It was 11:30 when the crowd dwindled onto the sidewalk. Was that her? Griffin thought it was her. So much time had passed. He couldn't be sure.

"You remember me, don't you?"

She said it first, smiling.

Griffin did remember Sedona Piper. Just like at the AAP, she had approached him here first, slipping away from a pack of women looking at their phones. "Here we are, trying to find someplace to go after this thing," Sedona said. "It never occurred to me I might know a local."

She looked different now. She wore a tapered dress with crystal beads sewn into the back, a spray of waves like a Japanese watercolor. For a psychologist working at a state school in Wisconsin, it looked like a month's wages.

"So, wow," Griffin said. "You clean up nice."

"What are *you* doing here?" Sedona replied. She said it with a puzzled laugh, staring down his black-tie three-piece.

"Undercover, of course," Griffin replied.

"Really?" Sedona straightened just a bit.

"Sort of," Griffin replied. "I have had quite the ride since we last spoke. I don't know if you heard about it."

"Hang on."

Sedona ran back toward where she had been standing. After a few words with her friends she returned.

"Who was that?"

"They wanted to turn in," Sedona replied. "We have a big room at the Hyatt. I told them I wanted to see more of Minneapolis."

"Wow, OK," Griffin said, unsure of his good luck. "I can give you the tour if you don't mind some dog hair in the passenger seat. We can head up Hennepin and I will show you the lakes."

"Sounds cute," Sedona said. "Reminds me of the guys I dated in college. But by the time we hit Uptown, I want a full explanation as to what drew you to this drug marketing group-grope."

౸

They made good time during the drive up Hennepin, a bustling roadway for young professionals en route to the high-end rentals circling the lakes of south Minneapolis. They made all the lights, turned right on Franklin, headed west towards Lake of the Isles, and by the time they reached Lake Street, Sedona had fully disclosed the circumstances placing her at an awards ceremony for the proprietors of drug advertising.

"I know what you're thinking," she said. "What's a talk-therapy schmo doing at a meeting that gives out crystal pill bottles?" She proceeded to tell him about "an awkward recognition shared between my department at UW Madison and that of team Jeremy."

It seems that Sedona's clinical program and the psychiatry department at the University of Dallas had shared in designing a public health campaign targeting bullying.

"My boss said the prize could help us pull more grants. I drew the shortest straw. Here we are."

"Speaking of Jeremy," Griffin said.

"Go on."

Sedona was admiring a stately Tudor the size of a small ocean liner.

"According to a guy I worked that party to ambush, Jeremy Elton was called in to organize placebo patients in the early trials of Bioferex. In another odd detail, tonight I also learned that this fake literary agent who came up here and snowed me after my article dropped—turns out he actually works for Krøhn-McGill too. So these people, they're everywhere."

"Get the fuck out of here!"

Sedona said it a little too enthusiastically. Maybe she wanted to fool around. There could be worse outcomes to this wretched evening.

"It's true," Griffin said. "But you were telling me about coming here."

"Yeah, I have family."

"In town?"

"Sort of. I'm from Rochester. My Dad was IBM. We left when I was nine."

Sedona rubbed her calf. It was toned and tan. Griffin hadn't been to the gym since the start of his downfall. She had the advantage.

"They retired a few years ago," Sedona continued. "They came up here to live in one of those condos by the Guthrie. It's a nice way to see them. We see a play, eat brunch. Back in Madison, it's just me and the cat in a place with an iron bathtub."

Griffin and Sedona drove for another half hour, talking about her job, his story of fleeting fame followed by the disappearance of his only source. He told her about his banishment from the profession and his interrogation at the hands of the *Times*.

Sedona told Griffin she thought Shivani Patel had been playing him all along. Griffin filed the idea for later consideration. Sedona lost her cynicism block by block, becoming sweeter as the mansions rolled by and the local alternative radio station played the sort of cool, strange songs they can only try out after midnight.

"You're going to be OK," she told Griffin, placing a warm hand on his knee, "I just know it."

They ended up at his place around one. It wasn't so much of a hookup as inertia. He moved closer and she rolled him against his fridge. This wasn't half-bad. A couple of jokes. They grabbed at each other in the dining room and they were in the bedroom a few minutes later. Sedona's dress landed on Griffin's desk. Everything else fell away as well, a rush of reflex and desire he'd nurtured since having their lengthy idea-exchange walking around a convention full of psychiatrists. He had been here before, too much, lately, but somehow it felt less scammy this time.

Griffin thought Sedona might be feeling something similar, but he knew better than to fall into that little trap. He suspected she was here out of something better than boredom, but he knew he could have been wrong about that one as well. She touched his face, pulled herself close to him, and they seemed to anticipate each other's movements like a couple with years of time together.

ɧ

"Wow," she said. "What do you think?"

Griffin looked up from his bed. It was a little after seven. Sedona had awoken first.

Christ, she had really found his Fran Tarkenton jersey? Part of his shock was that she was so relaxed. It had been so long since Griffin had woken up with someone who wasn't scrambling. Still. No one had ever taken the initiative to put on his number 10. It would have been alright. Except that she then asked him the strangest of questions.

"Who's Tare-keen-ton?"

"What?"

Sedona let the question drop, pulled off the jersey and ran into the bathroom.

Griffin got up to make coffee.

Though she had tried to redirect his attention, it bothered him. Who's Tarkeenton?

Did Sedona Piper from Rochester, Minnesota, really just mispronounce the name of the most famous athlete in Minnesota?

Griffin picked up Sedona's bag from a side chair, took a look inside, then froze as a corporate pass card tumbled to the floor. The laminated ID said her name was indeed Sedona Piper, and her picture was indeed gorgeous, but it said that her employer was Krøhn-McGill.

Griffin got dressed, finished making coffee, placed a cup on the bathroom sink for the spy in his shower, then returned to his living room. After another ten minutes, Sedona came out wearing her dress from last night.

"Walk of shame," Sedona said, straightening the hem of her dress with a brush of her hand.

"No shame, baby," Griffin said. "No shame in love."

"Uh-oh," she said. "Someone's using the L-word."

"Settle down, I'm a writer. Metaphor. Love, as in Love Machine."

Griffin waved two thumbs towards his chest in a half-hearted joke, looking out the window to disengage their connection.

"So, hey, Sedona Piper," he finally said, "you're like, my age, right? Mid-30s?"

"Close enough, " she said. "A lady never tells."

"And you grew up here in Minnesota," he continued, "like, in the 1970s?"

"Want to get some breakfast?"

She looked nervous, a little vulnerable.

"And you have no idea who Fran Tarkenton is?"

She gave him a funny look.

"That reason you came to the dinner last night sure sounds made up to me," Griffin said. He let out a slow whistle. Lee Majors got up, walked over to him and sat down.

"I don't think you came here for that award," he said. "I would have remembered that. I think you came here because you work in Pharma."

Sedona made a face of innocent surprise, like a toddler spying a Santa suit in the attic.

She corkscrewed her mouth in an affectation of offense.

"How about you tell me where you really work?" Griffin said.

Sedona stared at the floor, then her nails. She wasn't going to say it.

"Come-on," Griffin said. "I saw your badge in there, Krøhny."

39

"OK." Sedona looked at the ceiling and let out a defeated laugh. "This doesn't look strange at all."

"Let me guess," Griffin said, "you're not really a psychologist, but you play one on TV?" He bent down to pick up Lee Majors. The dog wrangled in his arms in a tangle of legs and tail as Sedona leaned against the door to Griffin's bathroom.

So, no, I'm not a psychologist, if you want to know the truth of it," Sedona said. "I'm more like a publicity cowgirl. What are you?"

"Nice try. Sorry to bore you, same person I said I was. The tag on you at the AAP said you were from UW. So, do you carry around secret agent paperwork or something?"

"Funny."

"Does your umbrella have blow darts in it?"

Griffin was being remarkably chill, if he said so himself.

"I was sent in to watch you at that thing," She said finally. Her head was down again. She returned to looking absent-mindedly at her nails. "You were press, you had asked about Breton at the front desk. Registration texted Krøhn-McGill that media was going in to hear him. Krøhn-McGill sent me in to find you and make nice. This is all S.O.P.

Which is a long way of saying that yes, we have fake tags for things like that."

"We?"

"They have way too many people like me."

"But you gave me that whole speech about psychologists being scientists and psychiatrists being whores."

"Yeah, well, you wanted to hear it," she laughed with a shake of her head. "It's kind of an easy sermon to rattle off when you get paid to read blogs all day. It isn't hard to parrot whatever shit one group of partisans wants to think."

"Compliments on the compartmentalization. But you even ripped on Elton. You, even like, put me on to him. He works for you guys."

"Again, all under orders."

"Just following orders. That's a new one. But why throw your man Jeremy under the bus?"

"They were nervous about him. AP was turning against Bioferex or something. That was the word in-house."

"AP?"

"America's Psychiatrist."

She made a little two-handed chorus line wave as she said it, as if to bring his cheesy nickname down a notch. "My guess is they wanted to give you a lane to take a run at him. They can only build people up. If a KOL gets too big, we need a journalist to take him down. We'd been trying to entice the bigger magazines to take a shot at him for a while. It's not an easy sell these days. You were the first one to take the bait. Your hubris got to you, didn't it? Or were you just broke?"

"Good one. All of this organized lying must be new for a kid from Minnesota," he replied. "But wait, you're not from here, are you."

"You're thirty-six Griffin."

Sedona had crouched down in heels and a tight dress like a pro as she began petting Lee Majors. "Not to burst your bubble, but seriously. Nobody takes a writer out to dinner and gives him the world." She gazed up at him with a theatrical look of sadness. "You didn't really think all of this good fortune happened because everybody loved your articles on cologne?"

Ouch.

"Tough talk for a girl in a shiny dress on Sunday morning."

"Oh, you sweet thing." Sedona rose up, walked up to him with tenderness and extraordinary messy hair, then put a hand on his face for a soft caress. "You really believed *Esquire* assigned you that work based on your ability. By the way, I like this dress."

Griffin pulled his head back and out of her reach.

"You even pointed out Shivani Patel to me," he said.

"Yeah, well, we didn't think she would *email* you. Not to mention, pull you in for a kiss in front of the Lancaster, Romeo. Welcome to our database, the part housing photos of lovebirds. You'd have to be crazy not to realize that she lives, like, in surveillance city. When we saw all the shit she actually told you, that changed the plan again. I'm pretty sure life is getting difficult right now for your little friend. She likes to spend money, you know. That gets tricky when your credit cards stop working."

"Why do you have to punish *her*?" Griffin said. "You guys sent Mitch in to help me get that story, remember?"

"It was only supposed to be a little story on pharma," Sedona said, "one that turned up the heat on Jeremy for being such an uncooperative ass. We didn't exactly go after Bob Woodward for this. Maybe the wine at that tacky steak joint went to your head. So when the article came out, yeah, now we had to play the zone. They sent Jeremy out to neutralize you on TV. We didn't know he was going to do it so irrevocably. You can't control everything."

"You knew Shivani emailed me?"

Griffin was too stunned to ask how they had known he had kissed her.

"We knew that a KM employee sent an email to a reporter?"

"But she sent it from a Yahoo account."

"And?"

Well that explained why Shivani had fled.

"Well, if you know so much about everything," Griffin said, "then you know that Jeremy Elton called me up after midnight the other night, right?"

Griffin thought he saw Sedona's face sag just a fraction, a reveal of new tactical thinking in progress. It occurred to him that her certainty of his naivete was of value.

"You know what's funny?" he lied. "I'm the only one who got screwed in all this. You and Shivani are both doing fine. Elton is doing fine. Bioferex is about to conquer the world. You all used me for your own purposes."

"Nice try," Sedona said, "I think you like her. Lee Majors!"

The dog looked up. Sedona gave him a little wave.

How dare she curry favor with his dog.

"No, I hope to never see any of you again," Griffin continued. He prepared to throw down the full appearance of outrage. She was still here after all, set on taking copious notes on his condition. Hopefully he could convince her to let on to her employers that he was vanquished, beaten and exhausted. Hopefully that would be enough to keep them off his trail.

"You don't by chance have a brush I could borrow," she asked, shaking out her beautiful black locks. Griffin was now heading through the kitchen to show her his back door.

"So, for future reference," Griffin said as he pulled open the door, "I only caught you in a lie because you were pretending to be a Minnesotan and didn't know Fran Tarkenton. You might want to bone up on the Vikings next time. Twins also. The fuck made you think you could pass yourself off as a local?"

"I took a chance." Sedona grabbed her bag and began striding behind him through the kitchen. "I saw you last night, figured I could deliver an update on Monday, score a few points with the company. Plus, you might not believe this, but I kind of like you."

She turned and put her head on his chest. She seemed momentarily defensive, even a little sad. She smelled wonderful. It was all lies. He reminded himself that. Then she straightened up.

"But yeah, Rochester, why *did* I say that? I suppose because nice guys are more likely to open up if they think you are from their home town. And lo, you are indeed a nice guy. So it worked."

"What are they going to do to her," Griffin asked.

"Shivani?"

"Not that I care."

He needed to act cold if he was going to get this last piece out of her.

"Digital tracking, probably. As long as she stays away from you there's no issue. I guess this means we won't be getting breakfast?"

Griffin stepped onto the deck leading downstairs.

"Let me guess: Seamus Cole, right? That's your boss?"

Griffin had seen him running the pack at the AAP.

Sedona turned and smiled weakly as she moved out onto his porch.

"See, I knew you were smarter than the average bear."

"Who works for a guy named Seamus?"

"He's worth forty-eight million."

"Killer name though, Sedona Piper, that is, if that's your real name."

"It is. And we never kill anyone, actually," she said as she started down the steps. "That's only in the movies. We just make sure to stay one step ahead of you."

Griffin watched her hobble the rest of the exposed staircase. An April snow was clumping everything in sight, cleaning up the walkway with big fat flakes. Watching her reach the bottom in stilettos and a mini-dress, he felt a mixture of anger, despair and embarrassment at all that had passed. The words came without warning.

"Do your parents know about you?"

She turned to him with an icy glare.

The mask had finally dropped.

"Well, what do you know," Griffin said. "Looks like a real person lives inside of you after all."

"I make $260K," Sedona shot back, the last ounce of sweetness having drained from her face. "My parents think I am a drug rep. All my loans are paid. I am OK with my choices."

"Have a nice life, psycho."

Aaaand, that sucked.

Griffin wasn't used to being nasty. He'd didn't like how it felt.

He had done it out of necessity. He needed to be the shithead, just this once, to have a chance at them giving up on the monitoring. But it had surely only given her more of what she expected out of men all along.

Griffin watched Sedona heading out onto the sidewalk, where she paused to light a cigarette, looking beautiful and lost. He called down to her.

"The cab stands are around the corner."

When he returned to his apartment, the text that awaited him made all that just happened seem small.

40

Shivani G. would have preferred the code on her boarding pass read SBH, for St. Bart's, or STM, for St. Martin. But when it came to off-shoring secrets, she was placing her bet with this journey that her Krøhn-McGill targets were old-school.

If her instincts were good, Shivani felt certain, they would have skipped the Caribbean getaways of A-listers to store their worst patient data at a longitude north of the tropics. This was why she was headed for BDA, FAA designator for the only runway in Hamilton, Bermuda.

Shivani had always known the firm kept an address north of the tropics, and this one seemed festooned with red flags. It sat in a cone of silence, for starters. Krøhn-McGill Bermuda went unmentioned in company meetings, and it was unlisted within the Krøhn-McGill digital storefront, letterhead or corporate report.

Bermuda was no tax haven, moreover. None could ever accuse her beloved homeland's colony of being anyone's Switzerland. What Bermuda did offer was a place to keep troublesome patient data secure from the probing eyes of researchers, regulators, and the aggrieved. Corporate records were sacred on this island, with local businesses finding safe harbor through decades of deferential prosecutorial customs favoring landowners and the stability of the tax base.

As a legal matter, once patient data came here it was no longer within reach of the United States court system. By harboring all records in Bermuda, each stateside demand for Krøhn-McGill Discovery could be terminated by stating that *Krøhn-McGill USA has fully abided by the Court's request to deliver all evidentiary materials in our possession,* and then giving them just the records stored out in New Jersey. That was her hunch, anyway.

஧

Shivani grabbed a cab from Hamilton and told the driver to take her to Ellis Beach, an exclusive hideaway with discretion, pink sand shoreline, obsessive attention to comfort and fully-stocked villas for those with the funds for all-amenity shelter. She grabbed her card for the Sea of Paradise Cottage, slipped into the complimentary sandals at the front desk, then followed a flagstone path lined with a fully stocked brook from the main building to a bungalow.

Celine Dion had just cleared out a couple of hours earlier, a detail Shivani's porter let slip and couldn't have made up if he wanted, as it was simply too weird. The hint of fresh fame in her living room seemed like a thoroughly decent welcome for a stay charging $9,600 a night.

Shivani had turned down the offer of complimentary butler service, but remembered to ask for someone to come do her nails at tea. Pausing at the sight of her own private infinity pool overlooking the calmest part of the Atlantic, she let out a long, slow exhale, distress she had been holding inside of her for years.

She was going to miss all this.

஧

Shivani had never lost the digits needed to reach the sole employee of Krøhn-McGill Bermuda, data operations manager Benjamin Breen. Breen was a fish out of water at Krøhn-McGill, stylish, funny and curious. The pair had shared weekends launching drugs and had always gotten along famously.

They'd fly him in with his encrypted laptop, and Benjamin and Shivani would hunker down for long weekends at the Plaza. The two would pore over Benjamin's data as Shivani pushed out papers. They would order in, take breaks to watch *Project Runway*, and run up the tab.

Shivani would ask Benjamin for confidential numbers and he'd read aloud from his view-only screen, holding a rainbow roll with chopsticks in his right, and if it was a minute past five, a glass of something red in his left. Shivani came to learn that Benjamin possessed as much ambivalence about his employers' rapacious financial practices as did she, although he was more careful not to let on.

Shivani hoped her accomplice had yet to gain knowledge of her flight from Krøhn-McGill. This was a gamble. She had flown the coop over three months ago. That said, Benjamin seemed like the rare staffer who could have let a season of company gossip escape him, including any coded memos that may have been generated concerning the abruptness of Shivani's departure. She liked her chances.

Benjamin would have accessed data Shivani never could get. She knew this data could give her leverage needed to get Krøhn-McGill off her back. She also hoped Benjamin's stash of compromising trial records might allow her to show the world that the biggest drug since aspirin was going to make a lot of people hang themselves. Shivani mostly needed release from her guilty conscience, those exhausting images of her aiding and abetting of it all.

Benjamin picked up on the very first ring.

"Sheevi G., you hot little fox, are you really going to make me talk shop with you on this deliriously beautiful day?"

"You're in Bermuda, love," Shivani replied. "Aren't beautiful days like socks?"

"That's what we tell the people on the mainland," he said. "We get a lot of rain, if you want to know the truth."

Shivani looked out at the sunshine. It *was* too glorious for her to be doing this.

"Well, you can tell it to me straight because I'm already here."

"Who are you calling straight?"

"I'm serious," she said. "I'm here."

"You're in Bermuda?"

"Someone wants an audit of the clinical trial workload going back to 2006, and it might as well be me, right? The thing is, it's all hush-hush because they sent me here on the down low. I have to have it all done by yesterday."

"Who could possibly want an audit?"

Benjamin sounded as if he had never encountered interest in his post.

"A buyer. That's all I can say."

"Cough it up!"

"If you insist," Shivani said, "some private equity wankers have been talking about a takeover. It's probably the usual beating of the meat, but one never knows, right, it could always be legit. You know finance, never stop not stopping. They might pay out a lot of cheddar, too."

Benjamin was officially intrigued.

"The money robots are always looking to get some Pharma, you know," Shivani said. "By the way, you heard none of this from me, girlfriend. Swear to god, if you email anyone in the 212 about my being here, they will treat you like venereal disease at the swingers club. I take it you've heard of the SEC."

"Wow, takeover talk," he said with blasé affect. "How very Nineties. This is me falling asleep. No worries about me letting the cat out of the bag. I don't think I have read their emails in years."

Shivani breathed a sigh of relief. She might really get away with this.

"Nice. So how do you do whatever it is that do you do here, my dear. I mean, besides all the sailing?"

"It's pretty sexy," Benjamin chirped. "I wait for boxes, log data, take a long lunch at the club and go home. Honestly, I think they just want me here to read catalogs and buy sandals. Hold on for a second, will you?"

Shivani could hear Benjamin clinking silver on china. Was it really still lunch around here? Her flight had left LaGuardia at five, and now it was two. She pictured the skinny and flirtatious Benjamin in a Ralph Lauren polo, picking at crab in some harbor room staffed with 25-year-olds.

"Young man," she heard Benjamin calling on cue. "What is the name of that gentleman working the host stand?"

Midday in Bermuda and must be like life with Lord Grantham.

Benjamin returned, he and Shivani traded details, and before hanging up, she had invited Benjamin to come by her resort later that afternoon. Benjamin made it to Ellis Beach in less than an hour. He had been admiring her bar when he asked her the question she had hoped to hear most.

"So, what time tomorrow should we start?"

"Why do you ask?"

"Because if you want to see the clinical trial paperwork, we could head over to the annex early."

"The annex?" Shivani asked in a tone meant to conceal her excitement.

"Yes, you know—cold storage. We don't talk about it on the mainland. It's a bit of a pain, being secret agent man."

"What's it like?"

"The annex?"

"Mm-hmm."

"Your basic hideously-appointed fortress that's costing them mightily. Temperature-controlled, movement-sensitive, moisture-monitoring, all of it in vain. In case you hadn't noticed, this part of the Atlantic is like a steam room in the summer."

"We store paper here?"

This was better than Shivani had imagined.

"Oh yes, love, it's mostly paper, in fact. Started coming over in containers about eight years ago. They hire the cutest guys to unload the boxes. It's a gun show, I won't lie about that. I stand around, give orders and scope without shame."

Shivani's head began to spin. She had always known Benjamin would have had access to electronic data. But the fact that her company shelved cartons of documents on this mid-Atlantic hideaway meant she may have finally gained access to unattainable Bioferex and Serotonal clinical trial patient records. Every last life that her product had destroyed would have been catalogued here. If she was ever going to atone for anything, getting all this to Griffin was her last job left.

41

The text from Shivani had confused Griffin and wiped clean his shock over Sedona Piper. After dialing all the digits, he heard the jingle of Shivani's UK ring-tone, a sound he recognized from Pink Floyd's "The Wall." As he waited for her to pick up, he paced his apartment with a mixture of anticipation, anger, and near apocalyptic distrust.

"Griffin. So nice to hear from you," Shivani purred.

Fuck this.

"Where did you go?"

He wasn't here to play games.

"Lots of places."

"Why are you calling?"

"I have an invitation. Why not come out to Bermuda? You can help me dig into the Krøhn-McGill dirty laundry."

"Forgive me if I need more detail."

Griffin had found the coffee cup used by Sedona Piper, picked it up by inserting a fork through the handle, and carried it outside to be dropped one story into his apartment building dumpster.

"Just so, so many questions," he said. "Starting with the previous one: what the fuck happened to you?"

"Well, I'm here now, right, and I'm going to get something on the bastards, that's a plus, and I think you would enjoy being a part of it," Shivani continued, ignoring his question. "We can find ourselves some details they can't hide behind all the usual fuckery. Then you can have it all. I bet that you'd go for that? We are talking incriminating paperwork here, exculpatory detail for your personal troubles also. I will even bring you out here in the front of the plane. It's the very least I can do."

Griffin thought about telling Shivani that the offer of extra leg room would definitely make up for her having triggered the permanent destruction of his ability to find work. Instead he circled back to his most-pressing question.

"You still need to tell me why you split on me."

"Over the phone?" Shivani asked. "It's so impersonal."

Griffin paused, exasperated.

Truthfully, a free trip to someplace warm didn't sound bad.

That said, he wasn't sure he wanted to get back in the business of pissing off the world's largest drug maker. The problem was, he couldn't think of a better answer than yes. So he told her to email him his reservation in the next two hours, "otherwise I'm heading down to Memphis to start over."

Shivani was right, the phone *was* impersonal. She sent the email in ten minutes. Griffin awoke early and flew four-and-a-half hours to Hamilton, whereupon he grabbed a cab to Ellis Beach, whereupon he requested directions to the bar.

Griffin was still wearing clothes from the mainland and carrying a bag $1,500 cheaper than customary for the resort by the time she sauntered in to the Sea Breeze Cocktail Lounge. He had been asking a coconut-scented mannequin what it was that a person did for fun around here when Shivani tapped him on the shoulder.

"Getting pissed alone in the bar without me?"

"Hey."

It surprised Griffin how cold you could be to someone so beautiful if you wanted. Nearly broken apart by the events of the past year, he had planned on keeping his distance from this treacherous mess with the gorgeous features. But now here she was pulling in for an embrace.

"I thought that Brits were uncomfortable with affection," he protested, obliging her as her hair draped along his face. Shivani ignored his question and pressed on with the charm.

"She's cute," Shivani said, motioning towards the waitress.

"Jealous?" he asked. "That would be a new wrinkle."

Griffin noticed Shivani's dress, a backless number she would have never worn to meet a reporter in midtown. Everything on her person now looked expensive and exclusive.

"Is this what they call resort wear around this place?"

He waved his hand in a complimentary flutter.

"Maybe. Have a thing for the birds now?"

She gestured towards the mannequin.

"Maybe."

Griffin placed a spear of mango into his mouth. Fuck this British hazard blinker in a party dress with her career demolition. He was going to eat, drink and enjoy himself, all of it on her tab.

"Never mind," Shivani said with a small smile and touch of his arm. "We'll always have the sidewalk in front of the Lancaster."

What was this?

Griffin was pretty sure there was ketchup on his collar. He was entirely not flirtworthy. He posed the question out loud.

"What is this?"

"What is what?"

"This, you putting on the charm offensive," he offered with a shake of his head. "Just so you know, I'm not going to let you kiss me again until you explain why you threw me under one of those big Manhattan buses with a Bioferex wrap along the side."

He started looking around the back bar. He wanted something better than the Pimm's Cup this weird colony handed you at every turn. "You have any anejo back there," he shouted towards the bartender.

Shivani paused. Either they didn't have nice tequila where she was from, or she was concerned that he was in no mood to begin digging into towering pallets of clinical trial paperwork.

"I know it was wrong of me to take time off," she said.

"Take time off? Is that what we're calling it now?"

"I can't imagine what it's been like for you to be accused of…"

"Making you up? In my first feature for a major magazine? A publication I'd dreamed of breaking into for decades? Yours truly outed as Captain Bullshit on cable news, while my parents tuned in to watch with their friends. Oh, it was excellent, babe, good times. But no, I bet you can't."

"I still don't get it," Shivani said, more puzzled than apologetic. "They've never done that to a reporter before. You must have made them nervous."

"Nervous. You say that like they are human. I doubt it. Sedona Piper told me Jeremy did this all on his own."

"How do you know her?"

Shivani made a face as she asked him the question, pushing him lightly. She would have known that Sedona Piper was on the payroll.

"Never mind," Griffin said. "I met her by mistake."

"Oh, my," Shivani smiled and let out a little laugh. "Very well, we all get a little lonely. But she would tell you Jeremy was a lone operator to try to get you complacent about the data, that seems inherently obvious."

Griffin told her the story about his late night call from Jeremy. Shivani began pulling strands of her hair behind one ear as she took in the information.

"I wouldn't have expected any of that," she finally said. "But I think it's good news."

"Yeah, it's been a veritable pleasure cruise."

"No, really. If Krøhn-McGill had wanted to throw you in prison, they would have done that yesterday. The fact that they have held back means they do not want discovery."

"Bravo, that's what my attorney Lee Majors said happened."

Griffin smiled at the joke about his dog offering him legal counsel. "You know why we're here?"

"Snorkeling, I hope." Griffin was looking at the Mai Tai recipe on a placard.

"Better. Documents. The nitty gritty. Paperwork far more damning than anything available on the mainland." Griffin noticed that Shivani was now talking quietly. "We can figure out what they were hiding." She pointed a manicured nail to a grove above the harbor. "This up there, this is where the accidents go to disappear." As she said it, Shivani had waved her fingers in a trippy, slow swirl, like a college sophomore dancing to Dave Matthews.

"So," Griffin replied, taking a pull from his drink, "I want to go over our plan. We're going to break into some deeply-sensitive Costco of clinical trial paperwork, sift through unknowably large vaults of impenetrable data, collect precisely the goods needed to nail the world's largest drug manufacturer to a cross, then spirit them out to vindicate ourselves to the world. All in spite of the fact that everyone loves Krøhn-McGill, Serotonal, Jeremy Elton, and nobody in journalism cares. Do I get to wear a Ninja costume?"

"I wish," Shivani said, tilting her head in a smile. "You'd look cute in a Ninja costume. If we look in the right places, we can probably get what we came for in under two hours."

"Pharma keeps paper." Griffin offered the statement as an expression of skepticism more than a question. It was also the opening moments of his beginning to take her plan seriously. Paper, now that he knew.

"Paper gives them a layer of deniability that cannot be fucked with in the event of a hacking," she replied.

"Or," he said, reaching for his drink, "we can snorkel."

He gave a little wave to the mannequin, who now seemed to find him interesting.

"Where's your sense of adventure?" Shivani replied, shifting her body to block Griffin's view of the local talent. "If we get the goods on these bastards, we both come out from under this cloud. If it all goes public, all the trickery, the deaths, everything bad in our short, shared past, we gain a measure of absolution. I know you weren't crazy about having written that love letter for *In the Zone* on Bioferex."

Well-well. It finally comes out.

"Touché."

Griffin shook his head. Having apologized, then pleaded, Shivani was now subtly shifting to a taunt. Then, with perfect timing, she threw him a lifeline.

"It wasn't your fault."

Griffin pushed his hair back from his face. His bangs held a shagged hedge where his hand last had left them. He was beyond exhausted. Those four words. He had to look down.

"And let me guess," he offered quietly, "the records here show Krøhn-McGill knew all along that Bioferex is a drug that gives people that horrible side effect called akathisia."

"You know about that?"

"A little bit," he replied. "You could say that."

"I think the records do say that indeed. But unless we find a way prove it, you and I are, and always will be, the ones who have lost their minds."

Shivani was now leaning on Griffin. She smelled like lavender.

"I'm not so eager to end this on their terms," she said. "Are you?"

Now she had draped her head onto his shoulder.

This girl. She was going to get him killed.

"They will hurt us," Griffin finally said.

"You look tired," she replied. "I say that's exhaustion talking. Go get some sleep. I will get a first pass at the paperwork in the morning. I'll shoot for three hours and then carting the good papers back to my cottage before the inevitable."

"Which is what?"

"Before someone in New York tells Benjamin how fired I am, and they send out their killers."

42

At ten, Benjamin had set Shivani up by a bank of windows overlooking the harbor, then logged onto his encrypted laptop, then placed his right thumb in a biometric reader before gazing into a hand-held iris scan.

The dual authentication procedure triggered a series of harmonic tones, followed by the tinny sound of a live voice from faraway stateside, a routine reply of "approval granted." After all the above had transpired, Benjamin plopped his laptop in front of Shivani.

"Here you are, doll," he whispered under his breath, "keys to the kingdom."

According to her hastily-crafted cover story, Shivani had been sent to Bermuda to make copies of documents for prospective buyers, paperwork supporting an investor's high hopes of billions in forthcoming sales thanks to a towering cache of drugs already in the pipeline.

It was the tale she used to gain access to Benjamin's read-only laptop, and it was how she justified asking him for the six carts of data she hoped would reveal that the company had known all along that Bioferex was deadly.

She had been unnerved by the discovery that a live monitor was required to open access to Benjamin's laptop, sufficiently so to decide she had better not ask more about the Krøhn-McGill database.

All told, there were over twenty boxes in the carts she had requested, plus a half-dozen spreadsheets Benjamin had opened on his laptop. It was a shit-ton of scanning to plow through before lunch, the hour in which she hoped that Benjamin would take off and bio-scan himself out of the room. She felt overwhelmed.

You wanted this, she told herself.

Getting her first look at raw data, tales of ordinary people whose experiences produced the numbers she had always taken on faith, Shivani marveled at the purity of its smallness.

To see all of this granular scratching of pencils and pens as the bricks and mortar of clinical trial research—these dull and desultory messages about patients and their families from the hands of doctors, nurses and trial intake secretaries. It was underwhelming and awe-inspiring all at once.

These were the human conversations behind her hundreds of publications and filing documents. Yet where she had only been shown columns of sorted and pre-tabulated data-points, here lay the crumpled and dog-eared worksheets, spiral notebooks, yellow pads and dictated case notes that had given rise to those numbers.

Her motherlode may have been ample, but diving in was dicey. How long did she even have until her presence in the vault would finally blow up? An hour? Benjamin was, in the end, a survivor. He may have played the part but he would have known why paperwork had been shipped six hundred miles into the ocean instead of a warehouse in New Jersey. He would also have known the wooing of prospective buyers did not require Shivani take possession of emails worrying about drug safety problems, the notes she had been seeking behind his back.

Shivani's best hope was that Benjamin trusted her, and that the firm would be preoccupied with the movement of electronic documents as she dug into paper. In another plus, she didn't see any cameras, at least not in the usual places.

ॐ

Most of the firm's dirty work would come trickling out in the protocols, which is why Shivani asked for those first. Protocols were the game plan for how to run a study. You filed them with the feds as a mandatory road map for the experiment, a sheath to keep the trial honest, true to first principles of science and controlled. The protocol said when the trial would begin, end, its hypothesis and its methods.

Shivani suspected Krøhn-McGill would have been changing protocols weekly to hide any rise in distress among subjects taking a new drug. She also assumed they would have been just dumb enough to brazenly record these developments so as to remember what they had done, all the better to do it again next time.

As Benjamin busied himself with online shopping, Shivani smiled at the moment she stumbled onto the first of these events, a bona-fide victory over the bastards she casually pulled aside for her own purposes.

On 10/25/10, Bioferex trial 627SD09X JRE/DF
PROTOCOL ADJUSTMENT 58:
HAM-D retroactively substituted in all analyses for AI.

It said it was for Bioferex trial 627, and that they would be changing the means of testing for distress, switching from a psychological questionnaire called the AI to a different one called the HAM-D.

The AI, or Agitation Inventory, was your standard mood-state questionnaire for every pill under review. It contained questions like *How many times in the last three days have you felt unlike yourself? And, How many times in the last three days have you wanted to do something you decided was too risky?*

An AI would have picked up early signs of akathisia in patients on Bioferex. This dull-sounding change in the game plan would have

301

meant CRO ripped it out to hide the appearance of a side effect. It seemed so brazen, and yet they had written it down.

A few minutes later, Shivani found another clue in the protocol rewrite, this time a doozy. In a change dated two months later, this one also for trial 627, Shivani read a notation changing the earliest allowable date-of-birth for trial participation.

A Post-it noted that shifting the allowable date-of-birth date had caused a previously-withdrawn patient (a Patient 378) to become too old to participate. Shivani couldn't tell why the 67-year-old male in question had withdrawn from the study, or if he had actually died. On first pass, however, it sure looked like this new eligibility criteria would have arbitrarily lowered the cutoff for disqualification in precisely the fashion needed to exclude the man in question.

All of this was hopeful, but with Benjamin sitting close by, Shivani declined to so much as greet the news with a fist pump. She pulled the sheet aside. She also remained mum upon finding a third suspicious alteration to Bioferex study 627. "PROTOCOL ADJUSTMENT 47:" the switch had drably noted. "Protocol changed to double the dosage of comparison drug."

This one had no innocent interpretation. By giving test subjects twice the dosage they had paired against Bioferex, PROTOCOL ADJUSTMENT 47 would make patients on a competitor drug appear more agitated, reducing the appearance of distress among people taking Bioferex. Shivani quietly pulled it aside.

"Surprise-surprise, no Bonferroni correction," Shivani mumbled upon reading the next sheet of paper destined to getting stolen, a page denoting the absence of an arcane formula used to balance comparisons in new subgroups. Skipping the step made Bioferex look less agitation-inducing. Shivani figured Benjamin would have no more understood what she was referring to than had she named a part number for a lawn mower engine.

But then he was behind her.

"So the buyers from China need to know about protocols?"

Shivani's response came faster than she could have predicted. She had been lying for so goddamn long.

"Of course they do, love," she laughed, "the protocol is evidence of progress in a trial. A trial turns a pill into an ATM."

Benjamin paused as he considered the thought. Shivani felt a wave of relief at the possibility that he was buying it. But instead of returning to his desk, Benjamin then picked up some of the sheets she had put to the side. He began to stare at them with a puzzled squint.

"So why photocopy protocol changes about *adverse events?*"

OK, Shivani didn't have a good answer for that one. When in doubt, play dumb.

"Do I look like I know what I'm doing?" She said with a laugh.

Benjamin laughed, then took the papers from her pile and put them back on the cart.

"I think these are parked in Bermuda for a reason. Show a buyer some of this and our stock options will be worthless."

He had said the remark a little loudly. Nervous, Shivani spent the next half-hour pretending to look for paperwork projecting sales for Bioferex. Soon Benjamin was standing behind her once again.

"Weren't you preparing a CSR on that indication?"

"Maybe."

"So why waste time on these? We can just grab the one you were working on from the database. How about I log into your portal so you can just grab the file and print it."

As Benjamin logged off a webpage for his Bloomingdales cart and clicked the Krøhn-McGill logo in his browser, Shivani panicked. The second he typed her name into the company system, Benjamin would know that Shivani no longer worked for Krøhn-McGill.

"Wait, Benjamin," she said. "Please don't."

"Why not? It will save us both time."

"I'm not there anymore," she said. "In the system, I mean. My access is down."

Benjamin looked back at her with a strange gaze of suspicion mixed with understanding. Or maybe it was just a dumb gaze. He was fairly unreadable.

"They don't know I'm here," she added. "This sale is *that* secret."

Benjamin paused, grabbed a marker from his desk and excused himself.

"Nature calls."

When he returned, his arms were now crossed.

"Well, they see you, you know."

He had barely whispered the phrase, nodding at a mirror.

Shivani mouthed a silent response:

"What?"

"They've had me under scrutiny ever since that security upgrade in '08."

He said it while looking in another direction. He rolled his eyes.

"Of course, they only turn it on when they want to. Personally, I think we are too dull for them."

At the realization that New York was watching her, Shivani felt her neck go cold.

"Lucky for me, I did my hair today," Shivani said with meek aplomb. She began pretending to rifle through her cart in a way meant to hide how stricken she had become. Her hands were shaking. She knew about jail on the islands.

Worse, Krøhn-McGill would be coming.

She looked up to see Benjamin making a light wave, his left palm facing her.

I know why you came here, his palm read in gold Sharpie.

He smiled.

Hoping to mirror his gesture, she waved back.

As he put up his right hand, the wording gave her a startle:

I will come for you.

After he gave his fingers a stretch, however, she saw the message correctly:

I will cover for you.

Benjamin then walked back to his desk, swiveled his chair towards Shivani, then leaned back with fingers behind his head.

In a final message he had written on his biceps for her, she felt the relief of her having trusted him. *You only have a day* read his right arm. *Then they will b here,* cautioned his left.

"Look at this," he said while turning towards the desk, pulling a dock master jacket over a white sleeved polo and gazing into the monitor.

"There's been some bad weather off the coast. All air travel grounded."

Shivani knew that already. She also knew the weather would be clearing by evening.

ふ

After an hour on the beach and one more spent snorkeling, Shivani grabbed her things and walked the thirty feet of shoreline into her room. Griffin was in the same spot where she had left him two hours earlier, immersed in carts of boxed records, confidential Krøhn-McGill material Benjamin had delivered by van from the annex.

Shivani understood Benjamin's Sharpie-on-hand communication to mean he would not be helping her find evidence of corruption, but wouldn't stand in her way, either. He too, had developed antagonism toward the firm, it seems, in his case, ever since it had fouled his island paradise with listening devices and hidden cameras.

That meant Shivani and Griffin had until early evening at latest to find something solid before the goons began arriving in private jets, piling into rented Ferraris, and setting out to canvass the small island in search of their data-stealing whistleblower.

It no longer looked like Celine Dion's home. A spray of clinical trial booklets had overtaken her moneyed living room. Folders were opened to tabbed sections. Pages of notes had been scrawled on yellow pads. Benjamin's encrypted laptop sat on a chrome and glass table and Griffin was on to his second Red Stripe.

"The reef fish are so much nicer to one another other than we are," Shivani said to him in place of hello. "I will miss this place so very much."

Buried in folders, Griffin didn't look up.

"I don't know why you picked out these cases, but they seem to have answered a lot of questions," he said.

"Why don't you tell me what you learned," she said, "and then I will tell you why I picked out these cases."

"Well, I started with this."

Griffin held up a pair of doorstop-sized binders marked *ROPFEN: Papers Submitted for Publication.*

"Ah, yes, my handiwork," Shivani exclaimed, tossing her snorkel gear into a wicker basket by the double French doors to the beach. She had a towel over her shoulders and was wearing gold sandals and a swimsuit. Griffin remained immersed in his crash-course on the trials of new drugs.

"This is what the public saw?" he asked. "The end product? Articles written for journals?"

"Bingo," said Shivani. "The six Bioferex trials that went into journals. They became dozens of lesser papers touting Bioferex for the prevention of everything. Our PR firm even sent one to you, if I am correct, something by Julian Powers to be touted for readers of *In the Zone.* Funny name for a magazine, I must say. What does it even mean… to be *in the zone?*"

"Engagement," Griffin said without looking up. "Flow. It's the magical state of easy speed in which time slows to a crawl and a fastball looks as big as a beach ball."

Shivani popped her head back in surprise.

"I had no idea a magazine about abs had such a seriousness of mission."

"It's never happened to me except for five minutes ago," Griffin said. "All this paperwork started out looking like a fastball, and now it seems like a beach ball."

"Well this is exciting," Shivani said. "Please go on."

"So as best as I can tell, these articles you wrote, and which I guilelessly reported as expected, they all draw from secondary source material—records I have piled over here."

Griffin then walked over to grab a box of Krøhn-McGill documents, lifting its lid and pulling out a zippered plastic envelope the size of a phone book.

"The CSR?" Shivani could identify them from the far side of the room.

"Clinical Study Reports, yes."

"I write those, you know," she said.

"Yeah, so you gave these to the FDA in exchange for regulatory approval, and they were usually so big the agency barely read them?"

"That was our hunch. I know they were filled with internal contradictions that never elicited a call-back. The firm was pressuring me to do the CSR for Bioferex as prevention. That's when I emailed you."

"But you wrote these FDA documents using data from other data, spreadsheets given to you by higher-ups, correct? And that data is these columns and rows of anonymized summary numbers that Benjamin has called up for you on the laptop over here, if I'm not mistaken."

Griffin motioned with his thumb to the encrypted rig.

"Nice work, by the way. Who gets a records clerk to messenger over the briefcase containing launch codes?"

"I don't think they are *that* secretive."

Shivani had decided to keep Benjamin's help on the down-low.

"I told him there was a buyout offer for the firm," Shivani continued. "He had to show them his thumb and left eyeball just to power this baby up. It could all blow up on us, for all I know. Literally. Boom. But you were asking about the spreadsheet."

"I believe you had called these 'Dimitri's trust-me numbers.'"

"Welcome to my nightmare."

"But Herr Dimitri gets his secretive numbers from somewhere else, doesn't he? Somewhere still closer to the source—the raw data. That, as far as I can tell, is this sprawling dump of case paper in your trials."

Griffin had moved over to rows of reinforced folders he'd lined up on a bleached cypress table, a quickie attempt to sort them into groups.

"Correct me if I'm wrong, but all of these records were churned piecemeal from centers studying Bioferex, then funneled to New York before getting off-shored for safekeeping."

"Sounds right."

"And somewhere between the truth-telling in these forms," he said, pointing at the cartons, "and the numbers in that database," he started pointed at Benjamin's laptop."

"…We lost just enough of the side effects," Shivani said.

"*That's* the reason we're here, right?"

"Yeah," she replied. "Please tell me you found something we can use, because I am too close to it to even guess anymore where that could be. It's why I brought you here."

Of all that she had said to him, only that last line was a lie.

Griffin picked up a folder.

"Here's something. It's the trial discharge sheets for a Mark Barry, a Participant 1431. After being randomized to Bioferex, one day our friend Mark walks out onto I-90 outside of Madison, then turns to face an oncoming semi, leaving behind a young wife and child. It was recorded as a suicide in the medical examiner's report, but in Dimitri's spreadsheet, I see that his manner of death has been coded AD."

"Accidental Death."

"You know the term?"

Shivani nodded.

"I see it a fair amount," Shivani said. "I have always wondered."

"Accidental Death, yes, an accidental walk out of a hotel, then an accidental stroll along two blocks of service road, before an accidental bounding onto I-90 timed for the appearance of a sixteen-wheeler. Mark was wearing no shoes, had no alcohol or drugs in his system except for Bioferex, but, yeah, all of it, one big *oops*."

Shivani had begun brushing her hair methodically.

She couldn't believe she had worked to make such lies credible. This was the real reason she had enlisted Griffin. She needed him to carry out this stone-hearted stare at the facts that so frightened her.

She walked up behind him and reached around to see the thing herself. Her decision to go diving in a metallic two-piece would have been destabilizing, except that she was heartbroken, and the two of them had just hours to strike at a firm that could easily destroy them both.

"Let me guess," she mumbled into her brush, "re-classifying Mark Barry's death as an 'accident' helped to move the swell of Bioferex suicides into an acceptable ratio."

"It got them closer."

"One death moved off the rolls. Is this enough?"

As she said it, Shivani had turned to look at Griffin, with her hands on her hips. He snapped out of his fugue just long enough to really see her. Was this enough, indeed. She was beautiful, and he would have noted that they were never going to be together, not on this trip anyway, especially given her habit of disappearing.

"No," Griffin said, looking down, flustered. "But I've already found, like, a half-dozen strange moves in all of these. I think that's all it would take to drop the signal below a threshold for safety."

"You're a quick study, my love." Shivani touched Griffin's arm but the moment had passed. She walked away, pausing to steal a pull of his beer before pulling on a wrap over her swimsuit.

"So, in addition to taking Mark Barry off the books," Griffin said, "here's three more events that got moved into placebo, all of them questionable. Failed Ambien overdose. Slashed wrist. Accelerated the family vehicle into a brick wall. The first and last ones survived."

Shivani was back to feeling overwhelmed. She had never heard any all these stories with Bioferex, only Serotonal, and only as gossip.

"So that's four cases of wrongly categorized events," Griffin said. "Which would almost be enough."

Griffin picked up the last folder he had set aside.

"Weirdest of all," he added, "it turns out it this final one came from a last-minute enrollee into the placebo arm, a volunteer who, two days later, guess what."

"Left us for good."

"Via a high bridge overlooking the Mississippi River in Saint Paul. I've driven it many times and it is not where a person decides to go swimming."

"I was kidding," Shivani said, frozen.

"Well they weren't," Griffin replied. "They found a guy named Danny Bryan. No known address."

Shivani felt a chill coming on. She dropped into an oversized chair, pulled the brim of her sunhat over her eyes and rolled some sand in her fingers.

"This would have been enough," Shivani said after a long pause. "Suicide is rare. Drug-induced suicide rarer still. The problem isn't that it's happening to eighty percent of the people taking the drug. The problem is that it is happening to five percent of the people taking a drug prescribed to millions."

She paused, got up for a glass of red wine, threw it over the papers and let out a laugh. Griffin looked at her and shook his head.

"Just so you know," he said, "you just vandalized proprietary data. Jeremy Elton is going to call you out on cable and your career will be destroyed."

"Oh we are leaving all of this right as it lays," Shivani said, "and as soon as we flee the premises, which has to be soon. But before we split, I think you need to know why I brought this back here, these papers." She waved her hand at the cart. "Because, as you can imagine, I could have brought anything back from that vault. I only had one chance to make my choices, and it couldn't be wrong."

Griffin looked at her.

"Jeremy was following this," she explained with a laugh.

"What do you mean, this?"

"*These* cases.

"I don't get it."

"Jeremy Elton was loading the placebo pool with self-harm in the in trials of Bioferex. He would have learned how to do that in order to make Serotonal look safe, then done the same for our bone pill in order to protect everybody who worked on Serotonal."

310

"Fine by me," Griffin said. "I never liked him anyway. Well, everyone likes him at first, so check that. The thing is, I can't exactly cart all this paper into my carry-on."

"You know," Shivani said, "there's still a possibility we haven't considered. Before this raw data is organized into a liar file, a beta version is created. It's the honest numbers. They build a file that's factual and once they get it together, higher ups start making adjustments to hide the all the death. If we can get the honest file, we can compare the before and after."

"Can I get those on a thumb drive?" Griffin asked.

Shivani pointed at the computer with a laugh.

"You could find it in here in under a minute. But that minute the download starts, it should be the last thing we do before jumping in the car. It will immediately be noticed in New York."

Shivani and Griffin packed their things and changed their ticket home.

Shivani put the thumb drive in her laptop and scrolled through the folders until she found what she was looking for.

"Here it is," she said. "Wish me luck."

In a click, one by one, the beta files of six Bioferex trials began popping up, all of it transferred into their six-dollar accessory. Prior to logging off, Shivani grabbed another file as well. "This last one is going to make your day," she said.

As an hourglass tallied the final batch being shuttled, alarms began to sound from the computer's over-engineered speaker, the same series of tones she had heard when Benjamin first logged on. This time, the voice that followed was of an order of magnitude louder.

"Identify yourself!"

It was male, with an eastern European accent. Shivani could hear chairs moving in the background as a microphone was situated and a Skype connection established. The camera in the laptop turned on.

"Mother of fuck," she mouthed to Griffin. "It's our friends in New York."

"Who has transferred this Krøhn-McGill laptop from company property?"

The two of them were standing behind the monitor, safe from visual identification. Looking at its reflection in the window, Shivani noticed Seamus.

"Patel, you are trespassing," Seamus called. "Security has disabled your connection and this external drive is being wiped."

Shivani reached to yank out the stick as Seamus continued his barking.

"Tell us your destination or we will find you and rescind all consideration for your having cooperated."

Shivani strolled to the front of the screen and picked up a folder.

"I don't believe you, Seamus. Your drugs are incompetent, why would your muscle be any better? PS, this is some fascinating paperwork. You should have showed it to me it when I asked for it. The first one hundred times."

"You knew exactly what you were doing for us." Seamus shouted. It was the first she had ever seen him show emotion.

"Don't you have some sweaters to order?" she replied.

Griffin walked to the front of the computer and leaned in.

"Dude."

He was smiling. He appeared as if his life was finally getting fun.

"Are you going to let her dunk on you like that?"

"Mr. Wagner, you are not to leave the island until we discuss the situation with your theft of trade secrets."

"Please, can we take a rain check?" Griffin said. "I'm going to be busy with my new story."

"We have told you all that you need to know. We will tell you more when the time is appropriate. Leave all documents as you found them and wait for our personnel team to arrive."

Seamus reached closer to the camera to push a button and the screen went blank.

Shivani handed the thumb drive to Griffin with a kiss on the side of his cheek.

"Find a magazine to put all of this online."

She then shut the lid on the laptop, picked it up off her table, and tossed it through the double French doors into the cottage's glistening infinity pool.

"I like that," Griffin said, watching the laptop sink.

"It was getting a little overheated." Shivani said. "All that negative Seamus energy."

"And this," Griffin said, looking at the thumb drive with dismay. "There's *so many* magazines that are going to want to print this... And from me especially...That was a joke, by the way. But I might know someone who will."

"Splendid," Shivani said. "We do have to get the fuck out of here. They may be clueless and amoral, but they will eventually arrive."

43

At a business desk in the lobby of the Ellis Beach Resort, Griffin placed the thumb drive in a padded envelope, wrote down an address in New Jersey on the outside, handed the concierge a hundred Bermuda dollar note and asked if she would mail it for him in the next thirty minutes.

He had already walked to an on-site computer, opened up the storage stick, counted all six Bioferex honest-record spreadsheets and uploaded them to a document cloud, a link he immediately forwarded to Alexander Breton.

The extra file Shivani had thrown his way was as remarkable as had been promised—a 60-page master file with every Bioferex trial participant's name, age, and trial center address. Griffin printed a copy, placed it in an envelope with his parents' address on the outside, then paid the receptionist to send that within the hour as well.

Travelling in separate rentals, Shivani and Griffin left the resort at ten after five. Griffin made it to the airport by 5:30, checked his bag and headed to the gate. Shivani had booked him on a flight to Minneapolis by way of LaGuardia, encouraging him to enjoy some downtime somewhere nice.

"Take a layover in the city if you like," she said before hugging him goodbye in the turnaround. "I can always code you in to the Lancaster."

It was sweet, if a nonstarter. Griffin told her he'd rather get back to Minneapolis.

At the time, Griffin had thought it was a smart idea to travel separately, as Krøhn-McGill would be looking for two of them in the same car.

He assumed he would see her in the airport. But when his plane started boarding and Shivani had yet to arrive, Griffin realized he could not call her because they had agreed to not use cell phones.

44

This was surely where a person would begin their journey to getting shoved off the Lafayette Bridge, if that's indeed what happened.

As Griffin reached the alley behind the ugliest of the University of Minnesota's eight copy shops, he found the porch of 116 Fulton, otherwise known as *New Changes*, the last known address of Danny Bryan.

A red bulb meant for mosquitoes glowed over a self-styled message of acceptance: *You are here now. And that is what matters.*

His knock was answered by a graybeard in sagging sweats and an enormous Harley T-shirt. The man looked as if he had just awoken from a nap, even though it was the start of summer and barely 7:30 in the evening.

Griffin introduced himself as a journalist then told Harley T-shirt he was writing about a young man named Danny Bryan.

"Well yes, Danny," Harley T-shirt confirmed. "That was a couple of years ago."

The pair sat down in the kitchen, an oversized grime-a-zoid under harsh fluorescent lighting. They sure knew how to decorate these places so you'd never want to return. The room had two refrigerators, one with a hand-drawn sign reading *Staff*, the other reserved for *Residents on the Heroic Journey to Self-Acceptance*.

If Griffin had to guess, this was a halfway house of some sort.

"Danny was from Menomonie, I think. The name is Terry, by the way."

"What was he like?" Griffin asked.

"Nice. Danny had been having a hard time finding work. He was a teacher, good with children. He taught art. He liked showing kids from the city how to copy Goya, the impressionists, Picasso. His room in the back had oils and a long table. He'd paint whenever he could. Art teachers are so screwed."

"Why was he here?"

"Why was he here?"

"Yeah, why was he here?"

"You mean, this particular residence?"

"I mean, what is this place?"

"We house psychiatric in-patients who have had cause to engage with the system."

Terry began eating from a bag of pretzels laying open on the table.

"This is a home for vulnerable adults."

Griffin was confused.

"That means, what, people with mental illness?"

"People at risk of harming themselves."

Wow. Danny Bryan was suicidal. That would explain the decision to recruit him as a placebo patent. Suicidal placebo-taking subjects would have been like gold to Jeremy Elton.

"Was Danny taking anything?"

"Ha. Danny would never take anything. He could always paint if he felt bad enough."

"What did he look like?"

"Handsome. Sensitive. Big mop of dark hair. Let me tell you, he worked it. Kid took a lot of females back there with only a promise to draw them in charcoal. We made him leave his door open, house rules with the opposite sex. But he didn't seem that interested in scoring, to be honest. They'd go back there, and he'd draw them, play some music, and the two would eventually go sit on the porch and smoke a little weed. This isn't a rehab, after all. He was always broke. I miss him."

"So what happened?"

"Well, you must know that part. He jumped off a bridge over in St. Paul."

Terry looked down for a moment, then off in the distance.

"I don't get it," Terry asked Griffin. "You said he was in a clinical trial?"

"Yeah," Griffin replied. "A bone drug called Bioferex. Maybe you've seen the ads."

"That doesn't make sense," Terry said, shaking his head. "Danny would never take anything."

"It would have pulled him some cash," Griffin said. "They could have told him he was getting a sugar pill."

"That's not how those work," Terry said, "because we've had people in them before. You don't get to know who gets what."

"Yeah, well sometimes they bend the rules," said Griffin. "Believe me, more than I ever realized. Do you remember anything about the night he died?"

"They found some of his things on the shoreline. They came to tell us in the morning. I guess they never found him. I remember it was a Tuesday in November. I think he was painting in his room and then someone picked him up in a car and he left."

"Did anyone get a look at who picked him up?"

Terry paused.

"Some guy in a top coat," Terry finally said. "Guy drove a nice car. Maybe a Lexus, I don't know. It's all there in the police report."

"No, actually, this isn't in the police report, because I was at the police station earlier today."

Another long pause. Griffin heard the ice maker in one of the two refrigerators drop a half-dozen cubes into a bin. Terry appeared to be marshaling himself back into the question.

"What'd the police report say?"

"It didn't say anything about him getting picked up," Griffin said, "I can tell you that. It did say the police talked to a witness. It said the guy had a nice car, but nothing about the make."

"It's possible I forgot to tell them about the guy who came by," said Terry. "It was a bad time."

Griffin wondered who would forget to tell the police about the last person to see his friend alive.

"That's possible," said Griffin. "It's also possible they saw where Danny lived, what kind of population you treat, then decided the case was closed. Think of how it looks, Terry. You have a guy who lives in a group home for people at risk of suicide, and who takes his own life. That about wraps it up."

"Stop it! Maxwell, get down."

Terry was calling to the cat. It had been clawing a couch with its entire headrest fully destroyed. Griffin was running out of questions. The next question asked itself.

"Did Danny have family?"

"I don't think so," said Terry. "He said his dad had never been in the picture and his mom died when he was thirteen. He'd paint portraits of her. You should see them. She had a lovely sadness about her."

"How do you mean?"

"Come take a look," Terry said. "We couldn't throw his things away. We have a lot of his drawings, his paintings."

The two walked into a living room, then into the converted front porch. It held a small bed and a big pine door on sawhorses with stacks of sketches, most of them portraits in heavy shadow.

They were of a high quality, no more than a couple of hours into any of them. Griffin began flipping through them, one by one. Lots of quick sketches of beautiful, broke-looking women who probably lived in the area. The pictures of his mother however were orders of magnitude higher in quality. The pair turned to leave, and Griffin stopped in his tracks.

It was picture of Jeremy Elton.

It was wild. He had his chest pushed forward, a comically large grin, glints of gold around his neck, and was wearing a pinstriped, double-breasted jacket. A blazing sun set behind him, just like the Serotonal ads.

Danny had turned Jeremy Elton into a Cadillac salesman for the afterlife.

"Who's this?" Griffin wanted to see if Terry knew who it was.

"Got me," said Terry. "Never really noticed that one. Looks like some sort of Hollywood producer."

"It looks like Jeremy Elton," Griffin said. "You know the guy, 'America's Psychiatrist?'" Griffin saw Terry shrug his shoulders a little too theatrically. They walked back to the door. "What had Danny done to get placed here, anyway?"

"You mean, how did he find this place?"

"Had Danny tried to kill himself back in Wisconsin?"

Terry shook his head.

"No, you don't get it. Danny wasn't here as a resident."

"The police report said Danny was a resident in a group home for psychiatric services."

"Yeah, that was their assumption, but Danny wasn't a patient. He worked here. He was not at all suicidal."

"You're kidding."

"Danny liked to be around people who were suicidal. He thought they made him a better person. He thought he knew how to help them. He would crawl in the hole with them and show them they have company. He was smart in that way, intuitive. You have to feel alone to kill yourself. Danny wouldn't let them. So, yeah, this was his night job."

Griffin was horrified. A minute might have passed, but it could have been two. He was walking towards his car, when Terry called him back to the porch.

"Come here, sir," he said. "There's one thing I never said."

"Ok, what?"

"Look. I don't care, I guess, what happens to me for saying this."

Now Terry was crying. Griffin saw an empty flask of Canadian Club on the counter.

"I didn't really tell you everything. I only hid it because he'd pay me on the side, a little something to get me through the until payday in exchange for access to our residents. I never wanted any harm to come to them, especially Danny. But yeah, our guy in the nice car, he recruited them. He said it was always for the placebo arm, so I figured where's the harm, you know. I wouldn't want the owners of this place to find out I was taking side money, but hey, now Danny's gone and I'm still going to lie to you?"

Griffin let the pause drag on.

"It's OK, man," Griffin finally said. "I lie all the time."

Terry began rubbing tears with a chubby fist, then the base of his palm.

"He liked our patients because they would smash up a coffee table, threaten to hurt themselves or stand on the freeway bridge to think it over. He liked them because we took all this down and kept good records that all went into the trial report. I didn't understand why he would want to put patients on placebo who were acting like ours. It's rare that any of them even attempted suicide. By the time that we get done with them, our residents are still suicidal, but less likely to follow through with it than most doctors."

"What about Danny?"

"Like I said, Danny got in the cave with them. He helped them laugh at the world. And I fucking sold him out because of some side money from a famous person. Not only that, I told him he had to do it. Yeah, well, I miss him. Fuck that guy.

"What guy?"

"Danny's ride that night. The guy you saw in the painting."

He pointed at the picture of Jeremy Elton.

45

Griffin took the last chair in the back of a conference room.

Mark Barry's widow had turned out to be a Susie.

She'd become an advocate for mental illness medications. Not only that, he found her name on a roster of speakers signed up to testify before a funding committee of the Minnesota state house. It seemed like a better place to ambush her than her front yard.

"Suzanne Barry is here to speak to our committee today," intoned the chair, a haggard public servant reading from a text on his flip-phone.

"I understand you're speaking on behalf of MISA? Thank you for coming, Mrs. Barry. You have ten minutes."

Susie Barry leaned into a microphone and proceeded to tell her story, presumably the same way she had dozens of times before, according to an extensive web history of her service as a spokesperson for the ubiquitous MISA. Susie explained how her husband Mark had died, then pivoted to the work done by MISA and how they had been her salvation. "I will always bless the day," she offered kindly into her microphone, "a nurse and young mother told me about MISA."

"I couldn't see it then. I did not want to take her advice. But I look back now and see that my husband was under terrible pressure at work,

322

traveling far too much and hiding his pain from us all, sinking into terrible depression. This is why MISA supports depression screening that is universal, government-funded and easy to obtain in our workplace, schools, or cellphones. This is why ending depression for good should be our collective goal just as we seek the same for cancer, heart disease and diabetes. Depression has lived too long in the shadows. It is why I am speaking to you today on behalf of this legislation."

Griffin had heard it all before. More screening, more psychiatrists, better awareness-raising, more pills. The pain of mental illness was surely real, and life was filled loss and great pain, but he struggled to square the circle. To understand how both depression and suicides had risen while antidepressant use reached all-time highs. Maybe he had read too much Alexander Breton.

Susie finished her remarks and filed out. Griffin approached her in the back of the room, introduced himself, asked for a minute of her time and reached into his bag. He found for Susie a photocopy of the clinical trial paperwork with Mark's name on it, one of just a handful of folders he had poached from the raw data he and Shivani had lifted out in Bermuda. He pointed at a line: *Barry, Mark, 31, St. Paul MN.*

"You know that Mark took his own life right? I mean, that's why you're here?"

Susie nodded.

"And you know the official cause of Mark's death was suicide?"

Susie nodded again.

"So would it bother you to know that, in the final report of the Bioferex study that had recorded his participation, Mark's death was changed from 'suicide' to 'accident?'"

Later that evening, Susie dug out the note from Mark's last night on Earth.

She hadn't looked at it in two years. She had only read it once. She never knew what to think about it. It was too strange. It was not really a suicide note, for starters. He hadn't mentioned her or Crystal or anything related to their life.

She had always assumed the note meant Mark was having battles with his sanity. Now it seemed different. Now it seemed like proof of deep confusion. It also seemed angry. That made Susie start to feel angry herself.

46

This one had been scheduled for months. Susie was expected to deliver the same speech she had always given. She could give it in her sleep. Now that the date was finally here, however, her head was somewhere else.

Entering the hall, Susie looked out at her largest audience yet. There must have 600 people in the chairs, easy. Not a bad room for her first time at *Discovery and Renewal*, the nation's largest cross-practioner gathering of psychiatrists, therapists, policy planners, treatment centers and advocates for mental health.

The crowd had only grown bigger following the decision, just a few months back, to link her keynote with the convening of a panel to announce a new indication for Serotonal. MISA had called in a half-dozen top psychiatrists, including the familiar presence of Jeremy Elton, all the top brass for Krøhn-McGill and lots of press. This was going to make waves, if she was really going to go through with it.

৯

After striding up to the microphone, Susie paused to collect herself, drawing strength with an image of Mark. She reminded herself that she was about to give a very different speech. Then she went for it.

She opened as she always had, reciting the same details of who she was, who Mark was, where it happened, and how she found out. She almost had to remind herself to venture off the script.

"I have long thought my husband's death could have been prevented," she said, reading from a note card to help her remember her new message. Her hand began shaking. "My belief was that if Mark could have only been treated, we would all be at Wisconsin Dells right now."

She paused for the laughter always given to the ice-breaker from a widow. It came so easy at these things. "I still believe that stigma is a terrible cruelty," she continued, "and that those subject to stigma are owed every last piece of our compassion and our witness.

"But in boxing myself in behind this one culturally freighted word, I did not until recently see the hole in my narrative. How if my husband did indeed have depression, it did not in fact go untreated."

Susie paused, looked around the room, letting her gaze rest on Jeremy Elton. He was flirting with someone next to him. He still had not begun listening.

"Far from being denied lifesaving medication due to the stigma of mental illness, I now come to learn that my husband was in fact being treated and with no ordinary pill but an isomer of the celebrated antidepressant Serotonal. It has come to my attention that Mark was taking rostangilorb, a chemical cousin of Serotonal, but a drug that had all the difference with Serotonal as the difference between Coke and Pepsi. I can say this now because, as many people now know, Serotonal is Bioferex."

The room had grown silent.

Susie heard the click of a camera and sensed movement in the back.

"Everyone who has heard my story knows Mark took his life in an aggravated manner, by walking out onto a freeway."

Susie realized her voice had grown thin. She thought about what Crystal deserved, a father, and how Krøhn-McGill had taken that away from her.

"Ernest Hemingway once tried to walk into a moving airplane propeller, and that possessed action was considered an attempt at suicide as well. But in his final note Mark doesn't apologize that he is about to leave us, or for his perceived failures or despondency. He doesn't say anything a depressed person might be expected to say. Instead, he writes down that he has been poisoned. It's fairly persuasive. But I'll let you decide. That's right, good times everyone, the widow brought the suicide note."

Susie held up Mark's notepad from the hotel bedroom, and with a wry stare over the faces in her room, began to read from it out loud.

"'I have been poisoned' he writes. 'One, who did it? Two is there an antidote? Three, could I stop this from happening to someone else? Four'—and this is the part that gives me strength—'if I do this, would they understand that I never meant it?'"

She folded the note and paused to collect her thoughts.

"I brought this in today because I recently learned something odd. It seems that Krøhn-McGill, not only provided my husband with Bioferex, they have listed his manner of death in their clinical trial reports as an 'accident.' Now, why would they do that?"

Susie addressed the question to the wide-eyed panel of Krøhn-McGill KOLs sitting behind her. The room began shuffling. Someone must have called out the waiters, because they had begun filing into the room to take orders from the tables. Her hosts' apparent panic only strengthened Susie's resolve to say what she had planned to say last.

"There are other irregularities," Susie said. "There is the statistically convenient suicide of a young placebo patient named Danny Bryan." Susie looked up from her notes as a team from Klein McGill began moving up the aisle. "We don't hear about guys like him because we let Krøhn-McGill hide raw data offshore. Although it's apparently beautiful, you and I can never see where they keep the records showing how my husband died. It was his life, but it's their property now. Our drugs are created, tested and promoted from within caves of secrecy, and this secrecy stole my husband's life. Thank you for your time."

Susie walked ten paces towards the foot of the stage, then remembered something she forgot to say. She turned on her heel and returned to the microphone.

"All of my blogging has been paid for by Krøhn-McGill, everyone," she called out with wonder. "They flew me here first class. They made me their marionette. I can't forgive myself for that right now, but I know that if Mark were here he would tell me I couldn't have known better."

Susie then pointed at Seamus Cole and Jeremy Elton, standing stricken at the side of the stage.

"But *you* two. He would have hunted you fuckers down."

A publicist from Klein McGill rushed to the mic.

"Well,'" the moderator said as Susie walked off the stage to scattered clapping. "Our advocates hail from all walks of life, and sometimes hold views held deep within the heart, if not the scientific consensus. Our wishes go out to them on their journey, and we would have it no other way."

"Now if I could turn your attention to the *big announcement…*"

Griffin came across Jeremy Elton as America's Psychiatrist was gliding out of the men's room.

"Ahh the reporter," Jeremy offered, noting the handful of bystanders who would be privy to their meeting, "I hope you are getting the help you need at this difficult time." He was hewing to his legendarily practiced warmth. "I remember when I called to check up on you that night, it was troubling, you were clearly intoxicated." He lowered his voice to a whisper. "All of it on tape, I should add."

Griffin didn't take the bait.

"You pushed Danny Bryan off that bridge, didn't you?"

Heads turned.

"What do you think this is, Mr. Wagner, the movies? You're accusing me of taking another life? You're worse off than I thought!"

328

Elton spotted someone in the distance and waved. "Charlotte!" he called out with joy. "Can I have a word?" He turned and headed down the hall.

"That's cool," shouted Griffin towards Jeremy's departing figure. "We'll see you later."

Then he flicked his Yoda doll at Jeremy's back, hitting him square between the shoulders. As it fell to the carpet, the toy began emitting its audio clip from the floor of the hallway.

"Do, or do not, there is no try."

Elton looked down, kicked the Yoda a dozen feet and began storming back towards Griffin. "Who the hell are you to treat me with such disrespect?"

The dumbest of ploys and it worked. America's Psychiatrist had finally lost his composure.

"Have you ever heard of the other Yoda, Jeremy," Griffin asked, reveling in the audience. The YODA in all caps? It's short for the Yale Online Data Archive. You should look it up if you ever decide to write your memoirs from prison, because they have all your little log-in and log-outs, the entire incriminating data trail you left when you moved people around to make Bioferex and Serotonal look safe. I'm no lawyer, but I think they call that research fraud."

His eyes blinkering, Jeremy leaned into Griffin with an eerie calm. He was trying to pull the monster back inside of him, but it appeared to have one last burn to get off its chest.

"That's too bad about your ghostwriter friend," Jeremy said with a whisper and gentle squeeze of Griffin's arm. "You'd think a person with her kind of smarts would know better than to drive twice the limit on a winding road. She left behind a lot of good papers, though."

Griffin was alone in an elevator as the door closed. He was still bleeding from a gash above his eye that he'd taken from his crash into the carpet. He had lunged at Jeremy Elton with all of his might, in the presence of multiple goons, the press, the head of the NIMH and dozens of deeply puzzled and Jeremy-worshipping mental health advocates who already thought Griffin was crazy.

Reams of Krøhn-McGill muscle had appeared to pull him off America's Psychiatrist with extreme prejudice, grabbing at Griffin's hair, ears, and one of them even curling his fingers under Griffin's rib cage before the entire lot of mobsters threw him out onto the loading dock. He may have suffered some kind of tear in a tendons at the base of his spine. It was blistering down there. He was going to have to get someone to look at that one. Numb, Griffin limped around the sidewalk for a full half hour before coming inside to go search for his car.

None of the pain seemed to matter. Griffin had never heard that Shivani had crashed. He'd had no way of calling her, she had never called him, and although that was weird, he always believed she would come looking. Now she was gone, and he'd have to carry the truth he knew in his bones: that her life had been taken by Krøhn-McGill. He didn't even know where she had been buried.

She would have been buried, right?

Tears filled his eyes and he choked back a sob. The door opened and a tall man got in.

"Hey Griffin," a familiar voice said, pressing a button denoting his floor.

If it wasn't Seamus Cole himself.

"It's always nice to see you," Seamus continued. "So. YODA, wow? Nice play. Wouldn't have predicted that one. I have to give you points for panache."

Seamus tried to hand Griffin a handkerchief.

"You got a cut on your head."

Griffin shook his head in silence.

"Well, for what it's worth, I would have bum rushed that clown

Jeremy, too," Seamus continued. "The guy's a menace. As is the shithead who works for us in Hamilton. Come to think of it, you ought to work for us. I like how you think. "

Griffin paused, then looked up.

"You have an insane way of showing it. You're going to jail. Fucking salesman."

"Rather coarse," Seamus replied. "But then again, you do hail from a bro mag, so no surprise there. No, Griffin, actually, I am going back to New Jersey to make another hundred million for the company and point-five for me. This month. So no, I won't be able to help with that plan. But listen, I have a question for you. You got a second for a question?"

"Fuck off."

"Super. First of all, *of course* I'm a salesman. Who do you think invented advertising?"

Griffin turned to stare at the door.

"Will this be on the test?"

"A lot of people think the auto industry invented advertising, when the first ads were written by the drug industry." Seamus was admiring his Rolex. "We now support the entire media, if you haven't noticed. Look around. All those big car ads? Gone. Groceries? Gone. Pick up a magazine, turn on the TV, ask about an illness on your web browser, flip through a medical journal. We keep all of those guys in business. Not bragging here, just facts." Seamus shrugged his shoulders, as if the power of his industry surprised even him.

"Jesus," Seamus continued, we spend more marketing a cholesterol pill than the federal government spends researching autism, Alzheimer's, epilepsy, the flu, MS arthritis and spinal cord injuries combined. I'll never forget the day someone told me *that*."

Seamus had begun looking at his phone.

Griffin wondered if he punched Seamus hard enough to shatter his skull, how much of that would come through on the security camera. These guys thought of everything.

Seamus shook his head.

"The government only created the FDA after learning we were marking up drugs 500 percent over what it cost us to discover and manufacture them. Thing is, today our markup is somewhere around 2,500 percent. Sometimes we raise the price of a pill just to make people want it more."

"All about done here, dumbass?" Griffin said. "I think this is my floor."

"If you think putting our data online will cause anything to change, I have bad news for you. No one went to prison over thalidomide, and that was a drug that caused babies to be born with flippers. Anti-depressant-induced suicide? SSRI homicide? Couple of deaths out in the sticks for every hundred lives we tell them it saves? That's a grey area, my friend. Reporters are in there right now filing stories far easier to get past their editors. The Extended Release version of Serotonal. It's exciting! It just is. This shit with Serotonal, with rebuilt reserpine, with Bioferex, whatever you want to call it. The FDA will give us a fine, we'll sign an integrity agreement, and the world will move on."

Griffin got out of the elevator.

"We had 19 percent profit margins in 2011," Seamus called as he held the door open to finish. "Every time you write about us—even our *side effects*—you say the drug's name, and we sell more drugs. You, my friend, you are working for me, and don't even know it."

"How am I working for you, asshole?"

"You are the so-called 'balance' the public considers out of fairness before coming down on our side and lining up for more pills. We stand for health, wealth and free TV. You stand for anger over a research trick. Good luck with that one."

Griffin gave him the finger.

"I know you have to go, bro" said Seamus, putting his phone back. "Get a stitch in that, will you, it looks like it hurts. But listen, don't be *sad* about this. She loved to go fast, and was a terrible driver. Truly. I'd taken more than a few white knuckle runs with her. Not to mention,

Pharma is all about over here in the states. We are going into China. And after that, India. Brazil. And you, Griffin, you are going back to writing about cologne."

48

WESTLAKE, Tex.—The late-afternoon arrest of Jeremy Raymond Elton, 48, on Wednesday was carried out quietly and without incident following careful negotiations between the University of Dallas, the Dallas Police Department, Krøhn-McGill Pharmaceuticals of Princeton, N.J., and the great state of Texas.

Dr. Elton was taken into custody after his weekly golf outing at the Vaquero golf preserve, abutting his home in the exclusive gated community of Westlake. Agents waited briefly for Dr. Elton, who had diverged from the agreed-upon plan in utilizing the Vaquero spa prior to his arrest, and therefore was wearing only a plush robe and sandals upon being apprehended.

Out of courtesy and respect for his prominent place in the community, officers allowed Dr. Elton to change into his medical lab coat before approaching federal marshals for the drive to his arraignment.

Dr. Elton now faces a suite of charges including aggravated research fraud involving misuse of federal funds and misappropriation of federal science funds. Observers believe that while Dr. Elton is expected to mount a vigorous and lengthy defense, he will need to do so without the assistance of his primary benefactor, Krøhn-McGill Pharmaceuticals.

Following his arrest, the firm released the following:

"We are saddened to learn of the charges filed today against our former product spokesperson, Dr. Jeremy Elton. While Dr. Elton's efforts have long provided a deeply resonant bellwether in our campaign for global health and healing, Krøhn-McGill trusts the wider wellspring of testimony for its products, freely and without undue influence.

"We will continue to do just that as Dr. Elton faces these troubling charges. We wish Dr. Elton all the best, and ask the courts to do their job as we continue to do ours—providing the public with the very finest pharmaceutical products for the treatment of life-threatening conditions, including Bioferex in the prevention of stress fractures, and Serotonal XR."

The caller ID said Trevor Drake.

Why the hell not. Griffin picked up the phone.

"Trevvie."

"Sexy Wagner. How come we never talk?"

"That was kind of your doing," Griffin said, "if I remember."

"Yeah, well we can hold grudges or we can move forward. No hard feelings?"

Griffin was thinking that one over. He let Trevor stew in the silence for once.

"You know what I want, Mr. Wagner?" Trevor finally piped up, a little more needy. "I want to give you a column. We'll even call it the G-Force."

Griffin rolled his eyes and looked out on his alley.

"We're hoping to get some long packages out of you," Trevor continued, denoting the high-paying, coveted stories assigned in groups. "How about you get back to crushing some service copy for me, bee-yotch?"

"I'll think about it," Griffin said out of kindness. "But I want three dollars a word. And you have to stop saying 'bitch' or even bee-yotch. It's a terrible way to talk about women."

"Three dollars a word?" Trevor was quiet.

Griffin let this pause hang in the air too.

"Repeat after me, the word 'bitch' is sexist," Griffin said. "There is no male equivalent. And then say 'I Trevor want to give you Griffin three dollars for each written word that we assign to you.'"

The pause was notable, but over soon enough

"All you had to do was ask," Trevor said. "Long packages are going to help us with the National Magazine Awards. It looks like *Esquire* is putting your piece up for the prize."

"Now that they put it back online," Griffin corrected.

"And I bet it's got an extra good chance of winning, given that Jeremy Elton is going to Leavenworth. I also heard some guy at the *New Yorker* is working up a two-parter on that data dump of yours, the leak that went public."

Griffin felt deflated. Of course the *New Yorker* would get the story he had made possible.

"You know what's funny, Trevvie?" he said. "When that flack first called to tell me about Bioferex, she accidentally told me the truth. She called it a 'killer' idea. And it fucking killed someone and not just anyone but the smartest woman I ever met. I should have never said yes then, so I am saying no to you now."

It took Trevor another half minute to sort out Griffin's reply. Once he finally understood that he was being rejected, Trevor launched hard into his redirect.

"No, no, *no*…come *on* now, that's precisely the *wrong* attitude. You have what our magazine wants. You are killing it, G. This is your *time*. We need *10 Kick-Ass Diving Watches for Summer* out of you. Look, in all honesty, I can't get you three dollars a word, I mean, this is still an industry in contraction. But we got more money than we act like. And they won't ask for every one of those watches back. Let us make up for some of your loss and great suffering. Send you somewhere warm. You could track down that Brit. She sounded cute."

"For the second time, she has died."

"Jesus." For once Trevor had no smack. "I'm sorry."

"Everyone's sorry," Griffin said. "Tons of sorry to go around. But I have to get out of this business, Trevor. It's not a good place for me."

"Is it *Buzzfeed*? I hear they are loaded with cash."

"No. Nobody. I'm thinking about hitting the festivals with my buddy, if you want to know. That's about it."

"O-kay. Well, seriously, we'll miss you, man. I mean, I will miss you."

"Me, too."

"Look, if you ever want to get a beer sometime, whenever you get out to New York."

"I'll do that," Griffin said. "Coming out at the end of next month, actually."

"Oh that's bad. I got to take my son off to see Reed. But let me give you my information."

Trevor rattled off a street name, house number and zip. He lived in the suburbs.

"Just put the Flecks on the envelope," he said, "not Trevor Drake."

Griffin paused, confused

"The Flecks?"

"I go by Trevor Drake for the magazine. It's one of those things they wanted me to do."

"Your real name isn't Trevor Drake?"

"No. It's kind of my pen name, kind of a work thing."

"What's your real name?"

"Cory Fleck. Gotta feed the fam."

"For sure."

Griffin felt bad that Trevor had never even had a real byline. It was the first non-sarcastic conversation the two had ever shared.

"So, Griffin."

"Yeah."

"Can I get the name of your editors at *Esquire*?"

"So, Cory, I'm coming out there to talk to someone about doing a book on Shivani. If you buy me a beer, I will tell you more about *Esquire* than you ever cared to know."

♋

Down by the boathouse on the east side of Central Park, at a spot along the path where runners step sharp to steer clear of dogs, Griffin paused in front of the third sketch artist working tourists for portraits.

His work looked better than the others. Kid had pinned up a half-dozen charcoals of angels, stranded-looking women anchored by bored expressions and cigarettes. They looked familiar, too.

"Hey these are great." Griffin meant it.

"Thanks." The artist pushed his hair off his face, and lit a cigarette.

"Are you here tomorrow?"

"Maybe. I'm still getting situated."

"Where are you from?"

The artist was studying Griffin's face. His eyes were squinting. He pointed at Griffin.

"I think I saw you on TV once."

"Yeah?" Griffin never got noticed anymore.

"My name's Danny. Nice job with that guy, Dr. Fuckendorfer, he's crazy."

Griffin froze.

"Danny Bryan?"

"Used to be. Now I go by my mom's name."

"From Minneapolis?"

"Sure."

"But I thought…"

"Don't tell nobody," Danny said with little shake of his head. "The guy pushed me. I tripped. Then I flipped. Then I zipped my mouth shut. I don't really remember much. Hit some under rigging. We used

338

to climb that bridge when I was homeless. Anyway, I got scared. All this bird shit in my hair. My head hurt so bad."

He pulled back his bangs to reveal a four-inch scar.

"You ran?"

"I figured if someone tried to do this, what will they do next, you know? Threw my wallet over the railing, climbed down after the cops went away and left town. A drug company will always find you when they need to."

Griffin thought about Shivani. What if she lived too?

"Yeah," Griffin said, lost in the thought. "They're mean, alright."

Danny had begun reassembling his bag with pencils and an oversize drawing pad.

"I gotta go. I'll see you again sometime. I work here now."

Danny turned and started to walk away.

"Jeremy Elton went to jail, you know," Griffin called to him.

Griffin felt proud, for the first time in years.

"I know," Danny called over his shoulder. "Thanks."

He flashed Griffin a peace sign and slipped into the crowd.

ACKNOWLEDGMENTS

This book is a work of fiction about a real side effect known as akathisia, and it is the culmination of a journey that began after meeting Kim Witczak while reporting on her story for *Minnesota Monthly* in 2007. I owe my editors at *MM* thanks for assigning the piece and I owe Kim an enormous debt of gratitude for sharing with me the story of her husband Woody's antidepressant-induced suicide. Kim went from being an advertising professional to sitting on the FDA's Psychopharmacologic Advisory Committee. Her example as an advocate for drug safety, transparency for conflicts of interest of medicine and data secrecy in clinical trials has been nothing short of inspiring.

The then-Mayo Clinic fellow, now-Australian clinical psychologist Brett Deacon introduced me to the work of Irving Kirsch and David Healy, after Brett brought Dr. Kirsch to speak to a very uncomfortable audience at Mayo Clinic. As someone who is irrepressibly drawn to the sight of academic discomfort I demanded to know more, and later followed Brett to Nice, France, to watch him debate SSRI efficacy questions at a European psychiatry conference. While there I was able to interview David and to report on SSRIs and suicide for *Men's Health*.

That experience set me on the difficult journey of reporting on akathisia, or trying to that is, then finding out the magazine industry found the subject a tough sell which is to say deeply anxiety-provoking, whereupon I set my mind to writing fiction.

I was grateful in the course of learning more about psychotropic drug side effects to meet or interview Paul Thacker, Mathy Downing, Wendy Dolin, Joseph Glenmullen, Carl Elliot, Joanna Moncrieff, Jonathan Leo, Irving Kirsch, David Cohen, Robert Whitaker, Peter Gotzsche, Leemon McHenry and too many others to count. I never got to meet Micky Nardo but I did read his blog 1boringoldman day after day after day. That which I got correct about this issue is entirely to their credit, and all errors are, of course, entirely on me.

For reading this manuscript in its early stages and providing patient observations, editorial assistance and feedback, my thanks are offered to my developmental editor Katherine Sharpe, as well as to Carl Elliot, Bob Fiddaman, Kristina Gehrki, Susan Golomb, David Healy, Billiam James, Victor Montori, John Rosengren, David Scott, Phillip Scott, Rick Scott, Tom Scott, Leslie Sim, Gary Taubes, and Robert Whitaker. For the kind use of private places to write, sincerest thanks to Patti Sim for the extended use of a high rise condominium overlooking the Lafayette Bridge. For the use of a lovely cabin in the woods, heartfelt thanks to Fred & Betty Beier. David Healy came up with the haunting title. My young son came up with the idea for a happy ending, one his daddy was far away too jaded to have imagined.

For tolerating my time in the delightful world of men's magazines, sincerest thanks are offered to my former editors and friends at *Outside, Men's Health, Details* and *Men's Journal*, including David Willey, Mark Jannot, Nick Heil, Chris Keyes and Peter Moore. They all made great magazines, and should in no way be paired with the fictional excess of *In the Zone;* it is their worst nightmare.

For publishing my often-unpopular if widely-shared magazine and newspaper essays on akathisia and similar subjects during this time, I owe a special debt of gratitude to Peter Moore at *Men's Health*, Bill Shapiro at *Men's Journal*, and Doug Tice at the *Star Tribune*.

Thank you to my two beautiful children for letting Daddy write when it got very frustrating for you. Thank you to the spirit of my dear and departed writing heroes, Colm Wood and Mary Judd Scott. You made me so hopeful about the solitary life. Thank you for everything else, ever and always, to Leslie for your undying faith in me, this and us.

The information contained in this book about the use of reserpine by Ernest Hemingway is based on the letters of the late, great Mayo clinicians Drs. Howard Rome and Hugh Butt, documents which are graciously archived and available for viewing from the John F. Kennedy Library in Boston.

I actually once shared a drink once with the elegant Dr. Butt at a neighborhood block party but forgot to ask him about Hemingway. It was quite a thrill.

Catharine Bliss

PAUL JOHN SCOTT is a reporter and writer who lives in Minnesota. His work has been published in the *New York Times*, *The New York Times Magazine*, *Men's Journal*, *Outside*, *Details*, *Men's Health*, *Cosmopolitan*, *Ski*, *The Columbia Journalism Review*, *The Star Tribune*, and *The Fargo Forum*. He is the recipient of a National Magazine Award for writing that appeared in *Outside*. He lives in Rochester with his wife and two children. This is his first novel.